THE ISLAND OF DRAGONS

GREGG DUNNETT

PART I

CHAPTER ONE

The snow began at midnight, falling thick and strong through the still air. Where it landed on the ocean it lingered for just a second, before melting away, but in the compound it settled, and the sand was cold and dry enough that it stuck there too. Only a strip of beach remained at the water's edge, where a whisper of swell pushed a tongue of seawater in and out. Just beyond it stood a figure, shining a flashlight out into the night.

A million snowflakes were illuminated in the light, dropping in perfect stillness through the windless air. Beyond them, many billions more, but also winks of color – the buoys marking out the prohibited area, flashing red in their steady beat. The figure watched the show for a while, marveling in the beauty, listening to the silence. But not too long, he was diligent, even after twenty years working here. He redirected his light, shining it over the high metal fence, checking, always checking. The reverse side of the signs reflected silver back at him, their painted sides faced outwards, warning that the compound was strictly private, protected by CCTV, alarms, and armed security guards. But the truth was Keith Waterhouse – the senior security guard – had never once had to fire his weapon. He'd only even drawn it once from its holster – years before, when he was unused to the animals that sometimes shuffled in the darkness during his nightly patrols. And because there were so many of them – rabbits, foxes, stoats and even small deer – then the stories he'd heard, about the pollution, about how this place was *dangerous*… well, he saw no reason to believe them.

Keith was a big man, but heavy set rather than overweight. He shifted inside his thickly padded jacket and turned back the other way, shining his light now on the dark, silent shapes of the buildings set back from the beach. Their outlines were softened tonight by the covering of snow. There were no lights here, the plant didn't work twenty-four hours, meaning it was only him and Miguel here, his younger, and much newer colleague. Miguel was back in the well-lit and warm control room, which protocol demanded was manned at all times. Miguel was an immigrant from Mexico – or somewhere down that way – and he didn't like the cold. Keith smiled at the thought. As he did so his flashlight illuminated the fog of warm air from his breath, sending a flurry of snowflakes billowing in every direction.

Keith turned and laid a second trail of footprints back up the beach to his truck. He brushed away the snow which had accumulated on his jacket and climbed in, then he clumped his boots together before swinging his legs inside. Then he started the engine and continued his way along where he knew the perimeter road lie, a couple of inches under the snow.

He kept the headlights dipped. Otherwise they just lit up the universe of fluttering white, but it wasn't hard going. He could follow the truck's own tire tracks, made on Miguel's earlier round when the snow was thinner. They were partially hidden now, but still showed. Even if they disappeared altogether, the road was marked out by wooden posts every fifty yards, painted with reflective paint. He felt quite relaxed, inspired and grateful for the beauty his job sometimes presented him with. He began to whistle.

A second later, he stopped. Ahead of him, clearly visible in the snow was something that shouldn't be there. A set of fresh boot prints crossing the road. It took him a moment to make sense of it. Even then, he was slow to react. Dangerously slow.

"Hey Miguel," he got on the radio. "Did you get out? By the generating equipment?"

A delay, a buzz of static, then the slightly accented voice of his colleague. "Get out?"

"Of the truck. Did you have a walk about? I can see footprints."
Another delay. Then, "No."

Keith pressed the button to transmit, but then released his finger, thinking. Miguel was a joker. He shouldn't joke about something like this, but he was young, and unlike Keith, he found the job dull. Chances were, Miguel had laid the tracks, and was now denying it, in order to wind up his older colleague.

"What kind of footprints?" Miguel's voice came through the radio now, and there was something in the words that told the story. Hard to pin down, maybe a little too casual. Keith smiled and shook his head.

"Oh no you don't *amigo*." He said it aloud, but not into the radio. He wondered how Miguel had done it. He must have stopped the truck somewhere to get out, and Keith couldn't work out where, and how he'd missed it. But then he figured it out.

He got out again, leaving the engine running this time, with the lights on. Miguel had stopped the truck up *ahead*, then doubled back here, probably walking along by the perimeter fence to play his trick. Keith shone his flashlight into one of the boot prints. It was smaller than his own size-twelve imprint. Miguel had small feet. Pigeon foot, he'd called it when Keith pointed it out. Smiling, and confident he had it worked out, Keith grabbed the radio again. He would play along a while.

"We have a single intruder in the compound. Kinda small feet though. Doesn't look very threatening."

He ignored the put-on confused response from his colleague. He would follow the prints from here to where Miguel had stopped the truck. It was a nice excuse to get back out in the gentle snowfall.

As he walked towards the fence his boots crumped through the fresh snow, his own boot-prints sharper and more defined that those he was following. Though there was enough definition to make out that the two sets of prints were going in opposite directions. Any moment he expected them to turn, where Miguel had moved along the fence. But they didn't.

Instead they ran right up to the fence. And beyond. And the fence, instead of being the secure barrier that Keith had seen night after night for so many years, now bore a large hole. The snow around it was trampled and messed up. The moment made him dizzy. Hyper-aware, but also confused, his mind pulled in all directions at once. The protocols he'd written and practiced for a compound breach swam into his mind, but they seemed distant, unreal paper exercises. He felt disbelief, a part of his brain still clinging to the idea this was part of Miguel's joke. And then the anxiety kicked in. He was suddenly aware of the hood he wore, and how it restricted his vision to just the world right in front of his face. He turned, swinging the light behind him, back towards his truck and the dark buildings beyond, but there was no-one there. Just two trails of footprints. His own, brand new, leading out to the fence, and the other smaller set, heading into the compound. But as he looked he had to turn his back to the fence, and he felt its threatening darkness. He swung the light back, illuminating the cut steel of the hole.

The words of his protocols finally prompted action. He got on the radio, keeping his voice low, and using the codewords he insisted that all security personnel learned for just such an occasion as this. But Miguel didn't know them, or refused to believe him. He had to resort to swearing at the man.

"Check all the camera feeds. There's a six-foot hole in the fucking fence! Oh and call the cops. Tell them to get someone out here right now." He slipped the radio into his pocket, and for the second time in his security career, he drew out his gun.

He may not have ever fired the weapon – a Glock semi-automatic pistol – within the compound, but he practiced with it every month, and the familiar weight of it felt comforting. But the grip of it felt wrong, through the wool of his gloves, and he ripped them off, discarding them into the snow without even realizing it. His mind was tunneling now, the shock and fear he'd felt falling away, leaving only anger and a need for action. A growing rage that his domain had been violated. He moved fast back towards his truck, careless of obliterating his own tracks, but avoiding those of the unknown intruder, as if that might alert them to his presence, whoever they were.

When he reached his truck he hesitated. A moment of decision.

Keith had long told his wife that his job was not dangerous. There was nothing worth stealing within the compound, and he was a visible deterrent, required by over-the-top environmental regulations. And his employers had made clear that if anyone did break in, they expected him to alert the police and monitor the situation from the safety of the secure control room. There were insurance considerations. Nobody wanted heroics.

And yet, his many years of service had left him emotionally attached to the place. So now it came to it, there was no real question he would act to defend it. He barely paused at all, just long enough to clamp his flashlight shakily alongside the barrel of the Glock so that he could fire into the pool of yellow light. Little white clouds of his own breath obscured his view. The snow no longer looked beautiful, it looked threatening, giving cover to an unknown adversary. He tightened his grip on the gun. He followed the footprints towards the buildings.

The prints came to a wall, and then split, going *both* ways. For a second he couldn't make sense of it, then he worked out the intruder must have gone one way, and then changed their mind, coming back and going the other. Meaning they were either to his left *or* his right. He looked down, trying to read the tracks, but he was no God-damn Indian. He guessed right, towards the entrance to the main building. His hands shook – the cold, he thought as the Glock rattled against the flashlight. Ten steps on and he saw something, not a man, but smaller. He swung around, checking the area around him to be sure no one was sneaking up on his blindside. Nothing. He turned back. What *was* that thing? A backpack? He came closer.

Keith felt the blood rush around his body. It was almost thrilling. His feet seemed to float over the snow. It *was* a backpack, placed in the doorway of the generator room, which had a kind of open porch, so that there was less snow here. Even so it had a fair covering, and he reached down to brush it off, surprising himself by how cold it was. Where the hell were his gloves?

Twice a year the firm sent him on courses where they ran scenarios – the protocol for a protest beyond the fence, what to do in the event of power outage, an incursion by boat into the buoyed-off area – that one happened often enough in the summer when the tourists were around. But what to do if someone cut through the fence and left their backpack against the generator room door? They hadn't done that one, which meant Keith was left to make his own decision. But by then, unknown to the big security guard, there *was* no right decision. By then he was being watched. A figure had rounded the corner forty feet away, cloaked by the darkness, as the big man played his light over the bag. He went to pick it

7

up, finding it heavy. The security guard hesitated now, he pulled out his radio again.

Away in the darkness, the other figure raised a hand. The screen of a mobile phone lit up softly, its brightness set to the lowest setting.

"Miguel. There's a package here of some sort, by the generator room. I can't see what it is." The security guard struggled to open the top of the backpack, and then abruptly stepped back, his last action before his final words.

"Oh Christ. I think it's a bomb."

In the next second the detonation ripped through him. A huge flash of orange yellow lit up the whole compound, turning the snow to gold, but it was a sight that Keith would never see. His heavy outer jacket, offering such good protection against the cold, was useless against the vicious flying metal. It tore into his torso, removed his arms, flayed his legs, and clove his head into two separate parts.

And as the light flared away, there was just enough time – had anyone been looking – to see the blood lying crimson and dirty across the pure white snow.

CHAPTER TWO

The cellphone, vibrating on her bedside table, woke Jessica West from her dream, but though it was still sloughing off her as she reached for the device, she'd already forgotten what it had been about. Neither did she care. The light from the little screen was so bright it hurt her eyes, but she made out the name of the caller: Black.

"What?" she managed, still sleepy.

"There's been another one."

She sat up a little in the bed, but not much, it was cold out there.

"Another what?"

"Another attack."

The remnants of the dream hit her now, something about throwing a stick for a dog, though weirdly, inside an empty shopping mall. Even weirder, she didn't own a dog.

"Can't it wait till the morning?" The two of them had been assigned to work the string of attacks on local chemical and power plants. Domestic terrorism in theory, but in practice such low level stuff that it didn't warrant a call in the middle of the night.

"Not this one. They've gone and killed someone."

West's eyes jerked a bit more open. She sat up more, suddenly alert. "Who?"

"Security guard. Guess he was there at the wrong time."

"Shit. He's dead?"

"All seven hundred pieces of him."

She swore again, then: "Where?"

"You might just like that bit, but I'll tell you about it on the way to the airfield."

"The *airfield*? Where are you?"

"I'm right outside your apartment. But wrap up warm, it's cold as hell."

The call went dead and West blinked into the darkness for a moment. Then she rolled out of bed, and fumbled about, finding some clothes. As she did so, she remembered what her partner had said, and added more.

Outside the street was silent, and appeared deserted, until Black flashed the lights in the black SUV. It was cold, she thought, as she crossed the road, but the forecast snow hadn't materialized.

"Why are they giving us a plane? They cost thousands of dollars an hour." West asked as she got in. She noticed the readout of the digital clock on the dash. Three twenty-seven. The temperature, thirty-two degrees. Freezing. She adjusted the heater, turning it higher, while Black started the engine.

"Because they don't have a boat I suppose. Though don't get excited. It's not going to be a Learjet."

West ignored the comment. "How do we know it's the same guy?"

"Same MO. Small chemical plant, same curved pieces of stainless steel. Bomb packed in a backpack. It all matches."

"Except this time he killed someone."

Black made his hand into the shape of a gun and pretended to fire it at her. "All except that."

West ignored that as well. "So where is it we're flying to?"

"Ah-ha, it's someplace you're going to find familiar I think." Black grinned at having information she did not, but he didn't hold on to it for long. That wasn't wise.

"Remember Lornea Island? You told me how you worked a murder case there, before you switched to the Agency?"

"*Lornea Island*?" West was silent for a moment, as the details came back to her. "Yeah."

"Well that's where it happened. Ain't it just your lucky night?"

The car pulled away from the curb.

* * *

Black was right about the plane. When they arrived at the airfield used by the Agency, they were let straight in and directed onto the apron where a propeller plane was waiting for them, its lights on and door open. Two pilots were aboard, making their pre-flight checks. They waited ten minutes aboard until two other agents joined them – also bound for Lornea Island but a different case, the Agency had to stretch its resources after all – then the door was closed and the aircraft taxied to the end of the runway.

The flight wasn't long, but dawn was already coming as they descended towards a wintry looking Lornea Island. West, who didn't fly too happily, was concerned about the possibility of ice or snow on the runway, but said nothing, not wanting to embarrass herself in front of her colleagues. She was still in her first year after graduating from the academy at Quantico, although with her time as a detective she had considerably more actual investigative experience than her fellow newly minted special agents. So instead she simply watched out the window as the aircraft side-slipped down, lower and lower towards the hopefully-cleared runway.

"I hope they fitted this with sleds" Black said as they got down to less than twenty feet up and the little Lornea airfield still hadn't appeared out of the side windows. But then the runway lights flashed beneath them, and a narrow strip of concrete appeared on both sides, snow heaped up on either side – the plows that had shoved it there must have started early. They bounced twice before the props changed angles and bit backwards into the air, roaring in protest as they slowed the plane down.

Out of the plane they found a car waiting, and West was first to grab the keys.

CHAPTER THREE

By the time they arrived at the site, a thirty minute drive to the northern end of the island, the site was busy with local law enforcement. West wondered if she would remember any of the faces, but though the uniforms looked familiar, there was no one she actually recognized.

"What have we got?" she asked the lieutenant in charge, a man named Jim Smith. She flipped her ID and Black did the same.

Smith inspected them both carefully before replying. "Security guard blown to pieces. Local man. A good man." He shook his head, and West was reminded of the slightly slower pace of life on the island, she could imagine the lieutenant with a toothpick in his mouth, one that he kept there the whole day.

"Mind if we take a look?"

A hesitation. Then a nod, and he led the way, through snow that was messed up from a hundred footprints from the parking lot of the compound, towards the buildings.

"They tell me there's been a string of these?" the Lieutenant asked.

"This'll be the seventh," Black replied. "If it's our guy."

"And who is your guy?"

"We don't know. We assume he's some wacko environmentalist nutjob, but he's careful, so we don't actually know."

"So why do you think it's him?"

"It's a chemical plant. It's an attack with no warning and no obvious motive. The bomb was in a backpack, and you said there were large pieces of silver metal found around the blast?"

"Yeah, and some embedded in the guard."

"Stainless steel?"

"Right. You have any idea what they are?"

"We have a pretty good idea."

The lieutenant stopped suddenly.

"And you wanna share that information, Special Agent?"

"They're pieces of pressure cooker," West interrupted, knowing how her partner would answer this. The lieutenant turned to her.

"What?"

"A steel pressure cooker. This guy likes to pack his bomb materials inside them. It initially contains the explosion, which means when it finally goes, there's more energy expended and more damage."

The lieutenant frowned.

"You remember the Oklahoma bombing? Same deal. Probably where he got the idea from."

Lieutenant Smith considered Black's interruption, still without moving.

"He mean to kill with it?"

West hesitated. "He hasn't so far. He's gone after low value buildings with minimal security, and always after hours, when there's no workforce on the sites. He doesn't even seem to want to cause too much damage, judging by where he's put the bombs."

"Doesn't make any difference though," Black said. "If he meant to kill or didn't. He set a bomb and blew a guy to pieces. That's still murder."

Smith looked to Black, and then back to West. The action gave her an air of authority and both men waited for what she said next.

"There's footprints everywhere, do we have a record of what was here before you guys turned up?"

"There were two guards on duty last night. Keith Waterhouse – he's the guy who died – and a younger guy named Miguel Lopez. Lopez says that Waterhouse reported he was following a single track of footprints. He said they were small. But it kept snowing after that which covered them over. Plus then Lopez freaked out and ran around like a madman. We've got photos of the ground, but it was a mess."

"He said they were small?" West looked at Black, and her eyebrows raised.

"But nothing we can get a cast from?"

"Everything's covered in snow."

"How about CCTV? Anything captured?"

"We've got boys looking over it now, but the compound manager – that's a woman named Claire Watson – she says the signs make a big thing of it, but they don't really have much. Nothing here to protect."

They arrived at the dead security guard's truck, the door still waiting open as if he might leap back in and continue his rounds. The police had made their own path through the snow, leaving the original tracks still visible, but their outlines were now softened by the covering of white, which had smoothed out any sharp edges. They could have been made by anyone – or anything. The prints connected the fence, where in the daylight a large hole was easily visible, and the largest building in the compound.

"Tracks that way lead through the fence and to a depression where a vehicle was parked. Then tyre tracks go back to the main road. Everything covered by snow though. We can't get anything useful."

"And the other way?"

"Where the bomb went off. It's kinda grim."

He turned, and led them that way, following the line of police footprints towards a large low building. The entrance porch was obviously damaged, parts of it hung down limply, and several windows were shattered. The snow around here looked odd, flattened and cleared in part, and trampled down in others. There were at least six people working, wearing the blue and white protective gear of forensic experts.

"You wanna get any closer, you'll have to suit up."

West watched for a while, taking in the scene, and trying to reconstruct in her mind how it must have happened. It wasn't too different from the other bombing sites she'd visited, and the thought of what would follow, a fruitless search through the debris – recovering parts of the bomb, but finding they'd been built to a recipe freely available on the internet, and carefully, with no trace of identifying material anywhere – depressed her.

"No, it's alright. But I'd like to speak to the manager you mentioned. Claire something?"

"Watson. Sure. She's over by the control room." He pointed towards another building, which had its lights on. "Go right on in, I'll be over in a minute."

Black and West walked across and opened the door, to find a woman in her forties just putting down her cell phone.

"Claire Watson? I'm Special Agent Jessica West, this is Special Agent Jason Black."

The woman nodded. She looked exhausted. "The police said you were coming. Said there's been other attacks like this one."

"That's only a possibility at this stage," West cautioned. "May we ask you a few questions?"

Watson nodded a second time, eyeing a low sofa in the reception area.

"You look tired. Let's take a seat. Early start for all of us."

Before she sat, Watson found a beaker of coffee, and emptied it into three cardboard cups. It tasted bitter, but the steam rising up and twisting around at least promised warmth.

"What does this plant produce?" West began, opening out her notebook and clicking a pen into life.

"Resins mostly. Thermoset resins." She looked at them blankly. Black looked back even more so.

"What does that mean exactly?" West prompted.

"Fonchem makes resins for all sort of applications. Abrasives, adhesives, chemical intermediates, coatings – you name it." She sipped her coffee. "We make some here, a lot more over on the mainland."

"Is it…" West paused and thought. "Is it particularly high value? Does it pose a risk to the environment? Any reason you can think why the bomber might have targeted here?"

Watson also thought for a moment, but she came up blank.

"I'm sorry."

"That's OK." West glanced at Jason, it was the same story as at the other bombing sites.

"There is the expansion though," Watson went on, suddenly.

"Excuse me?"

"The site. Fonchem, that's who I work for, who owns this site. They want to expand. Pretty much double it in size. There are quite a lot of local people who are opposed to it."

15

"Anyone in particular? Have there been any threats?" Black asked at once, but Watson shook her head.

At that moment the door swung open, and Lieutenant Smith walked in, stamping his boots on the mat and blowing his hands. He looked for the two agents, and beckoned them over.

"Excuse me Ms Watson," West said, as she got up.

She saw how Smith was looking at her cup of coffee, which she still held in her hand, so she offered it to the policeman, and he took a large gulp.

"Thanks. Your stainless steel pieces. You said he prepares carefully? You never find any forensic evidence on them? No DNA, no prints?"

"That's right." Black had joined them now too. "He's meticulous."

"Well he wasn't this time. We got a print."

The two FBI agents swung to look at each other. This was completely unexpected. A breakthrough in a case that had needed one for months.

"Can you run it?"

"Already have. I got the results here on my iPad. We're not so backward on the island as you Quantico guys might think."

West realized he'd been holding it in his hand the whole time, and now he clicked it on. "I got you a name too. Local man I'm sorry to say. Well, kid really. He's only seventeen."

Before she heard it, West felt a weird rush. Of foreboding. Like she already knew what name he was going to say. Though that was ridiculous. It couldn't be.

"Name of Wheatley. Billy Wheatley."

4

FIVE MONTHS EARLIER

"Come on Dad, we need to go!"

I've already got my stuff in Dad's truck, and I've checked twice around the house to make sure I haven't forgotten anything. It feels weird though, knowing that I won't be coming back here for months. Dad's sitting at the kitchen table, his broad back turned away from me. He decided now was a good time to fix the little outboard motor we found abandoned by the side of the road. He's got all the pieces laid out in front of him. But really he's just doing it because he doesn't want me to go.

"Come on, I can't miss the ferry."

"I could give you a lift across if you do," Dad says.

"I've already bought a ticket."

Dad hesitates. "Alright." He puts down whatever it is he's holding, and wipes his hands on a rag. "Alright. You got all your stuff?"

"In the truck."

"You got your computer? Your books?"

I sigh. "Of course I've got my books." I don't even mention my computer, I'm not going to *forget* that. "And I've left instructions for what to do about the campaign. I've left the printer loaded and ready, so I can email through new posters as I make them and they'll print automatically. If you could just take them and put them up, everywhere you can…"

"Yeah, I know." Dad replies, turning to look at me now. This is my current project. There's a stupid chemical company, up in the north of the island, that wants to expand, but if it does so it will destroy a sheltered bay which is a crucial nursery for seahorses. I'm trying to raise awareness so that it doesn't get allowed.

"You won't forget will you?"

He doesn't answer for a second, but then shakes his head. "I won't forget."

For a second I feel really odd. I felt it earlier too, when I was upstairs and still in my room. Knowing it was the last time I'd see it in months. I glance at Dad and can see he's feeling it too.

"Shit Billy. I just can't believe you're going to college. Already. It just doesn't seem…" He glances back and his eyes are welling up a bit. He shakes his head. "It doesn't seem five minutes ago that you were running around here, this wild little kid. Now you're leaving home."

I don't answer for a moment. I can't quite believe it myself. I've been looking forward to this for such a long time, and now it is finally here. "I'm not going far," I say in the end.

He looks up and gives me a smile. "It's a boat ride away."

"Every where's a boat ride away. From an island."

He doesn't answer this, so I go on. "And you have *got* a boat." Dad's work these days is taking tourists out to view whales and dolphins. I used to help him too, though he's learned how to find them pretty good now on his own, so he doesn't need me anymore, which has been useful as it's freed me up for my projects. The campaign, and other ones, you know what I'm like.

Dad's face breaks into a weak smile. Then he starts patting his pockets, like he's looking for his keys. In response I hold them up.

"Here." I toss them over and he catches them with both hands. But he thinks for a second then tosses them back.

"You drive Billy."

I'm surprised by this. It took me a while to learn to drive, and I did accidentally bump into a few things – there was a wall by the supermarket, a tree in a parking lot at Littlelea, and also a post when I was reversing, but it was so low no-one could have seen it. But anyway,

Dad's not been too keen on me using his truck since, so there's quite a lot of meaning in this gesture.

And maybe for that reason, as I go outside, it gets me thinking about when I was younger, like a little kid. Back then I used to love riding in the back of Dad's pick up, on the flat bed I mean. With my head up in the breeze, and feeling the wind make my cheeks wobble. It wasn't this truck of course, he had an old Ford then, and this one's a Toyota. It's funny how some things change, and some stay the same. Now I get in the driver's side and wait until Dad climbs in next to me.

"Are you sure about this?"

"Just keep your eyes on the road."

I start the engine and put it into drive.

"You are gonna be alright, aren't you?" Dad says after a while. I'd been paying attention, so it surprised me. We're just crossing over the river that divides the Littlelea end of the beach from the main part, where the tourist town of Silverlea sits. Then I have to turn right onto the main road that links up to Newlea. We need to make a stop there.

"Course I'll be all right. Dad, all over the country about a million kids are going to college. Why would I be any different?"

"Yeah, but they're all a year older than you."

For a moment I'm silenced by Dad's argument. I worked really hard this last year so I could skip a year of school. It didn't seem worth hanging about here studying stuff I already knew, not when I know what I want to do with my life. Might as well get on with it.

"Boston University has the best undergraduate Marine Biology course in the country. It's you I'm more worried about. Leaving you here on your own."

"Don't be." Dad smiles. "I've got Milla." That's Dad's latest girlfriend. He discovered this dating app about a year ago, and went through about fifty girlfriends in a month, but this one seems to have stuck. She's cool though, I like her.

We drive on for a bit, and I can sense Dad watching what speed I'm driving.

"If you actually want to get there, Bill, you might want to put your foot down a little."

I mostly ignore this, but accelerate a bit.

We come to the outskirts of Newlea, and I turn off the main road and over towards my old high school. Just before I get there I turn right and pull up in a little cul-de-sac. Normally I'd honk the horn, or use my cell phone, but I want to get out. I feel restless. Dad follows me, and together we go up the path towards Amber's house. In the window of the front room I'm pleased to see my latest poster. *Save our Sea-Dragons.* I said before they were seahorses, and they are really, but there's one species that's unique to Lornea Island, and the local people here call them Sea-Dragons.

"She's just getting ready." It's Amber's mom who opens the door, and when she sees Dad she gives him a look, like neither of them can be trusted to speak because they're both too emotional.

"Hello Mrs Atherton," I say, and she gives me the same weak smile Dad did earlier.

"Is that Billy?" I hear Amber's voice shouting down from up the stairs. "I'm just coming, can you load my stuff?" In the hallway there are two giant suitcases as well as an enormous backpack. I don't know why she needs so much stuff.

"I'll get them," Dad says, but I give him a hand, and so does Amber's mom. Together we wheel and heft the bags down towards the Toyota and heave them in, then stand there looking at them, like we're admiring what a great job we've done, or just marveling at the size of it all. But really it's like before, when no one wants to say anything because we're all a bit sad at what's happening. The moment is only broken when Amber's sister comes running out the house.

"Hey Billy!" she says to me, and her voice is so bright and alive I feel it for a second, what Dad and Amber's Mom are sensing, that this is the end of an era, that none of us are ever going to see each other again, although of course we are.

"Hey Gracie," I reply. She's eight now but she's still holding her toy rabbit. She doesn't like letting go of it after what happened last year.

"I wish you didn't have to go away Billy," Gracie says. And at the same time, Amber appears at the top of the stairs with yet another suitcase.

"I know," I reply. "But I'm coming back. And if you come visit I can take you to the aquarium. I know the manager there." Gracie doesn't really look too excited by this, and I'm glad that Amber comes downstairs at this point.

"Hi," she says breathlessly. "You ready? Don't want to miss the boat."

I mean to answer, but suddenly I don't think I can, so I look around her hallway for a second instead, not making eye contact with anyone. I can't believe I'm not going to see this place for such a long time. I can't believe I'm actually going. But Amber doesn't seem to be feeling anything.

"Come on!" she says, and leads the way outside.

Amber isn't going to college with me, she's already been, though not to a real university like Boston. She already did a design course, here on Lornea Island, but the problem is there aren't that many jobs here for designers, so she had to get one in Boston. But by chance her job starts at the same time that the fall semester begins, and she won't be too far away from where I'm studying. That's why we're traveling together now. And by the way, I should probably admit it was Amber who did the design on the poster. Though I did do the words. It just shows we're a good team.

"How are you going to move all that to your new apartment?" I ask, as she drags the third suitcase down to the pick-up. "It's massive."

"Well Billy, they have these new inventions in the city called cabs." She tips her head onto one side and looks at me. "Didn't you know?"

There's a bit of an awkward moment when we actually have to say goodbye to Amber's Mom. She hugs Amber, and then comes and hugs me as well, but I don't mind, because Amber's mom is OK really. She gives Dad a hug too. Then I get back in the truck and Amber jumps in behind me. Dad tries to protest and tell her to sit in the passenger seat, but she's already in, and leaning forward between the two front seats.

"Don't hit the gatepost this time Billy," she says, as Dad gets in.

"I won't," I reply, and give it a wider berth to make sure I don't.

It's normally only about twenty minutes from Lornea Island's capital, Newlea, which is more or less right in the middle, to the main port of Goldhaven, which is about three quarters of the way up on the west side. But even though it's nearly September, the island is still busy with tourists, so I try to drive as fast as I can, but we keep getting stuck behind people who are obviously looking at the views as they go.

"It's gonna be tight," Amber says, and I glance at the clock on the dash of the truck, a bit surprised. What with us leaving home late, and then stopping for so long to pick up Amber, and maybe just a little bit my driving, we might actually miss the ferry after all. In response I push my foot down onto the floor and then, when a straight bit comes up, I signal left and move out to overtake the car that's holding us back. It's not the longest straight in the world, and before we're half way past the car, another car rounds the bend in front heading towards us. Probably I should back off, and drop back, but I don't. Instead I push my foot further down into the floor. Dad's truck might be new to him, but that doesn't mean it's new, and it doesn't have quite as much power as I need, so we don't exactly leap forward. For about a second I don't think we're going to make it and almost start to panic, but then I see I've misjudged, and actually we've got plenty of room. Well sort of. As the car comes by it flashes its light and its horn blares. The sound gets all distorted as it shoots past my window.

"Doppler effect." I say, not to anyone in particular.

"Thanks for the explanation Billy," Amber replies tightly. "Good to know when I'm dead."

Dad just raises his eyebrows a little.

Goldhaven is pretty small. You can see the ferry as you come into town. I guess the fact it's still there is a good thing, but even so I drive right up to the front of the parking lot where you can drop off foot passengers. But then Dad tells me to go further, up to the booth where you have to check in if you're taking your car across. Dad's truck isn't going of course, but it's the only way we're going to make it in time with Amber's bags. When I wind down my window to speak to the woman in the booth, he leans across and explains, and after a moment's hesitation she waves us through. There's loads of space on the dockside, because all the cars and cargo that are going on the boat are already onboard, so I can stop right beside the foot passenger entrance. As soon as I stop, Dad jumps out and he's already got all of Amber's bags out of the truck, and waved to the ferry operative who's waiting by the gangway, a steel walkway that connects to a door in the side of the ferry. The guy comes down to check our tickets, and looks a bit shocked by all Amber's bags, and mine. And my bike.

"You've got about a minute to get that all onboard," he says. And we don't argue. We have to do two trips each, but we're able to load them all inside the ferry. And then we come back outside onto the dockside.

Amber gives Dad a hug, and then she goes inside with the last of her bags. So then it's just me and Dad there.

"Well Billy, I guess this is it." He says, and his voice sounds constricted, like he's choked up. I don't want to look at him, but I don't want to *not* look at him either.

"Hurry it up now please, we need to stow the gangway."

I turn to see the ferry operative with his high-visibility yellow vest and his radio, crackling away. I turn back to Dad.

"You're sure you'll be alright?"

Dad nods his head, and then he grabs me in a bear hug. "Come here Billy." I feel how strong his is, squeezing me towards him. But just as much, these days I feel how I've grown stronger too. I hug him back, blinking away the prickling of tears in my eyes.

"*Now* please. If you're going," the ferry operative says. There's actually two of them now, and I realize with a jolt that they're not coming with us. They're waiting for me to get on board so they can pull the walkway and leave it on the dock side. I nod and after a second I let Dad go.

"Be good Billy. And don't get into any trouble," Dad says, and I sort of half smile. Quickly I turn and jog up the metal ramp onto the ferry, my footsteps ringing out. As I step off into the hull of the ferry, they unlatch it and the walkway drops away, held up by steel cables from a crane overhead. Already we're moving. Only then do I hear Dad's voice behind me.

"Billy!" He shouts, he looks a little desperate all of a sudden, like it's suddenly gotten too much for him. He shouts something else, but I can't hear it with the judder of the ship's massive engines. Dad cups his hands round his mouth and tries again.

"Keys!" he yells, then makes an ignition-turning motion with his hands. I clamp my hand against my pocket, and feel his truck and house keys are still there. But by now the ramp is gone completely, and already the distance between the ferry and the dockside is widening. If I take Dad's keys with me he'll be stuck here, unable to get home. I pull my hand behind me to throw them across, but I don't do it. What happens if I miss? They'll fall into the swirling water beneath us, no one's ever going to get them out of there, and anyway they're not waterproof, they have a battery so you can zap the truck. Maybe I could zap it from here, and unlock and Dad could at least wait inside for a locksmith… Suddenly the ferry lets out a blast from its horn and it jumps me out of such stupid thinking. I look down, at the black water, swirling and foaming from the chop of the propellers, then at the distance to the dockside, growing with every second I delay. I pull my arm back again, and this time I send the keys sailing out over the gap. For a second or so they hang there, twisting in the air, then Dad's hand reaches up and catches them.

"Good boy Billy!" Dad yells, and he lets out a whoop. The two dock workers both clap ironically too, and I grin, but then I'm told to get away from the door and it's closed shut in front of me, so I can't see anything. I rush to help Amber drag our bags to the storage area, and then outside onto the deck, and I'm disappointed when I see Dad's truck is gone already. But then I see he's driven round, so he can watch the boat leave from the end of the harbor arm. The ferry goes so close I can just hear what he shouts out, when we glide by:

"Don't get into any trouble!"

I wave frantically, and then think of something. "Look after *Caroline* for me!" I yell, and he grins back, and hold up his hand, in the thumbs up gesture.

And then the rocky arm of the harbor is gone and replaced by a lively sea, blue topped with crests of white, dancing in the sunlight. I can't hear Dad anymore. But behind us I see the red of the truck shrinking into the distance of our wake, and for a very long time, he doesn't drive away.

CHAPTER FIVE

I stand at the stern of the ferry watching the island for a long time. It won't actually disappear – you can see the mainland from Lornea, and vice versa, at least on a clear day, but the features disappear, and there's something metaphorical about that. When you're on Lornea, you kind of see the stuff that happens on the mainland, but you don't really notice the details. That's what's special about it.

"Come on, you wanna get some food?" Amber says, and I'm surprised because I'd almost forgotten she was there.

We go to the café, and Amber queues to get two coffees, while I sit and look in my backpack for the sandwiches I made earlier. I'm going to have to be very careful with money – well, I'm going to have to *learn* to be careful, now that I'm at college, because everything is incredibly expensive, and even though Dad's a successful businessman now, running the whale watching trips, his boat is still mostly owned by the bank. Unfortunately I didn't have a lot of time this morning, so my sandwiches are a bit plain.

"Here." Amber joins me, sliding a plate with a much nicer looking sandwich on it in front of me, as well as the coffee.

"I made my own," I tell her, a bit confused.

"I know you did Billy." She gives me a smile. "I was a bit worried you might have made me some too." Her smile turns sarcastic, and she sits down. She takes a big bite out of her sandwich, and chews it loudly. I watch her, and think how I'm lucky that she happens to be moving to Boston at the same time as I am.

The ferry takes four hours, and the time goes too quickly. All too soon and we're going by little islands covered in seabirds and there's sailboats all around, and container ships, and airplanes taking off and landing from the airport, and ahead of us the skyline of a proper city, not like Newlea. I start to feel nervous again. Then we get closer still, so we can see the dock where the ferry berths, and then we're right there, and there's all sorts of shouts and clangs, and the whole ship judders as it slows down. And finally the ferry is in the berth, and then the doors open. We have to queue to get off, and we're almost the last to do so, on account of all the luggage Amber has, but she finds a baggage trolley on the dock, so we can wheel everything to where you have to catch the cabs. I think we're going to part here, but Amber has a better idea, and we share one cab, a minibus, to get all our bags in, plus my bike. I give the driver the address of my accommodation, and we sit watching the city slide by outside, slowly because of all the traffic.

I opted to live in an apartment in one of the main student areas. I wasn't sure, but Dad said I should make sure I'm in the heart of everything that's happening, though he doesn't really know, because he never went to college.

"Freshman?" the driver says, as he turns into a street that looks familiar from the photos on the university's accommodation website.

"Yes." I nod. He knows the address much better than me, and seconds later we pull up at the sidewalk. In front of us is a modern looking, three-storey building.

"You wanna come in and look around?" I ask Amber, and I can tell she wants to.

"Can you wait?" she asks the driver.

"I got the meter running." He replies, and she screws up her nose. Amber has to watch her money too, at least until she gets her first pay check.

"Fuck it," she tells me. "I'll get another cab later." So we unload everything onto the sidewalk, and pay the driver, and he drives off. Then she looks at me expectantly, and I realize I don't actually know how I'm going to get in. I don't have a key yet. I have to scrabble around in my bag to read the letter the university sent, and I realize I have to go to the accommodation office. Luckily there's a map on the letter showing where it is, and obviously I have my bike, and it only takes me two minutes to get there. But then I have to show about four hundred pieces of ID, and sign my name a hundred times, but finally the receptionist gives me a set of keys, one to get into the building, and another for my room. But then, when I come back, I can't see Amber anywhere.

A bit confused, I use one of the keys to open the outside door, and I see all Amber's bags are lined up inside. I go up the stairs and there's three front doors for three apartments. Number twelve, that's mine, has the front door open. I go inside and finally find Amber, in a super-basic kitchen diner, chatting to a guy with ginger hair.

"Hey Billy," she says. This is Guy. He's your housemate." She smiles, and Guy comes over to me and pumps my hand. He has a zit on his chin that looks ready to burst.

"Yo! Cool to meet you dude. This whole thing is gonna be so freaking awesome!"

We chat for a little while – well mostly Guy chats, talking a lot about all the parties we're going to go to, and how amazing they're going to be. Apparently he has an elder brother here, who's told him exactly what to expect. Then Amber suggests we look at my room. I think she does it to get away from Guy, but he clearly doesn't figure this out since he follows us. I unlock room three with my key. Inside there's a single bed, a chest of drawers and a desk. It looks a little bit like a prison cell.

"Awesome freaking view," Guy says – he's already at the window. "Way better than mine."

I have a look too, but there isn't really much of a view at all. The trees that line the avenue are blocking most of it, and even if they weren't it would just be buildings. It's nothing like the view from my bedroom at home, where I can see the whole sweep of Silverlea beach. All seven miles of it. I feel a burst of homesickness.

And that gets worse when, a few minutes later, Amber says she'd better go, since she still has to find her own apartment. I tell her I'll search for a Boston cab company – because the Lornea Island ones I have saved in my phone won't operate here – but Guy jumps in again, telling her to get an Uber, and I think even Amber thinks this is cool because we don't have those on Lornea Island yet. By the time we get downstairs, the car is already here, and Guy and me help to load her bags. Then she gives me a hug, and tells me she'll see me soon. She gets in the car, and Guy and me both watch it drive away.

"Wow Billy, she is *super freaking hot*." I turn to see Guy is shaking his head, like he's pretending he can't believe it. "Say, is she, like... I mean are you guys...? You know?"

I'm confused. "What?"

He makes one of his hands into a loose fist, and pokes a finger from the other hand in and out. "I mean are you like, *fucking*?"

"*What?* Me and *Amber*?" I'm not very impressed with Guy so far.

I give him a look, and turn to go back in, though I feel him following me up the stairs.

"So is there anyone you *are* seeing?" He persists, standing in the doorway of my room for a moment. I don't answer him, but instead of going back to the kitchen, or to his own room, he just comes in.

"I had this girl I was dating back home. Kinda dating," he says, then sits down on the bed. Just as I was about to put my backpack there to start unpacking. "I mean we were, you know. Just fucking really."

"Could you get off the bed please?"

"But we kind of split up," Guy goes on. "You know, she went to Berkley. The whole long distance thing..." He gets up when he sees I'm serious and I dump my suitcase onto the bed. "And I'm not worried. I mean like, I've been here a whole day and you should *see* the girls. They're *everywhere*, and they're *freaking* hot. I mean smoking." He's sat at my desk now, leaning back in my chair. "We're going to have such an *awesome* time."

"That's good." I think about telling him I need the desk, to set up my computer. Then I remember something Dad told me, how I have to make an effort, even if I don't want to.

"I'm studying Marine Biology," I say. "I chose Boston University because it has one of the best Marine Biology courses in the whole world. And because it's quite close to home as well."

Guy kind of nods and grins. "Supercool. I'm doing Law. Say do you wanna beer? I got some grass too, I don't know if you're into that?"

"You're studying *Law*?"

"Yeah. Why?"

I shake my head. "No reason."

"Shall I skin one up?"

"No. But thanks."

Guy nods again. "Cool. I'll just get the beers then."

After a while he leaves, and I start unpacking. I guess he's nervous, just like I am, and this is his way of showing it. While he's gone I connect my laptop to the Wi-Fi, but then he doesn't come back, because someone else arrives in the apartment. I hear Guy talking to them in the little kitchen lounge area. I don't particularly want to go out and meet them, but eventually I know I kind of have to.

* * *

It's another boy, a bit older than me, and dressed in sports clothes. Guy's given him a beer already and they're knocking them back.

"Yeah, so I bet it's gonna be three girls and three boys," Guy says, and I work out he's talking about the six rooms in the apartment. Then he spots me, standing in the doorway.

"Billy, this is Jimbo. He's in room four." I step forward and we shake hands. He's got a really firm grip, like he's testing me. Guy's holding out a beer to me this time, and I take it now, if nothing else I need something cold to fix my hand.

"Are you into sports?" Jimbo asks, then goes on. "You don't look like you're much into sports."

"No," I start saying, but he's not listening.

"I play a lot of hockey. Like *a lot* of hockey." He chuckles, and twists to point at the shoulder of his tracksuit, which has a badge sewn onto it. I notice that's in the shape of a hockey stick. He turns back to glance at what I'm wearing, hiking trousers (I like them because they have extra pockets on the thighs, which is useful to carry things), my best checked-shirt, then looks at Guy too, who's wearing jeans, but with a t-shirt and BU jumper. He seems disappointed. "I guess you guys don't play hockey?"

And then the front door opens again, and a girl comes in, carrying bags and looking nervous, and we all troop out to meet her. And then later on another girl arrives. The whole episode takes a while, but eventually I work out that alongside me there are five other members of the apartment. They are:

. . .

James (Jimbo) Drew, 18, from somewhere near New York and here on a sports scholarship to study sports science. Which isn't really a science is it? He's the one who told me to call him Jimbo, but I haven't decided if I'm going to yet.

Guy Musgrave, 19, from Dover, Delaware. He really is in the first year of a law degree.

Laura Collins, 18, from a small town outside Philadelphia. She's in the room next door to me. She's studying French History and has blonde hair and really big boobs. Even if I hadn't noticed this fact myself (which I had), Guy and Jimbo have mentioned it at least a dozen times between them.

Claire Leharve, which I think is a French name. She's 18 and comes from somewhere in Ohio. She's studying English Literature, and when she came in she was literally holding a copy of Wuthering Heights, as if it might protect her. Looks-wise she's the opposite of Laura, she's very tall and thin, and has no boobs at all. Neither Guy nor Jimbo spent long talking to her.

Sarah Ellingham, 18, from Connecticut. She's studying psychology. She has dark hair and I think she's actually quite a lot prettier than Laura, although not in an obvious way. She's the one Guy said was shy, and I suppose she is, because she hasn't said much yet. Maybe that means she has hidden depths.

And then there's me. So that means I'm the youngest in the house (it's an apartment not a house, but already everyone's calling it a house, so I'm going to do the same). But we're all freshmen, or freshwomen, if that's a term. Normally I'd look it up, but I don't really seem to have the time, even though none of us are actually doing anything, except sharing little details about the schools we went to, and why we chose to come here.

"Say, I heard there's a party tonight," Guy tells us all at one point, and it's clear he expects we're all going to go. "Let's get some more beers in and get out there." And then him and Jimbo go off together to the store to buy more beer – because we've drunk it all by then. When they're gone, the girls go back to their rooms, and gratefully, I do the same.

CHAPTER SIX

We all go out to a special student bar first. It's massive, and it takes ages to order any drinks at the bar. We all huddle together, because we're the only people we actually know, but actually the music is so loud you can't really talk. So I spend the time looking around at the other students. I don't know why, but I expected them to look really different to the other students in my school. I mean they are a bit bigger, but they're all wearing the same sort of clothes, and they look disappointedly similar. Like they're interested in pretty much the same things.

After a while Guy gets a message on his cell telling him to come to the party, so we go there instead. It's held in an apartment that's identical to our new one, only it somehow looks as though the occupants have been there forever. They've put up a few decorations – those foil-banners you can buy in Walmart, and their kitchen area is completely stocked with alcohol. And again, for a while, all of us stand together in the kitchen, and I get the sense that everyone else there is doing the same thing. Then Jimbo finds someone from the hockey club, and he goes over to their group, and we all watch a bit enviously, except Guy, who keeps pretending that we're having an amazing time. But then things get a bit better when a girl called Kate (I think she lives there) announces we all have to 'fire-extinguisher' cans of beer. I don't know what she means, so she explains we have to punch a hole in the bottom of a full beer can, and then shake it really hard and put it to your lips. Then, when you open the tab, all the beer gets fired straight down your throat, like it's being shot out by a fire extinguisher. I don't want to do one, but Kate forces me to, and I have to say it does make it easy to drink a beer very quickly. I guess things loosen up a bit soon after that, and my new housemates disappear. I bump into lots of people and I make sure to ask them all questions, like what they're studying and why, but then I kind of run out of conversation, and they usually wander off. Maybe I look a bit disappointed when they don't turn out to be studying Marine Biology with me. I guess it does disappoint me a bit.

A bit later on and the little living area is now a kind of dance floor, although there's a big difference between how the girls are dancing (quite well), and the boys (more like they're wrestling or playing football.) It reminds me of the seal colony I was studying back in Australia, and I look around for someone to tell this to, but there's only Kate, and she doesn't listen, instead she takes my arm, and drags me out of the room and into her bedroom. For a moment I get the wrong idea, but there's about twenty people in there, listening to more relaxed music and smoking pot. She pats the floor next to her, and I sit on the carpet, but just to be polite really, and to make an effort, like Dad said. But there's only so long you can sit in a room full of people smoking pot, and not actually smoke any pot, before you begin to question whether this is actually a worthwhile use of your time. So eventually I tap Kate on the shoulder and tell her I'm going back to the lounge. She gives me a funny look, then shrugs. From the delay in the two actions, I can tell Kate's pretty wasted.

In the lounge the dance/fight thing is still going on, although the boys have moved on to ripping down the decorations. I can't find anyone from my house now. So after waiting what seems a polite amount of time, I leave and walk home.

So that's my first experience of a college party.

* * *

I'm not the first up the next morning, Sarah is already in the kitchen making toast. She asks me if I enjoyed the party, and I tell her it was OK, and she gives me a funny look. Then I think I should tell her how it reminded me about the seal colony, with her studying psychology and everything. But I don't get the chance because she goes out. So I start to clean up instead. The room is a horrible mess. There's take-out food just abandoned where people left it, and someone has arranged all the empty beer cans into a pyramid shape in the window. I pick it all up and dump it in the trash can, which is already looking dangerously full. Then I open the refrigerator to get my sandwiches from yesterday, but they're not there.

"Oh man, last night I was so *freaking* wasted."

I look up, to see Guy walking in wearing a dressing gown, but open to show his underpants. I didn't have him down as a dressing gown type.

"Have you seen my sandwiches?"

"No mannnn. Hey, you sneaked off early didn't you?" He sits down and hold his head for a moment. Then looks up. "So did you?"

"Did I what?"

"Did you *do the business*?"

"What?"

"With that Kate? She was all over you, man. Did you slip her one?"

I look at Guy, not quite believing I'm going to have to spend an entire year of my life with someone who keeps talking like this.

"No."

"Oh." He looks disappointed, but then a bit hopeful. "Anyone else?"

"No."

"Mmmmm." He pulls his dressing gown closed and ties it up. Thankfully. "Me neither. But plenty of time hey Billy?" He looks around the room, and I think he notices the lack of beer-can-pyramid, but he doesn't say anything, because at that moment Laura pokes her head in. She looks very bleary eyed, and just has a towel wrapped around her, from the tops of her thighs to just above her boobs. She says good morning, and then turns around and goes into the one bathroom we have to share.

Guy nudges me.

"Oh my lord. Tell me you saw that? Tell me you saw those tits?"

I leave Guy to it, and go back to my room and check my emails. There's one from Steve Rose, from *Shark Bites*, the TV show, well *formerly* of *Shark Bites*. I worked with him in Australia, monitoring shark populations, and then he helped me when I had to stop a drugs gang from murdering Amber's sister. He's gone back to live in Australia now, but he's emailed to wish me luck, which is really nice of him. I start to reply, then get distracted as a new email comes in from the university. I open that, and discover I've been assigned my tutor from the Marine Biology department. It's someone called Lawrence Hall. I don't actually recognize the name, which is odd since I've studied the staff list on the Marine Biology section of the University website – I wanted to see how many I recognized from journal articles I've read – and I don't remember a Professor Hall. But there could be all sorts of reasons for that. He could have come to work here recently, and the university hasn't updated its website in a while. That's probably what's happened.

Even so, I'm quite excited about it, because having a really good tutor is super important. He'll guide me through which subjects to study, and that will have a big influence on my future career. For that reason, having a strong student-tutor relationship is important as well. So I decide that, even though my actual classes don't start for a few more days yet, I'll go and introduce myself to Professor Hall today.

CHAPTER SEVEN

The Marine Biology building is a little distance away from the main part of the campus, down by the harbor and next to the aquarium. It's almost brand new, and really well equipped, which was one of the main reasons I chose to study here. I go on my bike, riding along by the river, and it's a beautiful morning. In my head I go through the questions I want to ask Professor Hall – about what articles he's published, and what his specialisms are.

When I get there I lock my bike up and go inside. I have to scan my new Student card to do so, which is quite fun. The building has an exciting, busy feel, with lots of students and staff milling around, carrying folders and drinking cups of coffee – actually it's just as I imagined it would be. I ask at the reception desk for where Professor Hall's office is. She looks on her computer, and directs me to the third floor. So then I have a choice between taking the stairs, or using the amazing glass-walled elevator, which offers a view out over the harbor. Obviously I call the elevator.

I'm alone when I do so, but then I'm joined by a gaggle of girls. It's a bit sexist of me to call them a gaggle, but there isn't really any other word – they certainly don't look like scientists – and they're behaving in a very girlish way, giggling and whispering things to each other, and shaking their hair about as if they're in a shampoo advert. It all makes me feel a bit self-conscious. And inside the elevator I can't help but hear what they're talking about, a party that either happened or is going to happen soon, I'm not quite sure, and something about a boy one of them is sleeping with. I assume the last part, as that's the bit that's whispered, but it's fairly obvious. When the elevator stops at the third floor I get out, realizing only then that I didn't even notice the view. So I stop by the window to have a look.

It *is* a nice view. A lot nicer than my new room, though maybe not quite as good as the view from my house back on Lornea, if I'm being picky about it. I do like the islands here though. There's no islands in Silverlea bay. When I've looked for a while, I turn around and start to search for Professor Hall's office, and after a few hundred meters of corridor I find it. And then I'm nervous again, when I knock on the door.

At first there's no reply, and I start to think that maybe I should have emailed first, to make an appointment, when suddenly a voice replies from inside.

"What is it?"

He doesn't say if I should go in, or anything else in fact, so after a second I knock again, and again the same reply, only a bit more annoyed now.

"I said what is it?"

So this time I open the door a fraction. And inside there's a frankly wonderful sight. It's a room lined with bookshelves, and a couple of desks with quite good computers, and covered with papers and *work*. Proper work. There's posters on the walls showing different species of octopuses, and there's a glass tank filled with water with some pebbles and seagrass at the bottom. I squint to try and make out what else is in there.

"Yes? Can I help you?"

I turn quickly to the man at the desk. Professor Hall is almost exactly as I imagined him. He's quite old, probably in his forties, and he's sitting at one of the desks with a microscope in front of him. He looks friendly even though I've interrupted him, well quite friendly – no one likes to be interrupted when they're doing important work.

"Professor Hall," I begin. "I'm very sorry to disturb you without an appointment, but my name is…"

POP!

I stop talking, unsure where the noise comes from, and also because it's kind of obvious he's not listening to me. Instead he's staring intently at the tank, I notice now there's some kind of shrimp in it.

"Did you hear that?"

"Err…"

"Did you know there are over five hundred species of *Alpheidae*? Probably far more than that, but five hundred we know of?"

"*Alpheidae*… is that pistol shrimp? The ones that fire bubbles?"

Professor Hall looks up, he looks pleased. "Yes! Except they don't fire bubbles so much as generate a low pressure vortex by snapping their claw incredibly fast, producing a shockwave capable of stunning or killing much larger prey. Watch this."

He dips a wooden stick in the water, moving it near to where the shrimp is half buried in the sand, at the bottom of the tank. For a moment nothing happens, then:

POP!

It happens quicker than I can see it. Professor Hall turns to a digital thermometer he has pointed on the tank.

"The temperature, in a tiny area, is as hot as the surface of the sun. Isn't that incredible?"

"Yeah it is. Are you doing a study on them?"

"Actually no." Professor Hall looks up and looks thoughtful. "Sebastian here is more of a pet. Although I am thinking about it. Did you know the noise from snapping shrimps is so loud it can interfere with marine sonar?"

"No, I didn't know that."

"Oh yes. Extremely interesting invertebrates. Anyhow." He suddenly smiles. "What can I do for you young man?"

For a second I actually can't remember, but then I do.

"I just – I wanted to introduce myself, I'm Billy Wheatley. I'm one of the new students in your freshmen tutor group."

Professor Hall's face goes a bit dark then.

"No you're not."

"What?"

"You would be, if my name was Professor Hall, but it's not. He and I share an office, but I am not he." He articulates the last words very individually, so that even though it doesn't sound like it makes sense, it still does. I glance across at the other desk in the room. It looks kind of similar to his, but it doesn't have the fish tank.

"Oh. Sorry."

"No problem at all. If you'd been looking for Professor Little, then you'd be in the right place, since that's me. But I don't take any freshmen students. Professor Hall did just leave though, if you're quick you may be able to catch him. He'll be in the refectory."

"Oh. Right, thanks."

Professor Little smiles again, as if to say it was no trouble, and then leans back over his microscope. I'm about to back out and leave him alone, when I realize I can't.

"Erm, just one more thing…"

He lifts his eye from the microscope and, after a half-second's hesitation, gives me the same smile.

"Let me guess, you want to know why I named an *Alpheidae* Sebastian? Well it's a perfectly decent name for a shrimp, don't you think?"

"Erm, yeah. Only it's not what I wanted to know. I just wondered what Professor Hall looks like?"

"Oh. Yes. Look for the outrageously loud Hawaiian shirt imprinted with images of the Hibiscus flower. You can't miss him."

"Thanks."

"Thank you." He turns back to the tank, and a bit reluctantly I back out.

I take the stairs this time, since I need a little time to steady myself. Everything is so new, and so exciting, and I want to make a good first impression on the real Professor Hall. Plus it's only one floor up.

The refectory is quite large, and it has views all the way around the building, but it isn't full. There's maybe twenty people here. And I quickly scan around for a man wearing a Hawaiian shirt, and like Professor Little said, there's only one. But that can't be Professor Hall, because this man is far too young. Like, in his twenties young – with long black hair, a gold chain around his neck. And he's sitting with the girls I saw earlier in the elevator, they're all laughing together. I stare in confusion, and somehow he must notice it, because I catch his eye. And then I'd feel wrong if I didn't explain why it is I'm staring. So I move forward.

"Excuse me, are you Professor Hall? Professor Lawrence Hall?"

"No." He says, and I'm immediately relieved. I have made a mistake after all. Which is good, because this man can't be my tutor.

"Well technically I am, but I'm not a fan of the title. Makes me sound a bit too *uptight* if you know what I mean." He turns to the girls. "Just call me Lawrence." They giggle like they did in the elevator, and I feel their eyes on me.

"And you are?"

It's kind of an automatic reaction. I stick out a hand. "Billy. Billy Wheatley."

He raises his eyebrows to make me go on.

"I'm in your tutor group."

Then his face changes. It's like he panics. "Oh shit. *Now?*"

I don't understand what he's talking about.

"You've got a tutor group *now?*"

"Oh! No. No it's not until next week. On Wednesday, at three pm."

"Thank Christ for that." He looks relieved, and smiles. He's got a good smile but he knows it, I can tell by the way he turns to show it off to the girls. Then he looks back to me.

"So how can I help you?"

Still I feel the girls watching me. I start to wonder what they're all doing here. I start to wonder what I'm doing there, come to that.

"I just wanted to come and introduce myself. As it says in the course prospectus. The relationship between a student and a tutor is very important."

There's a silence. And as it stretches out I know I've said the wrong thing. I don't know why I added the bit about the prospectus – although it *does* say it there. It's like I wanted to provide evidence to back up my argument. Then one of the girls, the prettiest one I note, starts to laugh, covering her mouth a moment later, but it sets the others off. Then Professor Hall starts laughing.

"It's just..." I begin, feeling my face flushing hot.

"No, no. You're right. It *is* important. Something some of my second year students here would do well to remember." He raises his eyebrows at the girls, then leans back and stretches his arms behind his head. I think back to the questions I thought of earlier, about what his specialisms are. But I'm not going to ask them now. I'm not an idiot.

There's a silence, as they all stop laughing.

"Well Mr Wheatley. Consider yourself introduced." Professor Hall says, a few moments later. "I'll see you in our first session next week."

I think about asking whether there's anything I need to do before then, like read up on a subject or anything, but I guess he'd email us if there is. So instead I just nod and take a step back. Then I turn and walk away, but I can hear the girls are bursting into laughter behind me, and this time Professor Hall isn't doing anything to stop them.

CHAPTER EIGHT

By the time I get back, Guy and Jimbo are already drinking, and the pile of trash overflowing the trash can has grown a bit bigger. And over the next few days that's how it goes. That seems to be the pattern that most people are following. Drinking, recovering from drinking (and making a big fuss about how hungover they are), and then this absurd talk about how much sex they're having, or how they're going to get lots of sex at the next party. In short, it's almost exactly like high school was, only a lot messier because there's no proper adults to clean up.

I guess I'm a bit disappointed, but I'm still hopeful that it's going to change when the classes actually start, and I get to meet some of the other Marine Biology students. In the meantime I decide not to complain. It's not that bad. But I'd be lying if I said my first impression of college was great.

My first class is a lecture on *Cells: The Building Blocks of Life.* It's my first time actually taking a real class in one of the proper lecture halls, with the steep rows of seating, and the professor at the front behind a lectern. I'm a little bit early when I arrive, and I'm not sure where I should sit. Actually I'm fifteen minutes early, so the theater is empty, which doesn't give me much to go on. In the end I opt for the second row – near the front but not right *at* the front, I don't want to be the class geek. But then there are some geeks who do sit in the front row, as well as lots of more normal students who sit in little groups together in the other parts of the room. I kind of hope someone will come and sit next to me, but no one does. I take notes all the way through. I don't actually need to, because the whole lecture is incredibly basic stuff, but I feel the lecturer might be offended if I don't. I'm actually a bit surprised when it's over and she just leaves, telling us she'll see us next week. In a way it's a bit of an anticlimax.

Then I have a gap in my schedule, and later on I have my second class: *Introduction to Marine Biology.* Again it's pretty basic, because I've been studying this stuff since I was about eleven, but I expect it'll get tougher pretty quickly. In this class I take the time to look around a bit more. There's maybe a hundred other students, and most of them look much more serious, at least they're all writing, or typing things into computers. Which is quite cool I reckon.

The other classes I have are *Evolution and Behavior, Biodiversity* and *Physical and Chemical Processes of the Ocean.* Again, none of it is new, or difficult, but I suppose it's good to have a refresher. And as the days go by I do get to know some of the other students on the courses. In fact, it's hard to keep track of them all. But while everyone seems nice enough, I guess I'm still a little disappointed too – the Marine Biology students don't seem very different to the other students I'm meeting, at the parties and at my house. No one seems that committed to the course, it's more about how much they're drinking, and how much sex they're having.

* * *

I'm nervous when I get to have my first tutorial with Lawrence. I've understood now that he's only a PhD student who's doing teaching – that is, he hasn't even got his doctorate yet, let alone become an actual professor. And at the rate he's going, I'm not sure if he'll ever make it. As I suspected when I first met him, he still seems more interested in the girls he's teaching than about the subject (*Marine Ecosystems* – could it be more basic?) But it turns out to be a little more interesting than the lectures, because as least we get to answer questions in the tutorials (in fact I end up answering all the questions because none of the other students seem to know very much.) So in a way it's quite fun.

Then I get a call from Amber telling me we have to meet for lunch.

On the one hand it's hard to believe it's been two weeks since I last saw her, but on the other I can't believe it's been *only* two weeks.

It's easier for me to go to her than for her to come down to the campus, since she only gets an hour off from her work and I have large study gaps in my schedule (not that I particularly need them yet). So we meet in *Pasta Gusto,* which is just across the street from her office.

"So Billy, how's it going?" She asks, once we've both sat down. She's dyed her hair again, it's orange now – but only in bits. "How's my *college boy?*"

"Good." There's a pause, where we smile at each other, but it's just a tiny bit awkward. "How's your job?"

"It's cool. They're giving me a ton to do, but it's..." she tips her head to one side. "It's nice to see you Billy. Really nice."

For a moment I wonder if she expects me to stand up again and hug her – she kind of sounds like she's thinking about it, but then gets herself arranged instead, putting a phone I haven't seen before next to her, and tucking her bag on the seat next to her. Then she spots a waitress and puts her hand up, calling her over.

"You wanna beer?" She smiles. "I know what you students are like."

"You know what *I'm* like too," I reply, then frown. "Are you having one?"

"Can't. I'm still working." She orders a coke, and I have the same. "They got me working on this pitch for a re-brand of a bakery. But a big one. And my boss, he keeps having new ideas and getting me to start from scratch." She gestures to the phone. "That's why I've gotta have that on the whole day."

I don't really know what she's talking about. "How's your apartment?"

She looks up. "Oh, it's OK. Nicer than your place! I'm sharing with two other girls." She shrugs. "They're cool. Bit older than me. Hey, how's your lot? How's... what was his name? *Gary?*"

"Guy?"

"Yeah."

"You met him. He's a moron."

She grins at this, and I tell her about the whole lot of them, and how they either seem more interested in drinking than studying, or like the girls they hide in their rooms and I hardly ever see them. It's nice to be with Amber, I realize after a while. I can just be myself and relax. And I get the sense she feels the same, but at the same time I notice her checking her phone a couple of times, or maybe she's just keeping an eye on the time.

We both order pizzas, and I explain how the work is a bit disappointing, at least so far, and she nods, and when I've finished she explains how her pitch works. They have to basically design a whole new suite of logos and how the different products the bakery makes will get packaged. But they're up against two other design agencies, and the bakery will decide which one they prefer. If they don't win, they don't get paid anything. It's interesting but, well, you know, it's not *that* interesting, so I ask her if she's managed to do any new designs for the *Save our Sea-Dragons* campaign, and she gets a bit uptight and says she's already done loads for that. And then there's a few moments where we're both just eating the pizzas, and don't seem to know quite what to say. I guess it makes me realize how Amber and I are moving apart more quickly than I'd anticipated. I mean I'm sure we'll stay friends and everything, but we are on separate paths now, her into the commercial world, and me into academia.

Then before I'm even done eating, Amber's phone pings, and when she checks it she swears and says she has to go. Right then. She insists on paying for the meal, even though I try to stop her. She says she got paid already. So that helps, because my bank account is looking pretty empty already.

CHAPTER NINE

Nearly two months go by with me telling myself – and Dad, when I ring him – that everything's going great, when it isn't. Not really. It's a bit like with school if I'm honest, in that there's no massive problem I could point to, it's just the whole experience is somehow – I don't know, underwhelming. But then something happens that changes everything. Like *completely*. Actually it's not something, it's some*one*.

I didn't tell you, but just after the semester began I was selected for a special program, not here at BU but at a different university called Harvard. You might have heard of it, since it's quite well known (though it doesn't even teach Marine Biology). Anyway, Harvard University has a lot of money and likes to help out the other universities, so they offer a few special students – the ones from underprivileged backgrounds, or the really exceptional ones – additional courses, actually *in* Harvard itself. And I got told I fit into both those categories, so I was offered an extra class studying *National and International Law*. It was actually my tutor, Lawrence, who convinced me to go, since I didn't see the point, but he told me that Law is very important, given that it impacts upon the coastlines and the oceans. And actually it is very interesting, partly because it's actually something *new* to learn. The only problem is my Harvard class finishes at two on Thursdays, and then my *Physical and Chemical Processes of the Ocean* class starts at two thirty – which only gives me a half hour to get three miles across the city. Of course it doesn't really matter if I'm late for *Physical and Chemical Processes*, since it's super easy, and they don't take registers in college, but I still feel it would be rude. But anyway. That's why I was sprinting out of the Harvard campus just now, until I went around a corner too fast and literally smashed straight into a girl. She actually screamed like I meant it or something.

I stare at her as I pick myself up off the floor. Or bits of her. She's lying on her back, with her legs in the air, and there are books everywhere. It gives me a few seconds to consider what to do. I've already seen the students around here *are* different from the kids at my high school – they all look like they've got money. I don't want this girl to sue me.

"I'm really sorry." I say suddenly. "Are you OK? I was late for a class, and…"

She rolls forward, her hair all messed up and her face white. Even so her appearance stuns me into silence.

"You nearly killed me!"

Slowly she picks herself up and slaps the dust from her jeans. On the one hand she looks like any of the hundreds of other students around, in jeans and a kind of blouse thing, but on the other hand it's obvious she's different. She's *stunning*, and the anger on her face only makes her more striking. It's pushed a red color into her cheeks, where the rest of her skin is pale and clear. But I don't want to stare, so I bend down to pick up her books. I can't help but read the titles. They're all some sort of law textbooks.

"What class?" She says.

"Pardon?"

"What class are you late for?" She holds out her hands to take them, and as she does so she stares right at me.

"Oh it's not here. I'm at BU…" She's still looking at me, and there's a curious expression on her face that I don't understand. "It's, um, *Physical and Chemical Processes of the Ocean.*" I give a little cough, when she doesn't react.

"I know you." Her eyes narrow, and her forehead just creases a tiny bit, the skin still smooth, and kind of delicate. Her hair is this golden color, a bit like, a bit like… Well like sunlight. Or maybe more accurately dry Marram grass, but only when it looks beautiful like at the end of summer at sunset. Sunset in the sand dunes…

"I saw you on TV."

I snap quickly out of whatever it is I'm thinking and try to focus.

"I did, didn't I? You were that kid who stopped the – some drugs assholes. Only when they interviewed you on TV you only wanted to talk about the sizes of sharks. You confused the hell out of the reporter. It was hilarious."

Now it's my turn to frown. It's true I did end up helping to get some drug smugglers arrested about a year ago, well – in some cases arrested, in other cases killed, but that wasn't my fault. And while I did give a couple of TV interviews about it, and used the opportunity to try and explain the mitigating circumstances behind Steve Rose's scientific fraud, they definitely weren't *funny*. But you just try explaining all that to a girl you've just sent flying.

"Over on, erm…" She turns away and snaps her fingers. "Lornea Island, wasn't it?"

Dumbly, I nod.

"We have a house on Lornea." She smiles suddenly. Her whole face lights up, like the sun just came out. "My family I mean, it's just a holiday place," she wrinkles her nose.

I'm still holding her books, and though I don't know what to say, I don't want to give them back. It might mean she walks away, and I don't think I want that.

"So is that where you're from? Lornea Island?"

I nod again, although actually my background is kind of difficult to explain. "Yeah."

"Billy!" She exclaims suddenly. "It's Billy, isn't it? I remember now. I have one of those memories." She holds out her hand, and I have to clasp her books to my chest in order to free up mine to shake it.

Then her forehead creases again into a frown, but one of amused confusion, not anger.

"It was actually my books I was hoping for there Billy, but if you insist. I'm Lily."

So then I pull back my hand, just as she goes to shake it, and then I stick mine out a second time, and eventually we shake hands. Her hand feels delicate, the skin cool and soft. Suddenly she bursts into laughter.

"What are you *doing*?" I've no idea what she means, but I drop her hand at once.

"I'm sorry, I was just…"

"Don't worry about it." She stares at me for a moment. "Actually what *are* you doing?"

I pause. "I'm not. It's just your hand felt nice…"

"No, I mean – that was weird but - what are you doing *now*? There's someone I'd like you to meet."

I freeze. I've got my class. But then there's this girl. This incredible girl. But I haven't missed any classes yet. I have my attendance record to think of.

"I have my class."

"*Physical and Chemical…something?*" She smiles again. "*Processes of the Ocean.* I told you, I have that sort of memory. Is it hard? It sounds hard."

"Oh no. I've studied all the topics for the whole year, back when I was in high school… I mean, it wasn't a subject my school offered, I just studied it anyway."

"When you weren't catching drug smugglers?"

"That's right. Or murderers."

Her eyebrows shoot up.

"I also caught some murderers. Just a couple." I turn away and count in my head. "Actually three."

"Three?"

"I think it was three."

"You're even funnier in real life than on TV."

I frown again. "Do you want your books back?"

"You can carry them for me."

"What?"

"You can carry them. You're coming with me."

"But I have to get to…"

"No you don't. You just said it was easy, and I'm about to expand your education significantly in other directions. Come on." She turns and starts walking away, and I can't help but see how well her jeans fit her. Her hair swishes as she turns her head, and she sees where I'm looking.

"Come *on* Billy."

So I follow her.

CHAPTER TEN

She walks fast, so it's hard to keep up, especially since I'm still carrying her books clamped to my chest, and my back pack too.

"Where are we going?"

"You'll see."

I do soon enough, when we come to a little café. It's tucked away in the basement of a block of apartments on a street just off the Harvard campus. She skips down the steps and pushes open the door and a bell tinkles as she does so, and inside most of the customers look up to see who's come in. There's only about ten people, and it's one of those places where they let you linger and lounge about. Most of the seating is old leather couches. Against the left wall there are two facing each other over a low table, and three other people slouched in them.

"Hey guys!" Lily says brightly. Then she reaches behind her and grabs me by the arm, and pulls me forward, like she's presenting me as a prize.

"Who's that?" It's a man who asks, well, he's only a couple of years older than me, I'd guess, but he looks much more mature than me. Physically I mean, I don't know about mentally. I haven't had the chance to tell.

"I bumped into him," Lily explains. I assume she's using the term literally and metaphorically, but she doesn't explain how. "His name's Billy, and he's really funny."

They all – the man, and the two others, who are another man and a girl – look at me, as if I'm about to launch into a comedy skit, but obviously I'm not, so I just stand there.

"He doesn't look very funny," the first man says, but at once the other man interrupts him.

"Oh I don't know, James, the way he's dressed looks frankly hilarious." This second man is wearing little round spectacles, and he pushes them up his nose. But then he stands up and holds out his hand – not like I'm going to shake it, more like I can kiss it.

"I'm Eric."

I take his hand, still horizontal, and hold it for a second, then let go again.

"Charming to meet you. Any friend of Lily is a friend of mine. And James too, I'm sure."

I haven't got the first idea what's going on, but Lily takes my hand now and pulls me down onto the couch. The other girl moves along to make space for us.

"So you've met Eric, and sort of met James," she turns to him and gives him a smile. "This is Jennifer. There's also…" she looks around. "Where's Oscar?"

"He's got a class," Jennifer says, and she turns to me now. She's one side of me, and Lily is the other, and the thing is that both of them are stunning. Jennifer is much darker than Lily, dark hair and more tanned, and she surprises me by leaning in and kissing me. She only does it on the cheek, and her lips don't actually touch me, but it still takes me by surprise.

"So what? You know Lily or something?" It's James who asks the question. He's the only one sitting on his own, in one of the armchairs that completes the square of our seating, and he still sounds pissed. I'm about to answer when Lily does it for me.

"He's from Lornea Island."

"So?"

"So! He's from Lornea Island, *I'm* from Lornea Island. That's how I know him."

"You're not from Lornea Island." James says.

"I go there. Every summer." She turns to me. "Most summers."

There's a moment when no one speaks. And even though I'm sandwiched between the two most beautiful girls I've ever met, I'm kind of regretting coming.

"So why exactly is he here?" James presses on. The only good thing about the situation is that I don't feel I have to reply, it's obvious he's talking to Lily, and her to him. It gives me a chance to study James a bit. As well as being mature, in a physical way, I can see he's also very good looking. In the square-jawed kind of way.

"Calm down James. I told you, he's *funny*. I saw him on TV last year, when he caught a gang of drug smugglers. He literally blew up their boat."

This seems to take James by surprise. Lily keeps talking.

"I thought he could tell us about it. It'd be *entertaining*." She changes her voice just a fraction, but I don't know the significance.

"Alright," James concedes gruffly. "Go on."

Suddenly I feel everyone's attention shift to me, but Eric steps in at once. "Woah there. Where's our manners? First we have to offer the poor boy a drink, no?"

So then there's a bit of a debate about what I'm going to drink, and for a moment I feel a tinge of disappointment. These people seem so different to my housemates, but now it seems like they're just the same – only interested in drinking.

"Well, I've finished my classes for the day," Eric announces. "So I'm going to celebrate with a frozen banana daquiri. Perhaps you'd like to join me?" Eric stands up, and I notice for the first time how he's dressed. He's wearing a suit and a silk waistcoat. There's a chain coming out of it, so I think he might even have a pocket watch. But he smiles at me in a really friendly way, so I nod back.

"I'll have one too," Lily shouts at him, as he walks over to the counter, where he talks to the lady who's serving as if they're very old friends. Then he comes back and sits down. He kind of simpers, then looks at me very intently. "Frozen banana daquiris all round. They'll be just a moment. Now Billy, you're free to commence with your story."

* * *

I don't know exactly what to say, but I begin to recount the story of what happened last year, when I went to Australia with Dr Steve Rose, the famous marine biologist, to help monitor shark population off Wellington Island marine reserve, only I discovered that he'd been overstating the sizes of the sharks for several years, in order to make them sound more dangerous to the TV executives.

"Hold on," Eric interrupts my flow at this point. "You're talking about *the* Steve Rose – the TV guy, from *Shark Bait!*?"

"Yes, only he's not doing *Shark Bait* anymore, because of what happened," I say, then I get back to my story. "So I had to fly the drones – I have my own at home, so I'm very experienced at flying – and we used them for measuring the sharks…"

"Hang on, how does all this relate to the drugs thing? The thing Lily said?" This is Jennifer, she's turned towards me, her hair hanging down like a shining black curtain. It distracts me a bit.

"Erm." I take a slurp of the daquiri to refocus. They've arrived by this time, complete with those little paper umbrellas. Then I stare at it, wondering what it actually *is*. Whatever it is, it's tasty.

"That came later. I have this friend, she's called Amber…"

"Girlfriend?" Eric asks at once.

"No. Just a friend, but then she'd met this guy, this Italian guy who had sailed from Europe in a small yacht, and he'd met some guys somewhere in South America, and agreed to take some cocaine for them into the US. Only he got caught in a storm, and figured he could use it to pretend his boat had sunk, and make money selling the cocaine himself."

I stop for another slurp of banana daquiri, and this time I notice how everyone is silent, just staring at me.

"So he's hiding out, living on his boat in Holport, which is where I kept *my* boat, before it sank that is, and it turned out he had started seeing Amber when I was away and…"

"Hold up." It's Eric again. He raises his hand and acts like he's trying to work this all out. "So your friend Amber is dating a guy who faked his own death ripping off South American drugs smugglers?"

"Erm. Yeah."

"OK, carry on."

"Well, there's not much more to say. Somehow the smugglers found out Carlos wasn't dead – that's the Italian guy. And they found him, and they sent some guys to kill him and get the drugs back."

I take another sip of my drink.

"Carlos is the guy who stole the drugs?" This time it's James who asks.

"Yeah."

"So what happened?"

I think back, remembering how I took my kayak out, and saw Amber and Carlos having sex on the floor of his boat. I won't tell them that part.

"Well, they found Carlos and tortured him, but for some reason he told them *I* knew where the drugs were hidden."

"And did you?" Jennifer asks. Her eyes are really sparkling now. I glance from her to Lily, and then back again. They're both really beautiful, but actually there's no doubt which of them is more beautiful. It's Lily. There's something about her that just takes my breath away.

"Billy?"

"Huh?"

"Did you know?"

"Oh. No. Well not at first, but then I worked it out, because I actually saw Carlos when he was hiding the drugs. In a sea cave." I turn to Lily. "You know those caves down the west side of Lornea Island, in the marine reserve? I thought it was odd he was spear fishing there."

Lily's sets her face into a frown. "OK."

Eric sits back suddenly and his head gives a kind of shiver, like he can't keep up any more, but I press on. I'm almost there now.

"So I worked out where the cocaine is. But then the gangsters – I suppose that's what they are – they kidnapped Amber's sister, and told us they'd kill her if we didn't get their drugs back, it was worth millions, apparently."

James scratches his chin. "Then what?"

"Well then me and Steve went out to dive and get the drugs, and we managed to shoot the gangsters. Then we crashed my boat into their boat, and then the police turned up."

I sit back and wait.

"I told you he was funny," Lily says, and she looks at me, delight lighting up her beautiful face.

CHAPTER ELEVEN

"Wow." Eric says a few moments later. "Just wow Billy." He reaches up and clicks his fingers, then when the lady behind the counter looks over, he orders me another banana daquiri, even though I haven't finished the first one yet. And then they all start asking me questions, clarifying exactly what happened. I have to admit, it's fun to talk about now, even though at the time it wasn't fun to actually do. It's odd too, since I kind of expected that I'd have to explain all of this to the people in my house – after being on TV and everything – but none of them ever asked.

And the café where we're sitting has a real comfy feel, which I hadn't realized I'd missed, but now I think I have. My apartment (I still don't think of it as home) was sparse and bare when I moved in, and now it's filled with trash – I mean literally filled with trash, we've all got into a bit of a standoff over who should take it out, and as a result no one will. The trash can itself, a small plastic container which was in a corner by the microwave, filled up weeks ago and has been overtopped, like a river in flood. It's now buried beneath empty pizza boxes, beer cans and wine bottles in what Guy and Jimbo call the Trash Corner. They claim it's an improvement, since you can simply toss trash in the general direction and be sure to hit. And there's no need to take it outside. Obviously their thinking is flawed here. My room is reasonably tidy, but it's very small, and there's only one chair, by the desk, so you can't really relax there.

But this place – I look around – the sofas are all different, and all well used, but not in a worn-out way, more like they've taken years to bed-in, and now they're *just right*. I'm surprised, and a bit disappointed when James suddenly pulls out his cell phone, checks it, and announces it's time to go. I think at first he means just him, but all the rest of them start getting up to leave as well.

"Where are you going?" I ask, which is a bit forward of me, but just goes to show how relaxed I feel now, and how much I was enjoying myself.

"We have work to do Billy." James smiles at me, and it occurs to me it's the first time he actually smiled at me the whole time I was here. It's not the nicest smile either, he looks a bit sarcastic. The others get up, and they start leaving, and I panic for a moment that I'm going to be left with the check. I don't mind paying for what I drank, but ten Banana Daquiris must be expensive. But then I see Eric going to the bar. I expect him to pull out his wallet, or something, but instead he embraces the lady behind the desk, and kisses her on both cheeks. She does the same to him, like this is normal behavior. Then I guess he catches me looking, because he comes over to me and whispers in my ear.

"Don't worry dear boy, it's all on the slate." Then he touches my shoulder, gives me a look and says out loud. "I trust we'll see you again soon, Billy?" and then he looks at Lily, who looks at James, who says nothing, but turns and walks away and out of the café. The others follow him, except Lily, so that now it's just the two of us. She doesn't say anything, like she's considering what to do next.

"Why don't you come to dinner?" She says in the end, which I definitely wasn't expecting.

I've no idea if she means just the two of us, or everyone.

"OK." I say, after a moment.

"Good." She looks pleased with this, and she takes a pen and scrap of paper from the table and writes down a number.

"Text me yours. I'll set something up." When she hands it to me our hands touch a second time, and this time I savor how smooth her skin is. But it's her eyes I remember most, the way they sparkle when she looks up and says:

"See ya Billy."

* * *

I text her before I even leave the café, but she doesn't reply at once. In fact it's two days before anyone texts me again, so I start to worry if my cell phone might be broken. But then it chirps at me, a couple of days later. I'm actually still in bed, since it's Saturday, and I don't have any lectures. I have the phone charging on my desk, so I have to get up quickly to grab it, but then I see it's not from Lily. It's from Amber.

Hi Billy, I was a bit distant the other week. Super busy. Let's go out with your friends. I wanna meet Guy again!

I read it, and though I'm disappointed it's not from Lily, it also kind of makes me smile, and then a second text comes in.

It's Saturday night. You must have some party planned?

And then there's a loud banging on my door.

"Yo Billy, get your ass out here."

I don't know who it is, and then the voice gets harder to identify because loud music suddenly fires up from the kitchen. Whoever it is bangs on the door again, and then they shout again. I identify it as Jimbo this time.

"Get up you lazy piece of shit." We've all got to know each other a bit better now, this is just how he talks to his friends.

"What is it?" I reply.

"We're tidying." Jimbo says. "Get up."

"*Tidying?*"

"Just get your ass out here."

I consider ignoring him, since it isn't my mess, but I decide I better help, so I get dressed and come into the kitchen. Here I find that everyone else from the house is there and actually tackling the disaster of our communal living quarters. Jimbo is wearing pink washing up gloves and soaping up all our plates and cups and dishes – we ran out of clean ones weeks ago, but they never got washed. Claire is there drying up and putting them away, while Sarah and Laura are delicately picking up items from the mountain of trash and dropping them into black bags. Guy is sweeping, sort of, behind the row of chairs.

"What's going on?"

"We're having a clean-up. We're gonna start a rota." Jimbo tells me from the sink.

"I thought you liked the mess? What changed?"

No one answers for a second, then Laura does.

"I saw a rat." she explains, wrinkling her nose.

"Where?" My eyes turn to the Trash Mountain. "What? An actual rat?"

"I think so." She gives a shudder. I feel Guy come to my shoulder, and the four of us regard the pile of trash as if it might conceal terrifying monsters.

"I'm not 100% sure it was a rat," she goes on. "I was a bit stoned, at the time. But it was definitely something. And that is disgusting."

"And it's not good for bringing pussy home," Guy adds, causing Laura to shove him back to his sweeping.

"You want to help fill this up, Billy?" Sarah says, holding out her bag.

"Course he's going to fucking help," Jimbo shouts from the sink. "If he thinks he can get out of it he can fuck off." Which is rude of him, because of course I'm going to help.

"I can get my computer," I suggest. "I'm very good at spreadsheets. I could make the rota."

"Oh no you don't you lazy piece of shit. Grab a fucking bag."

So I do, and strangely enough it's actually the nicest Saturday I've had with the other guys in the house. Me and Laura and Sarah fill six bags of trash before we see the top of the actual trash can again, and then we slow down a bit, just in case Laura really did see a rat, although I'm doubting it would still be there, if she ever did see it in the first place. And at the same time, we get talking, about what they're studying, and how they're finding it. And it's funny, but now that I've met Lily and Jennifer, it's kind of made me more relaxed around my housemates – they seem... ordinary, but not exactly in a bad way. Laura has her hair tied back, and her skin is kind of blotchy. And Sarah still looks quite pretty – almost like a less glamorous version of Jennifer, Lily's friend. But nowhere near as stunning as Lily, so it makes her easy to talk to.

Laura picks up a plastic bag by its corner and tugs it loose from the now much smaller trash mountain. It comes free and drips trash-juice on the floor.

"Urgh, get it in the bag." I step forward and stretch open the black bag I'm holding, and we get it in. As we do so there's a rustling from the bottom of the pile.

"I saw something!" Sarah says, and we all stare, tense.

"It was just the pile settling back down," I say. I'm still sure we're not actually about to reveal a rat, that would be disgusting. But then Guy comes over with his broom. He turns it around and pokes the handle into the pile, hooking it under the partially broken-down remains of a trash bag. I remember setting it up, next to the can, after it overfilled. He lifts it, and we see a section of the floor we've not seen for a while, stained yellow. And then we see it. First a flash of brown fur, and then the scaly skin of rodent tail, disappearing deeper into what remains of the pile. Guy lifts some more.

"Oh my God!" Laura exclaims, and Guy screams too, as a dozen little pink bodies twitch in the sudden light. It's not a single rat, it's an actual nest of them.

CHAPTER TWELVE

It was me that had to deal with the nest in the end. No one else would go near it. I used an old cardboard beer box – the kind that carries twelve large cans – and cut down two sides to make a kind of scoop, with a fold-down lid. Then I put gloves on, cleared away the few bits of trash still covering it up, and slid the box gently under the nest. You could hear the little babies squeaking and chirping, but only just because Laura and Claire were squealing three times as loud. Sarah helped me close the box, and wrap tape around it to seal it. Then we carefully cleared up the rest of the trash, expecting to see the adult rats any moment, but they weren't there. We found a little gap in the skirting, so I guess they escaped under the floor that way. I blocked the hole up so they couldn't come back. We weren't sure what to do with the nest though. Jimbo and Guy wanted to dump it down the drain, but Laura wouldn't let them, and my suggestion to find a safe place somewhere in the wild was good in theory, but not much help in the middle of a city. In the end, Sarah and I carried it together to a park, while the others watched out that no one saw what we were doing. We slid it under some bushes and built up a little protective bank of sticks and leaves. I don't suppose they'll survive, but at least they have a chance.

And maybe you'd think, after all that, and spending the rest of the day finally getting the kitchen looking almost as clean as when we moved in, we might want to cook something in it, but maybe we were all a bit wary, hygienically speaking, and anyway, none of us had any food in. So instead we agreed to go out, together, for a proper meal out. I guess we were all feeling that we'd actually bonded a bit. And somewhere along the line I remembered the text from Amber, and I asked if it was OK for her to come along. The moment I mentioned her, Guy was all over the idea, and even though Laura looked a bit dubious for a second or two – because (in case you haven't guessed) she's obviously trying to get together with Jimbo, and doesn't want the competition, she obviously sensed the mood too, and didn't want to spoil it. So I text Amber and tell her to come as well.

After that it's really hard to get anywhere near the bathroom, since the girls are in there getting ready. Actually, the girls and Guy, who's just as bad. Jimbo sits in the lounge and drinks beer and watches sports on TV. It's hooked up to the internet, so he's able to get this really obscure hockey channel, and he tries to explain to me what the attraction is, although I have to admit he fails.

At about eight we all go out, to a pizza place. Amber comes along with one of the girls from her apartment, a girl called Susie, so there's eight of us around the table. And it's fun, in a kind of ordinary way. It's fun to recount the story of the rat's nest to Amber and Susie, who are both horrified. Then Jimbo talks about hockey club, and all the drinking they do, and Guy tries to flirt with Amber, who isn't having any of it. I talk to Sarah a bit, and decide she'd be nice if I wasn't more interested in Lily. But to be honest, the whole evening has that high-school feel I talked about before, only it's not quite, it's like we're all morphing from being just high-school students, into something a bit more grown-up, but it's like we're still playing at it, rather than it being who we really are. It's still not quite what I dreamed about when I thought of going to college.

Afterwards we work out the bill so that everyone pays for what they had, and then we go on to a bar. It's super crowded and we kind of all stand together, drinking and not able to say too much because it's so loud, but the same sort of things happen, and after an hour of that Susie goes home, and I'm about to as well, until Jimbo starts hassling for us to go to a club. I'm not going to, but Amber says yes, so we go to one that's supposed to be really awesome, but really it's a bit mixed. First we have to line up outside for a half hour, and when we get to the front they complain about my shoes, which are perfectly sensible waterproof walking shoes, and not sneakers at all, like the man suggests. It's Amber who gets him to let us in (it cost twenty dollars mind), and inside it's so loud you can't speak at all. Jimbo and Guy buy drinks and stand by the bar but the girls dance. I'm not sure who to join, until Amber grabs me and leads me onto the dance floor. I'm not much of a dancer usually, but she's good at making me relax – or maybe it's the beer. Anyway, after a few minutes of feeling a bit self-conscious, I forget about people watching, and just do what Amber does. And Sarah too. And for about an hour we're just there, laughing and bouncing and jigging around, as the place fills up around us.

CHAPTER THIRTEEN

The next morning is fun too. I get up, and I have a bit of a headache, but not too bad, and I get the feeling everyone else feels the same. The kitchen is only a little bit messy from the night before (we don't know who, but someone had a go at making a toasted sandwich when we got in last night, Sarah jokes it might have been the rats), but we clean it up and the girls make brunch for everybody. I have to write an actual essay, and I do so in my room, but with the door open, so I can hear the music that Guy is playing. It's kind of how I imagined college to be, at least a little bit.

But in a way, the little interlude is a high spot. The next day I have a tutorial, with Lawrence, and it's boring. I get annoyed at him because the work is too easy, and he gets annoyed at me for answering all the questions, but honestly if I don't, how are we supposed to move on? And two days later, the kitchen doesn't look too different to how it did before we cleaned it up. OK, there's no trash corner, we've learned that lesson, but I'm still the only one doing the washing up. And I'm not doing it for *everyone*.

So when I get a text from Lily I guess I'm excited. She simply tells me an address, and to come at eight. I look up the address on Google, and it looks like an apartment in one of the typical brownstone houses around here, although from the cars outside you can tell it's in the expensive part of the city. But I don't really know what to expect. I don't know what to wear, nor whether we're eating at the house, or going out, or anything.

I decide to walk there, in the hope it'll calm my nerves. And because I haven't really figured out the subway yet.

The apartment looks more impressive in real life than it looks on Google Earth, but I tell myself not to be intimidated and knock on the door. It takes ages for anyone to answer it, but when it opens it's Jennifer. She's dressed quite relaxed, in black leggings and a kind of chunky green jumper, but once again, she looks stunning in it, and it's nice to see how she greets me – I get a hug and a kiss on both cheeks, and I feel enveloped in her perfume, which kind of pulls me into the house.

"Billy – you came!" she says. "Come into the kitchen with us girls, ignore those stupid boys." She directs the last comment into a room on her left – I can't see inside, and takes my hand. I follow along, as if pulled by the scent from her hair, but I can't help also noticing that the lobby here isn't what I expected. I thought I was coming into a building divided up into lots of different apartments but it seems that Lily has the whole floor – that's assuming it is actually Lily who lives here. And the decoration is amazing, it's like being in a museum. The hallway is packed with antique-looking furniture and there are wooden panels on the walls, and actual oil paintings too. Hanging from the ceiling is an actual chandelier. I gaze around as Jennifer leads me along, and then through a door and into a kitchen. But it's not a normal kitchen. It's bigger than my whole apartment, even all the bedrooms. The decoration is similar to the hallway, just even more so. I only expect to see Lily, but Eric is also there. He's sitting on the worktop with his feet up, wearing a bright blue silk shirt.

"Billy will help us settle this," he says, as if I've been there for ages and just wandered back into the room. "The lovely Lily and I are arguing about the need for effective gun control in this country. I believe we need to ban all firearms, with the exception of those used where it's absolutely necessary to control wildlife populations. But *Lily* here wants to gradually *phase* them out, though she gives no details how that works in practice."

He talks really quickly, and as he does so he swings his legs down and, to my surprise, embraces me just as Jennifer did, including the kisses that are nearly but not quite on the cheek. But whatever he does, or says, it can't compete with how Lily looks. She's dressed in a nearly white dress, with flowers printed on it, and a delicate cardigan draped around her shoulders. She comes over and gives me a welcome hug as well, but without the kisses. I pay so much attention I barely realize Eric has spoken again.

"Yes. Well I think we need to get Billy warmed up before we hit him with the big questions in life." He holds up a bottle – it's just wine this time, white wine – and he pours some for me, into a giant, delicate wine glass. He slides it over the granite of the work-top.

"You're being deliberately idiotic, Eric. As usual." Lily goes back to the earlier conversation. She's making a salad, I notice. I've not seen salad in several weeks. "I'm simply pointing out that there are already millions of guns in circulation. If you simply ban them it won't make very much difference, and any approach needs to bear that in mind." Eric stares at her, then theatrically looks away.

"Actually, if you prefer," Jennifer interrupts, smiling sweetly at me. "You could join the boys. They're in the billiard room, discussing French Impressionist art."

I don't know if this is a joke or not, though I'm beginning to suspect it might not be, but either way, I haven't quite gotten over the house I'm in.

"Is this house all yours?" I ask. For a second I regret the question, but Eric turns on me with a big grin.

"Yes, it's quite something isn't it? The *Lily-Palace* I call it. Furnished for an exiled European prince, wasn't it? You wait till you have a piss – gold faucets."

Lily rolls her eyes and says nothing.

"It belongs to my grandfather, he's letting me live here while I'm studying. He wanted me to be comfortable."

"And she is. So *very* comfortable," Eric interrupts again, raising a toast to her with his wine glass.

"What does your grandfather do?" I ask. "He's not a prince is he?"

I suppose it's a stupid question again, or I work out it's a stupid question, from the awkward silence. For a few seconds none of them even look at me, but they exchange glances between themselves. Then Eric puts down his glass.

"Billy. Why don't I give you a tour of your palatial surroundings for the evening?" He turns to Lily. "Would that be acceptable? While you chop that tomato? I promise not to show him your boudoir…"

Lily's face, which is still serious after my question, suddenly breaks and she looks lovely again. Demure and beautiful.

"Be my guest. But please don't break any more vases."

Eric sends a look in her direction, but then trips over to me. Before I know what's happened he's plucked my own glass from me and put it down, and we're arm in arm. I can feel the thinness of his muscles through the shirt sleeve.

We go back into the hallway, and then into a room dominated by a huge dining table, set on a rug over a hard wooden floor. You could seat twenty people at it, probably, but it's set for just – I count quickly – six, and with what looks like really expensive plates and cutlery, with napkins and everything. I don't know if they're expensive or not, but they look it. The rest of the room matches the house. There's an enormous fireplace with a gigantic mirror hanging over it, and a large double window too, and when I step closer I see outside there's a big piece of lawn shielded on both sides by mature trees. Beyond the lawn there's a dock and the river, wide here as it meets the bay.

"This is where we eat," Eric begins. "Decorated for King George the eighth by the Parisian interior design genius Pierre Le Gustave, famous for having only one eye and three legs."

I look blank.

"I just made that up, but there will be a test afterwards." He stops. "Actually I just had to get you out of there before you got yourself into any more trouble."

If it's possible I look even blanker. "Billy, let me enlighten you with the rules of the Lily-palace," he slips his arm around me and leads me out of the room, back into the hallway, and then into another room. It's lined with bookshelves on every wall, with ladders for reaching the ones higher up.

"The library," He says. "Let's sit for a moment and contemplate." There are four red leather armchairs and he pushes me into one and takes another.

"The first rule of the Lily-palace is *you do not talk about the Lily-palace.*" He waits a second, then goes on. "You pretend, just like the rest of us do, that it's quite normal to live in a ten-bedroom mansion on the river with priceless antiques and golden faucets."

"But why does she…"

"Eh!" Eric holds up a finger to stop me. "You're forgetting the first rule of the Lily-Palace. You don't talk about the…"

"But…"

"Stop it. Billy. You don't *ask about*, you don't *look quizzically at*, you don't even *mention* the Lily-Palace. Not to your friends, your family." He fixes me with a hard stare. "Not even to your lovers."

There's a silence.

"I don't have any lovers."

I don't know why I say that. I guess I'm finding this all rather overwhelming.

"Oh Billy. You're very *revealing*. Like an open book. But it brings me onto the third rule. Up."

For a moment I don't know what he means, then he waves his hand at me to get out of the chair, and we leave the library, and go into another room. I guess you could call it a sitting room. It's a little bit more normal, and it has a TV on the wall. There's an opening at one end into a kind of sunroom that goes out into the gardens. Eric waves a hand vaguely around it.

"Living room. It's where she actually lives, here and the kitchen." Then he takes me back out. There's only one other doorway from the hall that I haven't seen, the one that Jennifer said the boys were in, discussing some sort of art, I think. We go there next, but even before we go in, I can hear they're still there. Eric pushes opens the door without knocking, and I see it's got a snooker table in it – I think it's snooker, I'm not sure of the difference between that and billiards, but it's obviously not a pool table because, like everything in the house, it's massive. Inside James is there, playing with another man I haven't met yet. I suppose this is Oscar. Both of them look at me like they'd much rather I wasn't here, then James forces a sort of smile.

"Billy. You came." He doesn't introduce the other man, but Eric does.

"And this is Oscar. You didn't meet before, but we told him about you."

I don't know if I'm supposed to go in there and shake his hand, or what, but he doesn't make any move towards me.

"Hello." I say in the end, and he just nods back at me.

"Your shot," James says, turning his back on us. So I guess the conversation is over.

"Let's look upstairs," Eric says. And then when we're going up the stairway he keeps on. "You'll warm to Oscar. And to James. As long as you remember the third rule…"

By now we're on the landing of the first floor, which again is lined with art. At regular intervals there are table type things with huge vases on them.

"That was what I broke," Eric interrupts himself. "One of those. Playing football. It was worth over a hundred thousand dollars. But apparently insured for several times that. So I made the family a profit, hence I'm still allowed in. But not with a football. Pick a door."

I do, and Eric takes me into a huge bedroom. For a second I wonder if it's Lily's.

"It's not. If that's what you're wondering. She sleeps in the very *grand* master bedroom. Not even I've been in there, only James. This is just one of the guest rooms."

He says James' name so quickly I almost don't catch it, but I do, and I stop myself from repeating it.

"What's the third rule?" I ask, after I've looked at the large bed, and admired a wardrobe.

"The third rule," Eric turns to me. He looks more serious now, even a bit scary. "The third rule of you being here Billy, is *you don't try and fuck Lily.*"

I'm completely taken aback by this.

"I wouldn't…" I manage, eventually.

"I know. I know you wouldn't. She's completely out of your league. Completely out of everyone's league. Except James of course. But the things is, she's just so gorgeous, isn't she..?" He smiles again. "Not exactly my type, of course, but that doesn't mean I don't appreciate how bewitchingly beautiful she is. All that milky white skin, clear eyes. Gorgeous cheek bones. And I suppose you can get away with *fantasizing* about it. When you're back at home. But if you make a move on her, when she's drunk, or when *you're* drunk, and she may give you that chance, because she can be flirty can our Lily. But if you act upon it, if you try to fuck her, then this whole place will collapse around you. Collapse into ruins."

I don't know what to say. But even through the warning, I feel a kind of pain. "That guy James, is he her boyfriend?"

Eric is silent. But then he nods.

"What about Oscar?"

"What *about* Oscar?" He frowns now. "He's just a… He's James' friend. He's nothing."

"He's not…" I don't know what I'm asking, and it seems Eric doesn't know either.

"He's not with… with Jennifer?"

Eric stares at me closely. "I think so. But why would you care? About her. Are you a particular fan of winning second prize?" He raises his eyebrows. "With Jennifer? I suppose you could try your luck there, but to be honest I wouldn't recommend that either."

"I didn't mean…" I struggle to make sense of all this. "I just mean, who *are* you all, to each other?"

Eric fixes me with a look before answering.

"We're just friends, Billy. We're just an ordinary group of friends. Now let me show you the roof terrace."

CHAPTER FOURTEEN

Not long after Jennifer calls up the stairs that dinner is ready, and we all go into the dining room. I sit in the center of the table between Eric and Jennifer on one side, and opposite James who has Lily and Oscar either side of him. And James kind of takes control now, but also he seems to be in a better mood now. He pours me more wine – red this time – and makes space on the table for Lily to put down a dish of what looks like little balls. I've no idea what it actually is, until she notices my face and explains.

"It's gnocchi."

"Mmmm." Eric says. "Homemade?"

"Yes, but not by me." Lily replies. "From the deli. And there's salad too, I'll just get it."

"I'll go." James gets up, and he smiles at her, looking completely normal and genuine this time. He leaves the room. When he comes back, the others start digging in, and after a moment, encourage me to do the same. I don't actually know what gnocchi is, but it seems to be a kind of soft pasta stuff, shaped into balls. It's pretty tasty actually.

"Did you come to a conclusion," Jennifer asks, addressing the question to James, "about which of the French impressionists was the best?"

"We agreed it was a tie," James replies, smiling broadly now. He really is handsome, it's hard not to notice. "Between Monet and Cézanne." Then he turns to me. "Maybe Billy can cast the deciding vote. Do you have a favorite painter Billy?"

I can tell that this comment could be made to belittle me, but actually it doesn't feel like it. It feels like a genuine question.

"I don't really know."

"I didn't either," James continues, without hesitation. "I couldn't tell my Pissarro from my Picasso..." He's interrupted.

"Or your Andy Warhol from your hairy asshole," Eric cuts in, but James carries on talking as if Eric doesn't exist. He just gives him a look.

"But we went to Europe last summer, to see them first hand. And it really is something." There's murmurs of approval from the others, and I understand he means they *all* went, together.

"The thing about art is, it's..." He stops, and stares off into space for a moment. "It's a strange mixture of money, mystery, scarcity-value, and a visible progression of skills and techniques, that you can trace through the artists, through history."

I guess he can tell I don't know what he means.

"OK, the money. Maybe seventy percent of the attraction is the value. They're called priceless, but each painting has a value, and it goes up all the time, because of the scarcity, there's a limited number, and since all the artists are dead you can't make any more."

He smiles. "Then the mystery. There are many more paintings rumored to exist, than are actually accounted for. But if you – if you have certain *connections* – you become aware that some of these paintings aren't lost, but hidden. Here in this house, for example, there's a Renoir, that isn't known about by any of the museums. By anyone."

"Is there?" says Jennifer. She sounds surprised. "I haven't seen it." Then I notice Lily is staring at James, she looks just a bit annoyed.

"It's in the master suite." Lily says, then gives a funny frown. "It's a bit risqué. It's called Nude in the River."

"No way!" Jennifer says, and James' explanation breaks down while Lily describes the painting, and promises she'll show it to Jennifer later on.

"So what are you into," James comes back to me, a while later. "If it's not dead French painters?"

Again I don't feel pressured by the question. In fact the opposite.

There's a real warmth to James now. It's a little weird, given how cold he was earlier, but I've sort of forgiven it.

"Well I've always been really interested in Marine Biology," I say. "I mean really interested."

"That's why you were in Australia, measuring the sharks?"

"Yes."

"I've never been to Australia," he ponders. "But that's good. You're lucky to have a passion in life, something of interest."

There's a silence, but Eric breaks it.

"These gnocchi are delicious Lily," he says, holding two up he's speared with his fork. "Beautiful balls of pleasure."

The talk goes on, and though it's mostly not about me, they each take care to include me in what they're saying, explaining throughout the dinner what it is they're studying, and some details about how they got to know each other. I learn they're all at Harvard, and they're all in their third year. Most of them are studying some variation of business, as in one subject with business as a second topic. All except Oscar, who's doing computer science, though that's about the only thing he says the whole dinner.

I get the idea that all of them come from families who run some sort of businesses, though they don't say which ones. They ask about me, and so I explain how Dad also runs his own Whale Watching business, and how I helped set it up. They all agree that's something they'd love to do sometime. Then I get invited to do what they're into, play tennis at a country club, and even to go sailing on Lily's father's yacht, although they don't actually set any firm dates. And all the while I'm trying to file away the information, and make sense of it.

After the pasta we have a main course (I didn't actually realize the pasta balls weren't the main course, until James and Jennifer took them away, and come back with chicken breasts, cooked in white wine). Then there's a dessert, which is something called a Pavlova – I'd *heard* of it, but never had one before – it's a kind of white crunchy stuff, with raspberries and cream – OK, but nothing special. But while we're eating this Eric reminds me that I talked about catching murderers, as well as drug dealers, and I tell them about my old high school headteacher, who helped to murder her father and her brother, and how I caught her. After that I help carry the plates through to the kitchen where Lily loads them into the dishwasher, actually into one of them. There's two dishwashers in this kitchen, which I think is a really good idea, just as long as you have enough dishes. But as I'm saying that to Lily I notice how her dress rides up her legs as she leans over, showing the bare skin. And I guess I fall silent. And then I look away when I realize Eric is watching me.

After dinner Oscar challenges me to a game of snooker. I don't actually know the rules, but he explains it to me. I'm not too bad either, because I've played a lot of pool in my time, they used to have a table in the Surf Lifesaving Club in Silverlea. You have to clear all the balls, just like in pool, only in the correct order, and you score different points for the different colors. However, Oscar is quite a lot better than me, and after about ten minutes he has sixty points and I've still not got any balls in. So everyone else suddenly starts supporting me. Oscar pots ball after ball, but then he finally misses, and I get a turn again, and the others start banging the table and cheering me on. I feel nervous as I lean over the table to take the shot, but when I strike the ball I can see it's going to go in, and when it does everyone cheers. Well everyone except Oscar.

He kind of smiles at me.

"Lucky shot Billy. I still win though."

After that James grabs me, along with Lily, and says he wants to show me some of the paintings he was talking about before. A couple of them are on the walls, or copies of them, but mostly we look through some huge books in the library, and I can tell he's genuinely interested, though I can't really see the attraction.

At about midnight though, when we're all in the sitting room that Eric showed me earlier, Lily gives a big yawn, and the others take it as a sign that the evening is over. We all say thank you to Lily, and I get another hug and a kiss, from her and Jennifer, and then we all leave together. Oscar and Jennifer turn right on the street, telling me they don't live too far away, but Eric has already called an Uber, which he says I can share. Inside I want to ask more questions about everything I've seen, and just who they all are, but I remember his strange rules, and I guess they apply to letting Uber drivers overhear. So I don't ask. And instead he drops me off, not letting me pay him anything again, and then the car drives away.

I'm still confused by everything as I walk back into my apartment. Confused and sort of on a high, not really believing or understanding where I've just been. There's a light on in our lounge, and I go in to see that Jimbo and Guy are both up, rolling joints and watching something about dirt-bikes on TV. Our own kitchen/living room looks *tiny*, even though it's quite a big room, with space for six people to sit down. And even though it's still mostly clean, it looks dirty and just bare compared to where I've just been. The Lily-palace.

"Billy, my main man." Jimbo puts on a terrible Rastafarian accent. *"You want a toke my brother?"* He offers me a puff on the joint, but I say no, and instead I go off to bed.

CHAPTER FIFTEEN

But I don't want to go to sleep. I'm still buzzing and I want to do some research. Even though Eric told me I mustn't talk about the Lily-Palace, he didn't say I couldn't Google it. So that's what I'm going to do.

I've got quite a good set up here, computer-wise. I have my laptop, and I bought a separate monitor after I arrived, quite a big one too, because I'm going to have to do work here at some point and I like to work on two screens. And I thought it would make me feel more at home.

So anyway, I minimize everything else I'm working on and open up a couple of new web-browsers – Google Chrome, Microsoft Edge, Opera, Vivaldi and Mozilla Firefox – you get different results on different platforms, so it's worth trying lots. Then I start typing in some of the terms I picked up earlier, hoping to get Lily's surname, so I can find out more about her. But it's harder than I expected. Either they were careful not to actually say anything that would let me find her online, or I was just a bit too excited about everything that was happening. Actually the latter is the most likely.

So then I remember that Lily texted me, which means I've got her cell phone number. I've tracked people this way plenty of times. Sometimes people put their phone number online, like in a Facebook post or something, so you can get them that way – which is pretty dumb, so I'm almost pleased when I see she hasn't. And anyway it's not a problem, it's fairly easy to access the database listings from the various phone companies. It is a little bit illegal though, so I hop onto the dark web to do it where I won't be tracked by bots. And it takes a little time too, because it's not like there's one centralized database of everyone's phone records. It's more that lots of different hackers have cracked the records from each of the major companies at different times. So you have to search through all of them one by one. Plus they're not always up to date, meaning if her number is newly assigned, then it won't be on there. Anyway – long story short, after a bit of digging around (if you really want to know I wrote a short program that creates a lookup table and ran that to automate the job), I discover it's not there. Her phone number isn't on *any* of the major networks used in the States. This is odd, and I don't know what it means, but I move on.

I try with the address now. I know *where* it is, obviously, but I don't know who owns it, other than it's Lily's Grandfather, or she says it is. But it's such an amazing place, there's got to be something about it online. One of the easiest ways to find out who owns a property is to see who's paying taxes on it, which you can find out through the local tax assessor's office. They usually have a website, and all you need is the address, and a bit of patience, because they're not the best websites. Annoyingly however, in the case of this tax office they also want you to pay a fee of a hundred dollars, and – get this – go down *in person* to pay it because they haven't even set up an online payment portal. And even if I was going to pay them (which I'm not) they're not open at – what time is it now? Three in the morning. Never mind. I'll check the County Records instead.

In most States the deeds and title documents of all buildings are publicly available. I have to hold my breath a bit when I check if that's true here, but I'm pleased to see it is, and there's no fee either. So then I enter the address and see what's listed, only to find a new problem. The records are only digitized back to the 1960's, and clearly Lily's Grandfather's house was built before then. So it's not listed on the indexed part of the site. It'll still be there, but I'll have to look through images of scanned in handwritten records. I am actually getting frustrated now.

It takes me another hour to figure out that they've organized it on a map basis. You have to find which grid square the street you're looking for is on their map, and then you can look through all the records for that square. Because it's a city, there's quite a lot of records, and you can't search them because it's just an image of a handwritten ledger. But eventually I find the correct square, and the correct street and there it is – Lily's address. Only there isn't anything listed against it. For some reason, while every other address has a neat handwritten block of text giving the deed-holder, for Lily's address there's nothing given. This is really odd. So I hop back onto the dark web and run a couple of searches for what this might mean, but I can't find anything, so in the end I leave the question on a message board and log off. These message boards, they're full of mega geeks who are totally into all this stuff. There should be an answer in the morning.

So that done, I log off and this time I actually go to sleep.

CHAPTER SIXTEEN

There's an answer waiting for me when I wake up, quite early as I have a nine o'clock lecture. I have to read it twice because I'm a bit bleary eyed from all my research, and it obviously isn't the name I need, it's just an explanation of *why* I can't see any records listed against Lily's address.

It comes from someone called Blackhorse. I haven't met him before. He tells me – actually I say he, but I don't know if it's a man or a woman, but I'm guessing man – but anyway, he tells me there are several reasons why a private residence might be 'access restricted'. It could be something really dodgy, like the owner being part of the Witness Protection Program, or because the owners work for military intelligence. In that case I'd need to proceed really carefully because there's all sorts of higher level securities that trigger red flags, and when they're secret they're super hard to wipe. Alternatively it could be something a lot less exciting, such as the owner of the property simply requesting that their records aren't made publicly available. As well as telling me all this, Blackhorse has asked if I want him to look into it further, and he says he won't even charge me. I think about the offer for a while, while I'm brewing up some coffee in the kitchen, but then I reply to say no thanks. It's probably the wrong thing to do, to run all these searches about Lily behind her back. And also, with these computer nerd people, you never *quite* know how stable they are.

It's a beautiful day outside, and it puts me in a good mood as I go into college for my morning lecture. The first one is the same as ever, going over topics I studied years ago, but I still go through the motions of writing notes, but it's so boring that in my head I start going over everything that happened last night. As I do so, I keep getting these visions of Lily. Lily laughing at the dinner table. Lily leaning in to kiss me when I arrived. Lily leaning over the dishwasher, her skirt rising up and showing her smooth legs. I'm actually so distracted I don't notice that a woman, sitting a couple of empty seats away from me, is leaning over to talk to me. Eventually she taps me on the arm.

"Hey! Are you OK?" She smiles, looking a bit concerned. I've actually noticed her before but we've never spoken. She's quite a bit older than me, and obviously really keen, as it's often just me and her at the start of the classes, before everyone else arrives. "You seem really distracted today."

"What?" I release my vision of Lily, though I'm disappointed as she drifts out of my mind. I shake my head clear and focus on the woman. "No. I'm… Fine."

She smiles reassuringly at me, and goes back to her notes. Then at the end, when the lecturer has finished, she moves a seat closer before I get up to leave.

"That was a tough one, wasn't it? I do struggle with all the Latin names." She rolls her eyes.

"Oh I wasn't…" I get what she means, but stop myself. I can't really say I wasn't paying attention.

"I'm Linda." The woman says, though I don't ask. "Linda Reynolds. I'm in a lot of your classes."

"I know."

"Right." She bobs her head to one side then the other, like she's thinking this over. "Well… I just wanted to say hi. And that you can borrow my notes. If you ever need." She gives me another smile. "Like if you've been up all night partying. And feel like your head's not on straight."

"I wasn't up all night partying."

"No?" She gives me a look and a grin, but then shrugs. "Well you know. In case you ever are."

Annoyingly, at that moment I feel a yawn coming on, and I can't stop it. Then I feel I ought to explain.

"I was sort of working. Last night."

"Ahhh," Linda looks suddenly pleased. "So you *do* put in all-nighters." She grins again. "We were wondering how you managed to know the answer to *every* question in the tutorials."

"It wasn't that sort of..." I start to say, but then I stop. "Who's we?"

Linda waves a hand. She's filled her bag now. "There's a bunch of us. Mature students mostly. We're helping each other out with the work."

I don't know what to say to this. So I don't say anything.

"I was wondering, maybe you'd like to join us? I mean, you're kind of mature yourself. In a young way."

I'm not sure what to say to this either. I definitely don't need any help with my work, but I don't want to say that, because it would make me sound really arrogant.

She smiles again, as the rest of the class files out around us.

"Actually we're meeting up today, just for a coffee. After *Chemical Processes*, maybe you want to join us?"

I'm sort of doubtful, I'm already younger than all the other students here. I'm not sure hanging out with the mature students makes much sense. But I don't want to be rude.

"Erm. OK. Sure."

"Great! I'll look out for you in class." She leaves, and gives me a wave.

I have a break next, so I go to the library. I try to read but I find I can't concentrate. I'm in a funny mood suddenly. I had all these ideas about college, before I got here. How it would be all research and experiments and fun. But actually it's mostly just reading about other people doing research. And it's all reading I've already done. I feel like something's missing, but I don't know what it is. So I don't read much, instead I just secretly watch the other students around me, with their headphones and their laptops and their giant Starbucks cups of coffee, and the looks of concentration on their faces, like they're finding it hard. I wonder what I'm doing wrong.

· · ·

79

But I cheer up pretty quickly because then I get a call from Lily. And she sounds fresh and full of life.

"Billy. What are you doing today?"

My schedule flashes up in my brain. It's my busy day, I have three other lectures after this break staggered, through the day and finishing at six this evening. But I don't get a chance to tell her this because she carries straight on.

"We're going to the beach. Do you want to come?"

"What?"

"The beach Billy. Like a big bath. With sand…"

"I know what… but I can't. I've got lectures."

"So?"

"So I *can't.*" I think quickly. Or try to. "I could come at the weekend." I say it a little hopefully. "Too late. We're going now. James has decided he's a *surfer.*" In the background I can hear a snort of laughter, it sounds like Eric. "It's his new hobby. His new *passion.*" She says that really sarcastically, and I can almost see her smiling at me, in her very-slightly goofy way. "And he says there won't be any waves at the weekend. So it has to be now."

I think – or maybe I wish – I could somehow move my lectures. But that's a ridiculous thought, and Lily interrupts it anyway.

"What classes do you have?"

"*Evolution and Behavior, Biodiversity,* and *Physical and Chemical Processes of the Ocean.*"

"OK. But didn't you tell us the other night your course was so easy you could do it in your sleep?"

"Erm," I start to reply. I might have said something like that, but I didn't use those exact words.

"So catch up later. When you're asleep. It's too nice a day now." She moves on fast, like it's settled already. "Where are you?"

"I'm in the library."

"BU?"

"Huh?"

"We'll pick you up outside. We're renting boards and wetsuits, so you don't need anything. Just clever old you." She hangs up. She didn't even say how long they'd be.

So I think about it for all of maybe thirty seconds, and then I get up to put my books back, get my stuff and go outside to wait for her. I feel a bit unsure when I'm there. Like I half-expect one of my lecturers to spot me and ask what I'm doing and where I'm going, but I know they won't because college isn't like school. You can actually *miss* lectures if you want to. There's no register, no Principal to report to if you don't turn up. You can do what you want.

Still it feels wrong. Until, ten minutes later when I see a big silver SUV come round the corner, and Lily's beautiful face peering out of the passenger window looking for me. Then she suddenly points towards me, and starts frantically waving.

CHAPTER SEVENTEEN

We drive out towards Nantasket Beach, which isn't somewhere I've ever been before. James is driving, with Lily beside him, and Jennifer and Eric are in the back seat. I'm in the middle (Eric got out to let me in – he said he gets car sick if he's not by the window). Then there's a third row of seats and Oscar is back there on his own, well – he's sitting next to a giant wicker hamper, I don't know what's in there, but I can smell it, and it smells pretty good.

It takes us about forty minutes to get there, with the traffic, and all the way they're chattering and excited, and it's really infectious. Not just because I love the beach, and I've been missing it. But because we're all going.

It's not busy when we get there. Kind of the same as Silverlea beach on a nice day, but during the week, when most people are at work. James seems to know where he's going, and pulls into a parking bay outside a little surf shop, and then he and Lily disappear straight inside. I don't follow them though, I just walk across the street and look out at the ocean, sort of drinking it in. It's not the most beautiful beach I've ever seen – there's a road running along the top, backed with buildings, and there's no cliffs or dunes or anything very natural, but at the same time, there's not a breath of wind, and the surface of the water is so calm it has a glassy look. Yet over the top there's a small swell that's rolling in, silvery and lazy in the afternoon sun. It's not epic, but even so, I feel it luring me out there. I shorten my gaze to take in the beach, pale sand, the tide out. There's a few dozen little encampments of people stretched out on their towels, or with sun umbrellas, but there's loads of space. The water's not busy either, just dotted with the heads and shoulders of a few surfers.

"Eric and Jennifer are going to wait on the beach, but you're coming in aren't you Billy?"

I turn to see Lily, standing with another guy. I don't know him, but I recognize the type right away. "This is Wayne, he runs the store here, I asked him to get you a suit and a board. Take whatever you like, it's all on my tab."

I realize I should protest at the generosity of this, and start to do so, but she stops me at once.

"Don't be silly. I dragged you here. And I'm going in." She smiles at me, a fresh, encouraging, excited smile. "Come on." So I glance back at the ocean, and then follow her and Wayne back into the store.

I've been in a dozen surf shops before, usually with Dad, and this one's no different, but I've never *rented* a board before. I've never needed to. Dad's always had tons of boards lying around. Usually people just give them to him, because they want him to ride on their brand, or tell them how to make them better. I've never rented a wetsuit either. Back home on Lornea, it's only tourists who rent wetsuits. Basically I'm just saying the whole thing is a bit weird, but I do my best to ignore that.

I can hear Lily is in one of the changing rooms, struggling into her wetsuit, and making quite a lot of noise over it. Meanwhile James is already in his, only somehow from the way he wears it, I can tell he's not used to wearing one. And then Wayne starts holding suits up against me to find one that fits. I look them over quickly, and take the best one – or the least worst. Then he shows me to the changing room. It's odd here too. Back home I'll get changed by the truck, and I won't really care who's watching, but now I feel self-conscious because Lily is still next door and there's only a curtain between us.

When I've got the wetsuit on I come out and the others are still choosing their boards with Wayne. It's only James and Oscar, and me and Lily who are surfing, the others have gone to sit on the beach. James and Oscar get their boards first, both taking a while to inspect the shortboard-style surfboards, but while I'm waiting I see there's a rack of paddleboards as well, and I surprise myself by asking Wayne if it's OK for me to take one of those instead. It surprises Lily too, since she asks why. I explain that, when the waves are small like today, it's much easier and you can catch far more waves on a paddleboard. And then Lily looks interested in that and says she'll do the same. So a few minutes later the four of us traipse over the road and down onto the sand. Eric and Jennifer are stretched out on the sand. They've got a sun umbrella from somewhere, though you don't really need it today. Eric gives us a wolf-whistle as we walk past them. Actually I get a weird feeling he's giving me a wolf-whistle.

I feel a bit odd as we walk down to the water. It's hard to explain exactly why, but it's like there's a meeting of two worlds. Or maybe more than two. When I was a kid I was really scared of the water, I mean properly terrified. And I had a good reason, since my Mom tried to drown me when I was a baby. But when I got over that I started surfing loads with Dad, and diving, and swimming and kayaking, and all sorts really. So now I feel very relaxed in the water, like I'm at home here. And I can see easily that Lily and James and Oscar don't – they're not holding their boards the right way, they didn't even know how to zip up their wetsuits (when I was younger they all had the zips on the back, but now they're always on the front). But at the same time, I keep expecting James or Lily to ask me a question about French impressionist painters, or snooker, or something that they all know about, and I don't. So it's a weird mix, if you know what I mean.

We wade out into the waves. It's still warm. James and Oscar lay on their boards and start paddling, and I jump up onto my feet on the paddleboard and start to use the long paddle to push me along. It's a really big board, and totally stable – I've got one at home that's about half the size, and I don't fall off that one either – but next to me Lily watches what I do and tries to do the same, but she tips forwards, and screams and falls right off, feet flying everywhere as she splashes into the water. From the shore I hear Eric calling out and laughing.

I'm a bit mortified, but she surfaces, looking shocked for a moment, before breaking into a smile, her hair plastered onto her face. She tries again, while I stop paddling and just wait where I am. She falls a second time. Still I wait there, turning to face the swells as they come in, so they don't knock me off.

"How do you do that?" She asks in the end, she's puffing from the effort of it.

"You just…" I try and think. "You just stand on it." It really isn't hard, not once you get used to it.

She tries again, but falls again, and she isn't smiling as much now, so I suggest she stays on her knees until she gets out through the waves where it will be calmer and easier. Then when that doesn't work either, I help her. I get off my board and let it trail out behind me, secured by the leash, and I push hers from the back until we're through the section on the break where the waves are breaking. All the while Lily is kneeling on her board, and helping a bit with her paddle. Eventually I get her into the lineup – that's the part where you wait to catch waves, just further out from where they break. Here it's easy, because the water stays flat. And here I give her a proper lesson, showing her how to get to her feet, while using the paddle to keep her balance. I show her the right place to stand on the board, and how to turn it. And it's easy – because paddle boarding is easy – that's why all the celebrities do it. Soon she gets the hang of it, and we paddle back towards where James and Oscar are waiting, and she calls out to them, saying 'look at me!', and I can see she's having fun again.

When a nice set of waves comes in I let James and Oscar take the first ones, because that's kind of the polite thing to do, and I watch them too. They both get to their feet, but they don't have the smooth, fluid style that the Lornea Island surfers do, like Dad and his friends. Instead they lurch up, knocking the boards from their path down the waves. Then they sort of flap about for a bit, waving their arms and trying to coax enough speed to make a turn. It's not really their fault, the waves are too small and slow for their shortboards – that's why I chose the paddleboard. So when the last wave comes in, and Lily is too far out to take it, I turn around and stroke into it.

The board I'm on is quite nice for surfing, as it happens. I zip down the line a bit, and then – just because I can – I step forward and hang my toes over the nose. Dad taught me to do this, and to hang ten, but instead of that I step right the way to the back of the board, since the wave is steepening in this section, and drive it around a couple of little turns, and then finally carve off the wave. Without falling I paddle back out to where Lily is waiting, watching.

"Oh my God. You didn't say you were an *expert*!"

I shrug. "I'm not." But I don't say anything else, because right away another set of waves is coming in, from a slightly different angle, and I paddle out to it, this time taking the best one, and I surf it on my back hand, leaning myself into the wave and casually dragging a hand for a few seconds. Again I carve off the wave at the end of the ride and paddle back out.

Soon I'm really having fun. James and Oscar are still struggling away, and there's not much I can do for them, so instead I concentrate on teaching Lily how to actually catch waves. Stand up paddle boarding is much easier than surfing, and if the conditions are right – like today, with smooth water with small waves – almost anyone can learn to ride proper waves, but there's a few things you have to get right. Like the way you stand. You start off facing forwards, but when you catch a wave you have to turn sideways, like when you're riding a skateboard. And you need to start paddling forward at just the right time, and do short, hard strokes with the paddle, so that you're going at the same speed as the wave when it picks you up. Once Lily gets all that she's able to catch the waves. The first one she gets she yells out in fear, and I think excitement, and her eyes are shining when she paddles back out (her hair mopped onto her head, and on her knees, a bit less elegantly than me, but she's getting the hang of it now). And it's obvious she's enjoying it, and that, well that makes me really happy too.

An hour later James and Oscar go in, and Lily says she wants to join them. I'm a bit surprised, I guess because I'm used to surfing with Dad, and he'll sometimes stay out for six hours. But we ride waves in together, and I get nice top-turn off the final section. Then we carry the boards up to where Eric and Jennifer are sitting, and James and Oscar are lying on their backs on the sand. They look puffed out.

"So you're a dark horse, Billy," Eric says when we get there. "You didn't tell us you were a *surfing champion.*" He looks at me with raised eyebrows.

"What?" Lily turns to look at me.

"We were watching you zipping around out there like some sort of…" Eric waves one hand as he searches for a word "…Hawaiian prince, and I got suspicious." He holds up his phone. "I Googled you." He starts reading from the screen. "Lornea Island Champion, several times over, plus winner of the *Big Wave Challenge*. Look at the size of that trophy!" He turns the phone, and Lily leans in to look. James does too, but from further away. I can't see the image that clearly, but I know right away which web page he's on. It's about a surf competition that was held on Lornea Island, and *I* didn't win it, *Dad* did, but the local paper is so bad at fact checking they got mixed up. They used a photograph of me holding up Dad's cup, and thought I'd won it.

Lily turns to me, a look of pretend outrage on her face. "I can't believe you sat in the back of the car the whole time we were driving here, and didn't mention once you were a bloody professional."

"I'm not." I protest. And I think about explaining, but then I decide I'd rather everyone just forgot about it.

Eric laughs, and James and Oscar say they're going to the store to get changed. I look at Lily to see if she's doing the same, but instead she's already reaching behind her for the zip on her suit, and she pulls it down. I'm a bit stunned, until she peels it down and I see she's wearing a bikini underneath, a white one. Then I remember I should look away.

"Here, do you want to borrow some shorts? I brought a spare pair." Eric smiles at me, and then tosses me a towel, so I get changed right here on the beach, while Lily peels off the rest of her wetsuit, then stretches out on a towel.

CHAPTER EIGHTEEN

I don't know who packed the hamper, but it's filled with amazing food. There's cute little sandwiches, some with cucumber and others with this special Italian dried ham, and a cold pasta salad, and then little pastries, and pots of olives and sun-dried tomatoes. I ask about it, and Jennifer shrugs, and says she picked it up from a deli, though she doesn't say which one. She seems to be into sunbathing, she's wearing a green bikini, which goes well with her brown skin, which is shiny from the sun cream she's put on. Actually it was Oscar who put it on, I notice, since he and James are back now. And for a little while, everyone just stays like that, sunbathing. Except Lily, who seems restless still. Right after James lays down next to her, she jumps up and then pushes me on the arm with a bat, and says we're playing beach tennis. So I take it and follow her a little way away, and we start hitting the ball to each other. We're both a bit rubbish at first, but soon get the hang of it, and we start trying to make it to a hundred shots without either of us missing, but every time we get close one of us feels the pressure and we miss, and pretty soon neither of us can get there because we're laughing too much.

But then she gets a serious look on her face, and tells me we're going to really go for it, so I stop laughing too. Then we get into a rhythm, sending each other easy shots, and concentrating more on the counting, and suddenly it's easy.

We get to ninety four shots, and it seems we're going to sail past one hundred. But then it's my turn, and I hit it back to her too carefully, so she has to lurch forward to get it before it bounces twice. She just manages to send it back to me.

"Ninety five. Don't mess this up!"

I hit it back to her, better this time.

"Ninety seven!" she says, as she gets to the ball.

The tension is actually getting to me, but this time my shot back is OK, she sends number ninety nine back towards me, with a little bit of a triumphant whack, but she mis-hits it this time, and I have to jump forward to reach it, but by now the sand is scuffed up, and I trip on a hole, and I completely miss the ball.

"Billy!" She yells at me, and then she runs forward, and she starts mock hitting me with her bat. And then somehow she's sort of holding onto me and sort of leaning on me and groaning, and I can feel the strap of her bikini top pressing into my chest – and I don't know where I should put my arms.

"You don't have an ounce of fat on you do you?" she says all of a sudden, and then breaks away. I wonder if she wants to start again, like before, but this time she gives up, and wanders back to the little camp. Oscar and Jennifer take the bats, and they have a go too.

I don't really know what's going on. I can feel there's some awkwardness, mainly around James, who's really sulky now. But I'm still a bit disappointed when, a little while later, he suggests to her that they go off for a walk. I kind of expect her to say no, but she doesn't. And they wander off, along the shoreline together. That just leaves me and Eric alone for a while, since the other two are still playing tennis. I don't say anything at first, instead I watch Lily as she gets smaller and smaller, walking down the beach.

"You're playing a dangerous game Mr Wheatley." Eric says. Surprised, I spin around to face him.

"*What?* What do you mean?"

"You know exactly what I mean."

"No I don't."

He raises his eyebrows at me, but then turns away, and I think he's dropped it. Until a moment later when he speaks again.

"She is beautiful though, isn't she?"

For a second I think about denying it, or pretending I don't know who he's talking about. After all, it could just as easily apply to Jennifer. But I notice he's looking at me again, and I sense he'll see if I lied. I nod.

"And lithe, and vivacious, and oh so sexy in that little white bikini. And let's not forget, insanely rich." Eric's not looking at me now, he seems lost in his own head. "And yet somehow she's still more than the sum of those parts." He smiles sadly, and a funny realization hits me, Eric *likes* Lily as much as I do. Though actually it's the second part of that thought that really impacts me. *I like* Lily. I *really* like Lily.

"But she belongs to James, and James belongs to her. And that's how it's always going to be." He says it with a real finality. I don't know why, but it grates with me.

"Why?"

It's Eric's turn to look confused. He turns back to me, his forehead screwed up. "*Why?*"

"Yes. Why?"

He doesn't reply for a moment, but the frown stays on his face. "Just because. That's why. They'll come back from their little walk, and they'll be hand in hand, and no-one will know what was said, apart from them, but Lily will stop her ridiculously obvious flirting with you, and James will stop moping about like an angry teenager, and all will be well again, in the golden couple. At least for now."

I don't reply, then he sighs, and – unexpectedly – smiles.

"Let me tell you something about the lovely Lily and the juicy James. They started dating when they were both fourteen, and they've known each other long before that. Plus their families *approve* of each other." He gives me a sickly smile. "He gets the *Bellafonte seal of approval*, in a way that you never will Billy. You never could."

"You like her too, don't you?" I say, feeling my face flush hot. I expect him to look shocked that I've worked it out. But instead he looks sad. He closes his eyes for a while, then opens them and shakes his head.

"No Billy. I don't."

"Yes you do, the way you're talking about her, it's obvious."

"There are none so blind as those who will not see."

"What?"

Eric reaches out a hand and with a shock I realize he means to touch my face, but he's slow and gentle, and I feel him pull open my eyes. It's totally weird, but I'm so surprised I don't do anything.

"Open them, Billy. Open your eyes. There's so much that you don't see."

I feel confused, frustrated. I've no idea what he's on about.

"I don't understand." He's not looking at me now, he's staring down the beach, where Lily and James are only just visible now, tiny figures in the distance now. Reluctantly he drags his gaze away.

"Keep your voice down. I don't want *him* hearing." He glances over at where Oscar and Jennifer are still playing bat and ball.

"Who?"

"His vicious little sidekick, that's who." Eric beams at me, and I figure out he means Oscar, though I still don't really know what we're talking about. Even so I'm desperate *to* know more. There's something fascinating about these people, all of them.

"Oscar's known James for even longer than Lily has. They go right the way back."

We're both watching them now. Still playing tennis. Jennifer's bikini bottom has got a bit caught on one side of her bum, so there's a little section of whiter skin exposed. Then she reaches down and smooths it out.

"To where?"

"Pre-school I think. They're closer than brothers."

"And you don't like him?"

Eric turns away from Jennifer's backside.

"Now why would you say that?"

I'm confused again. I don't know if I should turn back to him. But I don't.

Eric smiles. "Oscar and I get along fine. Just as long as I stay in my place, that is."

I realize I haven't paid Oscar much attention so far, and for the first time I study him. He's quite pale – he's taken his shirt off to play – but at the same time he's muscular, obviously strong. Yet as I'm watching, something else occurs to me. Something more important.

"Did you say 'Bellafonte'?"

"Hmmm? *What?*"

"Is that Lily's family? Is that her surname?"

Eric turns to me with a curious look.

"Yes."

I start thinking. I don't know how common that name is, but it doesn't sound too common. I'll be able to run a search now. I might not even need Blackhorse. But Eric seems to read my mind.

"I'll save you the trouble of Googling." Eric gives me a cold smile. "The Bellafonte's are one the East Coast's biggest industrialist families. Lily's grandfather built their fortune, making chemicals, but when he died the firm was split into two. Now one half is owned by Lily's father, the other by her uncle. I guess he thought it would stop them arguing over the money."

I listen, not really understanding, and thinking that there's absolutely no way I'm not going to Google for myself. But then something else occurs to me.

"So why are *you* here?" I ask suddenly, and this time it's him that doesn't understand, so I explain. "If Lily is with James, and Oscar is with Jennifer. Where do *you* fit in?"

Eric takes a long time to answer this, but when he does his voice is very serious. It's like he's given this a lot of thought.

"Lily is astonishing in many ways, but she's far from perfect." He says, and when I frown at him – since this isn't a real answer – he goes on.

"She's a *collector*. Of fascinating things, and fascinating people. That's why I'm here. I *amuse* her. And that's why James, and Oscar tolerate me, because I amuse her. But I'll only be here for as long as that remains the case, and then I'll be cast out." He's quiet for a moment. And then he continues. "But actually the real question, young Billy," he gives me that cold smile again. "Is why *you're* here?"

But I don't get a chance to answer that one, because Jennifer takes that moment to wander back, and lie down again on her towel, with Oscar beside her. For a few moments Eric and I fall into silence, until he starts asking me about my course, as if that's what we've been talking about the whole time. About a half hour later James and Lily come back into view, and just like Eric said they're holding hands, and when they get back they seem much more at ease with each other. And though Lily is perfectly kind and gracious to me, for the rest of the day, right up until James drops me off outside my house, it's not quite the same.

CHAPTER NINETEEN

Bellafonte. Lily Bellafonte. I don't google her as soon as I get home. I'm actually tired tonight. So instead I just roll her name around in my head while I clean my teeth and then go to bed. As I fall asleep I hear thumps and shouts from the kitchen, and the corridor outside my room. There's a bit of a party going on in our house tonight.

Then in the morning I sleep late, and when I do get up the internet isn't working in the house, so I go off to my classes first, but as usual, they're pretty basic, so instead of listening and pretending to take notes, I sit on my own and pull out my phone. And even with her surname, it's not easy to find her. But eventually I do.

Lillian Bellafonte, 18, daughter of Fonchem CEO Claude Bellafonte.

That's the caption beneath a photograph in the New York Times. It was taken at the Black Tie Gala of the Eastern Division Annual Business Awards of the American Chamber of Industrialists, whatever that is. It's definitely her, smiling a little bit shyly at the camera, and dressed in a white ball gown. She looks amazing. I glance up and around the lecture theater. Without meaning to I catch the eye of the woman I spoke to the other day, Linda something, the mature student. I look away quickly. It's odd too – Lily I mean – because I can't find anything on Instagram, or Facebook, or twitter, or any social media of any kind. *Everyone* has social media these days. Well almost everyone. In fact the only person I can think of who doesn't have it is me. I dig around a bit more, and I do find another couple of mentions of her, but no photographs, and nothing particularly interesting, so instead I focus on her dad, Claude Bellafonte, and though he's not exactly live-streaming every day either, it doesn't take me long to find out who he is on the Fonchem website. And then it hits me, what an idiot I am. *Fonchem.* I know that name. I look it up on Wikipedia to check, but right away I see I'm right. Here's what it says:

Fonchem Inc.
    Type: Private Industry Chemical Manufacturer
    Headquarters: Boston, Massachusetts
    Number of locations: 66
    Key people: Claude A. Bellafonte (CEO)
    Products: Chemicals
    Revenue: ~ $1.8 billion (2019)
    Number of employees: 4,300 (2017)
    Website: www.fonchem.com
Fonchem Inc. or Fonchem (previously Bellafonte Specialty Chemicals) is a publicly owned chemical company based in Boston, Massachusetts. It produces thermoset resins and related technologies and specialty products.

Founded in 1865, it's currently one of the larger chemical firms in the United States, although considerably smaller than the three largest firms. Until 2018 Fonchem ranked within the Fortune 1000 in terms of revenue, but has now slipped slightly. Fonchem has frequently been the subject of criticism related to the environment, human rights, finance, and other ethical considerations.

Fonchem is organized into two divisions: the Epoxy, Phenolic and Coating Resins Division, and the Marine Products Division.

Fonchem offers resins for a wide range of applications like Abrasives, Adhesives, Chemical Intermediates, Civil Engineering, Coatings, Composites, Crop Protection, Electrical/Electronics, Engineered Wood,

Fertilizers and Pesticides, Fibers and Textiles, Foams, Friction Materials, Furniture, Molding Compounds, Oilfield, Oriented Strand Board, Particleboard and Fiberboard, Plywood and Laminated Veneer Lumber and Refractories.

Corporate structure

Although Fonchem is shareholder-owned, it is still controlled by the Bellafonte family, notably by Claude Bellafonte, son of Arthur Bellafonte. Fonchem was formed when the larger Bellafonte Specialty Chemicals (BSC) was split into two firms upon Arthur Bellafonte's death in mid-2007. Roughly 50% of BSC formed Fonchem, while the other 50% became Eastfort Quality Chemicals (EQC), under the control of Arthur Bellafonte's other son Jacques A. Bellafonte. Both brothers are notoriously private and known to shun publicity.

See also: Formaldehyde

Then there's a link to a part of the page named 'sites' and I click it. I don't need to now, because I definitely remember now. And I think I must be stupid to not have recognized it at once. But maybe I wasn't too concerned about the name of the company. Frankly they all sound the same to me. But when I scan down the list of sites, there it is:

Lornea Island: Fonchem maintains a small facility in the north of the island, and is currently applying to expand its footprint to allow increased production.

Fonchem is the company that's trying to destroy the seahorse breeding zone.

* * *

I'm knocked sideways by this news. I really am, it's like the whole lecture theater is spinning. It's worse because the seats here are set really steep, so I feel I might actually fall down and to the front. I put my phone away, because I don't want to find out any more now, but I can't concentrate on what the lecturer is saying. All I can think about is the little bay up in the north of Lornea, where the seahorses live among the sea grasses, and how Lily's dad wants to destroy it. But I suppose I better explain. I mean I have the campaign, back home, but it's mostly directed towards local island people, so maybe you won't have seen the posters.

It all started – well I don't know when it really started exactly, since the chemical company – this *Fonchem* – has had its compound up there for as long as I can remember. Not that that makes it alright. But anyway, I'd better start from the beginning that *I* know about.

A couple of summers ago, Dad and I decided we would sail all the way around Lornea Island, in a small sailing dinghy that dad found abandoned by the side of the road. We sailed during the day, and then camped and caught fish and slept around a fire under the stars at night. It was really cool.

We set off from Silverlea beach, in late summer, and went down towards the south first, to take advantage of the north winds when we set off. We carried everything we needed inside the boat, and I really got to know the island better, and found habitats I hadn't known existed. But then, on the fifth or sixth day – I can't remember which – we got almost to the northern most tip of the island, and that's where we found the problem. We couldn't get past the land owned by Fonchem. The issue was they didn't just own the *land* where they have their compound, they owned the beach as well, and also the seabed that stretches out from the beach – for four miles out to sea. So they have this string of buoys running out protecting it, with notices everywhere saying that it's a maritime exclusion area, and anyone going inside it will be arrested.

You can't easily do a four-mile detour out to sea and back in a tiny little sailing boat, so we were stuck.

Only we weren't really stuck, because my dad isn't the type of person to give up easily. Or to listen to what signs on a buoy say. So he decided we would just sail straight through the exclusion area. But since it said there were armed security guards, and there was a pier with what looked like a gunboat tied up at it (it probably wasn't an *actual* gunboat, but it looked like one of those things from war movies), we decided to wait until it got dark, and slip through then. That meant I had the whole of the afternoon to explore the little bay just south of the compound, and the tiny island that protects it. And that's when I discovered the seahorse nursery.

When I say discovered I don't mean I discovered for science. Lots of people knew it was there, including me, it's just I didn't know exactly *where*. But I'd wanted to find it for ages, not just because seahorses are cool in general – but because of the endemic Lornea Island species I told you about – the Lornea Island sea-dragon. It's important to understand they're not actual sea-dragons. You only get those in Australia, technically Lornea Island sea-dragons are just a species of seahorse, but they have very wavy pectoral fins that look a bit like wings, and they swim more on their belly, like they're flying, so that's why the fishermen here called them dragons. Anyway, the point is, I figured the little bay tucked in by the Fonchem compound was their perfect habitat, so that afternoon I was really hoping I might spot one.

So I swam out with my mask, and I floated in the water above the seagrasses. It was a hot afternoon, and the water was warm and the sun felt hot on my back. But I didn't see anything, not for a long time, just the sandy bottom below me, and a kind of meadow of seagrass, that looked empty. But when my eyes acclimatized a bit better I started to see animals too – little flatfish, lots of mollusks and amphipods, and here and there a shoal of tiny silvery fish – too small for me to identify. But still I didn't see any seahorses. And then I noticed a piece of weed that didn't look quite right, and when I swam closer, I noticed it just very slightly dipped below another piece of weed – and there it was, a Lornea Island Sea-Dragon! It was only about three inches long, so it wasn't the most scary dragon you could imagine, but it did look a bit like a dragon, with its long snout and wavy fins. I watched it for ages, but unfortunately my camera had run out of battery by then, so I didn't manage to get any photographs or video.

Anyway. We didn't make a fire that night, because we didn't want to be seen. But when it got dark we packed everything up into the dinghy and paddled a little way out to sea without any lights on. When we were maybe a quarter mile off the beach, still on the legal side of the buoys, we checked with binoculars if we could see anyone moving inside the compound or on the beach. It looked quiet, so we started paddling like hell across the exclusion zone. It's only about a mile across, and we had the tide with us, but paddling a sailing dinghy is pretty slow, and you get tired, so when we were about halfway across we saw lights appear on the beach, and we knew they'd seen us. If there had been any wind, we could have put the sails up at that point (we didn't use them before because the sails are white, and would have made us easier to see), it didn't matter now, but then there wasn't any wind anyway. We paddled faster, but a few minutes later we saw they'd launched the gunboat. It could go about fifty times faster than we could, so there was no doubt it was going to catch us. But Dad had a clever idea. As soon as he saw the boat launch, he switched on his floating flashlight, and threw it as far as he could behind us. It was the only light around – except for the red flashing lights from the buoys – and the gunboat went straight towards it, while we both carried on paddling as fast as we could. By the time they realized what we'd done, and picked us out properly with their spotlight, we were almost at the buoys on the far side of the exclusion zone. We actually got out completely by the time they caught up with us.

And the security guard wasn't too bad really. He told us we shouldn't have done it, and it was dangerous and everything, but he seemed to understand that we couldn't have gone around by sea. In fact, he said that if we sailed around Lornea again, we should just let him know and he'd escort us through the cordoned-off zone. He was so friendly I even told him about the sea-dragons.

My first lecture ends, and thoughtfully I gather up my papers – mostly full of doodles – and pack them into my backpack, then I walk out and to the next building along, where I have another class. I see Linda, that mature student, and I try to give her a sort of smile to say hello, but this time she's talking to someone else, and she doesn't see me.

So I sit, on my own again, and keep thinking about what happened next.

It was announced in the paper, I think that's where I saw it first, or it might have been on TV, on the island's own cable channel. Anyway, the point is, the chemical company in the north of Lornea Island, Fonchem, had announced it wanted to expand its manufacturing base, and build a much larger dock for exporting its products directly from the compound. It was spun like it was *good* news – because there would be more money and jobs for the island – but I knew right away that it wasn't going to be good news for the sea-dragons. And I wasn't the only one who was concerned. It developed into a kind of battle between Fonchem and various proper environmental groups. And the Lornea Island Council is going to decide it now. They're going to give a final answer on whether the expansion is allowed or not. It's why I've been asking Dad to keep putting up the posters.

Except, I realize with a bit of a guilty feeling, I haven't asked Dad to put them up for a while. But then I've been busy, I'm doing a college course as well, and… And well, I'm also running around with the beautiful daughter of the CEO of Fonchem.

So I don't listen much to this lecture either.

CHAPTER TWENTY

I have Lily's number now, but I don't know what to say if I call her. And I don't even know if she likes me anymore, after what happened between her and James. But I suppose I get an answer to that a couple of days later when I get another invitation from her. She wants to have coffee on Saturday. I think really hard if I should go or not. Actually that's a lie. I'm obviously going to go. But I genuinely don't know what to say to her about Fonchem and Lornea Island.

As I cycle down to the coffee shop she told me to meet in, down by the harbor, I wonder if it's going to be all of them, or just her. If it's all of them I don't know how I'm going to say what I need to say. But if it's just her, then that will be odd, because it'll be like a date. When I get there, there's no-one there at all. So I lock up my bike and go inside to wait.

She turns up ten minutes late. Just her, and she's wearing a kind of pleated skirt thing with a white jumper. She looks – well I guess she looks *rich*, like the daughter of a family of rich industrialists who make all their money by destroying the environment. But then she does look really beautiful as well.

"Hey Billy, how are you?" She leans down to kiss me on both cheeks, since I don't get up, and I can smell her perfume. It's like I'm enveloped in it. She slips in the seat opposite me, and shakes her head.

"Urgh. Hard week. You?"

I stare at her. At her flawless skin, and her clear blue eyes, and her long hair, golden yellow, that falls onto her shoulders.

"Yeah. Me too." I reply. She gives me a funny look at this, and then the waitress arrives.

"So why did you want to meet?" I ask, when we've ordered. Lily gives me a funny look.

"What do you mean?"

"What did you want to talk about?"

"What do you mean *what did I want?* I wanted to see you."

I pause. "Why?"

She frowns, putting delicate creases into her forehead. "Are you OK Billy?" She seems to think for a moment and her expression changes. "Is this about James and me?"

I'm surprised by this, so I don't get a chance to reply before she goes on. "Because that's complicated…" She fades into silence, as the waitress comes back with our drinks. We both stay silent, even when she's gone, and Lily tears the corner of a sachet of sugar and pours it slowly into her coffee.

"James and I are very fond of each other. And we've known each other for a very long time, but…"

"It's not about James." I burst out, cutting in.

She stops, still holding the sugar. Then sets it down. "Oh." She frowns again. It's distracting because she has a very pretty frown. Then she takes a deep breath, and I can't help but be aware of how it makes her chest rise up and down.

"Well, what is it about?"

It's my turn to hesitate. But with a feeling that this might be the stupidest idea I've had in a long time, I pull out a plastic document folder of stuff I printed out at home. I open it up and pull the contents out. I find a photograph of a Lornea Island sea-dragon, and then a map I got off the internet of where Fonchem wants to expand. I put them both down in front of her.

"Your company. Your Dad's company. You didn't tell me they were the ones trying to buy up half of Lornea Island." I'm exaggerating there, quite a lot, but I'm angry.

She picks up the papers and looks at them, and then she looks at me.

"I don't understand."

I stab a finger at the map. "There. Fonchem. You're trying to develop this land here, including the bay, and it's going to destroy a unique habitat which is used by a species of seahorse that's endemic to Lornea Island. It's not found anywhere else."

She looks again, and as I feed her more papers, she looks at those as well. My posters, an article I printed out, with a photo of her dad, smiling in a suit.

"Oh." She says. And she bites her lip.

* * *

I take a sip of my drink, not able to look Lily in the eyes, while she forms all the papers into a pile and neatens them up.

"So you've found out what my family does?" There's an anger in her eyes that I wasn't expecting.

"Yes."

"And you're angry?"

I take a breath before I answer. "Yes."

"And of course you yourself, don't use any chemical products, in your life. You don't travel by car, or use detergents, or own any electronics?"

"I do. But I don't see why it's necessary to destroy wildlife habitats to produce all that stuff."

She looks away at this. I can see it was a powerful line.

"I'm sure they won't be destroyed…" She looks back suddenly. "Look, I didn't know anything about this until you just showed it to me. I wasn't trying to hide anything from you."

"But you knew I was into marine biology." A weird thought occurs to me. "Did you know I was running a campaign to oppose Fonchem buying that land? Is that why you made friends with me. Were you *spying*?"

"No!" Lily stares at me for a long time, and then she bursts out laughing. "No Billy. I'm not *spying* on you." She stops laughing. "I promise. And I seriously doubt your campaign has anyone worried in Dad's office. It's not the sort of place… It's…"

Her face suddenly looks serious again, matching mine. "Look Billy, we get opposition every time we open a site, or change what's made there, or expand a site, or do *anything*. It's a chemical company, that's just what happens."

"And you're OK with that?"

She looks away again. She seems more exasperated this time.

"Well actually no. I'm not." Suddenly she grabs my hand and pulls it towards her. "Look Billy, I can imagine what you must think of me. The rich-*bitch* daughter of a billionaire, owner of millions of shares. I have that giant house, and everything gets handed to me on a plate. But I'm not like that."

I got stuck at the word billionaire. I didn't realize she was *that* rich.

"You know what I'm studying?" She asks suddenly, and I have to think to remember.

"International Law."

"International *Environmental* Law. There's a difference. It's all about the attempts to control pollution and the depletion of natural resources. But not just to fight it, in small scale protests, but find actual solutions that can change the way *actual* firms operate. Firms like my father's.

"I don't have to study anything Billy. I could just go to parties and vacations and not do anything. We have more than enough money for that. But that's not what I chose. Doesn't that say something?"

Now I frown. I can feel it on my face. "So you don't approve of this?" I tap the pile of papers, but my voice sounds uncertain.

She looks at it, she seems frustrated.

"No. *Yes*, I don't know! I haven't… I'd have to study… My point is that I'm not who you fear I am. I'm not just… I don't know. I have to be a *realist*, not despite who I am, but because of who I am. But I'm on your side. I'm on your side Billy." She squeezes my hand, then lets me go.

Suddenly she spins around and starts digging into her bag, which is on the chair next to her. I have the strangest feeling she's about to give me money, to pay me off. She frowns again as she digs into it. But then she pulls out a card. It's from Greenpeace.

"Look, I'm a member. I've been a member for years. I don't know about these…" she hunts on the table for the picture of the sea-dragon.

"Seahorses."

"Right, I don't know about those, about that case in particular, but I *do* care about this stuff as well. I really do. In fact that's why…" she stops, and her eyes meet mine for a second, before she looks away. "I guess it's why I like you."

I don't know how to react to this, and there's a weird silence.

"What do you mean?"

"What do you mean, *what do I mean?*" She gives me a crooked smile, then looks away again.

"What do you mean *why you like me?*"

It takes her a long time to answer, and when she does, she just says: "I don't know."

Then there's another silence, which Lily breaks by asking me about my work, and the course, and lots of other questions that don't really mean anything. And then she has another look at the documents I brought. And we finish our drinks, and I realize she's going to go soon. And I really don't want her to.

"What were you saying?" I ask suddenly, when I get the sense she's getting ready to leave. "When you thought I was angry about James?"

Her face changes at once, and I can see her thinking what to say. But then she shakes her head. "Nothing. I just thought it might have upset you, that's all. Everything that's going on with me and James."

I want to ask her what is going on with her and James. But something in her face stops me. And then she gets up, and tells me she has to go. And before I can say anything else she's given me a hug and told me she'll see me soon, and she's gone.

And it's only then that I realize it's this – her and James, and where I might fit in – that worries and confuses me most about all this. More than the environmental angle. More than the Lornea Island sea-dragons.

CHAPTER TWENTY-ONE

The next time Lily calls she asks if I want to come out to dinner. But before I can reply she goes on, telling me it's Oscar's birthday, so they all want to do something nice. But from the way she says it, so quickly, I can tell she was worried that maybe I would think she meant just her and me again, like on a proper date. And then maybe because of that I felt the need to show her I wasn't thinking that, and also I do have other plans sometimes, other friends. Well – it all makes me do something a little bit silly.

"Actually I can't on Thursday." I say instead. "I'm seeing my friend. Amber." Obviously this isn't true, I haven't seen Amber for weeks.

"Oh." Lily replies, and then I sense she's going to say that never mind, perhaps we can do it another time, or something like that, and I panic right away that maybe there *won't be another time* – that I'll never hear from her again – so I go on, without thinking.

"But maybe I could bring her along. She's really fun."

Then there's a long pause, when I totally regret what I've just said, before Lily replies.

"Sure. Of course Billy. Of course you can bring your friend along." She just gently stresses the word friend, so that it sounds kinda weird, and I don't quite know what she means by it.

"I'll let the restaurant know."

So then I have a bit of a problem, since now I have to invite Amber to meet Lily and the others, and I haven't even told her about them. But it's not a massive problem. This is Amber we're talking about, she's my oldest friend, and we've been through a lot together, so going out to a restaurant isn't exactly going to be that difficult. So I think for a bit, and then I ring her and ask what she's doing on Thursday night. And while I do I get the idea that maybe *she'll* be busy, and I'll be able to say to Lily and the others that she wasn't able to come after all, and everything will just be easier that way. But then Amber says the only plans she had was dying her hair that night – which is just her funny way of saying she isn't busy. So then I ask if she wants to come out with me and my friends. And I can tell she's really touched by the idea.

So annoyingly, it's all arranged.

* * *

When Thursday evening comes around I cycle round to Amber's apartment. I figure it's best if we turn up together, so I can maybe warn her a bit about them. As I ring her doorbell I worry that Amber might have gone a bit too alternative in her dress, but she doesn't look too bad, in black jeans and a black t-shirt, with the name of one of the punk bands she likes on it. Her orange hair has gone too, turned back to a kind of dark blue/purple hue, which is the color I think suits her best.

"Billy!" She gives me a hug. "I'll just be five minutes. Dump your bike in the hallway. It'll be safer there."

She turns and disappears into one of the rooms – I've not actually been to her apartment before, and I guess she realizes this too as she shouts out to me from out of sight.

"Help yourself to a poke around. My housemates aren't in."

So I do, and her place is quite nice. Cozy, and much more like a home than where I'm living, although the whole apartment is probably smaller than the massive kitchen in Lily's house.

"So Billy, you're finally going to introduce me to your college friends huh?" I've finished looking around, and am back in the hallway, outside her room, but the door's open and I can see her at a mirror, putting on purple eyeshadow. I think it's called eyeshadow, either way, there's rather a lot of it.

"About time too!"

"Yeah. I just wanted to say something about that…" I begin, not really sure what I need to say here. "They're, they're quite into their culture stuff, sometimes." But maybe she can't hear me, she does have the radio on in the background.

"Is that Guy guy going to be there?" Amber interrupts me. "Get it? Guy guy? If so don't sit me next to him, OK?"

I tell her not to worry about that, and suggest hopefully that we should walk to the restaurant, so I get a chance to explain about them, but really I'm just delaying things, and when Amber sees where it is, she tells me I'm crazy and calls an Uber. And five minutes later we arrive outside a big glass-fronted restaurant which looks very expensive. Amber gives me a look before we go in, like this wasn't what she was expecting for a student night out. And I just know this isn't going to go that well.

Inside there's a man waiting at a kind of podium thing. He looks very well dressed, and he smiles at us a little bit confused maybe, at the way Amber is dressed. I only know what he wants because I've seen it on TV, so I explain, a little bit hesitantly maybe, that we're here to eat with Lillian Bellafonte. I'm only a bit surprised when he nods his head smartly and asks us to come with him. But Amber gives me a look and mouths *what the fuck..?* as we follow him. We go past lots of tables of diners, all sitting quietly and eating tiny amounts of food off huge plates. Mostly they're dressed in proper suits and dresses, I notice, while piano music plays quietly in the background. I'm kind of relieved when we get to the others, they're at a table tucked away a bit near the back of the restaurant, it's kind of cut off by a giant fish tank, brightly illuminated, and filled with fish, freshwater fish, like guppies, tetras and zebrafish. The others are dressed normally, or normal for Lily and her friends at least.

"Billy!" Lily stands up. She's wearing blue jeans and another white wool sweater. "And you must be…"

"Amber." Amber says, she smiles and I think she's expecting Lily to do the same, but she doesn't, or not really. Then Lily introduces the others, but she does so a bit quickly and half-heartedly, and James and Oscar barely stop talking to say hello. Then we sit down, the way the table is laid out, it's me and Amber at one end, kind of away from the others.

"We asked for this table," Lily leans in to say to me, "because of the fish." She gives me a smile, but then turns back to James, who seems to be half way through a story. I don't really follow what it's about, but I get enough to hear it involves someone suing someone else about some breach of contract. The others seem glued though, and when he gets to the punchline they all laugh loudly, all except Amber and me. Then there's a silence, and it's only really broken when James and Oscar pick up their menus, and start discussing what to eat. I glance at Amber, who's staring at me quizzically, and pick up my menu too.

The first thing I notice is the prices. I guess that's just a habit, but here they all look like typos, there's nothing for less than a hundred dollars, and the descriptions of the food is all in French, or most of it. James and Oscar start discussing, loudly, what's best – and it's all about the last time they had it, or when they ate that other thing in Paris, or that seafood restaurant in Florence, and it goes on for ages. Finally I hear Eric saying firmly that he's not hungry enough for a starter, so he's just going to have the turbot, and he fixes me with a look. When I find it on the menu, it's the cheapest thing, so I say I'll have it too. Amber leans in to whisper to me.

"What the actual fuck Billy? These are your friends?"

I don't know what to say, so I don't say much in reply. And when the waitress comes – she looks the most normal person here – Amber tells her she'll have the turbot too.

It gets a bit better after that. The table kind of splits in two. James, Oscar and Jennifer mostly talk amongst themselves – I don't hear what they're saying, but it sounds as though they're still re-living their holiday in Europe the other year. And then at my end Eric seems to do his best to make Amber feel welcome. At least, he actually talks to her. Lily is mostly silent. She seems torn between the two groups. But even Eric isn't his usual entertaining self, and plenty of times we end up silent at our end of the table, and just sort of passengers, listening to James and Oscar banter and bicker between themselves over details of their trip that we didn't go on.

"So Lily, what are you studying?" Amber asks suddenly, surprising me. I thought we'd settled into not talking at all.

"Oh," Lily looks startled. "Law." She replies. "And you? Err... Billy tells me..." She doesn't finish what she's saying, probably because I haven't said much about her at all.

"Design." Amber helps her out. "But I studied on Lornea, not here. That fun? Law?" She pokes at her fish.

Lily looks put on the spot by the question, and reluctantly turns to Amber. From where I'm sitting, next to Eric, I can see them side by side. They couldn't look any more different.

"I wouldn't call it fun. But it's important."

"Hmmm." Amber nods her head.

"I do like your hair color." Eric says, a minute or two later, and he tries to smile at Amber, but he still seems off somehow.

"Thank you Eric," Amber replies. "I like yours..." But her words are drowned out by a huge roar of laughter from the other end of the table, and it's followed by Jennifer giggling for ages, like she's unable to stop. And I kind of get the feeling it's fake somehow, from the way she glances at Lily at the end, to make sure she sees it.

"They probably shouldn't have lion fish in there," I say, suddenly. I know it's not the most appropriate thing to say, but I want to try to lighten the mood plus, it's been bothering me since I sat down.

"What?" Eric asks.

I point at the fish tank, and the large lionfish – *Pteriois* – swimming slowly behind the glass.

"Why not?" Eric replies. "Will they eat all the others?"

"Yeah, but the problem isn't in the fish tanks, it's in the wild. People buy them because they think they'll look good in their tanks, then when they eat everything else they dump them in the toilets, or release them into the ocean. And they've become one of the worst invasive species along the whole coastline of the Americas."

"No way?" Eric says.

"Yeah. They're incredibly efficient predators. They have very large mouths, and they drift up close to other fish, and then strike really quickly. But the real problem is how fast they reproduce. The females can produce 30,000 eggs every seven days. They just drive out native species."

"Really."

. . .

It gets better after that. At least, Eric gets a bit more talkative, and he and Amber seem to get on OK. But there's still a divide on the table, and Lily still doesn't say much. Meanwhile James, Oscar and Jennifer seem to be having a great time. They're laughing, and they keep ordering more wine every time they finish a bottle, which seems to happen a lot, but when they do, they don't even send the bottle down to our end. It's like Eric and Amber and me are at a completely different dinner. But eventually it ends, and then I start to worry about the bill. Before – when we were at the beach – I think Lily paid for all the food, and I sort of hope the same happens here, even though that doesn't seem fair on her, but I'm just worried about how much it's all going to cost. But that's not what happens. Instead James orders a round of what I think are brandies for himself and Oscar, and he asks for the check at the same time. But when it actually comes it gets given to him, because he's the one who asks for it. And after he looks at it, he announces loudly that we should all just split it equally, since that'll be easier. He looks at me as he says it. It's pretty much the first thing he's actually said to me all night. And right away Oscar and Jennifer agree equally loudly, and it's like it's settled when it isn't. I turn to Amber, and I can tell she's incandescent with rage, and I almost hope she's going to say something, but I can tell she's holding herself in. And so she and I just pay what we're asked, I think just to get out of there.

When we finally leave, James and Oscar and Jennifer say they're going to go onto a club, and they ask if we're coming, but I can tell they don't really mean it. So there's a painful five minutes, when they sort of pretend to be waiting to see if we'll change our minds, but really they're just waiting for a cab, and then they finally get in and disappear. Even then it still feels tense, because Eric and Lily are still here. Lily wants to go home, and Eric says he'll take her, so they get into the next cab. And then it's just me and Amber left.

"What the hell Billy?" she says to me, the moment it's just the two of us. "What the fucking hell was that all about?"

CHAPTER TWENTY-TWO

I can't really pretend it was a success of an evening, so I don't.

"*They're* your friends? The reason I haven't seen you in weeks?"

"They're not always like that. I don't know what was wrong with them."

"So what are they normally like? Just ordinary stuck-up rich assholes, instead of rich assholes intent on being as rude as fucking possible?"

"No... I..." We're still standing outside the restaurant, but there's no more cabs. "Do you want to call an Uber?"

"No Billy. I don't want to call an Uber. I don't have any money left."

I don't have any money left either, so instead we start walking, but Amber doesn't let up.

"I mean, what was she like? That one in the white sweater, the miserable one. What was her name?"

"Lily."

"Lily – what sort of a name is that?"

I don't answer.

"*I'm studying Law. It's important.*" Amber imitates Lily's voice, but in a mocking way.

"They're not always like that." I suddenly interrupt her. "They're really not. Something must have happened."

Amber turns to look at me now. "You know I'm actually still hungry?"

I frown.

"I can't believe I've paid two hundred dollars for dinner, and I'm still not full. And let's not even talk about that wine." Amber screws up her nose. At least Lily insisted on picking up the tab for that, otherwise our bill would have been much higher. "Do you want to go somewhere? Somewhere normal?"

So we walk back towards her house, and after a while we come to another restaurant, which I think is Malaysian, so not exactly normal, but Amber tells me I should try it, so we do. We go inside, and eat noodles, and they're good, and the whole thing feels normal – like it used to feel with Amber. She tells me more about how her life is going here in Boston, and what's happening at her work, and how she's dating a guy called Sean, who's Irish and works in a gym – none of which I had any idea about. She had a tough time a while back did Amber, when her boyfriend was killed, so I'm glad to hear she's seeing someone again. I tell her a bit about my housemates, and how they're OK, but a bit dumb, and I then try to explain why it is I like Lily, and even her friends normally. And we talk about my course, and why that's a bit annoying because it's too basic, and Amber tells me it'll get better, I just have to stick with it.

And then my phone rings, and it's Eric.

"Hello," I say. I don't go away from Amber, because it's not too loud in the noodle place.

"Billy." Eric replies, but he doesn't say anything else.

"Are you OK?"

"*I am.*" He sighs. "But I've just spent an hour with Lily crying her eyes out on my shoulder. And I just thought I should let you know."

He sounds weary, and I'm kind of shocked – or just somehow reluctant to be pulled back to thinking about where we've just been, and what happened earlier. I was feeling good, enjoying it being just me and Amber again.

"Know what?"

"To know why you had to sit through the most excruciating night in the history of the world," Eric replies.

"Oh," I say. "Why?"

But then he doesn't answer right away.

"Look, I don't know if I'm supposed to tell you this, Lily didn't… Well I couldn't get a straight answer out of her. But I thought…"

"Just tell me."

"Alright, alright" Eric sounds put out. "Don't you go getting all *dominant* on me. I don't think I can take any more major upheavals in my life."

"Please just tell me Eric," I soften my voice.

"OK. Well the reason tonight was so awkward is that James broke up with Lily this evening. Literally just before they arrived at the restaurant."

CHAPTER TWENTY-THREE

I don't see Lily, or Amber, or Eric, or any of them, for a long time after that. And to be honest, I'm not sure I want to. My course still isn't difficult, but there is a lot of work to do, and right now I've got a whole bunch of essays that I have to write, so for a while I'm able to lose myself in researching them. I actually got my grades back for my first essays, and while they were OK, I did get one B, and I don't want that to happen again. So I go to all my classes and I actually pay attention for a change, and I spend most of my spare time in the library, reading up on all the books and journals I was supposed to read earlier. A lot of the time they're books I've read before, but it's nice to lose myself in that world again.

On top of that I still have my law class over at Harvard University. I've figured out a new route now, which means I'm not in such a rush when I have to come back. But when I am there, I find myself keeping a look out for Lily. I don't really mean to, it's more like this automatic thing that I can't control, it just happens. But it doesn't matter anyway, since I don't see her. I guess I'm a bit disappointed about that. But every now and then I think about her. I wonder if I should call, or send her a message and ask if she's OK, and tell her I'm sorry about her and James – though obviously I'm not sorry, because I think he's an asshole – but I don't know if any of that is the right thing to do. So I don't. And then I start to think that maybe that's it, maybe I won't ever see her again, or any of them.

And that's when she sends me the text.

Can you do sailing?

I'm in the library when it comes in, writing an essay on plankton ecology and food-web interactions, which between you and me isn't as interesting as it might sound. So I don't know what to make of the text, and I even wonder if she might have sent it to me by mistake, as in, she meant to send it to someone else. But then she sends another one:

Sorry Billy, was a bit rushed just then, meant to ask if you're any good at sailing? Might need to borrow you if so...

I'm still not sure what to say, but this time I do text back.

I guess I'm OK

And then she doesn't reply but phones, which is awkward, because – like I just said – I'm in the library, but I don't want to put her off, so I quickly gather up my books and hurry outside, where I can talk more easily.

"Are you still there?" Lily asks, when I get outside and can talk properly.

"Yeah."

"It sounds like an earthquake."

"Sorry, I was just... No there isn't."

"Good. It's... The reason I'm calling. It's just because you were so good at surfing that time, and I figured you might be able to sail as well... And well. We're a little bit desperate, is all."

There's a noise in the background, I can't hear what.

"I've done a bit," I reply, a bit lost. And really what I want to say is how it's so nice to hear her voice, and how good she sounds – bright, and fresh, and happy. "Erm, my dad taught me a few years back. We found this boat abandoned, so we rebuilt it, and sailed it around Lornea Island."

"You're kidding?" She laughs. "My God, I *knew* it. That's absolutely perfect."

"Perfect for what?" I ask, but she's gone. In the background I hear her voice though.

"Dad, he's an expert."

"Are you busy Saturday?" She's back talking to me.

"No." I hesitate. I'm definitely not an expert.

There's more voices in the background. It sounds like someone's replying to her.

"Sorry, I'm at home. That's my dad. He's got himself into a stupid argument with my uncle at the yacht club. It's the final day of the season this Saturday, and…" She breaks off, and I hear her speak in the background again – "it *is* stupid, Dad." Then she comes back to me.

"They're both ridiculously competitive, so Dad challenged him to a bet. Whoever finishes in front at the weekend wins, loser has to buy the winner – and crew – dinner." She laughs again, but I just wait.

"So… We need crew at short notice. Ideally someone who can sail well. So I thought of you." There's a funny change in her voice when she says the word 'you'. Or maybe I think there is. Then I think about the little boat Dad and me fixed up and sailed around Lornea, and wonder what sort of boat Lily's *billionaire* dad might have.

"Um, you want me to come?" Is the only thing I can think to actually say.

"Yes!" Again her voice sounds bright, and fresh, and filled with joy.

"OK."

So then I'm committed to another social occasion when I'm going to be way out of my depth.

* * *

That night I have a dream that Lily's dad's boat is one of those enormous, ridiculous gigantic superyachts, a hundred foot long, with a dozen crew members and a helicopter on the back, and for some reason I'm told I have to sail it, only it doesn't even have sails, but it moves somehow anyway, because it's a dream, and I end up steering it onto the rocks, and then I wake up with Lily's dad – who looks like a pirate, only a pirate wearing one of Lily's white wool sweaters, and for some reason with a monocle – shouting and swearing at me, and holding a huge hose out of which dangerous chemicals are flowing all over me and all into the ocean. And I see Lily gasping in horror, at what I've done not at what *he's* doing.

And when I wake up I know it's just a stupid dream, yet I still can't shake the thought that this is going to be a disaster. But on Saturday morning, early, because that's when I'm told to get down there, I go to the marina where the boat is kept, and find a safe place to lock up my bike. I scan the basin of yachts, like a forest of masts, to see if there's any billionaire superyachts. There aren't, but there are still some enormous sailing yachts, and I wonder if Lily's dad's is one of these. So then I call Lily, like she told me, because there's a locked gate to get down to where the boats are moored. She comes walking up the pontoon towards me, waving, and looking happy. She's wearing a yachting jacket today, white and blue, with a fluorescent yellow hood. But I don't see which boat she came from.

"Hey Billy, beautiful weather. Perfect breeze!" She punches in a code and the gate swings open. I wonder if she's going to kiss me, or if I should kiss her, but in the end we both hesitate, and don't do anything.

"Come on then. I'll introduce you to everyone." She turns and leads me back down the pontoon.

"So which one's your Dad's boat?" I ask, as we walk out. The way marinas work, the smaller boats are always moored closer in, where there's less water and less space. So the further we go, the bigger her dad's boat is. She turns to look at me.

"Just out here." She points casually, but it's towards the one with the very tallest mast, an absolute monster of a yacht. It must be a hundred foot long, painted dark blue and towering over everything else.

"*That* one?" I stop. It's like my nightmare is coming true already.

Lily turns to look at me, a curious expression on her face.

"Are you OK?" She follows my gaze, and laughs. "No, not *that* one Billy. Who do you think we are? Internet billionaires? It's *there*."

She points instead to a much more modest yacht, the sort you might find in the harbor in Holport on Lornea Island, and at once I feel some sense of relief.

But as we get closer I see it is actually quite a bit bigger than the average Lornea Island yachts, perhaps forty foot long, with two wheels for steering, one either side in the cockpit. A man is bending over on the foredeck, struggling to move a coil of ropes.

"Wow." I say. "She's beautiful."

"Yes. She is. But she's not particularly fast, unfortunately. Least not the way Dad sails her. Come on."

She grabs hold of one of the stays, the metal wires coming down from the mast, as she swings herself aboard. I do the same.

"Hey Dad," she calls out. "This is Billy. I told you about him."

The man stops what he's doing and straightens up. He's quite slight, and he's wearing a blue knitted sweater with holes in it. He looks more like a fisherman from Holport than a billionaire. There's no monocle either.

"Hello," I say.

"Hello there!" He replies, and he walks back down the side deck, stepping carefully, until he's level with me. "Nice of you to join us." He shakes my hand.

"Billy's my expert sailor friend," Lily tells him.

"Really? Well, I certainly hope so. We're going to need every advantage we can get. I trust Lillian has explained the mission for the day?"

"Um, yeah, sort of. You have to beat her uncle, in a race?"

"Best of three races actually, but that's the general idea. Her uncle, my brother, he can be – over competitive, and I don't want to spend the entire winter listening to him bragging. So yes. Consider it a matter of life and death." He says this with a grin, so I know he isn't serious, but at the same time, I can sort of sense he is as well.

"First start is at ten, so I want to get out there. Do you want to go stow your gear?"

Lily takes me down below, and it's beautiful down here. Bigger than any yacht I've been in before, and fitted out in wood that's so well polished it glows like gold. There's a man and a woman, a bit older than me sitting at the navigation table, fiddling with the chart plotter. Another woman, older but elegant, walks in from a stern cabin, she smiles in expectation.

"Mum, David, Emily, this is Billy, I told you he was coming."

"Hello" I say, to Lillian's mom, because it seems most polite to greet her first. She takes my hand and tells me to call her Clara.

"David's my brother." Lily goes on, "and Emily's his girlfriend." I shake more hands. It didn't occur to me that the entire family was going to be here.

"Hi Billy, Lill's told us about you. You're going to be our secret weapon huh?" David's has a voice like a drawl, I can't tell if he's serious or not.

"Erm."

"I sure hope so, because Dad gets so mad when he loses. He'll probably throw you overboard."

"*David*," Lily's mom says. "Don't scare the poor boy. It must be frightening enough meeting the whole family like this."

"They're just *friends* mum," David says, in a way that I can tell means he's mimicking something Lily must have said before. I don't know how that makes me feel. I have no idea if I'm here as a friend or not. Well I guess I do know now, I guess I just hoped it was somehow something more.

Not long after we go on deck, and Lily's dad gives us instructions while he gets the boat ready to leave the mooring. I've done this a thousand times, but it's still a bit tense sometimes, because boats can be hard to move in small spaces. You usually get a sense of how confident the person in charge is, and actually Lily's dad seems quite relaxed, issuing instructions calmly, and the others do what they're told equally calmly. But there's an energy in the air too. It's not just us leaving the shelter of the marina, there's a steady stream of yachts leaving, each with crews on deck busily removing sail covers and preparing rigging, and the breeze is fresh too. We motor for a few minutes, but then we hoist up the sails, and immediately begin heeling over at a sharp angle as we cut through the water. Lily's dad is steering, and he points us towards a moored motor boat. Around us, other boats also put their sails up. Mostly they're white, but one boat has black mylar sails, to match its black-painted hull.

"That's *Abigale*." Lily pokes me in the ribs, though the sailing jacket I've been lent. "My uncle's boat. It's the same boat as this, but he had his made lighter, just so he can beat dad." She looks at me and raises her eyebrows.

I look over at the boat just as it changes direction onto a new tack, the great black sails start to spill their wind, until they're flogging as the bow glides right through the wind, and then fills in from the new side, and they press taut again. The hull surges forward, slicing through the water, now no more than fifty yards away. There's a man steering, and I see him turn to face us. Only not us, even from this distance it's obvious he's staring intently at Lily's Dad. I glance at him too, looking back, his face unreadable. Again I get the sense this is more serious to Lily's dad than he's prepared to admit.

I realize pretty soon though, that I'm not really here as the expert sailor after all. As we get towards the start line for the first race, David synchronizes his watch with the signals from the start boat, and as he and Lily's dad exchange instructions and tactics, and they don't ask me anything. I'm quite relieved actually. All that 'expert' stuff was just Lily winding me up. But that doesn't mean I'm just here for the ride, on a boat this big there's still plenty for me to do. Every time we change from one tack to another – which is a lot, while we're jostling for position, one boat among dozens – we have to release the sails from one side of the boat, and pull them in on the other. Lily and me are given one side, and Emily and Lily's mom do the other. Lily makes me do the winching. That is, I have to crank in the huge genoa sail at the front by winding the sheet around stainless steel winch as fast as possible. Lily helps by leading the rope the right way onto the winch drum, and I just turn the handle as fast as I can until David or Lily's dad – everyone else calls him Claude, so I suppose I should too – tells me to stop. Emily and Lily's mom do the same on the other side, and we get into a kind of battle to see which team can do it quicker.

I should explain about sailing boats here, just in case you don't know much about them. I didn't, at least not until Dad taught me. They're not like motorboats, in that you can just go in every direction you want. The way my dad explained it to me was like this: It's a bit like riding a bike on a very steep hill. The wind is the hill, and it falls from the top down to the bottom. So it's easy to go downhill, or even across the hill. But if you want to go up, you can't. It's too steep, and you have to go in zig zags. Like switchbacks on a mountain road. Each zig is called a tack. But then when you change from one tack to another – the corners – that's also called a tack (I told you it was confusing) but really you're just changing from one switchback to another. If that doesn't make sense, I didn't get it either, not until we got out there and started trying it. Then it's quite easy.

"Three minutes to the gun." David calls out, as we tack again and pull the sails tight. My shoulders are hurting from the effort of it, and I'm hot.

"Bearing off. We'll go a minute and gybe round then gun for the start." Claude shouts back. I don't know that much about what they're saying, so I just do what I'm told.

"Get that main pulled in! Going about…" Claude spins the wheel until we're running with the wind, and Lily pulls on the main sheet so the boom isn't able to sweep too fast across to the other side. Then he gradually hardens up on the new tack, and with the sails pulled tight, we're pointing right at the right hand end of the start line. About fifty meters back from it. There's a log readout on the instrument panel, telling us the speed in real time. It eases up, from six knots to seven. Seven point five.

"One minute to the start." David calls out. There are three boats just downwind of us, but another two upwind, positioned just a few meters ahead of us, giving them the upwind advantage. One of them is the black yacht, so close we can see the taut expressions on the crew's faces. They pull its sails tighter and it accelerates, moving a half boat-length in front of us. Then, amid shouts and noises and David's countdown alarm beeping, a canon fires on the cliffs on the shore. We see the smoke momentarily before the noise, and then twenty yachts all hit the start line together. For a few minutes I think we're all going to crash, or at least the race is going to be neck and neck the entire way, but actually we quickly begin to spread out as the faster boats take the wind of the slower ones, and pull ahead. We're about sixth, I guess – though it's not easy to say, because of the zig-zag thing I just told you about. David showed me the course we have to race, before we left the berth. We have to sail up against the wind to a marker buoy, then come back down wind again, then do it a second time, only not quite so far, and then come back down to cross the line in the same place where we started. It's all a bit pointless when you put it like that.

But it doesn't *feel* pointless, not now I'm doing it. It feels exhilarating and quite scary, and just really, really exciting. We're heeling over, bucking and smashing through the little waves, and there's spray flying through the air, and there's still two boats so close you could throw a stone onto their decks, one downwind of us, which we're beating, and the other upwind, which unfortunately is the black yacht. We tighten and ease the sails, trying to urge the speedometer up. Sometimes it's as high as nine knots, sometimes as low as six, and we see the difference in how the black yacht eases ahead, or we pull back closer. Then suddenly the black yacht rolls into a tack, faster than before, its sails only momentarily flogging as it changes onto the other angle of the zig zag.

"Tacking to cover," Lily's dad – Claude – says at once, and everyone runs to change the sails so we can go the other way too, following it. Then there's a moment of noise and chaos as we round up into, and through, the wind, our speed drops to three knots, then the wind presses the sails from the other side and we squeeze forward again. Five knots. Seven. Nine again. The water slipping past the rails beneath us is blurred. But even so, the black yacht is now further ahead, maybe two whole boat-lengths. And these are long boats. We're looking at its stern now, the name painted in red: *Abigale.* Then there's a hiss and a crackle on the radio, and a voice comes through, managing to sound smug even through the static.

"You need to work on your tacks Claude!"

David moves to the companionway, where the radio is. "Permission to tell Jacques he's an arrogant asshole?"

"Permission denied." Claude replies, but he looks up at the giant sails, and turns the wheel so we're sailing just a touch closer to the wind.

Ten minutes later and we've slipped further back. I've been watching the speedometer intently, we're averaging 8.5 knots. Suddenly I'm surprised when Claude talks to me.

"Don't worry Billy. We'll get him on the downwind leg." I turn to see him smiling, in a kind of rueful way.

"I can see you know a bit about boats?"

"A little."

He nods. "You done any racing before?"

I shake my head. "But I did do some research, after Lily asked me to come."

He looks surprised at this. "Research?"

"Yeah. Just about the racing part of things. So I knew the basics."

He chuckles. "Oh yeah. So what'd you learn?"

"Um." I'm not sure I can remember all the terminology, so I'm reluctant to try and repeat it all now.

"Well, obviously in a race it's mostly about who can get up the beat, or the windward leg first." I decide I'm not going to tell him my mountain analogy.

"Because you can't sail directly into the wind, and you have to zigzag towards it, the boats are actually sailing much *further* on this leg. But on top of that, the wind is never constant both in terms of direction and strength. So some parts of a racecourse will be windier, which makes you go faster, and some parts will be lighter, which makes you go slower. And on top of *that*, in some parts the wind will be blowing from slightly different directions, some of which let you sail more directly to the mark, and some of which force you to sail further away from it. So it's a bit like finding your way through a giant maze, where you have to read all this invisible wind to find the fastest route through. Plus, there's currents too."

I feel both Claude and David Bellafonte turn to stare at me. "That's certainly the theory."

We don't tack much though, not now we're actually racing. That's because the boat is so big and heavy, it takes a long time to get back up to speed when we do it, and because the right hand side of the course is obviously windier, so all the boats have gone this way. But as we cut our way towards the first marker buoy, the black yacht keeps easing ahead, and it makes the turn a full minute before we do. Then by the time we go around the buoy, and ease our sails to run back downwind, it looks miles away. We follow it downwind, putting up a huge spinnaker sail that pulls us back down to the start much more quickly than it took to get up here, and then there's a few moments of panic while we have to pack it away again. And then we start again, on the much shorter second upwind leg. We're even further behind now, and the mood on the boat sinks.

"What do you reckon David? Take a chance on the other side?" Claude says, when we're steady sailing back upwind again. I can sort of follow the tactics now. The black yacht has gone up the same side of the course as we did the first windward leg, out away from the land where it's windier, but if we just follow them, then the same thing is going to happen as on the first lap. We'll both be in the same wind, they're a tiny bit faster than us, so they'll stay ahead.

"We've got no choice," David replies. "We'll just have to hope they mess up the mark rounding."

But they don't. They go around a full five minutes before we do, and just after we round the upwind mark they cross the finishing line. Seconds later we hear the radio crackle again.

"That's one out of three Claude. You wanna give up already?"

We finish the race thirteenth out of the twenty five boats, which apparently isn't bad – according to Lily – but obviously no one's very happy, because the boat we wanted to beat was seven places ahead of us. We don't go ashore or anything though, there's another race straight after this one, and we have to sail about a bit while we wait for the final boats to finish, then there'll be another start sequence. In the meantime, Lily's mom brings out mugs of hot soup and sandwiches wrapped in tin foil that she had warming in the oven. They're really nice, but I somehow expected rich people to eat better than this.

There's less time than I imagine before we're starting again. And quickly the pressure builds up again. The start is incredibly important, you have to cross the line just as the gun goes, and moving at full speed – if you don't, it's like giving other boats a head start. But also, one end of the start line is a little bit more upwind than the other, so all the boats want to start at that end, at the same time. So there's lots of shouting and yelling, and boats changing direction. When the gun finally goes we're not quite so well placed as before, and the black yacht is already a few boat-lengths ahead. Just as before, it tacks off, to sail up the right hand side of the course, further out to sea where the wind is stronger. But this time there's something different.

"We need to tack," David says. "We need to follow them."

But this time Claude hesitates, and I can see why, it's obvious. The wind's shifted. You can see it on the water, and in the way the birds are flying, they're hanging in the air, just coasting on the up-currents flowing up the cliffs. The angle they're making against the shore has changed.

"OK," Claude says. "Prepare to tack."

"No!" I call out. "The wind's changed. Stay on this tack."

No one talks for a few seconds, because they're all surprised. Actually, I'm probably the most surprised. I think I was just getting into it more than I realized.

"It's windier out to sea." David replies, part to me, but then more to his dad. "We have to follow them."

I'd keep quiet, I really would if it wasn't so obvious that the wind has changed.

"But look at the wind inshore. The angle's better."

"You sure?" Claude asks. And suddenly I'm not. Not quite as sure. Because it's one thing to think all this in my head, and another to have actually said it out loud, now we're going to make a decision on it.

"The birds are flying differently to before."

Both David and Claude look, but then look back at me, frowning, like they don't see it.

"We're behind anyway. We're only going to chase them home if we tack. So let's stick it out." Claude says, so that's what we do. And now I'm super tense as we keep sailing left, while the black yacht moves further and further away from us towards the other side of the course. But soon we hit the wind shift, and we're able to tighten up our angle, and sail much tighter – more directly – towards the windward marker buoy. Suddenly we're sailing a shorter course than they are. All that's happened is the wind is bending around nearer to the shore, it did the same thing when we were sailing around Lornea. The wind is still slightly lighter inshore, but not by much, and we're still averaging eight knots on the log. We have to tack eventually, to sail back towards the marker buoy, and timing it right is crucial. But when we do, and we're back up to speed, we can all see we've reversed the position against the *Abigale*. Now we're comfortably ahead, it's ten boat lengths back. We go around the buoy ahead, and give a cheer as we pass them when we're on the way back downwind.

It's tense after that, but we stay ahead, and on the second, shorter beat back upwind, we make the same call, going to the left. This time the black yacht follows us, but it's too far back to catch us, and we finish the race fourth. This time Claude gives David the wheel and goes and talks on the radio himself, though I can't hear what he says. I don't care though, I have Lily beside me now, handing me more soup and sandwiches. She's grinning with delight, her hair tucked into a red woolly hat that matches the glow on her cheeks.

There's a longer gap between the second and the final race, and we eat more sandwiches wrapped in foil. There's a bit of a chance to relax now, and I start to wonder if I might be able to find some time to speak with Lily's dad. It occurred to me before that actually getting to meet him like this, I might be able to tell him about the issue of the sea-dragons – not maybe my campaign to stop his company expanding there, I thought I'd keep quiet about how it's me behind that – but maybe I could explain to him the reasons behind the campaign, the need to protect the seagrass areas. Before I met him I kind of assumed he wouldn't be the sort of person who might listen to this, but now I get the idea the opposite might be true. He actually seems a lot more decent and normal than I expected. But still, there hasn't been a spare moment so far. And before I can find a way to broach the subject now, we're in the start sequence for the third race.

It seems more tense this time, if that's even possible. I guess because it's the last race of the day. Actually, the last race of the whole season. There's more chatter on the radio, between lots of the boats, and more shouting, and the boats seem to be getting closer than before. A couple of times we have to tack away when other boats are aimed directly towards us. Boats on port tack have to give way to those on starboard, and it's like being in a parking lot in the summer at the beach, when everyone wants to position their cars to get into not enough spaces. It's chaos.

"One minute to go. Jacques's gone left." David calls out. Which means that the black yacht has stayed at the other end of the start line to where we aimed for in races one and two. I guess it means they're going to go up the same side of the course as we did in the second race. Because they're a bit faster than us, that means we'll lose our advantage.

"What side Billy?" Claude asks. "You still think the wind is better inshore?"

I look at the surface of the water. At the birds, but now there aren't any. They've flown away. Which is odd in itself. I hesitate.

"Need an answer. Go left or right?"

"Go left. Follow them left," David says. "We've got to."

I hesitate again, and I can see Claude is watching me. I nod. "Yeah."

So we do. We hit the line a few seconds after the gun, and quite a few of the other boats have seen the shift now, so the fleet splits. Half go inshore, the black yacht and us among them, the other half still go out to sea. We race on for a bit, but it's soon clear the black yacht isn't in a good situation. It's caught up too close to three other boats, which are all chopping up the water for each other, and disturbing the wind. We're luckier, out on our own, and this means the difference in our boat speed is evened out. We even creep ahead. So then the black yacht tacks early, abandoning this side of the course, and going for the other. But we stick to what's working, until eventually we have to tack as well, and sail towards the marker buoy. When we do, we all get to see which half of the course was better, and it turns out there wasn't really a better side, not this time around. So all the boats are going to arrive at the marker buoy at about the same time. It's going to be mayhem again, just like the start, as we all try to go around together.

"Careful Dad," David warns, as we close towards the buoy. The first yachts have already rounded, and are careering downwind back through the pack, just to add to the mayhem. We're aiming for the buoy from one direction, and we'll get there the same time as the black yacht, though it's coming in from the other side. The difference is, we're on port tack, while they're on starboard. That's another tactics thing, it basically means they have right of way, and we don't. I see Claude swear under his breath, as he has no choice but to ease off, and let the black yacht tack around the buoy before we do, but he cuts it close, so that we're only just in its wake, the water still frothy. But then something happens, I don't really understand it at first, I just hear Claude shout out, and look up to see the side of the black yacht is right in front of us, so close I could reach out and touch it. I see Claude spinning the wheel like crazy, to steer us away, and there's a horrible second before our yacht responds, and I think we're going to smash into the black boat. But then the rudder must bite, and we carve down away from the wind.

"Asshole!" someone shouts, and I see it's Lily's dad. "Crazy motherfucker." Then he seems to get control of himself. He concentrates on bringing the yacht under control again, and we head back up into the wind towards the buoy. But now the black yacht is much further ahead of us. We round, four boats back from them.

"Can they do that, Dad?" Lily asks. He doesn't answer until we're set on the downwind leg, our sails open, trying to catch them up again.

"Yeah. He can. He shouldn't, but he had the inside line and I took it too close." He looks super focused now. And super mad.

We all stay quiet on the way back downwind. Like if we're serious we'll go faster. When we get a swell underneath us, we cream forward faster, closing the gap, but then the wave will pass out from beneath us, and it'll pick up the *Abigale*, and they'll stretch out the lead again. I can see Jacques Bellafonte, steering on the other boat, he keeps turning round, and measuring the distance between us with his eyes. And on our boat, Claude Bellafonte is doing the same, only I can hear him murmuring, *come on, come on...*

When we round the downwind buoy for the final upwind leg, we're thirty seconds behind. This time Claude doesn't ask me, nor even David, which way we should go. Instead we follow the black yacht up the left hand side of the course, and somehow we creep closer. But not close enough. It rounds the final upwind mark still thirty seconds ahead, and there's nothing we can do. We pull out our spinnaker sail, and it cracks like a whip as it fills with wind. It's blowing a bit stronger now, and you can feel the pull of the sail on the yacht's heavy hull, as we cream through the water. Twelve knots on the log. Thirteen.

And then suddenly up ahead something happens. I don't know exactly what, but the colorful spinnaker sail on the black yacht, which should be taut and filled with wind, like half a balloon, *isn't*. It's billowing like a sheet hung on a drying line. And across the water we can hear the shouts, and they fight to get it under control. I see the reaction in Claude, he tenses, leans forward as he spots the problem, and then goes back to concentrating on what he's doing, steering the fastest path through the waves.

It only takes them thirty seconds to recover the lost rope, and the black yacht is up to speed again. But it's all we need. Suddenly we're neck and neck, side by side, running downwind, parallel to each other, and each taking turns to move ahead as we ride the waves downwind. Jacques steers his yacht towards us, forcing us to react and go the same way, to avoid a collision, but Claude does the same. We're closing fast on the finish line. Emily squeals out in excitement. *We're gonna win, we're gonna win.*

But I don't know if we are. It almost seems random as we take it in turns to have the lead, depending on who's on the wave. And we're all holding on, as it's like being on a rollercoaster. The finish line is twenty meters away, the black yacht two meters ahead, but it's at the end of its surge, and we've got the next swell. The push of the wave hits the stern of our boat, and we get a downhill boost. We're a meter behind, ten meters from the line. You can see the excitement on the people on the start boat. One of them is holding a starter pistol in the air. We can't be five meters from the line, and suddenly we must be level, and still we're being pushed faster, while they're still falling off the back of the wave they were riding.

Bang! The starter gun fires, and we surge across the line.

"Who won?" Lily asks, but no one answers, no one knows. Then the radio crackles.

"Sixth place to *Morning Star, Abigale* in seventh. Superb racing. Couldn't have been closer."

So we won.

CHAPTER TWENTY-FOUR

After that things go a little bit crazy.

At first we're still careering downwind at ten knots, but Claude rounds up into the wind, and we get the spinnaker down, and then we sail back towards the marina, and take the rest of the sails down as we get there. And gradually all the boats that were coming out in the morning, are now making their way back, but instead of a sense of anxiety and anticipation, at least on our boat, now there's a feeling of euphoria. I don't think I've ever felt anything quite like it.

There's loads of radio chatter too. I think that before I assumed Jacques was like some sort of villain in a Bond movie, but he's not really. You can tell he's angry at losing, but he congratulates Claude, and then David and Emily, on our boat, start talking with the crew on their boat – and you can tell they all know each other, and like each other too. But I don't mind. Lily is thrilled with what's happened, and everyone is working to put the boat away with huge smiles on their faces.

I'm not sure what's supposed to happen once we have the boat sorted out, but I soon find out. We go up to the yacht club, the actual building, where the bar is already packed with people. And there's loads of back slapping and cheering and retelling of the most exciting moments from the races. I don't really join in, but I still find myself dragged in, as

Claude, and even David seems determined to say it was my decision to go 'left' in the second race.

Then Jacques and his crew come into the bar, and there's more backslapping, and more cheering, and more drinking, but it's all good natured, sort of. Jacques insists that he had us, if his yacht hadn't nearly broached on the last leg. Then we go to dinner. It's a huge table, in a restaurant actually inside the yacht club, and when we get the menu this time it's all seafood. The prices are even higher than the other restaurant, but Claude keeps telling us all loudly that we can order whatever we like because Jacques is paying. And he's smiling at this, but in a kind of painful way, so you know he's really hating this part. All the while a whole team of waiters and waitresses are bringing plate after plate of lobster and shrimp and bottle after bottle of Champagne.

After a while it's clear that most people are full, and the waitresses clear away the shattered shells of all the seafood, and replace it with desserts, which frankly, are amazing. And then there's coffees and I think, brandy, and even cigars, and then some people start to drift away. And I think that maybe this is my moment. I see Claude is sitting talking to no one, but with his eyes closed as he puffs away on his cigar, and I push out my chair to go closer to him. What better chance am I going to get to talk to him about the sea-dragons? I'm sure now. I'm certain he's the sort of CEO who will do the responsible thing, if only he knows about the problem. But as I move I notice that Lily, sitting opposite me across the huge table, is looking at me in a funny way. It's hard to describe the exact look she's giving me, but then she gets up, and walks around to where I'm sitting, and she leans down and she whispers in my ear.

"Take me home Billy Wheatley."

And I guess I forget about talking to her dad about the sea-dragons.

She takes my hand and starts to walk away, so that she expects me to follow after her. So I get up, a bit surprised at how I'm unsteady on my feet. No one seems to notice us leave, or at least no one pays much attention, it feels like the heat has been sucked out of the party now, by virtue of how much sea air everyone's had. We're back in the bar now, out of the restaurant, and Lily stops, and turns to me.

"I'm drunk." She mouths, looking a bit dippy.

I blink at her.

"Take me home." She says again.

"You want to come to my apartment?"

She laughs at this, then turns away from me, and spins around, all the way around until she's facing me again.

"Maybe. But I was hoping for a hot shower, to wash all this salt off. And I've got a shower at my house that's big enough for two. Have you got one that big?"

I shake my head. "No."

She tips her head onto her shoulder. "Well in that case, I think mine is probably the better option. Don't you?"

I don't answer. I *can't* answer. Instead I watch as she steps away to the bar, which is quiet now. She asks the barman to call a cab, and he nods and picks up a phone. He speaks for a moment then holds up two fingers to Lily. I hear him say *two minutes*. She turns back to me.

"My hero. Conqueror of my evil uncle." She puts her arms around me, she leans her weight on me, then she rolls around, so we're kind of arm in arm, and she leads me through the bar and back towards the door where we came in. It's even quieter here. There's a few people coming and going, but the party is behind us. We go down the steps, towards the parking lot, and beyond it we see a city cab driving toward us. By the time we get down to street level, the cab's there and Lily pulls open the door and climbs in. She gives her address, and then we sit together in the back. We don't talk, but after a few minutes, Lily starts to let her hand creep towards my legs. First she just brushes them, but then her hand begins to crawl onto my thigh, like it's a spider, or a crab. I don't say, or do, anything. I just sit there, hyper aware of her hand, and what it's doing.

It's only a short journey, and Lily pays the fare, then runs lightly up to her front door. She leans in and unlocks it, and we both go inside. It's quiet inside. For some reason I don't expect it to be. I expect to see James and Oscar, playing snooker in the billiard room. But when I glance in there, it's empty, a game half-finished on the green baize.

"You want to do it on the table?" Lily sees me looking, and I'm almost terrified that she thinks I'm serious.

"No!"

"Then come on. Upstairs."

So instead I follow her. It's only the second time I've been upstairs here, the first time was with Eric, but he wouldn't let us go into her bedroom, but this time we go straight in, and Lily kicks off her shoes. Then she goes into the bathroom, turns on the light, and seconds later I hear the shower running. Then she reappears. She approaches me slowly. The light still isn't on in the bedroom, but with the light from the bathroom I can see the painting that James and Lily talked about. The nude one. I can't remember if it was a Pissarro or a Picasso. But I try to, because it's like I need something to think about instead of what's happening. Lily is standing a foot away from me, and then she reaches down and pulls her sweater up, and off over her head. I see her white stomach appear, and then the white of her bra. She pulls her arms clear, and tosses it aside. She breathes, I see how her chest rises and falls as she does so. Then she undoes her jeans, and pushes them down over her hips, until they're scrunched up on the floor. She steps out of them. Then she turns around, but still looking at me, she walks towards the bathroom and the shower, just wearing her underwear.

"Well Billy? Are you coming in with me?"

And I don't think I should tell you anymore.

25

TWO MONTHS LATER

"Billy Wheatley?" The words came both from Special Agent West, and the manager of the Fonchem facility, Claire Watson, who had been listening in from where she sat on the sofa, in the hours after the destruction of the bomb.

Lieutenant Smith, who had just revealed the name the police database had linked to the fingerprint on the broken shard of pressure cooker body frowned, not sure who to turn to next, so it was West who turned to the manager.

"You know that name?"

"Yes – I'm sorry, I shouldn't be listening in," she said, getting up. But she continued anyway. "He's behind this... I guess you'd call it a campaign, against the facility expanding. He runs this website, and puts up posters everywhere. They're all about some kind of fish thing. They're called sea-dragons."

"Sea-dragons? What the hell are they?" Black asked.

"I don't know exactly. But they're rare, and he claims they live here in the bay, and the expansion somehow threatens them."

"So he's an enviro-nut?"

"I don't know exactly... I guess..." Watson continued. Then the lieutenant turned to West.

"You know him too?"

She took a moment to answer, and with an apologetic smile to the manager, she pulled Smith and her partner away so they could speak in private.

"Yeah. I do. I used to work for the police, before I joined the Agency. This one time I got sent over here to work on a case of a missing teenager. A girl called Olivia Curran, you don't remember it?"

"The Curran Case? Sure, I remember it. Biggest case we had here in years." The Lieutenant screwed up his face, and then realization dawned. "Oh shit. That was *you*? You ended holed up in a cave with the woman who killed Curran, and Wheatley and his dad?"

"Yeah. That was me. His dad – Sam Wheatley – he got shot, and Billy and I had to swim him out, when the tide came in." She stopped, and her face was more screwed up than ever. "I got... I got stuck, in the entrance to the cave, and Billy came back to rescue me. He was only eleven. He saved my life."

"Yeah, I remember the case. I was just a deputy back then." The Lieutenant paused a second too, thinking. He went on.

"You maybe heard, but Billy Wheatley hasn't exactly avoided trouble since then. He formed this – detective agency thing, a few years back – started out as kids' stuff, but he ended up uncovering his high school principal as a murderer. Then just recently, he got mixed up in some drugs gang."

West stared in amazement. "Jesus. I didn't know."

"Oh yeah. He's well known on the island."

"And you're sure it was *his* fingerprints, on the shards of metal from the explosion?"

"That's what the database threw up." They stared at each other.

"How old would he be now?"

The Lieutenant checked on the file on his cell. "Seventeen."

West's brow stayed deeply furrowed, calculating. "So he's... what? He's still in *high school*? How's he gonna be bombing facilities across the whole east coast?"

"I have literally no idea. But that kid, I wouldn't put it past him to find a way."

West dropped her head into her hands. "No, there has to be some mistake here."

"Are you kidding me?" Black interrupted her. "We've been hunting this motherfucker for the last ten months, and the first solid piece of evidence we get, you want to excuse it away? Let's go nail him."

"I'm not saying… We should talk to him. Of course we should. But this… It can't be right. He's a kid."

"He's *seventeen*. You just said so yourself. And the Lieutenant here said he was mixed up in drugs a while back. Come on Jess, you realize every piece of shit we end up busting was once a sweet little kid. With big doe eyes and…"

"Alright." The sharpness of West's voice stopped him. "I just think… I think we need to go in cautious here. Something about this doesn't feel right. Doesn't feel right at all."

She turned to the lieutenant.

"It's your case," he said, watching both of them. "We'll play it however you want."

West took a deep breath, thinking. "You have an address for him?" The policeman nodded.

"Let's not go in too heavy. Let's just see if he's there."

CHAPTER TWENTY-SIX

The two special agents traveled together, following the lieutenant in a squad car, with another following behind. The island looked nothing like West remembered it, covered in its blanket of snow. But the day was heating up now, and the covering was rapidly melting away, the roads were slushy and wet. The little convoy made its way towards Silverlea, and took the turn off for Littlelea, the tiny clifftop community where Billy Wheatley was listed as living, with his father Sam Wheatley.

They turned off the Littlelea road into a driveway, and West had a clear recollection of coming here, years before, that time to arrest Billy's father. They rounded a corner, and were presented with the same view, the whole of Silverlea's broad stretch of sand, laid out below them.

"Whoa!" Black said, and West just met his eyes.

"Truck's here," she said, pulling her eyes back to the parking area outside the little house, where a red Toyota pick-up sat. It looked in better condition to the one they'd found those years before, but then the whole house did, better maintained. They both got out, and with the Lieutenant, went to the front door. When they knocked, the door opened at once.

"Sam Wheatley?" West remembered him clearly. He looked a little greyer on top, but it was the same guy she'd dragged out of the cave entrance, the same guy she'd sat and talked to in the hospital in those weeks afterwards.

"Detective West?" Wheatley cocked his head onto one side. He took in the other officers too. "What is this?"

"No it…" West hesitated. "It's Special Agent West now." She stopped. "Is your son… Is Billy here?"

"Billy?" Wheatley frowned. "No! Why would he be here? More to the point, why are you here?"

West hesitated so long that Black took over. He flipped open his ID and showed it to Wheatley.

"We have reason to believe your son may have some information regarding a bomb attack on a chemical facility last night. Is he here please?"

Sam Wheatley barely registered the ID. "Excuse me?"

"I'm sorry Sam, I know this is a shock," West found her voice again. "It's a shock to me as well, but my partner is correct. We do need to speak to him."

There was a silence as Sam Wheatley looked at all of them, staring back at him, without friendly expressions on their faces.

"Well, like I said, he's not here."

"Where is he?" Black demanded at once.

"I don't know, and if I did I don't think I'd tell you."

"Obstructing a federal investigation is a felony crime…" Black began, but West cut him off.

"Sam – could we maybe come inside? And talk about this. It may be there's some mistake but we do have to get it cleared up."

There was a silence while Sam Wheatley considered, but then he stepped back from blocking the door.

They all took a seat at a small kitchen table. Except Sam, who stayed standing.

"So what the hell is all this about then?"

No one answered him.

"Could you please tell us where Billy is? Is he still living here?"

"No."

"*No?*"

"He's at college."

"College? He's seventeen?"

"He's a smart kid. They bumped him up a year."

The officers exchanged glances at this.

"I see," West was the one who spoke. "Which college?"

"Boston. Boston University. Why is this important?"

"And he's there now, you believe?"

"Yeah. He is."

"You have an address for him there?"

Sam Wheatley didn't move for a while, but then he started rummaging in a pile of paperwork on the work top. Eventually he found what he was looking for, a letter with the letterhead of the BU Accommodation office. It listed a room let out to one B. Wheatley.

"You mind if we keep this?"

Sam shrugged. "You mind telling me what this is all about?"

"OK." West met his eyes and nodded slowly. "OK." She said again, then took a deep breath.

"My partner and I have been investigating a series of bomb attacks on chemical plants within the eastern states. The latest one took place last night, and your son's fingerprint was found on shards of metal from the bomb."

Sam was silent, then after a while he laughed. "Bullshit."

"The company in question is called Fonchem," West went on. "I understand Billy was engaged in some form of protest against it?" She indicated toward the pile of papers where he had fished out the letter from the accommodation office. On the top was a small poster that said in large letters: SAVE OUR SEA-DRAGONS. Below it, in a smaller font, were the words. Stop Fonchem. Sam Wheatley stopped laughing.

"*Fonchem?*"

"Yes."

He opened his mouth to speak, and his lips even moved, but no sound came out. Then he turned away. When he looked back his face was resolute again. Determined.

"No. There's no way Billy would do anything like that. No way on earth."

"We think the bomber is a committed environmentalist. With an agenda to force these companies to reduce their impact. Cut their waste. That sort of thing. I know Billy was very keen on marine animals. He sent me a lot of stuff about it. Papers he was writing."

Sam Wheatley just stared at her.

"What's he studying Sam? What subject is he doing at college?"

His jaw jutted out before he answered. "Biology. Marine Biology."

A few minutes later, Black asked the police lieutenant to sit with Wheatley, and took West outside.

"Look Jess, I don't know quite what's going on here, but we need to send a team to his student address. Right now!"

She didn't answer. But after a moment she nodded, only the action was so slight her partner didn't notice it.

"He's seventeen, we've seen he's got a grudge against the company, and his goddamn fingerprint was on a bomb fragment. That's enough to convict, let alone arrest him!"

"I agree." West snapped back. "I just… I just don't understand, that's all."

"Look," Black tried changing his tone. "Remember the psych analysis we had done? Said the bomber or bombers was most likely interested in environmental causes, and of *above average intelligence*? This kid is at college a year early. Everything fits. You might not like it, but it fits."

"I said yes OK? Phone it in. Get a team there to pick him up." West stopped suddenly.

"What?"

"Well if he's here, setting bombs on Lornea Island, then he isn't going to be there, is he?" Her eyes widened as her mind started working. "Get onto the port, the ferry companies. We need to stop him if he tries to leave the island."

Two hours later and a report came through. Two cars had gone to pick up Billy Wheatley at the address given by his father, Sam Wheatley. And while he was registered to that address, and his housemates confirmed he did live there, he was away at the time, and none of them had seen him for a couple of days. Black snapped down the phone, inside the Newlea Police station where they were now waiting.

"They say where he was going?"

"No. They didn't know. Said he was a bit of a loner. Didn't tell them where he went."

Black formed his hand into a fist and squeezed. He looked at West. He began pacing up and down.

"OK." West said. She looked resigned to something she didn't want to do.

"We need to put out a public alert. We need to pick him up, wherever he is."

CHAPTER TWENTY-SEVEN

The alert went out as a photograph of Billy Wheatley, taken from records the police already kept – along with a plea for anyone who had seen him to contact a hotline without delay. The number actually reached the switchboard in Newlea police station, in the center of the island, but any credible sightings would be routed immediately to the two FBI agents. For their part, they went to have a very late lunch, West seeking out a diner she vaguely remembered from her earlier stay in the town.

But though they got there, and even ordered food, they never got to eat it. Just as the waitress had left their table Black's cell phone went. He barked his name, then listened for a moment, then he covered the microphone and relayed the information to West.

"We've found him. Ferry company says he drove onto the afternoon sailing."

"Shit. Has it sailed yet?"

Black asked the question. His face hardened at the answer.

"It's gone. An hour ago. But it hasn't docked yet. The boat's still sailing. He's on the ferry now."

West looked pained. "When's it due in?"

"Forty minutes." They stared at each other for a long moment.

"Can we get that plane again?" Black asked, not entirely seriously.

"I'll try." West pulled out her cellphone and started dialing. At the same time she kept talking. "Phone the ferry company back, get them to slow the boat down – say they've got engine trouble, say they're sinking. Anything to slow them down. I'll get us there."

Thirty minutes later they were at the island's small airfield, and by a combination of offering a large sum of FBI budget, and sheer luck, had managed to commandeer a helicopter and a rather elderly looking pilot, who had taken a painfully long time to climb into his flight suit, and wipe the condensation from the inside of the chopper's windshield. But he was now finally pouring power into the aircraft's main engines. They lifted off, circled once – needlessly, as far as West could tell – and then finally started moving eastwards towards the sea, and the mainland beyond. They flew low over the water, and West spent the entire flight scanning below them for the ferry, while Black coordinated the welcome committee on the ground.

"We can land in the port," Black shouted at the pilot, as the sprawl of Boston began to fill the view in front of them. "They've cleared space." He turned, and continued only to West, having to shout loud to be heard above the noise of the motor.

"We've got four agents heading there now. They're minutes away."

"Has the boat docked?"

"I can't get them on the phone." He checked his watch. "It was due in ten minutes ago."

They both scanned the water below them, looking cold and grey in the winter light.

"There!" West said, as they rapidly closed upon the land, and the much larger docks here on the mainland. A small car ferry was turning around, almost at its berth now, only minutes away from docking.

"*Shit.*" Black said. "We're not going to make it."

"We better." West replied.

They landed on the harbor-side, and almost before the two agents had climbed out, the pilot saluted, and then lifted off again. But neither West nor Black even saw him as they were busy bundling into two black saloon cars that drove them to where the ferry was now edging sideways into its berth.

From ground level it didn't look so small. It was the type with a bow that lifted up to allow cars to drive on board. West remembered it from her earlier trip to the island, years before. She directed one pair of agents to wait by the foot passenger exit, a gangway that was hoisted onto the ship as it was tethered to the dockside. West and Black, and the other pair of agents, waited on either side of the off-ramp at the bow, ready to stop each car as it drove off. With a series of shouts and clangs, the ship settled into her berth, and the bow was raised. Black went to work with the ferry dockhands, giving them instructions to allow the vehicles out slowly, one by one. As they exited the ferry, expecting to drive out of the port and away, they were instead stopped by the FBI agents, who checked the license plates, examined the faces of the passengers, and searched to make sure Wheatley hadn't snuck onboard the vehicles. It was slow going, and no one was pleased for the interruption to the normal docking procedure.

Three long hours later, the line of vehicles waiting to exit the ship had dwindled and finally stopped.

But none of them had contained Billy Wheatley.

CHAPTER TWENTY-EIGHT

West got on the phone to the other agents, by the foot passenger exit, but they'd seen nothing. The only people who had used the gangway to exit were two little old ladies, and they'd spoken to them, just in case they were a seventeen year old kid in disguise. They weren't. Then she saw Black waving his arms at her from inside the steel cavern of the ferry's interior.

"He's still on board. His car's here."

Issuing instructions that the other agents should continue to monitor the ways off the ferry, West hurried aboard, and caught up with Black by a single car that remained inside.

"They take license plates when they come aboard. This is the plate he registered when he made the booking. He must have seen us stopping the cars. He's still aboard."

"OK." West looked around, relieved to have an answer to the boy's whereabouts. She nodded. "OK, we're going to have to search it then."

Black relayed the news to the ferry operator that their return sailing was going to be delayed even longer, West redeployed the other agents to search the ferry. Within twenty minutes a ten strong team were working with the ferry staff, going through all the different decks examining any space that a seventeen year old could hide. Half an hour later, another thirty agents joined the search.

In the meantime an FBI vehicle recovery truck drove onto the boat and lifted Wheatley's car onto its back, wrapped it in tarpaulin, and took it away to the Agency's Chelsea offices. West watched, her phone ringing every ten minutes as the ferry company implored her to finish the operation and let them get back to work. Outside, on the dock, she could see the lines of cars and trucks, their journeys interrupted by what she was doing. And still the search teams found nothing.

In the end they did three complete sweeps.

"He's not on here Jess," Black said, after the third was complete. They were standing on the open air deck, an iron railing the only thing protecting them from the ferry's slab side drop down sixty feet into black harbor water.

"How sure are you? There's a hundred places to hide on this boat."

"And we've searched them all. He's not here."

West suddenly snapped. "Then where the hell is he?" She ran her fingers through her hair, and turned to her partner, meaning to apologize, but there was no need.

"Look, we know he got on. And we got here *before* the ship docked. We searched every car, so there's no way he got off early. And we have searched every inch of this boat, and he's not on it. So that leaves one option..."

She breathed hard, and then lifted her head to look at him. "What's that?"

"You notice the TVs in the café? Tuned to a local news channel. It's been on the whole time we've been searching. Three times while we've been on board, it's shown the appeal for information. So if he was on here, he'd have seen it.

"What if the security guard's death was an accident? What if this Billy isn't such a bad kid, like you've been saying, and this whole thing just went horribly wrong? What if he saw we were on to him, and he knew there was only one way out?" Black looked up and outwards, back towards the open water where the ferry had come from. Then he looked down again, at the sixty foot drop to the water below.

"What if he just jumped off?"

CHAPTER TWENTY-NINE

West insisted on one final search of the ferry, before calling the agents off and releasing the boat back to the control of the operator, which let the frustrated crowd of new passengers back on. But still she stayed, from a position that allowed her to watch both the bow doors and the foot passenger gangway. Yet still there was no sign of a teenager trying to sneak off. Eventually, seven hours delayed, the ship's horn blared out, and with a volley of shouts, the mooring lines were cast off. On board there were still four agents, with instructions to blend in with the passengers, and keep an eye out just in case Wheatley had somehow managed to evade the searches of the ship. And when it did finally dock on Lornea, in the small hours of the morning now, it would again be met by local police, checking every car.

West herself met Black early the next morning, at the FBI regional headquarters in Chelsea. There had been no reports of Wheatley during the night, and the ferry had finally been allowed to continue its normal operations. However, a request for CCTV images had turned up a hit. West and Black gathered around a monitor as a series of images were emailed across. They came from a camera covering the check-in booth for vehicles at the Lornea Island dock. The system was old, and mostly meant for show, to dissuade tourists who had to queue to leave the island from yelling at the ferry staff. But still, it showed a jumpy black and white clip of Wheatley's car arriving and a lone occupant presenting a ticket. West froze it when the face was briefly upturned and pointing towards the camera.

"Is that him?" Black had a print out of the photograph they had used on the appeal for information in his hands, and he looked from one to the other. "It could be," he answered his own question.

There was a slightness of stature, to both images, and after replaying the clip several times, they concluded that if it wasn't Wheatley, it had to be his twin brother. West stared at it a long time, trying to reconcile how the slight, precocious eleven-year-old she had known, had turned into this young man.

"Doesn't change anything." Black said. "We knew he got on. And we know he didn't get off."

They spoke to the Coastguard, which confirmed that there had been no reports of a body floating in the waters between Lornea and the mainland, but also that there rarely was, on the not infrequent occasions that someone went into the water from a vessel, either by accident or design. The problem was the depth of the water, and the currents, which tended to pull a body out to sea, not onto the land.

"Could he have swum ashore?" West asked, already knowing the likely answer. She had a history as a competitive swimmer, so had no particular issue imagining someone fit and healthy covering the distance, even if they'd gone in midway between the island and the mainland. But she knew the distance wasn't the main issue.

"It's forty two degrees in the water right now," the coastguard agent replied. "Without a wetsuit, or survival suit, you're looking at half-an-hour absolute maximum, but it's much more likely that the cold would slow down the muscles quicker than that. People think they can swim, but their arms and legs just stop working. We've seen people drown in just a few minutes. And that's if he didn't black out when he went over the side of the ferry."

West ran her hands through her hair again, and was only dimly aware of Black putting a cup of coffee on her desk.

The car was an enigma. There were no records showing any vehicles registered in Wheatley's name – though he did have a license to drive. And running the license plates from the car recovered from the ferry quickly showed it be a rental from a small car hire firm in Boston. Their records showed it had been rented three days previously under the name of *Hans Hass*, aged twenty-five-years old. According to state and federal records, Mr Hass didn't actually exist.

"Hans Hass?" Black said, as they pondered this discovery. "Weird name. Do you think it could be an anagram?" He grabbed a blank piece of paper, and wrote the letters down in a large circle, and started trying different combinations. West watched him for a few moments, then turned back to her computer, where she typed the name into the search bar of her web browser.

"Hans Hass," she read, a few moments later, "was an internationally famous marine biologist and underwater diving pioneer. He was known for being among the first scientists to popularize coral reefs, stingrays and sharks, becoming something of an early celebrity in the field. He was particularly known for his pioneering use of technology, including underwater cameras."

Black stopped what he was doing, looked at his results for a moment then screwed the paper into a ball.

"Hmmm."

The hire firm kept on file photocopies of the documents Hass had used, and these were quickly shown to be fairly crude fakes. Meanwhile the forensics team examining the actual car found no end of fingerprints and fibers, as might be imaged with a rental. Most were not on record, but plenty were found to come from Billy Wheatley.

In the afternoon, West and Black went to search Wheatley's Boston apartment. It was clearly a moment of great excitement for his housemates, who gathered outside while the team broke down the door to his dorm room. West told Black to wait outside with the other students while she pulled on a pair of silicone gloves and went inside.

It was a fairly typical student room, not unfamiliar to her from her own student days. The bed, wardrobe and desk were all cheap, and well used, but the computer equipment on the desk wasn't. Wheatley had an expensive looking second monitor, alongside that of his laptop, which looked expensive enough on its own. The computer was quickly unplugged and taken away, for further investigation.

Most of the paperwork in the room seemed to relate to the course Wheatley was studying, yet West did find a wire frame document holder, on the windowsill, which held various different designs of posters for the campaign against Fonchem. They focused on the habitat destruction for sea-dragons, and from these West learned they were a type of seahorse type creature that was only found in this area. The room was neat. Nothing else looked out of place or wrong.

After the search, West and Black interviewed Wheatley's housemates, one after the other, in the apartment's communal dining room. They got the same story from each of them. Wheatley hadn't adjusted well to college life. He didn't go out with the others. He didn't seem to have made any real friends there. Most of the time he stayed in his room, doing stuff on his computer – they didn't know what. A lad named Guy Musgrove seemed to be the most forthcoming. He claimed to have been the one to make the most effort with Wheatley, in the first weeks after they both arrived.

"You said he was a loner," Black led the questioning, while West sat back and watched. "Did he *ever* go out?"

The boy shook his head, his eyes wide with the excitement of what was happening. "We kind of made him, a few times when he first got here. But he was…" He looked away, and seemed to be searching for the right word. "Kind of arrogant, you know? Like he was too good for us."

"Uh huh," Black nodded. "You ever see him with other friends? A girlfriend, anything like that?"

"No. He didn't seem to have any other friends. He was like a loner. Say, you guys are *really* saying he was actually doing a bombing campaign, the whole time he was here?"

Black scratched at his ear irritably. "We're not saying anything. We're asking you what he was like, when he was staying here. That's all."

"Sure."

"So, he have any girlfriends? Or other friends we might want to talk to?"

Musgrave shook his head. "Oh wait, there was someone."

West sat forward. "Who?"

"A girl…" Musgrave thought for a while. "She dropped him off, when he first got here. She was," he turned to Black, with a smirk on his face, "you know, she was hot, in a kind of punky-goth way."

"She have a name?"

Musgrave thought for a moment. "I don't know. Amber something. That's all I know."

CHAPTER THIRTY

They spoke to Wheatley's tutor, a PhD student named Lawrence Hall. He suggested meeting in the cafeteria on the top floor of the Marine Biology building, saying his office was a mess.

"What was Wheatley like as a student?" West began, sizing the man up. He was good looking, but seemed to know it, and he dressed for attention. Hall didn't answer at first, instead forming a steeple with his fingers while he considered the question.

"Unusual." He finally responded.

"How so?" Black asked, and the man turned to him instead.

"He wasn't like any other freshman I've tutored," Hall went on. "He was unusually precocious. He knew a lot, and he wanted to show people how he knew a lot. He dominated the few tutorials he actually attended."

"He didn't attend that often?" West cut in.

"At first he did. In fact he came to see me before we were even due to meet. Right here, as it happens. And for the first few weeks he would be waiting outside the door before the session started. But more recently, he missed a couple of weeks. And the ones he did get to, he seemed distracted. Less engaged."

"Would you say he was the kind of guy you could imagine had some kind of secret agenda? Some kind of secret life? Like running a bombing campaign, against chemical companies?" Black asked, and again there was a long delay while the tutor considered this.

"I can. He's exactly the kind of guy I could imagine doing that," he answered in the end.

* * *

"What kind of a question was that?" West asked when they got back to their car, parked in the lot below. It was the first thing she'd said since they shook hands with Hall and left him, still sipping on his cappuccino.

"Huh?" Black frowned.

"You wanna ask it in a more leading way, or can't you think of one?"

"What? What's up with you?"

"What's up with *me*? How many students has he taught who have gone on to run secret bombing campaigns? How many students has he even *taught*? The guy's barely twenty five years old himself."

"Hey! I was only asking if he was the sort of kid who might do something like this. And once again, the people who knew him recently all find it easy to believe it. It's only you who doesn't."

"Well he's not going to know, is he. He's not going to know that." West pressed a hand to her brow. She'd hoped that a report of a young man, climbing frozen and exhausted out of the water, would have emerged over the preceding days, but they hadn't. Nor had watches being kept on his home on Lornea Island, his student address, and his father's boat, which was big enough to live aboard, turned up anything. His bank account hadn't been touched in three days, and his cell phone had last pinged from midway across the island, apparently showing Wheatley on his way to catch the ferry. Her own phone rang, interrupting the discussion before it could turn into a row.

West listened, and then turned to Black. "They've got into his computer."

They hurried back to the office, and went to see the technical analyst who had been tasked with gaining access to Wheatley's laptop. He sat with the computer at his desk, plugged in to what was presumably his own system, cables linking the two.

"I'd say he was *extremely* paranoid," the technician said, answering another leading question from Agent Black. The man wore a short-sleeved shirt, even in winter, and had narrow, thin arms that were painfully pale. "He had two passwords to get through, the first is the regular one you put on a set up on this type of system, you know when you set up a Linux system?" he paused, and it was West who answered.

"No."

"Oh, well you have to put in a password, and with this type of system you can't just access the source file and read what they are, like you could with most people's set ups. And anyway, like I said he had two passwords," the man explained. He seemed to be happier talking to West than Black. "But then I realized this wasn't a standard Linux installation at all. It was something else, a kind of custom crossbreed."

"So what does that mean?" West gave an encouraging smile.

"Well, Linux is a recreation of UNIX, but this was more of a continuation…"

"No, I mean did you get in or not?"

"Oh, right. Well yeah. You see for the first password he used a randomly generated combination of letters, numbers and symbols. Technically that's impossible to break, but if you can throw enough computer power at it, you can just try every possible combination and get through that way."

"So that's what you did?"

"No way. It would take like, longer than all the time left in the universe. No you see the weakness of passwords like this is you have to either remember them, which is hard, or store them somewhere, which means there's a weakness. He had a password vault set up, and luckily it's one we already cracked. So I was able to try all the passwords from there as his main password. And bingo."

"So he's paranoid, but not too bright?" Black asked.

The analyst frowned at once. "Oh no, I wouldn't say that. I mean, maybe, like if he was an expert on FBI methods and was assuming we'd try and get in, then yeah, pretty dumb. But if he was just an ordinary citizen going about his business, then I'd say his level of protection was extraordinarily high. It just depends." He shrugged.

"So what have you actually found?" West was keen to move things on.

"That's where it gets interesting. He liked the dark web."

West drew in a deep breath, not liking the sound of this. "What was he looking at?"

"Who knows? That's the beauty of the dark web, at least, if you have the correct software installed, which permanently erases your search history. And he did."

"So you don't know?"

"Not really. You see whatever you look at on the regular internet is tracked, because the internet provider and search engine both keep their own records, which you can't access, but that doesn't happen on the dark web. You can look at something, delete the records, and poof. It's gone." He smiled appreciatively.

"So we have no idea what he looked at?"

"We have some idea. He had his software set up to delete the searches automatically, but not right at once. You can change the setting. I guess some people like to be able to go back and find the same page they had open before. Google doesn't work so well on the dark web, so you kind of need a way to find stuff."

"I don't get this. What are you saying? We know what he looked at? Or we don't know?" Black asked.

"What I'm saying is he had a delay on when his history got deleted. He didn't delete his last week's searches." The man turned to his second screen, which had a web browser open, on a number of tabs. He clicked the first, and immediately the screen changed to the car hire firm which had provided the car Wheatley was driving.

"What's that?" Black asked.

"Terms and conditions. He was looking at what he needed to hire the car."

West and Black both leaned in closer to look. "What else is there?"

The technician showed them the other tabs. "He sourced the documents here. A credit card bill and driver's license in the name of Hans Hass."

"Both fake?"

"Uh huh. They were made by someone with the name Blackhorse."

"Who's that?"

"No idea. Looks Russian. He doesn't seem involved though, beyond providing the documents."

"You find anything about bomb making?" Black asked. "Specifically how to make a pressure cooker bomb?"

"No. But like I said, he deleted all his previous searches on the dark web. He could have searched for it."

"And the information is there? I mean if he had searched for it. The information was there to find?"

"Oh yeah." The analyst's fingers flew on his keyboard, and seconds later a list appeared on the screen.

"What's that?"

"There's loads of places you can find how to make a bomb online, anything from a simple pipe bomb to a nuclear device, if you can find the material. But this is a kind of portal that lists them all."

The man scanned the screen, the words reflecting back off the coating on his glasses.

"Here." He clicked a link, and the page refreshed with the colorful images and instructions for what looked like a recipe, only the pressure cooker being used was being filled with fertilizer and wires.

"I thought they called it the dark web," Black muttered. "Looks like a page on making soup."

"Did he look at this?" West clarified. "Is there any evidence to suggest he looked at this?"

"There's no evidence he *didn't*. But wait, I have more."

He clicked off the page, and went instead to one of the last tabs on what had been Billy Wheatley's screen. It showed a Google map, but the contents blurred out.

"OK, first up. This is the Fonchem site in the north of Lornea Island. This he was looking at."

"Why's it blurry?"

"Ask Google, or actually ask Fonchem. Military and some commercial sites are obscured. You can apply to Google and make your case. A lot of chemical and pharmaceutical sites do it, to make it harder to see what they're actually up to, but check this, it's clever." He clicked to the next, final tab. It showed a blueprint.

"Every state and county keeps a record office of all buildings, and you can download it. They're just a lot harder to find. But he found it."

"So what is that, what we're looking at?"

"It's the blueprint of the building that was bombed."

CHAPTER THIRTY-ONE

They worked together on the report, West paying particular care to make sure there were no claims which weren't strongly supported by the evidence. It was broken down into sections.

There was considerable evidence to suggest that Billy Wheatley was responsible for the attack on the Fonchem facility. Rental car records, and data from his computer, showed he faked an ID in order to rent a car, which he then booked onto the Lornea Island ferry on the day prior to the attack. He was then seen leaving the island, on the day after the attack. In total sixteen of his fingerprints were identified on the remaining fragments of the bomb casing, strongly indicating he was at least present when the device was made, if not responsible for its manufacture. The single trail of footprints reportedly seen by the murdered security guard, and their small size, was consistent with the size of Wheatley's own feet. And Wheatley had an ongoing campaign against Fonchem, something he didn't even try to hide, which may, in his mind, have provided a motive for the attack.

The autopsy on the security guard had by now confirmed that he was killed by the detonation when the device exploded. It had caused so much destruction that it was impossible to ascertain exactly what had happened. It was possible Wheatley had timed the device to explode when the guard was there, or it might have been an unfortunate accident – none of the other bomb sites had involved any injuries or deaths.

Interviews carried out with all those who had known Wheatley during his brief time at college had all told a similar story. He was quiet and polite, and clearly highly intelligent, but also reserved, and appearing to be more interested in his own private projects than taking part in the typical freshman activities. The details of his private projects had not been shared. He had an 'air' about him, a sense that he was different. Arrogant was a word that came up a lot. He appeared highly capable of carrying out the work tasked to him, yet unmotivated by it. His attendance to classes had started well, but slipped in the weeks before the attack.

The computer equipment recovered from Wheatley's student apartment revealed an interesting absence of information, which in itself was damning. He had installed and employed an array of software and devices designed to prevent leaving any sort of electronic trail. His cellphone, which was not recovered, was discovered to have been loaded with software that projected a false position, to anyone who tried to track it. Though this program was legal, other software and apps installed were not. In total he seemed to have gone to considerable lengths to leave false trails, and to hide his true online activities, and physical locations. This was considered the likely reason it had been difficult so far to place him at the locations of the other bombings the agents were investigating. But with sufficient resources and time, it was thought likely that these defenses would fail, and information would come to light which demonstrated he was directly involved in the other attacks.

Finally, there had been no sightings of Billy Wheatley since he was captured on CCTV driving the rental car onto the Lornea Island ferry over two weeks previously, a ferry which he did not drive off. There had been no activity on any of his electronic devices, nor anything from his multiple online accounts and aliases. Watches placed on his student address, his family home on Lornea Island, and on the few actual friends he was known to have, in particular one Amber Atherton, had not seen any contact from Wheatley, nor any evidence to suggest anything other than he had perished that night. And while Wheatley's body had not been found, this was perfectly consistent with the likelihood that he had either fallen, or more likely jumped from the Lornea Island ferry on February 2nd.

It was therefore the conclusion of the investigating agents, that the perpetrator of the string of domestic terror attacks on the Fonchem Chemical facilities was one William 'Billy' Wheatley, and that he had died, most probably by suicide, on the evening following the final attack.

When the report was finished, Black read it through, looking satisfied.

West however, did not.

32

THREE MONTHS EARLIER

I'm still here. I can't believe it. It's the morning now, and I'm *still* here. At Lily's house. The Lily Palace. But not just that, I'm actually *in her bedroom. With her.* Well actually she's asleep, but she's right next to me. This is the most amazing thing that's ever happened to me. And I've had quite a few amazing things happen to me.

I sort of want to get up, because I feel like I'm filled with electricity, but also I daren't move, because I don't want to wake her up. I want to tell you what happened, but I don't think I really should. It's kind of private, you know? I'll tell you a bit. Just so you know what's going on.

We came back from the meal at the yacht club, and we came upstairs, and I didn't know what was going on, not really, and I think I was a bit drunk too, and Lily said she wanted to have a shower, and then she took off her clothes right in front of me – well not all of them, she left on her underwear, but even so, and she went next door into the shower – she has a bathroom that leads right off her bedroom, and not just a little room either, it's massive, and after a while I heard the water running, and I didn't know what to do, so I just stood there, and then I heard her calling me, in this really soft voice, so in the end I went in there, and she was in the shower, and I couldn't really see, because of all the steam, but she didn't seem to mind, and she told me to come in and rub her shoulders, so eventually I did. But then she screamed and said I had to take my clothes off first, which I guess I must have forgotten to do, but then she helped me, and it was really *funny*, which I wasn't expecting. Not at all. And then, well, I think I really should stop there, but maybe I could just say that we *didn't*. Didn't stop I mean.

I'm not that experienced with girls. I mean, I'm not that experienced with girls in *that* way. Or at least I wasn't. I suppose I am now. I kind of always knew I'd have to do something about it. But I never expected... I never expected it would be with *Lily*. Very gently I turn my head to look at her. Her golden hair is all ruffed up on the pillows, and her mouth is slightly open. I can't believe I've kissed that mouth. She's... She's perfect, even when she's asleep like this, I don't think I've ever seen a more beautiful girl. It makes my heart beat funny. I think it's making me feel ill.

"Billy..." She suddenly murmurs to me. She's not asleep after all. But her voice is so soft and lovely.

"Billy, will you please stop staring at me?"

I turn away at once, and look at the ceiling instead. "Sorry."

I try to concentrate on it. It's different to the room in my apartment. There the ceilings are low, and there's a cheap light bracket. Here the ceiling is high up, and there's a swirly round coving thing above a kind of mini chandelier fitting, I don't know what you'd call it. Suddenly Lily moves, her hand slides across my stomach, and then she starts to pull herself on top of me. The next thing I know she's lying right on top of me, her long hair making a kind of curtain shutting out the outside world, just her smile and her scent, and oh God. It's happening again.

* * *

We get up at eleven thirty, in the end, so I don't know if I should call it breakfast or lunch, but we eat pancakes, and drink lots of coffee, and then Lily wants to go for a walk, because it's a nice afternoon. My clothes are still a bit damp from last night, but Lily puts them in the drier, while I wait, just wearing her dressing gown. And then when they're only a bit damp still, I put them on and we go out. We walk along the river, and we don't talk that much, but Lily keeps resting her head onto my shoulder, and looking at me and smiling. And it's almost too much for me to cope with.

I'm almost pleased to get back to my own apartment, and my own space, where I can make sense of everything that's happened. I've got a girlfriend. Lily is my girlfriend.

Well, she's *sort of* my girlfriend.

CHAPTER THIRTY-THREE

Over the next week I go around there twice, and both times I don't come back until the next day. If you know what I mean. And I still can't believe it's happening, not to me. It's odd though. On the one hand it's kind of easy, everything feels natural and fun, but on the other hand, it's a bit – I don't know – difficult to relax. At least when we're not – you know. Sometimes then it's like we don't quite know what to say to each other, which is odd when you think about it. But it's not a big thing. Then the third time I go around though it's different. I can tell right away.

When I come in, I expect her to stand there looking at me in the way that she does, or maybe even to actually kiss me, and I definitely want to kiss *her*, but when I try to do so she backs away. And right away a fear hits me, like a physical blow to my guts, that somehow it's over, already.

"What's wrong?" I ask.

"Nothing's wrong," she shakes her head. Her hair shimmies in both directions at once. "Come in." She stands back so I can put my bike inside, and I do so, but I feel awful now. Sick. I've spent the whole day thinking about her. About what we're going to do, and now it's not happening, and I don't know why. I don't know what to say.

"Are you sure nothing's wrong?"

"Of course I'm sure!" she sounds normal – no, she sounds like she's trying to sound normal, but actually she's stressed. But then she mouths to me. "Eric's here!" And I understand. But before I can respond his voice calls out from the kitchen.

"Is that the young mariner Billy?"

So then the evening goes very differently to how I expected it. And I think differently to how Lily expected it too. We stay downstairs for a start, Eric's brought ingredients to cook, but he leaves Lily to cook them, and he and me sit at the table, drinking wine that he pulled out of the chiller. He didn't bother asking.

"So Billy," he says, when he's poured three large glasses. "Tell me all about your triumphant success last weekend. At the sailing thing."

"How did you hear about that?" Lily interrupts from across the room.

"I have my sources. Outside of you, I mean." He turns to me. "Yacht club website. There was a report of the race."

I look at Lily, and she frowns at this, but goes back to cutting slices of cucumber.

"You know, I went out on the family yacht once." Eric shudders at me. "I was violently seasick, the whole time we were out there. Literally I was either hanging off the side, or throwing up onto Lily's mother. I don't think she's ever quite forgiven me."

"Mom's OK," Lily sweeps up to the table and deposits a bowl of potato chips between us. As she leaves she lets her hand just touch my shoulder as it pulls away. It's so subtle I'm not even sure it happened. "It's Dad who has the problem. He struggles a little bit with the idea of me having a gay friend anyway."

"Lillian!" Eric sounds shocked, though he's just pretending. "I haven't come out to Billy yet. He's innocent of these things."

Eric pretends I didn't hear this and goes on. "So? Billy? Tell me all about it."

So I explain, about how there were these three races, and we ended up winning on the last leg of the last one, and the whole time Eric sips white wine and selects potato chips, one after the other and carefully crunches them in his mouth.

"Mmmm. Quite the hero. And was there a celebration?"

"We had a meal," I say. "In the yacht club."

"That's not what I mean."

"Supper." Lily interrupts again. She puts a serving platter of pasta on the table, then goes back and adds a salad, and no one says

163

anything, except asking to pass the plates around, and top up the wine.

"James is a very good sailor, did you know that Billy?" Eric asks me, a few minutes later, when we're all eating. "He was a regular out on the family yacht. Both yachts I think, doesn't he sail with your uncle sometimes, Lily?"

She gives him a look, then goes back to her food.

"Do you think Billy is likely to go out with you again? Another ride?"

"Oh Eric, just come out and ask it will you?"

Lily's voice is suddenly angry, and it's followed by silence.

"Ask what?"

"Whatever it is that's on your mind."

Eric swallows what's in his mouth, and looks a little bit hurt for real this time. "I'm merely curious of the status of two of my friends."

Lily looks at me, then back at Eric.

"Are you?" Eric goes on, his eyes on her only but his eyebrows moving right up his forehead. "*Did* you?"

She gives the slightest shrug, and Eric's eyes go wide.

"Oh my." He takes a deep breath, and finally turns to me. He picks up his glass, and raises it in a toast.

"I knew it. I *knew* it."

"But I don't want anyone to know." Lily goes on, hurriedly. "Not my family, not James. Especially not James."

I want to ask why not. But I don't, and Eric just nods, like this makes perfect sense.

"I don't want to spoil – what we have. All of us."

Eric keeps his glass raised, and holds it out towards Lily. Eventually she picks hers up as well, and they clink them together.

And for a second it's like both of them have forgotten I'm here at all.

After dinner we play cards. Still in the kitchen. It's a game I don't know, but apparently they all played it a lot when they were in Europe, on trains and waiting around in airports and hotels. You have three packs of cards, and you have to get rid of all your cards, but if you don't remember the rules correctly you end up with whole handfuls of them. It takes me a while to learn the rules, but when I do I start to quite enjoy it. But then Lily says to Eric he should probably call a cab, because she's tired. Then he gives her a look and asks if it's for one, or for two, and he means whether I'm going with him. And I don't know at all. But she tells him I've got my bike here, so I'd be able to make my own way home. After that we all go out into the hallway, because we can see on Eric's cell phone that the Uber is here already, and I start to get my bike ready too, though there isn't much to do – it kind of is ready, just by being there.

Then Eric gives Lily a hug. A proper one, that goes on for ages, and says something to her that I can't hear. Then he surprises me by giving me one too. And just as he lets me go, he whispers something into my ear too.

"We should talk. I'll call."

Then, without pausing at all, he goes on, much louder. "Well I shall be off. Alone. Be careful cycling home young Billy, the night may hide many dangers." And he pulls open the door, and walks through, leaving it open for me. I hesitate a second, and then pick my bike up, to take it outside as well. But Lily puts her hand on it and presses it back against the wall. She doesn't say anything, she just shakes her head, then goes to shut the front door again.

So I stay again.

CHAPTER THIRTY-FOUR

I don't exactly know why Lily doesn't want anyone to know about us, but I'm not going to risk ruining it by telling anyone. And I do sort of understand. I mean, take Guy and Jimbo, in my apartment. They go on and on about sex all the time, but for them it's almost – I don't know – it's almost like a competition, or like they're stealing something. They want to have sex with girls and then pretend it didn't mean anything to them. Then they can run away, laughing, and try and have sex with another girl, and the more hurt the first girl feels about what happened, the better. Not that I think they actually get much sex. Not as much as they brag about, anyway.

But what me and Lily have is nothing like that. Nothing at all, so *I* don't want to tell them either.

And if I'm not telling the boys, then I can't tell the girls either. I'm not quite sure what their attitude to sex is, because I don't speak to them very much, but I do know that if I told any of them, then Laura would probably find out, and she'd tell Jimbo, and then they'd all know.

And I suppose there's one other reason that I don't want the girls to know, and that's Sarah, the quiet, dark haired girl in my house. And that's because I quite like her. Not in the same way as Lily, or not as much as Lily anyway, but I just like that she's different to the others, and I don't want to disappoint her. Not that it would, of course.

Then there's Amber. I'd really like to tell her – because I do kind of want to tell *someone* – I guess that's why I keep going on about it with you, because a bit of me really wants to tell the whole world, just because of how incredible it is, how incredible it feels. But I can't tell Amber, because it really didn't go well when she met Lily, and she really didn't like her. So I don't know what her reaction would be.

So I just keep pretending that nothing's happening at all. I go to my classes and tutorials – most of them – and I do my essays, either in the library or in my room with the door shut. And I'm kind of present in college life, but at the same time, I'm not really present, because in my head I can't stop thinking about Lily, and wondering when she's next going to call or text me saying I can come round.

* * *

Eric calls, like he said he would. He wants to meet and discuss 'the situation' whatever that means. I suggest we go to the coffee place where we first met – the one with the banana daiquiris – but he says it's the wrong time of year, and that he'll come to me. In the end we meet up in the cafeteria on the top floor of the Marine Biology building. When he turns up I ask if he wants a drink but he insists on getting it, and has to wait in a line until he orders.

"Ahhhhh – Mr Wheatley." He sits in the booth opposite me and slides a cardboard cup of coffee over to my side. "Can't you just smell that fresh sea air." He makes a big thing of taking a deep breath. "Seaweed, and… fish." He looks around, studying the other students before turning back to me.

"You know I can actually see it?"

"See what?"

"That…" he lifts a hand and rubs his thumb and forefinger together, like he can't quite pin down what he wants to say. "Certain *Marine Biologist* look." He grins. "It's… like *practical geek* isn't it? Lots of highly durable fabrics." He looks around again and then grins at me. I glance over at the table where my tutor usually sits, but he's not there today.

"I'm sorry Billy. I'm being a bit bitchy." He smiles now. "So how are you?" he asks next, sipping on his coffee and staring at me. "How's life treating you?"

"I'm OK."

"How are things?"

I'm about to answer this when I realize he's not finished. "…With *Lily?*"

So then I change my answer, looking left and right to make sure no one can overhear. "They're OK."

Eric keeps his eyes on me the whole time. "Just OK?"

I don't know what to say to him. I don't know what he wants. The truth is things with Lily are amazing. But that's private. I don't want to tell him that.

"That's good. In a way," he smiles now. "It's probably better if things don't go too far beyond 'OK', if you know what I mean."

He flashes the smile again.

"I don't know what you mean."

He looks back at me, and his face drops when he sees mine. "Oh shit. She's really got to you, hasn't she?"

"What?"

"Lily. She's…" He stops, thinks for a moment, then goes on. "Billy, on a scale of one to ten, how smitten would you say you are?"

I don't answer, but I can't keep a look off my face.

"Oh Christ. That looks like an eleven Billy, or even a twelve. This is bad. Very bad." He takes in a deep breath, like he's calming himself down, then continues. "Look Billy, I came here to warn you not to hurt her – I'm very protective of my Lily – but I see now I've got this the other way around. She's more likely to hurt you." He sighs. I don't get it.

"Why would she hurt me?"

It's like he doesn't hear me at first, then I notice Lawrence, my tutor has come in, and Eric's eyes are scanning him up and down.

"Why would she hurt me?" I ask again.

Eric turns back to me. "Huh?"

"What are you talking about?"

Eric waves a hand, he looks distracted. "Oh, it's all this family business stuff." He gives me a half smile, like the sort when you've discussed something for too long and it's gotten boring, but I don't have a clue what he means.

"What family business stuff?"

Now Eric frowns. "The takeover. Well the takeover *attempt*."

I'm still lost, and it must show on my face.

"What takeover?"

Now he looks shocked. "You don't *know*?"

"Know what?"

"Oh my." Eric shakes his head. "What do you talk about in those quiet moments in between…" he stops. "Or maybe there are no quiet moments…"

"Eric, can you just tell me what this about." And finally that stops him messing about.

"OK. Billy. I'm sure you've noticed that Lily's been distracted in the last few days. The reason why is her uncle, who owns one of the biggest rivals to Fonchem – that's her dad's company – has issued a hostile takeover bid to Fonchem. It's all over the financial press."

I look a bit vacant.

"I guess you don't read the financial press," he goes on under his breath. "Not enough fish in it." Then he sighs. "A hostile takeover is where one company makes an offer to the shareholders of another company to buy the shares, and replace the board of directors against their wishes. Lily's uncle wants to take over Fonchem, and kick her dad out. That's why she's upset."

He tells me more about it too, but the thing that worries me the most, is I didn't even know she was upset.

CHAPTER THIRTY-FIVE

The two final spot balls on the table were right over the top pockets. They prevented any other balls being sunk there, and if the other player got a chance to come back to the table, he would pot them easily. Worse, that was almost bound to happen, because the black was up that end too, meaning the only way for the kid to pot it – ginger haired, twenties, kinda geeky-looking – would be to bounce the black off the top cushion so that it landed in either the middle pockets or down the near end. The kid weighed it up now, pretending to be more pissed than he really felt at the bad luck that had left him in this situation. There was nothing riding on it. It was just a few games of pool with his buddy, another geeky looking kid who swigged Budweiser and began to grin as he watched, knowing the game was going his way.

The kid whose shot it was bent down to take it. He didn't see the line, even a pro-player wouldn't. He was just going to punt it hard and hope for the best.

"Hundred bucks you don't make that shot." The words came from neither of the two players, but a handsome, blond-haired man, taller and bigger built than either of the kids playing.

"What?" Ginger hair stood up from the table, sounding scared.

"Hundred bucks. You. Don't. Make. That. Shot."

"What?"

"Is that the only word you know?"

"What? No. *Heck.* No. I just mean I don't wanna bet with you."

"Why not? You a pussy?"

Ginger hair looked to his friend for support, but he'd backed away, happy this wasn't happening on his shot. "No. I'm just… I'm just playing a game here."

"Yeah, well I'm playing a game too. Come on. Hundred bucks." James smiled, with a bit more warmth in it, and he pulled a wad of notes out of the pocket of his jeans. He held one up. But the kid shook his head.

"No. I ain't… I don't wanna…"

"Come on…" James peeled off another note, then three more. "Here's five hundred bucks. But that says I can make it for you."

"*What?* You? You wanna take the shot now?"

"Yeah." James nodded, waving the notes a little closer to the ginger haired kid now.

Then the other player got involved. "Look man, how about you just leave it, huh?" His voice had come out squeakier than he intended, and his eyes darted nervously about. He looked like he regretted opening his mouth already. James turned to look at him.

"It's alright little fella. Your buddy here's his own man. He can decide for himself if he's interested or not." The ginger kid's eyes were fixed on the cash.

"Five hundred bucks says I can make that shot." James repeated, his voice soft. "Against your one hundred."

The ginger kid paused.

"You wanna bet *five hundred bucks* you can pot this black, and if you make it I only have to give you one hundred?"

James nodded.

"And if you don't make it, you'll give me the five hundred?"

"That's it. You got it."

"What are you doing Paul? Let's just get outta here?" The second player said. But the ginger haired kid – Paul – wasn't looking at him. He glanced at the table. At the shot he'd been about to fire off, with no hope of making. Even if this crazy guy was some kind of pool shark, there was still no way he could make the shot. It was basically impossible. Besides, this was now a challenge to his masculinity. Why should he run away? The way he'd done his whole life.

"Alright. But put the money down. So I know you're not gonna go back on it."

"Absolutely. No problem with that." James took the notes and pinned them to a table under his half-empty bottle of beer. "Now show me yours."

"What?" The ginger haired Paul froze.

"Show me you've got a hundred. After all, you're gonna have to give it me in thirty seconds."

Paul didn't believe this, but he nodded and fumbled in his pocket for the wallet which James had already noticed, and from it he pulled out a note of his own. He showed it, tentatively to James, who waved his hand at the table.

"Put it down." He said, as if talking to a slightly simple child.

Paul looked to his friend, who shook his head, lightly, so that James wouldn't notice him. But Paul turned away, and did what he was told. For a second all of their eyes were on the table with the cash, then they all slipped back to the other table. With the near-impossible shot.

"May I?" James held out his hand for ginger hair to hand him the pool cue.

"Oh sure. Sorry."

James bent down to line up the shot. He pantomimed for a bit, his whole arm shaking like he couldn't control it, and then he straightened up again, to chalk the end of the cue. While he did that Oscar silently approached the table where the cash was pinned, just as James lined up the shot again, but this time gave a huge sneeze. Ginger haired Paul couldn't stop himself from laughing, and James did too, but then he pulled himself together.

"OK. Watch and learn my friend. Watch and learn." He slammed the cue into the white ball, and sent it careering into the black. It took all the energy, and bounced off the end cushion at a hundred miles an hour. Randomly it careered around the table, at one point it came close enough to the middle pocket that it could have gone in, but it didn't. Eventually is slowed and stopped.

"Ah shit!" James exclaimed loudly. "I *really* thought I had that." He held out the cue for Paul again, who looked delighted.

"So I… So do I win?" He asked, grinning. He had slightly goofy teeth and his freckles colored with the thrill of it.

"I guess you do." James turned to the other table, where the cash was pinned under the beer bottle. But then his face dropped, because the bottle was there, but the cash wasn't.

"Hey?" James exclaimed, louder still. He looked to Ginger Paul, and then the other kid. "Hey did you? *What the hell?* Where's that money?" James turned back to Ginger Paul, moving intimidatingly close.

"Did you move it?"

"No!"

James turned to the other kid. "Did you?"

The other kid looked scared again, but didn't get it either. Neither of them had noticed Oscar at all, much less seen him slip the money from under the bottle before leaving the bar.

"Oh man, that sucks," James said, shaking his head. "That really fucking sucks. You got ripped off." Ignoring the two kid's anxious looks, he went to walk away.

He met up with Oscar a couple of streets away, by the white SUV.

"Fucking gorks." James said, unlocking the car.

"That was a stupid risk." Oscar replied as he climbed into the passenger seat.

"Oh come on. They were asking for it. They'd been on that table the whole fucking night."

"I'm serious. I'm not doing that again. Not for a hundred lousy bucks."

"It's not *just* a hundred bucks." James grinned as he pulled the ginger haired kid's wallet from his pants pocket. "I went back. Made out I thought *he'd* taken the cash before I took the shot. Said it put me off. Little fucker shit his pants, thought I was gonna hit him. Slipped it out nice and easy." James gave a narrow-eyed smile, and tossed the wallet across the car.

"How much?" James asked, once Oscar had opened it and looked inside.

"Two hundred seventy."

"And credit cards?"

"Sure, but we can't use them."

"Why not?"

"Because I don't want to go to jail, that's why."

"Alright, alright. You sure there's nothing more?"

Oscar sighed "Yeah I'm sure. You wanna check for me?"

"No." James sounded chastised.

"Turn right here." Oscar told him, then he used his sleeve to wipe the wallet, removing any fingerprints. By the time he was done, James had already lowered the window and steered the car close to the side of the bridge. Oscar glanced backwards and forwards, then tossed it casually out into the water below. In the semi-darkness there was no one around to notice.

James rolled the window shut again.

"Shit. Less than four hundred bucks huh?" James mused.

"Uh huh." Oscar replied.

"You wanna go back and ask if they've got any more?" James turned suddenly to Oscar and grinned, but Oscar didn't smile back.

"Are you bored?"

"What?"

"Are you bored? Frustrated? How's it going with that – what's her name?"

"Which one?"

"I dunno. The cheerleader one. Isn't that the latest?"

"Brooke? Yeah, she's fine. She's all over me."

"I don't doubt it. But maybe..." Oscar stopped, and James' face tightened this time.

"Maybe what?"

"Maybe it's time."

"Time?" James pretended not to understand. Oscar took a deep breath.

"Time you got things back together with Lily."

James didn't answer for a long while.

"I'm kinda sick of hanging out in dead end bars too."

"You think I'm not?" James snapped the words back, and there was silence for a while.

"Then I don't see the problem. The two of you have split up before. You fuck around like a stud dog for a few weeks, wear yourself out and get back together... And I can see you *want* to – all these stupid risks you're taking, ripping off dumb assholes for three hundred bucks. You're deflecting. You're putting it off. What I don't understand is *why*. Just get back with her, and things can be back to normal."

James didn't answer, but his face darkened.

"What? Come on man, tell me. I'm your oldest friend. You're not worried she found out about Brooke?"

"It's not that."

"Then what?"

James drove on for a while, looking fixed ahead, but then he started speaking again, through gritted teeth.

"There's been a *development*."

"What development?"

"OK you're right. I guess I was ready to get back with her. So I went to her house – I've still got a key. Only..."

"Only what?"

"Only she wasn't alone, was she?"

Oscar looked confused. Then he smiled as understanding dawned. "Oh man, you're shitting me? You walked in on Lily..." he almost didn't want to say it, but he did – "*fucking* someone?"

He turned to James, and from the blackness on his friend's face he stopped smiling.

"Shit. What did you do?"

"I left. They didn't see me."

Oscar considered this.

"You see who it was?"

"Yeah. Yeah I saw."

James drove on one-handed for a while, picking at his teeth.

"Well? Who was it?"

James waited until he'd removed whatever it was that was annoying him.

"It was Billy."

CHAPTER THIRTY-SIX

I wouldn't say I'm bored. I mean, I don't want to sound ungrateful, it's just... it's just it would be nice to do something other than hang around in Lily's house and, and – well, go to bed. She's texted me again, asking if I can go round tonight, when my classes are finished, so that's what I'm going to do, but this time I'm going to suggest we go out somewhere. Just for a change.

When I get there she's dressed in her staying-in clothes. I've learned the difference now. If she's going out she'll make an effort, with make-up and whatnot, with her hair extra shiny and with clips in. But if she's staying in she wears more comfortable clothes, and she just ties her hair up. Like today, she's got leggings on, and a long sweater that comes down to her thighs. It's not that I mind, I mean she genuinely looks amazing whatever she's wearing, it's just interesting to note.

"Hey Billy," She says as she opens the door, and I notice how she checks the street behind me before she closes it, but I don't say anything. When the door is shut and I've put my bike against the wall she leans on me and starts to kiss me right away, which is nice but like I said earlier, it's not really what I want to do tonight.

"What's wrong? Are you hungry?" she gives me a grin, like she noticed that I eat a lot.

"No. I mean yes." There's a smell coming from the kitchen, I don't know what it is, but it smells really good.

"I am hungry," I begin, and I tell myself to do it. Because if I don't we're going to end up eating and then just going to bed. "But I also thought..."

"Thought what?" Lily pulls away from me and looks me full in the face. She looks confused.

"I just thought that maybe we should..." Her eyes, which are so big and blue, follow my every word.

"Should maybe go out somewhere? Afterwards, I mean."

Her look turns from confusion to something else. A little bit of hurt maybe.

"Out?"

I have to break away from those eyes, so I walk into the kitchen, towards the source of the smell, and there's a bottle of wine open. I pour myself a glass of wine, and have quite a big swig from it.

"Are you getting bored of me already?" Lily asks, watching me from the doorway.

"No." I feel a kick of emotion that I didn't expect, and it feels like this isn't going at all how I meant it to. "No, it's just... just I'm a bit fed up with always being here, you know, being hidden away and everything."

And all of a sudden it's almost like we're having our first row.

"Oh." She says, and suddenly she won't meet my eye at all. "Oh, so this house isn't good enough for you? Is that it? I've been baking all afternoon, but now you don't want it." She comes in and picks up her glass now.

"No, it's not that. It smells great. I just, I had this idea."

"What idea?"

"After dinner, can you pack a swimsuit?"

"What? It's freezing outside!"

"I know."

I refuse to tell her anything while we're eating – she's made a sort of pie with chicken and vegetables and it's really good – the pastry is just the right sort of crunchy on the edges and not soggy underneath. And then she goes upstairs to find a swimsuit and I come with her, and a bit of me wants to change my mind when I see the bed, and see her holding lots of different bikinis and things against her, asking me which type is most suitable for whatever we're doing. I have to tell her I don't know for sure we'll be able to use it, and that confuses her even more. Then we book an Uber, even though she does have a car, a little Audi, but we've drunk quite a lot of the wine now. I get it on my account, so I don't have to tell her where we're going.

It drops us off down by the waterfront, and I lead her towards the aquarium.

I don't completely approve of aquariums. I think it's best if animals get to live their lives naturally, but on the other hand, they do give people a chance to see marine animals in realistic looking situations, and there's some evidence that this leads to them better respecting the natural world. I read an article about it in National Geographic once. And a lot of aquariums, like this one, also do a lot for research and conservation. That's how I got to first meet Kevin. He was only the day manager when I first met him, and I was quite young, and to be perfectly honest I think I annoyed him a bit because I kept coming up with suggestions for other animals they could display, and for how they could do it, and also offered to bring them animals that I collected. But as I got a bit older, and a bit more sensible, he became the deputy manager, and now he runs the whole aquarium. And now we're quite good friends.

"Why are we going to the aquarium Billy? Isn't it closed?"

"It is for most people," I reply, leading the way. "But not for everyone."

It's not Kevin who meets me at the door, they have a security guard, but Kevin's told him what I want to do, and he lets us in, and locks the door shut behind us. Then he looks Lily up and down and raises his eyebrows in surprise, and winks at me and tells us to have fun and not trip any alarms. Then he waddles off back to his room.

"Where's he going?"

"He has a little room. It has all the CCTV, so he'll be keeping an eye on us."

"But what are we doing *here* Billy?"

"I wanted to show you around." I smile at her.

Most of the lights in the tanks are on timers, because fish are used to the rhythms of day and night just like we are, but there's some light in the hallways – kind of the same as if there was a full moon. But it always looks different at night anyway, because there's no people here. I take the lead, showing her the first few zones – that's how they have the animals arranged, in zones. It's all a bit basic, but it's kinda fun too.

In the Amazon zone they have about fifty red-bellied piranhas that actually do look quite menacing. The display says they can form feeding frenzies and strip an animal of all its flesh in minutes, but that's mostly a myth, it only really happens during times of starvation. Mostly they just eat insects or seeds that fall in the water. There's also a really fat iguana called Susan. The Africa zone has tilapia, giant perch, a couple of pig-nosed turtles, and lots of otters. They don't like people much, so they're much happier at night when no one's around, and we get to see them playing, which is cute because there's some pups too. There's a zone called The Abyss, which is supposed to be about animals from the deep oceans, but of course they can't reproduce the pressure of the real deep oceans, so it only has pictures of creatures like the Dumbo octopus, and then some fish from shallower seas that just happen to look scary or odd, like conger eels and nautilus. But Lily doesn't seem to mind. I'm able to explain to Lily what all the animals are, and what makes them interesting, and she goes from one display to next completely transfixed. So that when we finally get to the big tank in the middle of the tropical zone, she's forgotten what I asked her to bring.

It really is big by the way, the size of a large swimming pool, but deeper and there's a glass tunnel that leads underneath it – it's kind of the grand finale of the warm seas part of the aquarium. You see the pool from above first, so you can't quite make out what's in the water until you're standing right above it.

"Are those sharks?"

"Yup. Black tip reef sharks, nurse sharks and epaulette sharks. And rays, and zebra fish, and guitar fish, and a few tuna, and a turtle, he's called Norman."

"Norman?"

"Yeah, he's a loggerhead. You have to be a little bit careful of him, because one time he bit someone, but you just push him away and he gets the idea."

Lily looks at me. "Are you suggesting I go swimming in *there*," she points at the giant pool. "With sharks?"

"I thought you might like to. It's really nice and warm." It's actually so warm in the water that the atmosphere up here, out of the water, is uncomfortably hot.

"Are you serious?"

In response I go to the storeroom door. You wouldn't really notice it if you didn't know it was there, and I key in the security code to open it. Inside there's a few diving masks hanging on hooks. I grab a couple. "You can get changed in here if you like. Out here is all on the CCTV, so the security guy might be watching."

"Oh my God. You *are* serious." She doesn't go inside, but walks back to the pool and half-way out across the bridge. She looks down, and I join her, seeing all the fish cruising around. Mostly the different species act pretty much the same here as in the wild. The open ocean fish cruise the tank, and the reef fish guard their holes and nests on the fake corals. A large black tip shark comes near to the bridge, its dorsal fin just breaking through the surface.

"I can't swim there. Not with sharks."

"They're only small sharks." I say. "Come on, it's fun." I let her watch for a while, then lead her away to the storeroom.

I let her get changed in private. It seems more proper that way, then when she's done I quickly change too. When I get out she's still staring down at the sharks.

"Are you sure about this?" She asks, biting her lip. "Have you done it before?"

I've done it loads before, the animals here are completely used to the aquarium staff and volunteers snorkeling in this pool – that's why I'm allowed to do it tonight. But I decide to play a trick on her. I just shrug a bit, and I see how much she tenses up.

"You haven't?! Then I'm not."

"Relax, just watch out for Norman." I climb the barrier of the bridge, and lean out over the water. Then I fix the mask over my face and let go.

It's lovely, being engulfed by warm water, it always is. I let myself sink down, to the bottom of the pool. With the splash I made, all the fish initially keep away, but after a few moments they come back, inquisitive to see what has just joined them. But I don't stay long. I surface to see Lily still on the bridge.

"Come on!" I call.

"Are you sure?"

"Of course I'm sure."

"Oh for Christ's sake." She slowly climbs over the barrier too, but holds on tight to the railings.

"Come on!"

She lets go, and screams as she hits the water.

I can see how panicked she is at first, she won't even put her face in the water, even though that's the best way to calm down, by seeing what it is that's scaring you. But slowly, when nothing attacks her, I manage to persuade her to put the mask on properly, and first to look down, and then to take little dives under the water and around the tank. The fish are very good at not coming too close, except for some of the sharks that don't seem to care. They actually brush against us as we're swimming, and we can feel how rough their skin is. Norman comes to see us too, but he's not in a nippy mood.

We swim around the strange glass bubble that is the tunnel. It's weird how it always looks distorted and odd from when you're inside it, looking up into the water, and it always looks really limiting and small when you're *in* the water. There are other viewing ports too, and we swim around them all, looking out at the public spaces like the fish do. Finally we swim circuits of the whole pool, along with the mixed shoal of fish, and then with Norman, holding onto the rim of his shell, and letting him pull us through the water. Then – because it's nearly midnight – I say we should probably get out of the water now.

We both get changed in the storeroom this time – only because I forgot to suggest we should bring any towels, but they have some in there. And I look away from Lily as she peels down the swimsuit, but she's going on and on about how amazing it was to feel the sharks, and she notices me looking away, and tells me to look back, and then she can't stop giggling at my reaction. And I have to remind her, again, that they have CCTV in the main part of the aquarium.

And then we get let out, back into the street, and we decide to walk home, because it's a nice night. And when we finally get back to Lily's house, and Lily starts kissing me the moment we get inside, I don't stop her this time.

* * *

"You know," Lily says the next morning, when I wake up. I'm late actually – I ought to be at a class, but it's not one I really *have* to go to. Lily draws the drapes back to let the daylight in. She's already been downstairs and I can smell the coffee. "I've been thinking about what you said yesterday. About how we've been hiding away here." I kind of struggle up onto one of my elbows, and rub my eyes with the other hand.

"You have?"

"Yeah. I have. And you're right. We can't go on like this, hiding away, as you put it." She smiles to show she's not mad. "We need to open up to the world. Beyond Eric I mean. Be brave."

"A bit like before. When we did lots of things. That was fun."

"Yeah. So…" She takes a deep breath. "I was thinking that, before we do, before we tell the whole world, we should get everyone back together first. To clear the air. You know, Eric and Jennifer and Oscar and… …and James." She looks at me for a second as she says the last name, then looks away again.

"Oh." I say.

"He's part of the group Billy. And Eric says he knows about us anyway. But he's OK with it. I mean – he ought to be. He's the one who broke up with me." She smiles again, but it's a little more forced this time. "And I heard that he's got a new girlfriend. Some cheerleader called *Brooke*." She screws up her nose, as if this is a really stupid name. "I guess we could invite her too."

"*Invite* her? Invite her where?"

"Round here. Before we – you know – before we get *seen out*. I was thinking I could invite them all on Saturday. Would that be OK with you?

It wasn't what I meant really, about going out more. But I guess it's a step in the right direction. "OK. I guess."

Lily smiles. "There's coffee downstairs. But then I have to go to class. But you can stay. Have a shower, let yourself out."

So that's what I do.

CHAPTER THIRTY-SEVEN

"*Billy*? Lily's dating Billy?"

"No. Not..." James looked away, still driving slowly through the night-time streets. "They're not *dating*. At least, it's not gonna last, it's just a..."

"A what?" Oscar pressed him, the shadow of a grin on his lips.

"I don't know what. That's the problem. She's never done this before. Much less with...."

"Hey come on," Oscar turned to his friend. "There's no way she's gonna choose a runt like that over you!"

James didn't answer.

"Oh my God," Oscar went on. "That explains everything. Your dumb ass behavior tonight. Picking on those nerd types." He chuckled, then when he spoke again his voice was serious. "So what are you gonna do?"

"Do? What am I gonna do?" James drove on silently, as if this was the first time he'd been able to think clearly about the issue. "I'm going to get her back, that's what. And I'm going to fuck that little prick right up, too."

CHAPTER THIRTY-EIGHT

I don't go over to Lily's on the Friday night, because I have to work, an essay (The Meaning of Biology and Its Different Fields – so still really basic stuff). Then, just as I'm about to leave my house on Saturday afternoon, I get an email from back home. It sort of throws me. It's like two worlds crashing together.

I can't tell you who the email comes from because I set up the system to be anonymous. I thought it would encourage more people to use it, but now someone has, it's actually a bit annoying since I can't contact them to ask more questions. I guess I should explain. The email came through my website against the expansion of the Fonchem site in the north of Lornea Island. After I discovered that the bay just to the south – which Fonchem wants to take over – is an important breeding ground for Lornea Island sea-dragons, I was worried about them being so close to a site where they make all these horrible chemicals, so I set up an anonymous tip line, where people could email through reports of chemical spills or environmental damage. And then – well to be honest, then I forgot about it, because no one emailed, and most of the time I didn't even remember to put the anonymous tip email address on the posters. But I did put it on some of the posters, and now someone's emailed me.

Whoever it is has included photos, and they're sitting on my computer now. They're pictures of the high tide line, you can't see where exactly, but I looked at the metadata from the photos – that's additional information most cameras capture when they record images, it tells you the date, and what equipment was being used, and on cameras with built in GPS it also includes location data – so I know it's in the bay south of the Fonchem site. And there, dried up and dead, and looking almost identical to pieces of seaweed, are three little corpses of sea-dragons, their tails curled up. But I still want to ask questions, like how many there actually are, and whether there's been any strong winds there in the last few days, that might have thrown up unusually large waves and washed them ashore. Or, whether there's been any residue on the water surface, or on the sand, that would indicate a spillage, or some other reason why they might have died. But I can't do any of that, because I don't know who sent the email. So instead, I just study it for a while, and then I'm in a rush because I said I'd get to Lily's house in time to help her get things ready for tonight. So you can see why I'm a bit conflicted. One half of me is campaigning against a chemical giant probably poisoning the sea, the other half of me is sort of in love with the daughter of the CEO of the exact same company.

When I get there, Lily's decided we're going to have a games night. She thinks that will give everyone something to focus on. So they're not all thinking how weird it is that she's with me now, and not James. While she's cooking, I follow her instructions, going into the library and bringing out all the games they have in the house. I like the library in Lily's house. It's not a massive room but all the walls are just bookshelves, from the floor to the ceiling. There's even a ladder on rails, that you can slide left and right to get at the books which are too high to reach, and I spend a bit of time climbing up and down and looking over the books. But I find the games in the end, they're in a cupboard made of really dark wood, and there's pretty much every game you could think of. There's Scrabble, Monopoly, Risk, various different types of charades-type games – I don't really have a preference for which one we play, so I yank them all out and take them through to the dining room table. Then I make a fire in there, because it's a cold room, and the weather is turning now it's the fall.

Eric is the first to arrive, and he gets all over-excited when he learns we're playing games. But I can tell Lily is more like me, still nervous about how tonight's going to go. And when the others arrive –Jennifer and Oscar and James all come together in his big SUV – I have to take a deep breath before I open the door to them. But pretty soon I can tell it's going to be alright after all. Oscar has a bunch of flowers he's brought for Lily, and Jennifer gives me a kiss on both cheeks, like she might have done before me and Lily got together, and when James sees me, his face lights up into a big friendly smile, and he slaps me on the back. There is a bit of a moment though, when he sees Lily.

"Hello," James says to her, when she steps out of the kitchen to greet everyone. And everyone kind of freezes, like they're watching to see how each of them reacts, but it doesn't last long, and they have a sort of half-hearted embrace.

"Hello James," Lily says. "It's nice to see you."

"It's nice to see you too. You look well."

"Is your new girlfriend not here?" I ask, because I remember that Lily said she would invite her, and then I regret saying it, because it's – well it's not the right thing to say, is it? But I've said it now. "Brooke isn't it?"

James turns to me, and his smile is a bit forced at first, but then he relaxes again, and almost laughs. He shakes his head.

"I wouldn't say she was a new girlfriend, Billy," he replies. "We went on a couple of dates, but it wasn't really working." There's a silence, but James keeps on, and breaks it. "But hey, no need to talk about that. Let's keep things happy. I hear we're here to play a games marathon, and I intend to destroy you all."

"I don't think so," Oscar interrupts, and they're both being playful, and Lily has to stop them by saying we have to eat first.

Dinner is delicious. Lily has really made an effort, and I learn a bunch of new Italian words like 'bruschetta', which is a kind of toast with garlic and tomatoes and olive oil, and 'crostini', which is sort of the same thing, only with smoked salmon and watercress – but either way they both taste amazing, and there's these little goat's cheese tarts that I can't stop eating. And everyone compliments her on how good everything is, which she seems to like. James sort of dominates the conversation, but not in a bad way. He's actually much funnier than I ever thought before. He tells us a story about how he found a goat in his dorm rooms, which sounds bizarre, but it turns out it belonged to a friend of his who was trying to get into one of the 'final' clubs they have at Harvard university.

I didn't know anything about them, but James explained, they're these private society clubs that are really exclusive, and even if you get invited into them you have to do an initiation test. And for James' friend he had to keep a goat for a week, only he left his door open and it wandered off. They all had to search the whole building for it, and only when they'd all given up did James come back to his room, and find it was in his bathroom, eating the shower mat. Everyone laughs at this, except for Eric, because for some reason he's not in a very good mood.

After dinner is cleared away we get the games out. There's a mini argument about what to play, Oscar says we should play *Risk*, but James wants to play *Monopoly*, so the pair of them end up having a vote. I vote for *Risk* but neither Jennifer nor Lily know how to play *Risk* though, so we decide on *Monopoly*.

I read an article on *Monopoly* in *Science* magazine. About how odd it is that it's become a cultural institution, even though it's essentially just a game of chance. You can only move to the place where the dice tell you, and then the only choice you have is whether to buy that property or not, and only then if you happen to be the first one to land there. You might as well just take it in turns to roll the dice a dozen times and see who has the highest score at the end. It would be quicker, and there'd be fewer arguments too.

It's funny how it sucks you in though. I follow the only tactic that makes sense – to buy everything I can at the start, and hope I get lucky. Which is pretty much what everyone else does too. So after a while all the properties have been bought, but no one has a full set, which you need in order to build houses or hotels, and push the rents really high – I'm sure you know the rules. So then the bargaining starts. Eric has gone for the stations (which is a very poor tactic by the way) and practically bankrupts himself getting Lily to sell him the last one. She's then got the money to buy from Jennifer and James and get two full sets. I have two of the yellow properties and one red one, and James has the opposite, so we do a deal. And meanwhile Oscar gets a set of the dark yellow properties, after doing a deal with Jennifer, who gets the light blue. Then we all start building houses. Pretty soon we're split into three different levels of power. There's Lily and Oscar, who are both the most powerful with two sets each. Statistically speaking, it's almost certain that one of them is going to win. Then there's Eric and Jennifer. Eric only has the stations, and Jennifer only has one low value set, so it's just a matter of time before they both get wiped out. And then there's James and I, who are sort in the middle – we've each got one, mid-value set. We're unlikely to win, but we've got enough money and other property to stay in the game for ages.

At this point you could make a mathematical model of the game, using a random number generator as the dice. You could run it a few thousand times, and work out the exact percentage chance we'd each have of winning. Of course it wouldn't give the exact same *outcome* every time, because the dice rolls are random, but it would be interesting to do.

But actually it might not work, because it would miss out something important to Monopoly. It would miss out how you can gang up on people. I don't know how you'd build that into the model.

After we've been playing about two hours, Jennifer has a really unlucky run. She throws a double, which makes her land on Lily's second most expensive property, and then she has to throw again, and lands on Lily's *most* expensive one – which also happens to be the most expensive property on the whole board. And even though it's not Lily's fault at all, everyone blames her, and keeps blaming her when Jennifer doesn't have enough money or property to pay the rent due. So Jennifer's the first to go out. She pretends to be really upset about it, but actually you can tell she's only half-pretending, like she's pretending to pretend, to cover up that she really is a bit pissed.

Eric goes out next, also after landing on one of Lily's properties, so she gets the stations back. He gets a little bitter too, and even makes a comment about how she must have learned to be so ruthless from her father. Everyone laughs, everyone except Lily that is. She's now isolated, but still kind-of enjoying herself because she can't really lose the game now. So then, when it's James' go, he thinks for a long while, as he's holding the dice, but then doesn't throw them. Instead he suggests that he and I do a merger. We're the two weakest players left, and he says it's the only way we stand any chance of surviving. We'll remove his character, the car, and just keep my boat. He's right, of course, that is a good tactic, but then there's a bit of a row over whether it's legal to do this. Only it's an old box and the rules book is missing some pages, so we take a vote to decide it, and it's only Lily who's against it. So after that James and I are about the same strength as Oscar, with Lily still way out in front. So the only real question is whether James and I, or Oscar, is the next to get unlucky and land on an expensive property. It's a bit tense for a while, but then we squeak through the toughest bit of the board, and hand the dice to Oscar, and he gets whacked by Lily's hotel. After that it's only a matter of time before Oscar is toast.

Three turns later, we knock Oscar out of the game, and take over all his properties, and then finally the balance of the whole game shifts. Now we're actually stronger than Lily – in terms of statistics and probability, much stronger, although she doesn't seem to see it. That's because she's still got tons of money, but you could run the model from this point and ninety nine times out of a hundred she'd be paying rent to us faster than we are to her, until she'd eventually run out and have to start mortgaging property, and then she'd be finished. Basically, we're gonna win.

I guess I get a bit excited by this, maybe even a bit overexcited, but it is really late now. Jennifer is curled up nearly asleep on the sofa, with Oscar beside her stroking her hair. And Eric has found some brandy and is swirling it around a giant glass while poking at the embers of the fire. Lily keeps yawning, but it won't take long now, for us to beat her, I mean.

"How about we call it a draw?" James says, just when I'm about to roll the dice.

"What? No way!" I say, a bit louder than I mean. Lily looks at the board, and I can tell she knows she's doomed.

"It is nearly two in the morning." She sounds tired. "Billy – would you accept a draw?"

A lot of me wants to say no, but I can suddenly see what James is doing. He's trying to make himself look good in front of her. And me look bad. Trouble is, I'm still a bit sucked in.

"How about we just count up our assets, and see who's got the most?" I suggest, but Lily groans. Between us we've got all the property and more money than the bank. It would take a while.

"No, come on Billy. It's super late," James says. Then he leans in and goes on very quietly in my ear. "Trust me, she'll appreciate you giving in." He gives me a smile.

I look at Lily, and she looks back, a funny expression on her face. So with a bit of an effort I agree.

"OK. Let's call it a draw."

Eric and Jennifer give a couple of mock cheers, and James quickly sweeps all the pieces off the board, like I might change my mind. Then he starts trying to call a cab, because everyone's drunk too much to drive. Only then it's so late he can't get one for another half hour. We can hear because he actually calls a cab company, I don't know why he doesn't just use the Uber app.

"Why don't you stay here?" Lily asks, while he's still on the call, asking if they're sure they can't come sooner.

"No – we've imposed ourselves enough for one night," James says, covering the speaker on his cellphone with his hand.

"Don't be silly." Lily replies. You know I've got plenty of rooms here. Just stay. Then you can drive back in the morning."

James looks as though he's going to have one more go at persuading the cab company, but then he changes his mind, and tells them not to bother. So suddenly everyone's staying.

I feel a bit awkward then, because I'm not suddenly sure if *I'm* staying. I still have my bike here after all. And then Lily goes upstairs, to make sure the spare rooms have covers on the beds, or something like that, and I find myself the only one downstairs. Eventually I have to make a decision, so I creep upstairs and to Lily's room. And fortunately she's left the door a little bit open, so I look in, and she's already in bed, but looking at her phone. She looks up, and sees me there.

"I didn't know if you were coming."

"I wasn't sure if you wanted me to."

"It's up to you."

So I go in and shut the door. And without really saying anything more we both go to sleep.

CHAPTER THIRTY-NINE

The next morning Lily wakes me up suddenly by blowing into my face. As soon as I open my eyes she kisses me quickly, and then prods at my nose.

"Monopoly is a stupid game, and you are a stupid boy."

It's quite late, but I'm still a bit sleepy, so I don't reply. I think I just blink at her.

"Remind me never to play it with you again." She kisses me again, but before I can kiss her back, she rolls out of the bed and goes to the bathroom. I think she's going to come back, or maybe I hope she is, because she seems in a much better mood, but instead I hear the noise of the shower running.

When I'm a bit more awake I check my phone, and right away I see another anonymous email came in the night. It has more pictures of dead sea-dragons washed up on the beach by the Fonchem compound. So then I'm back to feeling conflicted. I know I should say something to Lily about it. Even if she can't *do* anything about it. Even if they've just been washed up by some bad weather, which is quite possible. Because what if they haven't? What if her father's company is responsible for discharging dangerous chemicals into the ocean and destroying a valuable habitat?

"Are you OK?" Lily is out of the shower. She's got a towel wrapped around her and she's rubbing at her head with another. Her sudden appearance jolts me back to my strange reality.

"You're not still bitter about last night?"

"What?"

"Losing the game." She sits down at her dressing table, and I see her in the reflection.

"We didn't lose."

"About not winning then? About not destroying everyone and dominating the world?"

"No."

She frowns. "What then?"

I think for a few seconds, then I pull up the picture on my cell phone again, and turn it around so she can see.

"What's that?" She turns around to face me properly.

I explain. "It's a picture of the beach to the south of the Fonchem facility on Lornea Island. You remember?"

"Of course. But what is…"

"They're sea-dragons – well seahorses really, but dead ones."

"Why? How?"

"I don't know. It could be a chemical leak. From the facility."

She looks horrified. Which is nice, in a way, because I was scared she might not even care.

"Well, how do you…? I mean, how come you've got this picture?"

But just then there's a knock on the door, and we hear Eric's voice. "Breakfast will be served in five minutes." He waits a moment and then goes on. "I do hope I've just interrupted you two having sex." And Lily throws something at the door.

"We've just finished!" Then she turns back to me. "We'll talk. About this. But let's have breakfast first."

* * *

The others must have been up for a while, because James has already been out to get bagels and croissants, and Eric has found a waffle maker and already has a pile of them on the kitchen table. And Jennifer, whose hair is all ruffled up behind her head, is making coffee. We chat, about nothing much, and then the others drift away.

"So tell me," Lily says when we're the only ones left. So I start to explain, about how I set up the site, and how I think that Fonchem might be leaking something into the water.

"You should tell your dad," James says at one point. I hadn't noticed him coming back into the kitchen, but he must have heard the whole thing.

"I will. But are you sure it's chemicals? Could it not just be natural? I mean don't things die sometimes? There's only a couple in the photos?"

I hesitate. I've been asking myself the same question.

"I don't really know."

"Fonchem's not one of those really bad firms," James says suddenly. And he's looking at me more than Lily. "They have really high environmental standards, and there's no way they'd deliberately do this." I see Lily smile at him gratefully.

"I mean it, Billy. And if Lily tells her dad about this, he'll look into it. Properly."

I let the subject go. I didn't want to talk about it with James. It seems Lily doesn't want to either because she gets up and leaves the room. So then it's just James and me left.

"By the way Billy, I never got your cell phone number," he says, out of the blue. He pulls out his phone, and waits, until I call out my number. Then he gives me a call, and – a bit surprised this is happening – I add him to my contacts, and type the name: *James*

CHAPTER FORTY

I'm not completely surprised when he calls me, a couple of days later. He asks if I want to go for lunch with him. When I don't reply right away, he goes on, and says that there's a few things he wants to say to me. That's the only reason I agree.

"Great. How about tomorrow?" He gives me the name of a burger joint that's half way between the two colleges.

"Oh, and don't worry about the tab. This is on me."

So the next day I walk out there after my morning lectures have finished. I don't take my bike because I don't want to lock it up off campus, where it might be stolen. I don't know if that's likely, but I guess I have a strange sense of foreboding about this meeting.

I meet James as I arrive, him walking from the other direction. He greets me like we're old friends, or at least good friends. We go inside and take a booth by the window. The restaurant has table service, and at first James studies the menu like what he's going to eat is the most important thing. He looks up after a while, and sees me watching him.

"Order whatever you want Billy, it's on me," he says again. So I do. I choose a double bacon cheeseburger, fries, and a salad, because since I've been seeing Lily I've kind of got into eating salads. When I finish ordering James turns to the waitress and smiles.

"I'll have what he's having." He smiles, and she smiles back. She's pretty, not Lily-pretty, but then not many girls are. But she obviously likes James because she can't take her eyes off him.

"Oh, and a couple of beers too."

She smiles back at him and takes a while to write it down, looking up at him over her pad, and fluttering her eyelashes. Finally she leaves, and James tears his eyes from her behind to look at me.

"I bet you're wondering why I asked you here?"

I give a sort of shrug, to show I am, but it's not a big deal. But then I'm irritated when he doesn't tell me.

"How did it go with Lily's dad?"

"What?"

"Those dead seahorse things? By the Fonchem site? Did she talk to him?"

"Oh." I don't go on. The truth is I don't know. She told me she'd speak to him, but I don't know if she did, and I haven't liked to bring it up again. It's awkward. It's not like it's *her* company exactly.

"Lily's touchy about Fonchem." James goes on, speaking very casually and easy. "It's one of the things I learned about her. One of the things." He does a half roll of his eyes. "You gotta see it from her perspective. She didn't ask to be born a part of the Bellafonte dynasty. And maybe when she does inherit it all, she might want to do things a different way. But right now, there's very little she can do to influence the way the company is run." He stops, and gives me a moment to argue if I'm going to, but I don't.

"She's not one of these girls who has her dad wrapped around her finger. He makes business decisions. Regardless of what she says."

I still don't answer. It's like he's building a case against things I haven't even said.

"And also, think of the kind of company it is." James goes on. "Think of what they do." He pauses. "Chemicals, pharmaceuticals. We all love to hate them, right up until we find out we use what they make, every single day of our lives." He leans back in his seat, glances down, and laughs a little. "This table here. It's not a solid piece of wood, you see that? It's resin bound hardboard." I look, you can see at the edge he's right.

"Almost certainly made with resins manufactured by Fonchem, or one of the companies like them. And you might say, well we don't *need* hardboard tables, we could use real wood, but if all the furniture in the country was made of solid wood instead of hardboard, that's millions more trees cut down every year. Billions maybe."

I don't answer. Though I could point out that you could use sustainable forests, where trees are replanted as they're cut down, but I get the point. And it's kind of what I've been thinking, when I've said how conflicted I've been feeling seeing Lily.

"And it's not just hardboard, it's *everything*, our whole lives…" He looks around, searching for another example, and grabs the ketchup bottle, made of plastic. He puts it down again. "But you know this Billy, you're smart. Anyone can see that." He sits back, and the waitress comes back with the beers. She sets James' down very carefully, right in front of him, and straightens the glass, then puts mine down without hardly looking at me. James flashes her a smile, then goes on, still talking to me.

"She's grown up in that world, where everyone's a hypocrite. Where we all use the products her family's company make, but we're the first to lay into them for daring to make them in the first place." He stops, and takes a long sip from his beer. Then a few seconds later he speaks again.

"Let me guess, she said she'd speak to him, and then she's said nothing more about it?"

Eventually – and carefully – I nod in reply, and James gives a look that says *I knew it*. He looks away, out the window. When he looks back he nods too, much more vigorously. Then he drums his fingers on the table, like he has a tune in his head.

"Tell me Billy, have you ever wondered about us? About the five of us, I mean. We're kind of an odd group, don't you think?"

I frown as he says this, then I try to keep my face neutral, because obviously I've thought that a lot, but I don't want him to know.

"There's a reason for it." He stares at me now. It feels like his blue eyes are piercing into mine.

"What reason?"

"I need to know I can trust you, Billy. I *think* I can trust you. But can you promise me you won't repeat what I'm about to tell you. Not to anyone?"

"What is it, you're about to tell me?"

He keeps staring for a second, than breaks into a grin. "Come on, stop messing. This is serious."

So I shrug again, and when he keeps waiting I tell him. "OK, I won't tell anyone."

"You gotta promise. I swear, I've never told *anyone* else this. But you're... You're kind of a part now, too."

"OK. I promise." I don't really believe in promises like this. In a way I wish I'd thought to record this.

But he nods and seems happy. He takes a moment to compose himself before he goes on. "There's a bond, between the five of us. That ties us together."

James stops, and waits.

"What bond?"

He fixes his blue eyes on me. *"We do things."*

We're interrupted again, by the burgers and fries and salads. And again the girl serving takes care to place James' plates carefully in front of him, and dumps mine down. Again he smiles his thanks with a flash of his white teeth, and I have to admit he is pretty handsome, in a very obvious kind of way. The waitress goes away, and James reaches for the salt, but it's nearly empty. He has to shake hard to get any out. He offers it to me when he's finished.

"What sort of things?" I ask, not taking the salt.

James munches through a few fries before answering. "Nothing illegal. Or at least, nothing very illegal, and certainly nothing where anyone can get hurt." He looks up suddenly, and smiles again, his face open, and sort of glowing with a sort of excitement. "Look I'll start at the beginning. That's why I wanted to buy you lunch. To explain this to you. You deserve to know."

I just wait.

"Lily and I first started dating when we were thirteen. She was my first proper girlfriend. My only proper girlfriend." He glances at the waitress, but just for a second. "Look I know this sounds crass, but we knew each other because our parents went to the same country club." He shakes his head at me. "Her family has a load more money than mine, more than almost anyone there. But I don't wanna deny my own privilege." He stops. "Come on, you gonna eat that or what?"

We both stop, and he takes a bite from his burger. I've lost my appetite, so I eat some lettuce. When he's finished chewing he goes on.

"I'd liked her for ages, I mean – look at her. When we finally got together, I couldn't believe my luck. Even more so when she finally let me sleep with her." There's a pause, when neither of us says anything.

"And she told me about her family, about what they do, and what it's like growing up that way. And I went out on the family yacht, and got invited to barbecues, went skiing with them, all that stuff…" He waves a hand, casually. "I was even allowed to stay over at her parents place – have you seen it yet?"

He whistles, but I shake my head. "Man, it's a proper mansion. Makes her place here seem like nothing." He takes another bite, and chews it carefully.

"Jennifer was her best friend growing up. Oscar was mine. It seemed sort of fate that they should get together, and then the four of us became very close. Almost, *unnaturally* close." He stops and puts his head on one side. "You know what Oscar's dad does for a living?"

I don't, so I shrug.

"Good. He prefers it that way." He waits a beat. "He's an arms dealer."

There's another silence, but this one is more because I'm shocked.

"He sells weapons, in the Middle East, Africa. Wherever a highly dubious government or would-be government can raise the money to buy them." He sees my eyes go wide. "No, not like that. He works for an arms manufacturer. This is all legal. Legal, and highly profitable." He pauses, and has another go with the salt.

"But yeah – I understand that look. Then you have pharmaceuticals – that's my folks. And Jen. Her old man's a defense attorney." He shakes his head again. "No, nothing too exciting, but he represents rich folk who haven't paid their taxes. He takes a huge chunk of their money but stops them going to jail."

James takes a break for another swig of beer. Then he goes on.

"So. Arms. Chemicals, big pharma and law. All of us, the product of some pretty fucked up industries, and yet the four of us, we seem to have anything we want. Life is good. Only it isn't, is it? Not really. Not if you don't want to be a hypocrite.

"We used to go on and on about it. On ski vacations, yacht regattas. Around the pool in Lily's folk's place. And then one day, the opportunity came to do something about it." He grins.

"What?"

"You pick things up, OK? Growing up like we did. People talk, say things they shouldn't, thinking we're just kids, spoiled kids who aren't gonna bite the hand that feeds them. Oscar found out about a deal someone was doing, selling weapons to a country that was on the banned list. And we worked out we could stop it, just by leaking it. An anonymous email to a journalist, another to the regulator. They wouldn't even get punished that much, they'd just – it just killed the deal. So we did it.

"That was the first. I guess we got a taste for it. We became these – I don't know – *secret crusaders*. It tied us together, it made us stronger – I'm talking about Lily and me, Oscar and Jennifer – the four of us, it made us invincible. We were different from everyone else. We didn't need anyone else."

I'm completely silent. Listening, not really knowing what to think about all this. And now James is quiet too.

"What are you thinking, Billy?"

"I don't know."

He laughs. Sort of. "I guess this is hard to take in." He half-smiles for a few seconds, then it fades and he's left looking seriously at me.

"It didn't happen at once. We didn't decide to become – whatever we are. It was a gradual thing. You see Oscar was always into computers. Ever since I met him. He's doing a computer science major now. And he's – I don't know, you know that Facebook was started here? At Harvard?"

I nod. Everyone knows that.

"Well he's like one of those guys. He could invent the next Bitcoin or YouTube – probably will one of these days. But right now he's into hacking. Big time. He breaks into the email servers of companies, searches for evidence where they're breaking environmental rules, or where the rules need toughening... Sometimes we have to do a bit of covert operations – that's my favorite part," he grins. "It's exciting. It's nothing fully dangerous, but sometimes you have to take a risk or two."

"What type of thing?" I hear my voice ask.

"The worst we've done? We broke into a guy's apartment to get a letter from his bank. You need it sometimes to get someone's identity, and break passwords." He grins again. "He wasn't there, but Oscar still had to disable the alarms, and it was a rush being in there."

"Why are you telling me this?" I ask suddenly. I feel like I don't want to be here. I don't want to know this.

"Because you're with Lily now. And you have to know. What binds us together. What we *are*."

"Does Lily know about this?"

James grins again. "Yeah. Lily knows. That's why everything went so fucking crazy when you came along. Suddenly it wasn't just the five of us anymore, but six."

I'm silent. Completely not hungry any more.

"You said five, when did Eric get involved?"

"That's a good question. Lily was in a shared apartment in her freshman year. He was in the room across from her. He just attached himself. Inserted himself into our group, and eventually she told him about what we do. He loved it, you know what he's like."

I'm pretty stunned. I've heard of some crazy things in my time, but this is wild. Certainly not what I expected. And I try to make sense of it, try to understand James' reason for telling me now. I think I know.

"Is this about me and Lily? The other night, you were trying to make me look bad, when we were playing Monopoly. Are you trying to get back together with her?"

James looks suddenly shocked. "Trying to make you look bad? That was just a game…. I was… Oh man, I was trying to help you." He stops, and takes a deep breath. "I told you I started dating Lily when I was thirteen, we've been together ever since." He hesitates, fixes me with his blue eyes again. "Until this month, she was the only girl I'd ever slept with." His eyes don't move. "Can you imagine what that's like?" He looks away before me, reaching again for the salt cellar before finding it's still empty.

"I promise you…" He doesn't finish the sentence. Instead he looks around, and sees the waitress from earlier, standing on her own a few tables away. Then he looks at me again, meaningfully. He gets up, still holding the salt cellar and, with a glance at me, walks over to her. I can't hear what he says, but a minute later I see her laughing, and changing the salt for a full one from the counter. Then he says something else, and she gives him a long look, where she's trying to make herself look more beautiful than she really is, then she scribbles something on her pad. She tears the sheet off and hands it to him. Then he comes back and sits down. He puts the paper on the table between us. It has a name, Clara, and a cellphone number.

"Lily is amazing, Billy. She really is. I'm always going to be a part of her life, and she's always going to be a part of mine. But the truth is she was holding me back. And I was holding *her* back. I promise you. I only want the best for Lily. And if she thinks that's you, that's good enough for me."

CHAPTER FORTY-ONE

I'm doubtful. I mean. It could be true, what he's saying, but it might not be. It could be a trick.

"Does Lily know you're here? Telling me this?"

James sits back. "No. She doesn't."

"So if I tell her about it, is she going to confirm it all – this stuff about you working – I don't know what you call it, undercover, like some band of vigilantes?" I watch his face carefully, to see how he takes this idea. "Or is she going to ask what I'm on about?"

"I don't know." James looks like he finds the idea interesting, but not concerning. "She might admit it. Or she might not."

I wait. I don't know what he means by that.

"We swore to keep this secret. You can understand why. It was only the four of us who knew. And I've never told anyone else. Not until today. Lily was the only one who ever has. When she told Eric. So I don't know what she'll do, if you tell her you know. "

"OK. I will then. I'll ask her."

James makes a face like he's weighing that up. "It's your choice Billy. But..."

"But what?"

He takes a deep breath. "If it was me, I'd wait until she tells you."

"Why?"

"Because then you'll know she really trusts you. That this isn't just a fling – for her. That she thinks it's going to last."

There's silence between us. I open my mouth to reply, but suddenly it's too dry.

"And – you have to consider how it's going to look. Remember I said she's touchy about Fonchem?"

"Yeah?" I say. It's about all I can manage.

"So, if you go to her wanting to know all about what we do… think how that's going to look? When she knows you're upset about what her family firm is doing?"

"I don't understand."

"Think about it Billy, what is she going to think you're really after? Her or…"

I try to do what he says, to think about it, but I don't know what he means.

"She's going to think you want something *done*. To Fonchem. For us to do what we do, to her company. And she's not going to take that well."

There's another silence at our table. I really need time to take in everything James has said. To process it. But I don't have time.

"How do you know?"

James waits a beat, then suddenly leans forwards. "Two reasons. One, because I know Lily. Probably better than anyone else, and I don't mean to be disrespectful here Billy, but I know her better than you. That might change, when you've been through enough of her moods, the highs and the lows. But not yet."

"What's the other reason?"

James takes a long slow breath before answering. "Two, is we made a pact. That we wouldn't ever target our own firms. Fonchem's off limits for what we do."

CHAPTER FORTY-TWO

I have to take a walk after everything I've heard. I end up by the river, watching the swirling water rolling past below me, and in a sudden flash I miss the beach. I miss the island, where I can get away from everyone on empty sands, where the water is right beside me, not channeled into a concrete-banked river, and the path that runs alongside flanked by a four-lane highway. I have to sidestep joggers, earbuds leaking tinned music, mom's with prams, people taking their dogs for their walks.

One the one hand, everything that James has told me is ridiculous. Why would they do what he said? Why would anyone do it? But on the other, *I* did some stupid things when I was younger, so why wouldn't anyone else? And it's definitely true there is some strange bond between them all. I guess it's why I was interested in them in the first place. Plus they have led unusual lives – the four of them at least. They're all rich, in a way I've never experienced, so maybe that does lead you to do strange things.

If James was simply lying to me, and I ask Lily about it, then he's going to look stupid. She'll tell me the truth, and we'll both know he's trying this strange trick to break us up. It'll backfire on James, and only make me and Lily stronger. But James isn't stupid – he's far from it – so he'd know that. Which kind of suggests it might be true.

The other possibility is that Lily would deny it, even though it is true. Which would mean… I guess it would mean she doesn't trust me, like James said. Or at least, she doesn't feel safe yet confiding in me. Or she doesn't think I'll be around long enough to risk letting me in on the secret. I don't like the thought of that at all.

OK, how about if she *does* admit it. What then? I walk on, sidestepping a fat man jogging, with his headphone cables bouncing up and down. To lose the image, I look at the river, a goods barge coming down it now, the water dark in the dying afternoon light. An image hits my mind, unbidden – it's me, under the water, that sunny summer afternoon, in the north of Lornea Island, when Dad and me were waiting to sneak through the restricted zone, by Lily's family's chemical plant. When I spent the whole afternoon in the warm water, diving amid the golden sands, the water pure and clear like liquid glass, all the way down to the seagrass beds below, with the pipefish and sea horses, and the Lornea Island sea-dragons.

If she does admit it – I drag myself back to reality. I don't know, it's all too confusing. But then another thought forms. Something I wished I'd thought to ask James earlier. Are they *still* doing it? What they do. Is Lily secretly doing all this stuff with James and Oscar and Jennifer and Eric, behind my back? The whole time I've known them?

Before I get anywhere near making sense of it, I get a call from Lily. She's just back from her classes and she's obviously in a good mood. And I know she's going to suggest I come round to her house, or maybe even that we go out somewhere, but before she does she starts telling me about a funny thing that happened in her lecture. It wasn't that funny, it was something about how the lecturer broke the projector. But when she's finished I can't bring myself to laugh, and I guess she picks up that I'm not in a good mood. But instead of asking what's wrong with me, she gets uptight, and suddenly the conversation is going about as badly as it can. And then even though I knew she was going to invite me round, suddenly she doesn't. She tells me she's going to hang up now, and I know I should say something, to stop her, to undo this moment that doesn't define what we have, but I don't have the words to do it. I stay silent. She tells me again she's going to hang up, and she sounds distant and upset, but I just let her go. And the feeling it leaves me with, it's like actual pain. It's like my stomach has been punched.

CHAPTER FORTY-THREE

I decide not to ask Lily anything about it in the end. James is right, if she told Eric, then eventually she should tell me, and I need to give her the chance to do so. In the meantime, it sort of goes back to how it was before. We meet, in the downstairs coffee shop with the comfy couches. We go to play pool, we have dinner at Lily's house.

But then I get an odd text from James. He invites me to his dorm room. It's odd, because I haven't been there before, in fact I'd never even thought about where he lives. But I say yes, because I suppose this is just his way of us getting to know each other better. And then he sends a second text, asking me not to say anything to Lily or Eric. Which seems even weirder.

* * *

He lives in a kind of shared set of dorm rooms. It's sort of similar to where I live, only it's a lot nicer. Instead of only having one room to himself, like I've got, he has a set of rooms – there's a kitchen, a living room, a bedroom and a bathroom – so it's more like a proper apartment. When I get there, Oscar is cooking in the kitchen. He gives me a fist bump to say hi, then tells me to grab a beer from the refrigerator, and goes back to a recipe he's following.

"What is that?" I ask, looking at what he's making.

"Pot roast."

"No, not that, *that*." I point at what he's cooking it in. A massive saucepan, but different somehow too.

He turns around, looking confused. "Oh. *That*. It's a pressure cooker. My mom uses them a lot. It's the only way I know how to cook." He watches me a moment, then goes back to chopping up carrots.

We talk about nothing much for a while, then James asks me to lay the table for him, which I do, but a bit confused, since I still don't really know why I'm here, nor why it had to be a secret. It is true I've been getting on better with James and Oscar recently, but I'm still closer to Eric, and to Lily of course.

I finish with the plates and cutlery, and then Oscar gives me a shout and asks me to bring his pressure cooker in. So I do. I go to pick it up with the cloth so it doesn't burn my hands but he stops me, saying he's already let it cool.

"I need the cloth," he tells me, when I look confused. He takes it from me and uses it to open the oven door. I shrug, and do what he asks, carrying it through and putting it on the table. I think how it's probably good Lily isn't here, she makes the table look much nicer than this.

"What's this all about?" I ask, when – a few minutes later – the three of us are sitting down and eating Oscar's pot roast. It tastes OK, but nothing amazing.

"I love Billy's directness, don't you?" James says to Oscar, who gives a bit of a laugh.

"Billy, you remember you asked me if we're still – operating?"

I nod.

"And I said we might be. Well, we just might be."

I wait for him to go on, and he does, but on another tack.

"Did Lily ever get back to you about those dead sea horses, by the Fonchem site on Lornea Island?"

I look from one to the other. "No."

"Do you think she even told her dad?" James' eyes are level on mine.

"I…" I shrug. "Maybe. I don't know."

"Do you even care?"

"What? Of course I care."

Neither of them speak. But then James nods his head. "Good. Good.

Because Oscar's come up with something." He turns to Oscar, who puts down his fork.

"There's a public meeting on Lornea Island next month, where they'll decide whether to grant the extension of the Fonchem site. It'll go through, it's guaranteed to, because Fonchem has spent a ton of money on the idea that it'll create much needed jobs, and there's no risk. It's how they operate – not just Fonchem, every firm like it. Except..." He glances at James. "Except, there's your campaign, about the sea horses." Oscar stops.

"No one's paying any attention to my campaign, in fact I haven't even paid it..."

"But that's because you have no evidence." James cuts me off.

I don't reply.

"I told Oscar about those photographs you showed me, and he did a little digging into the Fonchem mail servers. He found..." James stops. "Actually Oscar, could you explain this? I've never understood what it is you do."

Oscar's eyes narrow in the way they do when he smiles.

"OK. This is complicated. But I'll do my best. They run a virtual box with a Kali Linux instance, and when you boot it with the mail server ISO you can see that..."

"Woah there!" James interrupts again. "This is gonna be easier if you use plain English. So that Billy can understand?" James shoots an apologetic smile in my direction. But I just watch him a second then turn back to Oscar.

"Where do you get the server ISO?"

Oscar's eyes widen slightly. Just for a second. He glances at James, then turns back to me.

"I queried it from DNS records."

"*What?* They had them open?"

Oscar hesitates, he seems to be thinking hard. Finally he goes on. "Yeah. That's the point. It was *all* open, which is why I figured they must be using a third party app, with end-to-end encryption."

I nod. I can see where this is going. But also that James is a bit left behind.

"Hey! What? What am I missing here?"

So I turn to him and explain. "Normally you wouldn't be able to just access someone's DNS via a simple query. You'd need to run port scans against a DNS *range*, and find it that way. But if it's open then the whole *thing* is open. You can't send private emails, they may as well be left on a public message board."

"Or put on Twitter," Oscar continues. And he's right.

"*What?*" James says again.

"I didn't know you knew this stuff, Billy?" Oscar says. And I shrug. "I don't really, I'm not an expert."

Oscar gives me a sly grin.

"Do you wanna just maybe carry on with the explanation?" James tells him, and he does.

"OK. Bottom line is. Once I was in I ran a series of keyword searches, on all the company emails, around the times when you got the reports of the dead fish on the beach. I wanted to see if anyone was reporting any problems at the site, anything that might have caused it. You'd be amazed, just how stupid some people are, they still think email is private."

"And?" I lean forward. I didn't think of doing this. I mean I wouldn't do it anyway, it's completely illegal, but maybe if it had occurred to me. I just didn't imagine the DNS would be listed.

"What did you find?"

"Nothing."

"*Nothing?*"

"Nearly nothing. Except this." He stops and takes out a printout from the pocket of his jacket. It's an email from a woman named Claire Watson. I scan read it, and it seems to be a report of yields from the Lornea Island site. There's one bit where someone has used a highlighter to turn some words yellow:

Our issue we've discussed on Sqrbt. I'll update there.

"What's Sqrbt?"

"I don't know," Oscar says, "But Squarebot is a private end-to-end encrypted company communications system. So I'd guess it's a reference to that."

I hand it back. It figures, any sensible company these days isn't going to discuss sensitive matters on email. That's why platforms like Squarebot exist.

"I don't see the point."

"The point is," James interrupts us. "They're not *using* email. They have an issue, but it's too sensitive to talk about. And it's ongoing." He looks at Oscar. "We reckon it's a leak."

"Why?"

"Your dead fish. It's either a leak or they're dumping. And as much as I don't trust a single chemical company, I don't think Fonchem would dump. Not with Lily's dad's knowledge anyway."

"Well," I start, but then I stop talking. I'd already assumed it must be a leak. Or it could be a leak – if it's not just the result of an onshore gale that whipped up enough waves to wash some animals ashore, that can happen.

"Billy, are you done eating?" James asks now. And when I say I am, he goes on.

"Can you clear the table. I've got a map I want to show you."

So I help by grabbing the big pot and taking it through to the kitchen. I go to rinse it in the sink, but James tells me not to worry, he'll do it later, so I just dump it on the side instead. Then I go back through to the other room, where now there's a giant blueprint unrolled on the table.

"What's this?"

"It's the building plans for the Fonchem site. The current one – you can see where they want to extend down here." I lean in and look. It's interesting to me, because on Google Earth it's all blurred out – companies can request to do this and sometimes Google says yes, if they accept that there's a security risk for publishing accurate maps. I've no idea really what I'm looking at though. It's just a series of buildings, and pipelines, and storage areas. I turn to James and look.

"The Fonchem Lornea Island site makes resins, mostly, and you need a lot of heat to do that. So we reckon, if there's a leak somewhere, you'd be able to see it, if you could *see heat*."

Now they both look up from the map and stare at me, in this really weird, expectant way. It makes me feel uncomfortable, the way they're both looking at me. But then I understand what they're getting at.

"Infrared?"

James nods, smiling.

"Fitted onto a drone?"

"Uh huh."

"Fly it over there and…"

211

"That's right. We figure if we can get images – actual pictures showing there's a leak from the current facility – they'll be forced to fix it. But more importantly, there's no chance they'll get the go ahead for the site extension."

"Even better, Lily doesn't have to find out we had anything to do with it." Oscar finishes.

Maybe I should explain, because it's both really simple, what they're suggesting, but also – well – *audacious*, I suppose. Possibly illegal, I'm not sure – I'd have to check if there are any restrictions of drone flying in that area. You see, all objects emit infrared energy, known as a heat signature. An infrared camera (they're also called thermal-imaging cameras) detects and measures the infrared energy of objects. The camera converts that infrared data into an electronic image that shows the apparent surface temperature of the object being measured. So something that's cold, like a pipeline, would show as dark, you'd hardly see it. But a leak – a leak of something hot – would show up bright white. You wouldn't be able to miss it.

"Have you got an infrared camera?"

"No," James says. "We don't even have a drone, or know how to fly one, but you mentioned…"

"In Australia," I remember, I told them when we first met. "I used them to monitor white sharks – and I knew how to fly them, because I have one at home."

"Exactly." James says. "So we thought you might want to join in the fun."

CHAPTER FORTY-FOUR

I probably shouldn't, but I get a bit carried away by it all. It's kind of exciting to be doing something like this. More exciting than my course anyway – I do hope that gets a bit more challenging next semester. I do feel bad about not telling Lily of course, but I *can't* tell her – James is right about that, anytime I mention her family's business she's touchy about it. And obviously I don't tell anyone else, and that includes Eric. Apparently Oscar hasn't even told Jennifer.

There's the problem of how to get there. I assumed at first we would just go in James' car, but when I suggested that he gave me a look like he couldn't believe how naive I was – I forget how they're much more experienced at this sort of thing. So Oscar asks me if I can handle booking a rental car, and then the ferry. I think it was a bit of a test. And while it might sound easy, it's not as straightforward as you might think. Even if I wanted to rent the car in my name, I couldn't because I'm too young. But obviously I don't *want* to do it in my name because that would mean leaving a super-obvious trail. Oscar told me he could help me get fake documents together, but I didn't need help because I asked my dark web contacts to source them for me.

I had a bit of fun with the name, I choose Hans Hass. That's a joke, he's a really famous marine biologist who came up with something called the Energon theory. It says everything boils down to the transfer of energy, which implies there can be no right or wrong. So even though what we're doing is a little bit illegal, that doesn't make it the wrong thing to do, because there is no right or wrong. I tried to explain this to James and Oscar, but I don't think they really appreciated it.

I'm surprised how fast it all moves though. I mean, I understand that we have to get the evidence before the public meeting on Fonchem's expansion. But it still seems a bit rushed.

We meet at James' again to go through the plan. I'll pick up the car – I might have to show my fake documentation, but it's more likely I'll just need to show the email receipt that I've paid. And James is going to repay me when we get back – they have a little fund set aside for covering the costs of their operations. Once I've got it, I'll take it onto the Lornea Island ferry. Oscar and James are on the same boat, booked on separately as foot passengers. I don't know what names they've used – we're going to pretend we don't know each other, wherever there's any chance of us being on CCTV. Then, once we get there, I'll pick them up just outside the ferry terminal. We'll drive to my house to pick up my drone, and then we have to wait until it gets dark, which will make the images clearer. From there we'll monitor the site, and come back on the morning ferry.

I'm excited. It's going to be fun.

CHAPTER FORTY-FIVE

I've been on the ferry quite a few times before, but never under a false name. It's a really weird feeling. I walk around as Hans Hass, then buy myself a coffee and an actual newspaper in the café – because that's what someone called Hans would do. And I sit reading. I feel sure that Hans Hass would have been a smoker, but obviously you can't smoke indoors these days, so I make do with a slice of cake. I see James, while I'm eating it, and he makes eye contact for a second, but other than that we pretend we don't know each other. I don't see Oscar at all.

As the ferry docks, the drivers have to go back to their cars, so I line up, and then wait until the bow doors open, and slowly we drive off. It's weird to be back on Lornea. Weird but nice. I like it this time of year, when it's empty and cold.

I see James and Oscar just past the entrance to the ferry terminal, and slow down to pick them up. They've both got big backpacks on – part of their disguise as foot passengers, and they fill up the trunk. Then we drive south, down through Newlea, and out towards Silverlea. This is the trickiest part of the plan. I just have to hope Dad's not home, so I can go in and grab the drone, without being spotted. If he does see me, well it doesn't matter, but it's going to be a bit hard to explain. I don't have a plan for how to handle this until I actually arrive in Littlelea, and then – instead of driving right up to the house, I park on the road a minute away. I tell James and Oscar to wait for me. Then I cut through to the cliff path, and run along that until I can see the house. No truck, I'm in luck.

I have my key, so I let myself in, and run up to my bedroom. It's the first time I've been back since going to college, and it's strange to be back, to see the bed I've slept in since I was just a little boy. It makes me think about Lily. How I'm not little any more. How I'm a man now. It almost makes me think about what I'm really doing here, and whether it's such a great idea after all – but I don't have time, not with James and Oscar waiting in the car. So instead I grab the drone and quickly check it over. The battery won't be fully charged, but I can give it a boost from the socket in the car. I chuck it all in my bag and get out of there.

Then we drive back the way we came, but this time past the ferry terminal in Goldhaven and right up to the northernmost tip of the island, where the Fonchem site is. We decide to wait until it gets dark. It's unlikely there'll be anyone around, especially this time of year, but there might be someone walking their dog, around the footpaths that surround the fence, so it makes sense to be cautious. But then it's too cold waiting in the car, so we drive away again, and wait in a bar, where we get some food. There's a TV on in the corner, and it says it's going to snow. I hope not. That could be a problem, for the drone I mean.

We don't talk much as we wait, there's a ball game on the TV, and James and Oscar watch that, while I get on with converting the camera on the drone to infrared. I had to buy a kit to do it, and it was $350, but James said he'd put it on his credit card. It's pretty simple, so when I've done that I do a little research on my phone on how to set the drone up to fly in the snow. I find out you can do it, but it's not exactly recommended. There's a risk that the batteries will lose voltage, which means the drone will crash, or you could get moisture in the electrics, or an ice buildup on the body of the drone, or even the rotors. And if any of that happens it could crash as well. I explain all this to James, but he seems more concerned that we maintain the pretense that none of us know each other.

It's not fun, by the way. I thought it was going to be fun, but now we're actually here, James and Oscar are both quiet, and very serious, and I'm not enjoying myself at all. I think I liked the idea of doing this a lot more than actually doing it. But I'm here now, so I'll finish what we've started. But after that I'm not going to do any more of James' plans.

At eleven we get back in the car, and drive back to the site. It's already started snowing now, big fat flakes that are lit up by the headlights and flutter like moths. The road hasn't been treated, and hardly any other cars have come this way, so we have to go carefully to avoid skidding off, but at least it's flat up here in the north of the island, so we don't get stuck. We leave the car half-hidden behind some bushes, and walk up to the fence, there's a sign on the outside warning of security cameras, and CCTV and it makes me shiver. Or that could be the cold. Then I go back to the car to get set up.

First I check the voltage of the batteries. They're both at 100%, and I've kept them warm while we drove here by sitting on them. I don't want to let them get cold now, so I slip them in my pocket. At the same time I take a roll of gaffer tape and use it to cover up all the vents on the drone's body. That should keep the snow out. I fit the infrared camera, and check it's communicating properly with my phone. Then I sweep the snow off the roof of the car, I'll use that as a launch pad – so the exhaust from the rotors doesn't blow up a blizzard the moment I try to take off. Finally I fit the drone batteries, and I'm ready to go. James and Oscar stand around looking nervous.

I have the drone set up so I can see what the camera sees in real time, on the screen on my phone, which is mounted on the drone's controller. It's getting covered in snow, and my hands are freezing, but I can see clearly enough. I put it on the roof, and step back, then push the throttle. I don't go too hard, like it said on the instructions for flying in the snow, because they cause the battery voltage drop. A second later, there's the buzz of the motors, and I take off, hovering at head height.

"It works!" I say, out loud. It's the first thing any of us have said in a long while. James and Oscar are right beside me now, looking at the camera. I spin the drone around, so the infrared camera is pointing at us, and you see the three human heat signatures, mostly on our hands and faces, and the air where we're breathing out. The hood of the car is also a deep red, from the heat of the engine block underneath. But everything else is black.

I push the drone higher, up to the height of the trees that are sheltering us, forlorn and leafless, and then higher, so that I'm right up in the clear air. Only it's not clear, the snow is really heavy, and you can see the flakes running past the camera, crazy thick. There's a lag in controlling, which I've never seen before. And because I don't have the normal camera feeding back to the screen, it's super hard to control where I am, or where I'm supposed to be going.

"What's it doing?" James asks.

"I don't know." I reply. I don't want to say this, but it's getting pretty obvious. "I don't know if this is going to work."

I covered up the lights on the drone body, so although we can hear it, hovering somewhere above us, we can't see it. And I can't see where it is from the screen either. There's a button I can press that will bring it home though, so I try to push it a bit further, aiming it towards what I think is the Fonchem compound, before shaking my head.

"This is hopeless. I can't see anything with the snow." I try to gain altitude, but the drone won't do it. I press the home button.

"I'm bringing it back."

For a few seconds there's silence, total silence, as the snow absorbs all sound. Then we hear the burr of the rotors again, and they grow louder, until the body of the drone suddenly appears at head height in front of me. Carefully I catch it, and power down the motors.

"I can't see where I'm going with just the infrared camera," I say. "If it wasn't so cold I could fit a second camera, and use that to steer from. But in this temperature, the drone wouldn't get off the ground." I'm gutted. Despite how I'm not enjoying this, we still came to do a job, and I'm disappointed that it's not going to work. Again though, James' mood doesn't seem to match mine, which I don't understand. He seems quite cheerful about this.

"Never mind Billy. We've got a plan B."

"What?"

"Forget the drone. Pack it away, but grab the camera. And meet us at the fence." And then he and Oscar trek off through the snow, where I can't see what they're doing.

I do what he says. I unbolt the camera, and put all the drone equipment back in the box. I'll have to dry it off properly before I next use it. I wonder if I should take it back with me to college, or leave it at home. Both are a bit problematic – if I take it, Dad might wonder why it's not in my bedroom, and if I leave it there, I'll have to pack it away where it was, and it might not dry properly, which could damage it. I'm still pondering this when I shut the car and follow James' and Oscar's footprints towards the fence. And when I get there, I'm stunned.

There's a large hole in the fence, big enough to crawl through. You wouldn't even need to crawl.

"What are you doing?"

"Breaking in. We can still do this." James replies. His voice is calm.

"What? But this wasn't the plan."

"Plans change Billy." Oscar says. His voice is almost menacing. He turns away from me and starts packing the tools he's used back into his bag.

"Is that an *angle grinder*?" I spy what he's holding, a battery-operated power tool. Heavy and bulky. "Why did you bring that?"

"Billy," James ignores my question, and he sounds different suddenly to how he's been all evening. Now he sounds like he did when we were at his apartment, planning this. I realize there's two James' the one I first met, who's arrogant and aloof, and another one, who's charming and friendly – the one who wants you to do things for him.

"We can still do this, without the drone. Just go in and film as much as you can with the infrared camera. It'll still work from ground level. It might even be better."

I want to say no. To tell him to go to hell, but I tell myself to remember why I'm here. What we're actually trying to do, even if I suddenly don't much like my co-conspirators.

"What about the security guards?"

"There aren't any." James replies.

"What about the signs?" My voice is indignant.

"They're just signs. We've done this before Billy. It's easy. That's why we're here so late when it's cold. If there are any security guards – which is unlikely – they'll be tucked up somewhere nice and warm. Probably watching porn."

I look at the hole. There's a flat area on the other side, and in the distance, the dark shapes of buildings. It does look deserted, but I still don't want to go in there. I turn to James and Oscar, and they've both staring at me. Both bigger than me too. I don't really have a choice. This plan, it's not going to work, that's obvious now. To me at least.

"This is stupid," I say.

"Why?"

"It's not going to work. There probably isn't even a leak to find."

"There might be. And we've come all this way." James stares back at me.

"Without the drone, we'll never find it."

"We've come this far. I'm paying for this Billy. The ferry, the rental car. We're doing it for you. I don't want to leave without even trying."

I stare back at him, feeling how I'm angry now. Then I turn away, and hold the camera up at the fence, pointing it towards the distant buildings. But they're too far away. I pull it back down again.

"Come on Billy. You gotta take this shit seriously. Think why you're here. You wanna do something good in the world? Huh? You've come this far. Don't let yourself down now."

I don't believe him. I don't believe he cares about this, but I don't have much choice. So I'll go in. I'll get some footage, to show them both this is a waste of time. Was always a waste of time.

I get down on my hands and knees, and I crawl through the fence. Then I start walking towards the dark buildings in front of me.

CHAPTER FORTY-SIX

It all goes crazy. It all goes madly, horribly wrong. I don't even know what. I don't even know what *to say*.

I can't even hear. I don't know if you're talking to me now. I don't know if you can hear me. My ears are screaming at me. It's like when you're doing scuba and you dive too deep without equalizing. Only you can't swallow to make it go away. I might even be deaf.

There's been an explosion. I know that much. Not from the noise – there wasn't any – but from the light, and the pressure wave. They came, not at the same time, but a split second apart – like the way you can measure how far away a storm is by timing the difference between the lightning and the thunderclap. I can't say how close it was this way though. But I was close.

I saw a man. Twice. The first time he had no flashlight, and I flattened myself against the wall I was by. I was terrified. But I don't think he saw me. The second time he was on the other side of me. He had his light on this time. And that's when the blast happened. Right where he was. Right on top of him.

I pick myself up, I've fallen over in the snow, like I'm making a snow angel – I'm not, it's just I can't even stand, I'm so disorientated. I can't hear – the crump when I take a footstep is gone. I don't know what to do. *What the hell exploded?* Are James and Oscar OK? *I've got to get out of here.*

Before someone comes, to see what the explosion was. I don't know what to do. *What the hell happened to the man I saw? Is he... is he dead?*

I turn, to see if he's maybe there, lying in the snow like I was, only actually injured. If so maybe I can help? But what if this is just the *first* explosion? *I don't know what's happened!* Maybe the whole site is going to blow up? And I shouldn't be here. I've broken in. And there's security guards. They'll come to check what's happened. And they'll have first aid supplies. I've got nothing. I make a decision. A coward's decision. I turn again, and I run for the hole in the fence.

* * *

I expect to see James and Oscar there. It's like I can visualize them, helping pull me through the small gap in the fence, so when they're not there I can't make sense of it. Their bags are gone. They must have heard the explosion. They must be back at the car. So I struggle through, and I press on, back to the car. But they're not there either. What the hell?

It's quiet now – silent again, with the snow coming thicker and harder than ever. And it's dark too. There's no glow from a fire, coming from inside the compound. Whatever blew up was just that, an explosion, but not a fire. Did James and Oscar go inside the compound? To check on me? I stop, dead still in the snow. It's the only answer that makes any sense. And I've left them there.

I retrace my steps, before I can change my mind. I have to get them. To get us all out of here. I get to the fence, and crawl through again, and once again I set off across the snowy open ground before the buildings. But it's quiet. I can't see James or Oscar.

I call out to them, but I don't hear anything, not even my own voice. I come closer to the building from where the explosion seemed to happen. And that's when it happens. I come so close I almost kick it. Even in the darkness I can see what it is, just from the shape. It's an arm. A human arm.

I stare at it. Blinking, shocked, for a long while. I don't know how long. Then my brain starts working again. It's not James's nor Oscar's. I know because it's wearing a watch. A big silver watch, and the sleeve looks different. It looks like the sleeve of one of those reflective jackets that workmen wear. Or security guards.

I step forward again, terrified now about what I'm going to find. Expecting to see James and Oscar dying in a pool of blood and melted snow – but no, they were waiting at the fence. Why would they be here? OK then, the man whose arm that was, it's possible he could be alive still, that he might need help.

But he's not. There's other bits of him. Like hunks of meat in the snow. I feel sick, but I don't throw up. My head's spinning. Everything hurts.

* * *

The next thing I know, I'm back at the car. Still no James and Oscar. I almost kick myself when I think to call James on his cellphone. Why has it taken me so long? But then he doesn't answer. It goes to voicemail – I can only just hear it – and then, when I ring back a second time – to leave a message asking where the hell they are – it doesn't even go to voicemail anymore. I just get a weird tone that I don't understand.

I go back to the fence – and there's movement inside now – a guy with a flashlight. A truck, so I know it's not James and Oscar. Then the lights come on. All inside the compound, in the buildings. An alarm starts blaring out. I can see the site of the explosion more clearly now. It doesn't look big, not as big as it looked when it happened. Not as big as it felt, close up.

I go back to the car. Still no sign of them. Could they have been *captured*? By the security guards? And if so, what should I do? There's no point waiting here. I'll just get caught as well. But if they have been caught, then I'll have to give myself up too. Or should I?

I'm cold. I'm tired. I'm shaking. Maybe I'm in shock. Definitely I'm in shock. But I can't just stand here, out in the snow, waiting until the police pick me up. I try James' phone again. I still get the same strange tone, but this time I wait longer, and a woman's voice comes on – the sort you get from the telephone company – telling me that number isn't valid. Isn't recognized. I check the screen of my phone. I didn't type it in, I just used the number dialed. It *can't* have changed.

I know I have to leave. The place is lit up like a football stadium, and there will be police coming. A man died. And I was right there. I don't know what this means. But I get in the car, and I start the engine, and then the noise of it freaks me out, even though I still can't hear it properly, I can feel it, vibrating my head, and I know that other people will be able to hear it, and I might as well be advertising where I am. So then I start moving, keeping the headlights off. Four hundred meters down the road, I turn them on, because otherwise I'm going to wipe out into a tree. Then I drive further away. Two miles down the road, a trio of police cars come toward me, their beacons flashing red and blue against the snow of the road surface. They scream past me, one after the other, and even though I can't make myself not look across at them, no one from inside the cop cars pays me any attention.

Somehow, without really even meaning to, I get away.

CHAPTER FORTY-SEVEN

I drive home. I don't mean to, but there's nothing else I can do. Nowhere else I can go. And this time I don't bother about trying to hide, I just drive up to the house, expecting to see Dad's truck on the drive, and the lights on – but it's late, so the house is dark. And then I realize Dad's truck isn't here after all. He must be staying over with his girlfriend.

When I realize I'm still on my own, I want to cry.

I go inside, and put the heating on, because I'm seriously cold. I look on Dad's computer, for news reports about what's happened, but there aren't any, not yet. I make coffee, and then don't drink it. I pace up and down. It truly feels that none of this is real, but then why is my hand shaking so much? Why, when I look outside, is there a rental car – taken out in the name of *Hans Hass*?

* * *

I force myself to drink the coffee, and tell myself I have to make sense of this. And slowly I do. There's been an explosion at the site. The chances of it happening when I was in there are incredibly slim, because I wasn't doing anything to trigger one – but there's no other explanation. An industrial accident. And when it happened, James and Oscar must have thought I was caught in it, maybe they even thought I was killed. *I* had the keys to the car in my pocket, which is why they didn't go back there – they thought it was useless to them, so they tried to escape on foot. Or maybe they were caught by the security guards, I can't really make sense of it.

I try to work out what to do. Coming here was smart. James and Oscar were here with me, earlier in the day, so they might come here, if they think I'm still alive, so I should stay here, stay awake, in case they turn up. They'll be cold.

But that's crazy – they left the car – so they won't think I'm here. They think I was blown up. Maybe they'll be in that bar we waited in. No – that's closed, it's what, four in the morning now. I have a horrible fear about them, stuck out in the snow, all night, but I don't know what to do. I ring James' number again. Still the same dial tone. I don't have a number for Oscar.

Somehow I sleep. I have to. I wake super late – about eleven, and everything comes rushing back to me, and abruptly I'm sick. I just about get to the toilet in time. After that I decide I have to work out a plan. Somehow James and Oscar must have made it. They *must* have. They'll be on the boat, headed back to Boston. I'll do the same. I'll catch the ferry back to college. I'll tidy up here, so that Dad doesn't know I was ever here. And hopefully I'll see James and Oscar on the ferry, and all of this will be OK again. Well not OK exactly, because we've had the incredible misfortune to break into the Fonchem site just when it happened to blow up. But it wasn't our fault, and everyone will see that.

And if they don't. Thank God we were careful, with the false papers and everything.

A half hour later, and the house looks like I left it. I even take the time to put the drone back, and pick off the gaffer tape from the vent holes, so there's nothing to show I was here. Apart from the tire tracks in the snow outside. I suppose Dad might think it was just a delivery, or a sales call, when he sees them, and my footsteps going up to the door and back again. Either way, I can't do anything about them, it would look worse if I tried to rub them out.

I lock up and walk back to the rental car. When I try to start the engine it protests, because of the cold I suppose, but eventually it catches, and I turn around to drive away. I expect to see Dad's truck coming in the opposite direction the whole time I'm driving, away from Littlelea, and out to the Silverlea turning. But I don't.

Then I head north again. Back towards Goldhaven, and the afternoon ferry.

CHAPTER FORTY-EIGHT

I'm here early, the first car in the queue to board the boat. I have to show my ticket at the booth, the man there gives me a strange look, when he sees my name. I notice too, they have a camera pointing at the cars as they come through. I can't avoid it, but I wish I'd thought to put a hat and sunglasses on. I could have taken some from home, if I'd thought of it. I wish I hadn't used a foreign name now too. I should have been David Smith or something, no one would look twice at a name like that.

Then, while I wait to be allowed to board, I walk around, and check all the other vehicles. I have this crazy hope that somehow James and Oscar might have managed to get a car, and that everything will be alright. I walk up and down, and stare inside all the other cars, and some of the other drivers look back, like they're angry at me for staring at them, but I don't care, because none of them are James or Oscar, not even disguised. And it's not even hard to be sure. The sailing is only about a third full, the dock bleak and cold. I run over to the foot passenger waiting area, in case they've somehow managed to walk here, but they're not there.

I go back to my car just before we get called forward. I'm not very comfortable, driving onto the ship, even at the best of times. I don't like the way the metal plates clank under the tires, and it feels like you could easily drive off the side by accident and then the car would sink in the

black, cold water before you'd have a chance to get out. But now it's
worse. There's a finality to it, that suddenly closes in on me, like the steel
hole I'm driving into. I'm *leaving*. I'm getting off the island, leaving
James and Oscar here. And I've no idea what happened to them. I just
left them. I left them in the freezing cold, in the middle of the night, miles
away from anywhere. I killed…

"Hey! Lookout!" I'm shocked back to reality by a bang on the hood of
my car. Then the ferry worker that did it, comes to the side window,
angrily gesticulating for me to roll it down. I do what he says.

"You look where you're going!" He tells me. "Nearly ran into me!"

I mumble an apology. Eventually he grudgingly accepts.

"Over there. Carefully." He points to where he wants me to park the
car. I nod, and roll the window back up. When I get there I sit still for a
few moments, my stomach is cold as a block of ice. I realize I've just
accepted something. Something awful. And something obvious, I
suppose. Something you've probably already worked out, but I haven't,
not till this moment.

James and Oscar are dead. They must be. They would have realized
they couldn't escape in the car, because the keys got blown up with me –
or that's what they thought. And they couldn't stay, because the police
would have caught them, so they tried to get away on foot, on a freezing
night. But they weren't dressed for it. They had no equipment. They
would have got colder and colder, probably they would have thought
they could flag down a car, or find an outbuilding to shelter in, but
there's nothing, up there in the north of Lornea. No one goes there,
there's nothing.

I think of how cold I was, driving back, even with the heater on full.
We were out in the cold for ages. It wouldn't have taken long for the cold
to get to them. They'd have got disorientated. Hypothermic. I've seen
what it does to people, we learned about it in the Surf Lifesaving club.
How it makes people go mad, they think they're hot, they take off their
clothes, and that just kills them faster.

No. That's crazy. I'm just over-tired and stressed. They'll *be* here. On
the boat. Somehow, they'll have found their way, and they'll be on this
ferry. Suddenly I'm in a hurry. I grab my things, and get out the car, and
hurry onto the passenger deck of the boat. I take a seat in the café, by the
window, so I can watch the foot passengers come aboard. I'm just in

time, because they haven't let them on yet, so I can see them lining up and then boarding. There's only a few people. The same ones I saw before.

None of them are James and Oscar.

And then my eyes turn, as if pulled by an invisible wire, to the TV screen, playing in the corner of the café. I hadn't paid it any notice before, but now I can't ignore it. Because it's got my face playing on it. The volume is down but it has subtitles on, delayed from the pictures a bit.

Island police hunt Billy Wheatley over murder of Fonchem Security Guard

I feel my heart rate scream upwards. I feel everyone in the café suddenly staring at me, making the connection. They don't, they ignore me, but I stumble up anyway, knocking over my chair in my rush to get out of there. I don't know where to go, I push open the heavy sea-door, out onto the deck. My mouth's hanging open, my eyes filling with tears at the biting cold wind. They think I'm a *murderer*. But I'm not. I had nothing to do with the explosion. I didn't kill that man.

But… I watch below me, as the last the of the foot passengers climb on, and the ferry workers take the passenger gangway down. I feel the deep throated judder of the ship's huge engines. I look down, at the black, freezing water, where I could hide away from this, where no one would find me. Where this wouldn't be real.

Because I didn't kill that man… but I *did* kill James and Oscar.

PART II

CHAPTER FORTY-NINE

There was no clear moment when Amber Atherton knew that Billy had died, no before and after, only a growing sense of awareness and understanding of what was known, and what was not. But if there *was* one point that served as a divide between the two realities, it was when Billy's father, Sam Wheatley, phoned to invite her to the memorial service.

"I was thinking you might like to," Sam's voice was low as he spoke, he sounded broken, exhausted. "Maybe say a few words. You knew him better than anyone."

Amber clutched the phone tightly in her hand, the only thing she could do to reduce the feeling of vertigo. It was as if just below her there was a spinning black vortex that threatened to swallow her up. This couldn't be real. And yet it was.

"I don't get it," Amber replied. "This still doesn't make sense."

On the other end of the line, Sam was silent for a long while. Then he began again, explaining how every other possibility was now exhausted.

"He's gone Amber. I know it's hard. The police know he got on the ferry that afternoon, and he didn't get off. It only leaves one option." His voice was firmer now, but still filled with pain. Pain that he would live with for the rest of his life. They both would.

"I still don't understand."

"They think he saw the TV news on the boat. They'd issued the appeal for information by then, and there were pictures of him all over it. He'd have known the police were on to him. They believe he thought it was his only way out." Sam continued.

Amber was silent. Feeling the frustration bubble back to the surface.

"But out of *what*? What did he *do*? You're not telling me you believe he killed that guy?"

There was another silence, a long one, before Sam spoke again.

"They have his fingerprints on the bomb parts, Amber. I don't think they'd lie about it. I don't think they *can*."

Amber felt the vertigo again. She remembered the story Billy had told her about when he was a baby, and Sam had been falsely accused of drowning his sister. The police, together with Billy's mother's wealthy family, had joined forces to protect *her*, the real culprit. It showed the police *could* lie. But she didn't bring it up. Why add to his pain? And why would they in this case. It didn't make sense. But then none of it made sense, the whole thing was crazy. Madness. Billy would never make *bombs*.

Or would he?

She said nothing, but thoughts and memories about her friend chased each other around her mind. Billy was... impulsive, careless. He acted according to his own moral compass of what was right and wrong, which had little to do with the actual law. And certainly he was bitterly opposed to the expansion of the chemical plant – he'd pushed for much harder wording on those posters. But it was a giant leap from a poster campaign to a bomb. And why – what would be the point? There was no question that he could build a bomb. That he knew how to do it, and could find the resources. Of course he could. Billy was brilliant like that. He could do it as a lunchtime project.

She wanted to hang up. To somehow turn off this madness. But she knew that wouldn't end anything. The pain, the questions, they would still be there.

"Billy would never blow up a security guard," she said in the end, more firmly than she really believed.

Another pause, and Amber knew that Sam was chasing the same twisted thoughts around his mind as she was.

"I know that. Not deliberately."

* * *

There had been no search and rescue operation. By the time it was thought Billy had gone into the water, too much time had passed. The water temperatures were too cold, and no one knew where he'd entered the water, meaning the potential search area would be far too large. Nevertheless, Billy's father had put to sea, along with almost the entire fleet of fishermen from Holport, and tried to conduct their own search – both as that cold afternoon turned to black night, and from the freezing dawn the next day. But nothing was found, and everyone out looking knew by then it was only a body they were looking for.

In the days that followed, Amber was simply numb. Believing there must be some mistake and waiting for the confirmation. But when the FBI agent came to interview her – a woman, who claimed to have known Billy years before – she told Amber she had been at the ferry port herself. Had directed the search of the ship when it came in, and that there was no possible way he could have gotten off. And yet there was still something she was able to cling onto – one of the agent's questions was whether Billy had made any attempt to contact her, since that day. It proved they too were not 100% sure, at least not at that point. And in the days that followed she sensed – rather than saw – the presence of other agents, waiting outside her apartment, following her to work. Keeping watch. If they were watching her, then they weren't sure. They wanted to be certain he was dead.

But the days flowed rapidly past, and there was no contact with Billy. And either the FBI watchers got better at hiding, or they left her alone. And the slim chance that a mistake had been made seemed to contract further into nothingness. It was winter, cold and bitter. Billy wasn't at home on the island. He wasn't on his father's boat. He wasn't at his college apartment. He wasn't *anywhere*. And though she checked her phone hundreds of times a day, near-panicking if it ever fell below thirty percent battery, for fear she might miss his attempt to contact her. He never did.

A week passed. Then two. Then three weeks. And still nothing. Except the call from Sam.

"You don't have to, if you don't want to." Sam repeated. "Say something I mean – at the memorial service. But please come. I don't know if many will."

CHAPTER FIFTY

In the end the little church was two thirds empty. Almost certainly it would have been fuller, had Billy Wheatley not been painted in the island media as a cold blooded murderer in the weeks before – after all a dead person cannot sue for libel. But perhaps it might not have been much fuller anyway, Billy was not a boy who went out of his way to make friends.

But it was an odd affair, with no casket on show, no body to bury or dispose of. And the subjects of how he died, and the still unresolved mystery of why he decided to bomb the chemical site were both off-limits, by unspoken resolve. Amber had initially rejected Sam's call for her to speak, but as she traveled over on the ferry – the same boat that Billy had apparently jumped from – she changed her mind, and wrote something as she sat in the café, perhaps in the very same seat he had occupied as he discovered the police knew what he had done. She fingered the edge of the paper now, wishing she had had more time to consider what she wrote, had not penned it in such an emotional place, in such a dazed frame of mind. She barely listened to Sam as he spoke, nor to the priest who led the service. But when he said her name they cut through, and she found her legs working on their own, pushing her to her feet.

There was a microphone, a thin metal wire that stuck up from the wood of the pulpit. At first she leaned in, too close to it, and her first words warped and echoed around the little church. She shrank back, shocked, for the first time looked out at the audience. Most of the seats were empty, the ones that weren't were mostly working people – fishermen from Holport, whom Billy had pestered, and grown to know, through asking what they were catching and where, so he could map it on his species charts. There was her own mom and sister of course, poor Grace was taking it worse than anyone. Billy's old science teacher from high school had come. It was he that recommended Billy skip a year and attend college early, that he was getting bored with the too-easy work of high school. Had that decision been the one to condemn him? Or was Billy's downfall all his own doing? The police were there too, sitting at the back, watching. Still watching. Wanting to be quite sure. She turned around, seeing what they were seeing. The backdrop of the church, the little altar. Father Evans standing with his hands folded in front of him, waiting for her. She unfolded her paper, began to cry, and began reading.

* * *

After it was over they went to Sam's house in Littlelea. Some of the fisherman's wives had cooked, and there was far too much food for the dozen or so people who turned up. The whole time Amber kept wanting this to be a mistake. That somehow this still couldn't be real, but the evidence of her eyes and ears couldn't be ignored. And when she knew she wanted to leave it felt somehow disrespectful, that she should stay to the very end, but Sam sensed how she was feeling and suggested to her mother that she take her home. And so Amber left, sitting on the back seat with Gracey, so she could let the little girl rest against her side as they drove away. And when she got back to her childhood home, where her bedroom was still just the way it always was, she cried and cried and cried, until there were no more tears inside her and she felt empty and bereft.

CHAPTER FIFTY-ONE

There was little point in hanging around, so the day after the memorial she booked a place on the ferry back to the mainland. She'd been given compassionate leave by her firm, and had no fixed day when she was expected back, but there seemed no reason to delay it. If anything she preferred the idea of being at work, alongside people who hadn't known Billy and therefore wouldn't be mourning his loss. Let their carelessness and concern for other things rub off onto her.

She took the bus from Newlea to the ferry terminal in Goldhaven, and when it dropped her off she sat, shivering from the cold, in the breezy foot passenger shelter on the harbor side. The ferry was late getting in, she saw it appear on the horizon and slowly grow larger. She remembered the last time she had caught the ferry off the island, that time it had been her and Billy who were late, rushing in with Sam in his truck, and dashing aboard at the last minute. Now she watched the ferry slow as it came through the harbor walls, its great engines churning up sediment from the bottom. It edged closer to the dock, thin mooring lines were thrown ashore, then reeled in by the dock hands, until the much-thicker lines were hauled up. The gangway was hoisted into position, and after a few minutes the departing passengers began trickling out, while the huge bow doors of the boat disgorged cars and trucks. Still she thought of Billy, of what he had said to her, about Fonchem, and their campaign to stop them. Still it nagged at her, the idea that he might do something as radical as bombing it, as stupid. It didn't make sense. None of it made sense.

There was an idea, a thought in her head. It didn't make sense either. Sam would have said something, Billy would have said something, if it were true, if he wasn't gone. *But* – but if there was just a *chance*, then shouldn't she check? Before she went back to her life, before she tried to forget about him and move on? The flow of vehicles leaving the boat eased and stopped, and the reverse happened, new vehicles drove in, ready for the return voyage. The other foot passengers around her were lining up now, ready to go aboard. But Amber wasn't among them. Inertia glued her to the plastic seat as she watched the line shuffle forward, and then disappear altogether, as they went aboard. She was alone now, the last foot passenger in the shelter. She felt like the last person on Earth. An announcement came over the tannoy, the final call for foot passengers to board. Finally, Amber got to her feet. She shouldered her backpack, and walked towards the gangway. But just before she stepped on it she stopped.

"Fuck it." She said, to no one but herself. And she turned around.

CHAPTER FIFTY-TWO

There was a bus back to Newlea, but it wasn't due for a half-hour, and she waited in the desolate shelter until it arrived. The lurid colors of a tourist map stared back at her from the glass of the shelter, printed to help tourists orientate themselves with the island, and decorated with cartoonish images. A pair of children playing on the Silverlea Sands, two more searching for silver at Northend. Cartoon men fished from the pier at Holport, as an oversized, friendly-looking image of the ferry sailed past, white smoke puffing from its funnel. But she didn't look at those. Instead she searched the gaps between the cartoons, between the towns and the places where the visitors flocked. Thinking.

When the bus finally arrived she sat right at the back, even though it was almost empty. She used her cell phone to call her old school friend and near-neighbor, Kelly. Amber had never been popular in school, but her and Kelly had become relatively close, mainly as a result of how they lived in the same street. Amber explained very little about the situation, but begged if she could borrow Kelly's car, just for the day. Luckily Kelly didn't need it that afternoon, and agreed. Amber thanked her, and hung up the call.

A half-hour later, and Amber was walking back into her old street. Grace was at school, and her mother at work, so the house was empty. Even so, she found herself going up the drive. She let herself in, went upstairs and dumped her bag on her bed. But as she left the room she caught sight of herself in the mirror on the wall. She stopped, frowning deeply at her reflection. Then she sat down on her bed and pulled off her boots. She inspected them, one after the other. They looked perfectly normal, and she nearly put them back on. But something stopped her. Instead she yanked open her wardrobe, and fished around in the bottom until she found another pair, an older pair that hadn't made the cut when she was packing to move away to her new life on the mainland. Suppressing the sense that she was actually going crazy, she pulled them on, then threw her newer boots back in their place. Then she considered. If this was worth doing, it was worth doing properly.

She checked quickly around her old bedroom for a second, then dropped back down the stairs and into the kitchen. She rummaged around in the crazy drawer – the place they kept for the little stuff that didn't live anywhere else, and eventually she found what she was looking for, the little metal spike for removing the SIM card from her cell phone. She had to concentrate to use it, but soon she had the little rectangular chip in her hand. She wasn't sure if that was enough, so she found some silver foil, and wrapped it up in that, finally putting it carefully into her purse. Then she thought again, and decided she was satisfied.

She was as vague as she could be with Kelly, saying she just had some things to do before she left the island. Kelly wasn't suspicious at all – they'd each lent their cars before, the island's less than regular bus network tended to encourage such generosity – nevertheless Amber promised to have it back by the evening at the latest, when Kelly had to get to work. And with that she set off.

It would have taken her far longer than one afternoon to search all the island's creeks and coves – the east coast was riddled with cliffs and caves, and the west coast mired with swampy inlets, but Amber had an advantage. There was only one place she needed to check. She didn't really believe she would find anything there, but nevertheless, she wanted to look.

Forty minutes later she turned off the proper road and onto a muddy track. The temperature was warmer now, the snow long gone, and replaced by deep brown puddles, that she had to steer around for fear of leaving Kelly's car sunk up to its axles. As she drove she couldn't help but reflect on the previous times she'd been here. The first, in the back of a panel van, with the kidnappers who had taken her sister. That seemed several lifetimes ago, and was understandably something she had tried to forget. The second, just under a year ago, with Billy, after he'd finally revealed his latest, 'secret' project.

And for once it was actually a cool project, at least as she saw it. It wasn't about rescuing some crustacean population, or counting seagull eggs, but actually something genuinely neat. A few years before the two of them had helped Billy's father set up a whale watching business, and one of the – admittedly fairly major – perks, was they were able to use the boat when it wasn't needed for the business. That boat, the *Blue Lady*, was sadly no more and its replacement, the *Blue Lady II*, was too large and expensive for general leisure use. That had been a particular blow to Billy, who always seemed to have some reason to need to be on the water. And for weeks and weeks she had known he was up to something, Billy and his Dad, behind her back. Eventually they'd let her in on what it was.

She remembered the gleam in Billy's eyes as Sam drove them both here. There were puddles then too, but he threw the truck through them without concern, and they emerged at the end of the lane with muddy water streaming off the sides. But Amber had barely noticed. She'd known exactly what it was she was supposed to be looking at. Bishop's Landing was one of the smallest named places on Lornea Island, and consisted of precisely one small wooden boathouse/workshop, one rickety wooden jetty stretching out into one of the island's innumerable creeks, and the long, lonely lane they had just driven down. There was nothing else, and no other buildings for miles. Except that now there *was* something else. A small wooden yacht sat tied to the end of the pier. A wooden yacht that needed a ton of work.

"What's that?"

"It's my boat." Billy beamed. "She's called *Caroline*."

Amber couldn't help smiling at the thought. Even though it was madness, the boat was about twenty seven foot long, and once upon a time would have been a real beauty. But now the paint was peeling off, what rigging it had hung limp and damaged from blistered spars. Many of the porthole windows were smashed or missing, and the cockpit was covered with black, oily tarpaulin. Seemingly oblivious to this, Billy led the way down the jetty and jumped aboard. The yacht didn't move, its keel was lodged in the mud.

"Where did you get it?"

"She was abandoned. I found the previous owner online, and he said I could have her. For nothing. Isn't that incredible?"

Amber had looked around, it needed so much doing, you'd have to pay most people to take it away. "I guess. But why's it *here*?"

"Well that's why it's a secret. You know how much berthing costs are. We can't afford to keep her anywhere else. But no one knows about this place. No one ever comes here, so it's free, *and* there's a workshop. It's perfect."

She'd looked at the near-wreck again, trying to see it as he clearly was. "Perfect for what?"

The plan, as she'd understood it that day, was that Billy and his dad would come to fix the boat up, as and when they had free time. She'd protested, saying Billy *had* no free time, not with cramming two years of high school into just one year, alongside all his other projects. That it would overtake his other, more important demands on his time. And maybe her lack of faith had offended him a little, because he hadn't mentioned the yacht to her again, and she hadn't asked, assuming it must have been one of the projects that fell from favor and would be quietly forgotten. It wouldn't be the first. So as she drove down now it wasn't with high hopes. She assumed that if the *Caroline* was even still here, it would have simply fallen further into disrepair.

She crested the final rise in the track, as it led up to the flood embankment which cut off the view of the water. She held her breath as she did so. The image that she had in her head – the image that had forced her to turn away from the ferry to the mainland – was of a beautifully restored yacht, bobbing on silvered water, perhaps with a wisp of smoke coming from a new, stainless-steel chimney, indicating that a little wood burning stove warmed a cozy cabin.

The car's tires slipped a little on the gravel as she climbed the embankment, but she revved harder and they bit. And her heart sank. The boat was there, but it looked much the same as it had the previous time she'd seen it. If anything it looked worse, there was more tarpaulin, presumably covering more rotten wood and missing windows. Amber stared at it a long while, the engine still running. Then she turned it off.

There was a sudden silence, that slowly revealed itself to not be silence after all, but a low moan from the wind, and the lonely cawing of some seabird. Billy would have told her what type.

Suddenly she was crying again. What had she really been expecting, coming here? A miracle, that's what. That the police, the FBI, Billy's father – that they could all be wrong, and Billy somehow could be still with her. That the best friend she'd ever had, the boy who she assumed she would love as a brother for her whole life would be here, hiding away and living life the way he always had. But it was nonsense. Of course it wasn't real. The police weren't wrong, the FBI hadn't made a mistake. They saw him onto the ferry, and they saw he didn't get off. Abruptly she got out of the car, needing the cold wind to blow the now sobbing flow of tears from her face. And her feet seemed to take her automatically, down to the head of the jetty, and then out onto its rickety wooden boards. She picked up a rock as she walked, not knowing why but knowing she intended to smash it against the boat, to damn it for having given her false hope. She went right up to the Caroline, raising the rock, wishing she'd taken more of them. Before she threw it she saw that some work had been done. Presumably Billy's dad – it looked well done. She wondered what Sam would do with it now. Would he finish restoring her now Billy was dead and had no use for a boat? What would any of them do?

She didn't attack the boat with the rock. Instead she just let it slip from her fingers, into the muddy water.

The wind hadn't dried her tears, quite the opposite. They flowed, fully, for the first time since she'd learned of Billy's death. Perhaps because this was the first moment she truly believed. Now that she had looked Sam in the face. Now that she had been to his memorial service. Now she had come here, and confirmed he was nowhere. Not hiding out in his secret project but *dead*. Drowned. Gone. How was she supposed to go on? Now that Billy was gone.

"Can you stop crying please?"

The words, which came from nowhere, stopped her dead. She looked around. There was no-one. Not on the jetty, not on the boat. But then the tarpaulin was lifted from underneath, and Billy's head appeared, a look of frustration and irritation on his face. "And whose car is that? Why didn't you come in your mom's car? I was watching for that one."

Amber was speechless. Literally unable to form a single word.

"You better give me your phone. I can scramble the signal, so that no one will know you've come here, but I can only go back half an hour." He came fully out of the tarp now, and into the cockpit, standing up. His hair was scruffy and messed up. He held out his hand.

"*Come on.* They'll be tracking you. I have to be quick to make use of the delay in the data. Make it look as though you're at home."

"You're not dead?" Amber managed. With the back of her hand she swiped tears from her cheeks.

"No. But why did you take so long to come here?" Billy looked irritated again. "And can I have your phone, *please*?"

Automatically she handed it over, and Billy disappeared out of view, pushing the tarp more out of the way, and revealing the steps down into the cabin. He didn't tell her to come aboard, but after a few moments she did so anyway. This time when she stepped onto the wooden deck it tipped a little under her weight. *Caroline* was afloat this time.

She lifted the tarp, and looked underneath properly. And then gasped. The inside of the yacht, which had been a mess of twisted electrical wires, warped wood and mildew, with an inch of oily water sloshing over the floor, was now entirely different. Now it looked polished and beautiful, almost completely restored. But the way it was set up was nothing like any yacht she'd been in before, instead it more resembled a high-tech control room, perhaps like the interior of one of those vans you see on movies, used for running a hostage situation or secretly monitoring a gang of mobsters. There were three computer screens set up on the saloon table, each of them apparently running some program or another. Billy himself sat in front of them, Amber's phone in his hands and a puzzled look on his face.

"Where's your SIM card?"

"I took it out."

"Oh."

"Will that work? Can they track it when it's out?"

"They shouldn't be able to. But you should wrap it in silver foil. Just in case."

Amber looked in her purse, and after a moment pulled out the SIM card, which she had previously wrapped in silver foil. She held it up to show him.

"Thanks." Billy took it off her, and unwrapped it. Then he slotted it into a machine she recognized. He'd shown her it before, it was an external SIM card reader. She couldn't remember exactly why he had it. Then he turned to one of the laptops, which was connected by cable to the reader. A moment later he looked up.

"You took it out at your house?"

"Uh huh."

"That's quite clever." He extracted the SIM and wrapped it up in the foil again. Then he took it, and the phone and opened a small microwave oven that took up most of the space in the galley. He put them inside and closed the door.

"I changed my boots too. In case they were bugged."

Billy frowned at this, as if it wasn't something he'd considered. Or at least, that's how Amber took it.

"You didn't say whose car that is. It's probably OK, because I can see you weren't followed. I was watching you come down the lane." He tapped a couple of keys, and one of the screens switched to show two camera feeds from the road she'd just driven down. Amber glanced at them, but didn't really look.

"But you should still move it. Park it behind the boatshed."

Amber ignored him. Instead she stared around at the incredible interior of the little yacht, that was no longer a wreck, and at her friend who was supposed to be dead.

"Billy, what the hell is going on?"

CHAPTER FIFTY-THREE

He wouldn't tell her. He wouldn't answer any questions until she had gone back to the car, moved it behind the wooden boatshed where it wouldn't be seen by anyone who happened to come down the lane. When she got back, she found he'd put a kettle on the gimballed stove, and was preparing coffee.

"Billy, you have to tell me what's going on. I thought you were dead," Amber said, as she sat down.

"Is the tarp fully over?" he replied.

"Yes. And the car's moved and there's no one around for miles, and by the looks of it you'll be able to track it if anyone comes close and presumably launch missiles at them." She answered. "Now tell me what the hell's going on. I actually thought you'd killed yourself."

"No you didn't." Billy answered at once, as he measured three level spoons of coffee powder into the French press, and carefully folded the packet back up, then wrapped a rubber band around it, and put it back into the wooden locker.

"What?"

"You didn't *actually* think I was dead. If you did you wouldn't be here. And you wouldn't have done that to your cell." He turned to look at her. "I'm actually a bit annoyed it's taken you so long to come here."

Amber's mouth formed a word of protest, but it wouldn't come out. She dropped it.

"Why didn't you just *tell* me?"

"How?"

"I don't know. Called me. Sent me an email. Something."

"I couldn't. Any of those things and they'd have known. They're watching you, and Dad, and me, or at least all my old accounts, which is all they think is left of me. I did think about sending you a coded message, but the FBI have people who are way smarter than you are. They'd have cracked the code before you would. Then they'd have known I was alive and before too long they'd have found this place. And I can't let that happen. Not until I have enough evidence."

"Well thanks." Amber said.

Billy turned to look at her quizzically, then turned back to the coffee.

"Hang on." Amber stopped him. "Slow down. I don't understand."

"I know." Billy frowned. "That's why I'm making coffee. I need to explain it all."

He poured two cups and handed one to Amber, who sat down. It *was* warm and cozy in the cabin, despite the computers everywhere.

"What is all this?" she began, casting her eyes around.

"It's all old stuff. From the loft. Dad brought it down."

"Your dad? So he knows? That you're alive?"

"Of course he does."

"But... But he's just held a *memorial*. For your death."

"I know. I told you. We have to make it look like I really am dead, or they'll find me."

Amber paused to take a sip of the coffee. It tasted bitter and harsh, but she appreciated the hit it gave her. For a second she smiled, wondering if she should pinch herself, but knowing there was no need. This was too weird to be a dream. Billy was alive!

"Who's going to find you? Who's watching you?"

"The FBI. If it had just been a normal murder it would be left to the island police, but because it was a bomb, it's classed as domestic terrorism, and that's a federal offense."

The casual way he talked about it reminded Amber what he'd been accused of doing, something she'd succeeded only in suppressing, because it was too awful to think about. But now, here, she knew it had to be faced.

"The bombing... Billy... did you..? I mean..."

"Did I *do it*? Of course I didn't. What do you take me for? It was James and Oscar. You remember them."

Amber stared at him. It took her more than a few moments to place the names. "Those two rich assholes you were hanging about with? At the restaurant? *Why*? I don't understand." A memory floated in her mind. Saying the exact same words to Billy's father, a few days earlier.

"Billy, you need to explain."

"I am explaining, you keep interrupting me!" Billy paused to take a sip of his coffee. "Say, you didn't bring any food did you? I have to ration everything I have, Dad can't come too often or he might be noticed."

Amber considered answering, but decided against it. Instead she tried to work out what she needed to understand most to make sense of all this.

"Why were your fingerprints on the bomb that killed that security guard?"

Billy's lips thinned, and his brow furrowed before he answered. "Well they weren't really. But I suppose I was tricked."

"What does that mean?" Amber shrugged helplessly. "What does that even..."

"They weren't on the *actual* bomb, just the outer casing. They used a pressure cooker. They're quite good for bombs because they initially contain the explosion, just for a few microseconds, but then they fail and it magnifies the forces. Sort of like a lens."

Amber waited until it seemed he was done. "And your fingerprints?"

"Oh. I touched it. James and Oscar invited me to dinner, in James' dorm room, and they cooked with a pressure cooker. I thought it was weird at the time, but I didn't figure out why. They made me pick it up, and I guess they must have been super careful to not touch it themselves. Then they put the bomb inside, so mine were the only prints."

"OK." Amber said slowly. "Why?"

"I don't know. I'm trying to find out." Billy went back to his computers, typing something quickly.

"But *you* planted it?" Amber went on. "The FBI agent, she said they know you were there? You made a fake identity to rent a car? You booked the ferry?"

"Hmmm. Yes. Sort of."

"So you were there? You set the bomb?"

"No. I told you. I didn't know there was a bomb. When the explosion happened I thought there must have been an accident on the site."

"But what were you doing there?"

This time Billy took a deep breath and told her, explaining about the plan to fly the drone above the Fonchem site, to use an infrared camera to identify the supposed leak, and then to send the evidence to the island's TV and newspapers, influencing the public meeting to decide on the site's expansion. Amber listened, asking questions where Billy was hazy or skipped on the details, which was often.

"But what did that have to with James and Oscar? I didn't think they even liked you. It certainly didn't look like you liked them?"

"I didn't. They didn't. But I thought they were OK for a while. Like I say, they tricked me. I think it's to do with Lily."

"Lily?"

"You remember her…"

"The rich bitch?"

Billy turned sharply. "She's not a rich bitch."

Amber caught the change in his tone, but decided she would worry about that later.

"Whatever. What does she have to do with it?"

"Nothing. Nothing at all. At least I don't think so. It's just when I started going out with her, James got jealous and that's when he planned to set me up."

"Did I just hear that right?" Amber stopped him. "Did you just say you started going out with the rich bitch?"

"She's not…"

"OK. Alright, alright. But still. How the hell did that happen? She's like…"

"What?"

Amber didn't reply, so Billy pressed her.

"She's like *what*?"

"I don't know." Amber looked away.

"Are you saying I'm not good enough for her?"

"Fuck no." Amber's head snapped back around. "She's not good enough for you. But even so, you'd expect someone like that to date a certain type. And it's not you."

The tension in Billy seemed to ease a little.

"Look, when you say going out with – what are we talking here? Did you..?" Amber's voice faded out, and when Billy just stared back, his forehead still creased and dark, she just asked him outright.

"Were you sleeping with her?"

After a pause, he nodded.

"Christ Billy. And she was going out with James, he's the good looking, arrogant one?"

"I don't think he's good looking."

Amber let it go. Trying to recap in her mind. It still didn't make sense.

"But the FBI agent told me they thought this bombing was just the latest in a series, that went back before you even went to college. That's before you even met this *Lily*, so that couldn't have been about framing you. Why were they doing it?"

"I don't know. I'm trying to find out, but there's a lot that doesn't make sense. That's why I'm pleased you're here. At last."

Amber picked up her coffee, only to discover it was cold. She had no idea how long they'd been talking. She put it down, and Billy saw the problem. He picked it up and took it to the little microwave. He took out the phone and SIM card and heated up the coffee. While Amber was waiting she got up and stretched, her fingers easily touching the roof of the cabin as she reached upwards.

"How did you get here?" she asked, when he set the coffee back in front of her. "Everyone thinks you're dead because you got on the ferry but didn't get off. Did you jump in?"

"No. It was freezing. I'd have died for sure."

"Then how did you..."

"I was freaked out. I had a feeling there was something odd going on, when we were waiting to test out the drone, and I'd already decided I wasn't going to have anything more to do with James and Oscar. There was something not right with them. But I had no idea what was really going on." Billy paused. He got up and went to a cupboard, and pulled out a packet of cookies. "I was kind of saving these for a special occasion. But I guess this kinda counts." He offered them to Amber.

Amber waved them away. "Go on." But she had to wait until Billy had taken and bitten into one of the cookies. When he continued the explanation there were crumbs falling from his lips.

"When the explosion happened I went to look. I saw someone had died, I could tell he was security from the bits of jacket, and it was obvious there was nothing I could do to help. I was pretty scared, I thought there might be another explosion, that the site was blowing up. And I thought we'd get blamed, even though we had nothing to do with it." He took a deep breath, then pulled a second cookie from the packet. "Are you sure you don't want one?"

"I'm sure. Go on."

"OK. I went back to where we'd parked the car. I thought I'd find James and Oscar there, waiting for me. But I didn't find them. I waited ages. I went looking for them. So then I figured they must have thought I died in the blast, and since I had the car keys on me, they must have tried to escape on foot. In the middle of the night, when it was freezing cold."

Amber didn't see how this connected to her original question, but she didn't interrupt. Billy's answers had a way of getting there via routes she never expected.

"I drove back home, to Littlelea. I thought they might find their way there, even though it's miles away. But they didn't, I waited the whole night, and the next morning. And then I went to get the ferry – we all had return tickets. I prayed I'd find them there, alive. But when I got to Goldhaven I looked all over the port, and I couldn't see them anywhere. When I got on board the boat I looked all over there too, but I couldn't find them." He stopped.

"And?"

"And I couldn't leave. I felt like I'd abandoned them. I saw my face on the TV in the cafe, and I didn't know *what* was going on. I thought they were probably dead but I had to try to find them. I ran back down to the car deck to drive off the boat, but the car was totally boxed in by then, there was no way I could get it out. So instead I just ran off the boat, just before they closed the bow doors."

"No one saw you leave?"

"I guess not. I wasn't even trying to avoid the ferry workers, but they were all up the other end of the ship, so no one noticed me. But then I was stuck. I went into the terminal to see if I could rent another car, but they had a TV playing and that had my face on too, and then I saw the police saying the explosion was from a bomb made out of a pressure cooker. Then I was completely freaked out. I just didn't know what to do. What it all meant."

"What did you do?" Amber asked after a moment.

"Well I realized I wasn't going to rent a car anymore. And I worked out I didn't need to search for James and Oscar. That somehow they planned the whole thing."

CHAPTER FIFTY-FOUR

"How did you get here, it's miles?"

"Oh that was quite fun, actually."

"What?" Amber stared incredulously. Then she shook her head and grabbed a cookie. She took a bite. "Go on."

"Well, I knew that coming here was the best thing I could do. Dad had finished most of the inside by then, and he'd started sleeping over, so there were blankets, and some food. But I didn't have any transport, and like you say, it would take miles to walk, and someone might see me."

"So what did you do?"

"You know the boatshed in Goldhaven? Past the old ferry dock?"

Amber raised her eyebrows. "No."

"Oh, well there's a boatshed there, and there's a few old kayaks and things stored there. I took one of those."

"I thought you said the water was freezing cold."

"I did, but I wasn't going to get wet. It was calm and still, and paddling for seven hours made me pretty warm."

Amber sighed. "OK, so you stole a kayak and paddled here. What did you do then?"

"I didn't steal it, I borrowed it. Dad took it back, the owner will never know I used it."

"Alright, you *borrowed* a kayak. What then?"

"I did the only thing I could do. I just waited. I figured either you or Dad would come and find me soon enough. Dad had to wait four days before the police weren't parked outside the house. I'd pretty much run out of food by then."

Amber looked around, at the computers set up. One of the screen was still showing the camera feeds from the lane she'd driven down.

"And all this?"

"I told you. I got Dad to bring all my old computer gear. I needed to protect myself in case the police come looking."

"But you can't... I mean you can't just stay here. Why can't you *go* to the police? Tell them it was James and Oscar who did it. Tell them about this pressure cooker?"

"It's not the police, it's the FBI," Billy reminded her, and she glared at him.

"OK. I can't. Not until I have evidence. I don't really know why James and Oscar framed me, but they obviously expected me to blame them. They're ready for it. And they've been clever."

Amber shook her head in confusion. "How?"

"Look at this." Billy grabbed one of his laptops, and spent a few moments opening a saved webpage. "This is from James' Facebook page. He posted it on the night we broke into the compound. It must have been planned out in advance."

Amber looked at the screen, which showed a series of photographs posted to James' account, with the caption: *Chilling at home*. There were three of them in the images, James, Oscar and the other girl – Billy reminded Amber she was called Jennifer. They were sitting on a sofa, watching a movie and eating potato chips.

"I've checked the metadata for the images, if that's what you're thinking," Billy looked morose. "They changed it, so it has the right date and time for that night. Of course it's not difficult to change the metadata, you just program the camera with the date and time you want it to imprint on the images. But even so, there's three of them that will claim they were in Boston when it happened. Plus James and Oscar left their phones there, so their cell records will look right too. Like I said, they were clever."

"You've still got to try! You've still got to tell them. You've got to put your side of it."

Billy took a while answering. "I keep wanting to. But think about it. What's actually going to happen? That bomb killed the security guard, and I'm the only person linked to it. That's *murder*, as well as domestic terrorism. In fact, I researched it, and because of how it happened they'll class it as aggravated murder. The sentence is life without parole. Plus they'll think I faked my own death to escape, which is going to make me look even more guilty. And I don't have any proof that James and Oscar were ever here, while they've got loads of proof they weren't. If I go to the police now, I'll go to prison, and I'll never get out."

"But you can't just sit here forever, pretending to be dead." Amber's happiness at finding Billy alive was slowly being replaced by a frustrated understanding of just how much trouble he was in. She remembered her interview with the FBI, the woman agent had seemed calm and decent, but there was no doubt she was serious. Of course they would prosecute him. They had plenty of evidence. In their minds he was guilty.

"The FBI agent knew you, by the way."

"What?" Billy frowned, surprised for the first time in the conversation.

"She met you, when you got involved with that case with Olivia Curran. Years ago. She said you were eleven the last time she saw you."

"I didn't meet any FBI agents on that case. What was her name?"

Amber searched her mind. "I don't remember. West. Agent West."

"*Jessica West?* Detective Jessica West? She was with the police, not the FBI?"

Amber shrugged. "I guess she changed. Anyway, she knew you. I just thought I'd tell you."

Billy frowned but didn't reply.

"So what are you going to do?" Amber said again, a while later. "You can't just wait here forever." She was feeling the pressure now, she had to get the car back to Kelly. She had to explain to her mom why she was still on the island. But her own issues paled to nothing when she held them up against Billy's.

"I'm not quite waiting here forever. I was waiting for you, because I've got a sort of plan."

There was a change in his voice, and Amber snapped to attention.

"What plan? What can I do?"

Billy didn't answer her, but instead got up again and walked to the fore cabin, she saw inside it was still a mess of cardboard boxes and sails. He picked up one box and brought it back. He opened it in front of her. She recognized some of the contents.

"Oh no. Not this again."

CHAPTER FIFTY-FIVE

Years before, when she had first met Billy the two of them had started a detective agency. For her part, Amber was simply bored with her life, and wanted to capitalize on the notoriety that Billy had already established with his involvement in the Olivia Curran case. And it was kids' stuff, barely serious – although once they managed to attract one client, a rich, batshit-crazy old woman, the attraction of getting some of her money had kept Amber interested. One result of the madness that followed was that Billy had developed an obsession with collecting all sorts of spy gear. He had listening devices, covert trackers, and a pile of software on memory sticks and CDs that she didn't understand at all. And while it had seemed cool to her for a while, she'd quickly lost interest. She knew that Billy probably hadn't, but it was a couple of years since she'd seen any of it, but now here it all was, piled up in the box.

"What's this?"

"It's my old kit I kept. Back from when we had the detective agency."

"I know that. I mean what do you want to do with it?"

Billy didn't answer at first. He pulled out what looked like a cellphone charger from the box, but one which, Amber knew, would also secretly record and transmit audio from wherever it was plugged in.

"Ideally I'd get you to buy some new ones. These are a bit old now." Billy went on. "But they should still work."

Amber didn't reply, and Billy went through how they operated, showing her one cell phone charging device that secretly listened in to conversations, and another that was able to actually record video.

"But what do you want me to do with this?" Amber interrupted him.

"Lily's got this house. In Boston. I need you to find a way to get inside, and set all this stuff up."

Amber was silent for a few seconds. "Why? You said it wasn't her that did it."

"I know. But she's back with James. So he'll be there. And he might say something incriminating. If he does, I need to record it, and take it to the FBI. That way they might believe me."

"Why would he say something incriminating? Does she know about it?" Amber asked, but Billy shook his head.

"He might say something though. They must talk about it, and it might give us a clue as to what this is all about. Something we can focus on. Of course it would be better to set up it all up in James' rooms, but I can't think how you'd get in there, plus Oscar might find it. He's very suspicious."

"Well how am I supposed to get into her place?"

"Just go round there. Say you need to speak to her. Say you're feeling sad about me dying or something, and heard that we were together. She might be feeling sad too." From the look on his face Amber realized that Billy really needed this to be true.

"But how do I..." she waved a hand over the box of electrical covert gadgets. "How do I install it? What do I do?"

At once Billy seemed happier again. He showed her what to do. How the phone-charger devices were the easiest, you just had to plug them in, they were pre-programmed to record and transmit, whenever they picked up sound, and you could even dial into them remotely. They drew power directly from the mains. But that wasn't all Billy wanted.

"The hardest thing is this, but it's also the most important." He held up a USB stick.

"What is it?"

"It's really good. You need to install it on her laptop, and it will let me see everything she's done, plus I can get more audio, wherever she takes the laptop. But..." he hesitated a second.

"But what?"

"Well, you need to be careful. She doesn't have the quickest laptop, so it'll take about two minutes to install, and while it's running, it'll be visible what you're doing. So you need to make sure she doesn't see what you're doing while it's installing."

After that he pulled out another box, this time one from a store and in it was a new cell phone. Billy explained it was a pre-paid cell that wasn't tied to anyone. In theory they should be able to use it without danger of it being tracked, though to be on the safe side he'd installed peer-to-peer encryption, whatever the hell that was. But there was one more thing, something that he didn't seem to have prepared. Billy asked her to buy him a new computer. He scrawled down a list of specifications, telling her to have it delivered to the Silverlea Surf Lifesaving Club, where his Dad could pick it up and deliver it to him, in case the FBI were monitoring her purchases.

It was only when she was driving away that the weight of it all hit her. She'd driven there, a tiny bit of her wondering if there was some mistake, but mostly needing to be sure, to allow herself to truly begin to grieve. She was leaving with her world blown apart, having agreed to a crazy plan that she didn't understand, and seemed utterly futile. Yet with no idea what else to do.

Back at home – her old home at least – her mom was surprised to see her, but Amber explained how she's failed to get on the ferry, and instead needed time to think, to get used to the fact that Billy was gone. It wasn't hard to keep her face downbeat and somber, as if he really was dead. The truth was he might not be dead, but he was truly in a heap of trouble, and there seemed little chance of him getting out of it. Worse, if she really was going to do what he asked, then surely she would be guilty of aiding and abetting a felon. She didn't know what the penalty for that was, nor did she care to look it up.

Instead, when she was in her room, late that night, she typed in the specifications for the computer Billy had asked for. And then, after a few moment's shock, she called him on the burner phone.

"What is it? Have you done it already?"

"No! I've just seen how much this computer costs."

"Oh. Right. Yeah, it's the cheapest I could find."

"It's seven thousand dollars. For a computer."

"I know. But you've got your savings, after Dad bought us back out of the business."

"I know I do. But I only have seven thousand dollars left."

"That's why I choose that computer. I could really do with a slightly better one, but I can boost that one with bits I have here..."

"Billy! It's seven thousand dollars. Do you really need a computer that powerful?"

There was a silence, and she could imagine him, sitting there, surrounded by nothing but marshland, a little bubble of tech, protecting him from the full weight of the Government's justice machine. She didn't understand it, but she realized he was pitifully out-gunned.

"OK. I'll get it."

"Make sure you send it to the Silverlea Surf Lifesaving Club. You've done work for them before, so it won't look suspicious."

Amber nodded, and then told him she would do it now. Then there was a moment's silence.

"Thanks Amber," Billy broke it after a while. "Thank you for believing in me."

Then the line went dead.

CHAPTER FIFTY-SIX

There were four long hours on the ferry the next day to think about it. Five if you included the bus there and the wait to board. Amber used them to try to make sense of what she was doing.

There was no doubt she believed Billy. At least, she believed he hadn't been behind the bombings. She wasn't beyond imagining that he could have been involved in some kind of campaign against Fonchem – the fact that he agreed to fly his drone over the site demonstrated that. But a bombing was a million miles further than he would ever go. There was no way. Whether or not James and Oscar really were the guilty parties though – she only had his word on it, and she knew he'd been wrong before, maybe on more times than he'd been right. At the same time, inviting him to dinner, and using a pressure cooker, which they encouraged him to touch – well that was just weird and too much of a coincidence given how one was used to house the bomb. Plus of course they had traveled with him to Lornea, at least if Billy was telling the truth. But she had no idea why they had attacked the site – and while it was possible the final attack had been to frame Billy, that couldn't have been the reason behind the earlier bombings. So what did all that mean? Billy seemed to have no answers for those questions. He didn't even seem that interested.

Was it possible they would talk about what it was all about in Lily's house? Might they incriminate themselves? Possible, she supposed, but it seemed crazy unlikely.

But should she get involved? Was she really going to risk her own future to do something that seemed incredibly unlikely to even help? What if she got caught? What if this Lily bitch saw her plugging in the listening devices, or fiddling with her laptop – assuming she could even get in the house, or even find the laptop? Would she call the police – the FBI? And what would they do? Amber didn't like to think about that, so instead she focused on the more immediate problem of how she was supposed to do it. All she had was an address for where Lily lived, and Billy's insistence that she had to put the devices in the kitchen, where Lily charged her cell, and where she spent most of the time.

* * *

She went the very next day, taking the metro, with the listening devices hidden in her purse. She walked up and down the street where Lily lived twice before daring to walk up the path. On top of her nerves she couldn't quite believe the size of the place, a huge house, right on the waterfront. But that was exactly what Billy had described. It was early evening. Amber hoped that Lily would be alone, she probably had only one shot at this.

Amber hadn't been sure if Lily would remember her, and it seemed for a moment she didn't. She opened the door and frowned, the lines in her forehead creasing. Amber noticed the slight shadows under her eyes. She looked less perfect than before.

"Yes?"

"Hello Lily."

Lily suddenly made the connection, but obviously struggled with the name, so Amber told her.

"It's Amber. I'm Billy's friend."

"Yes, I remember."

"I wonder if I could speak to you. Just for a moment."

Lily looked uncertain, and for a second Amber thought she might close the door in her face, but she didn't. Amber pressed on. "Please. It's… I wouldn't have come if it wasn't important."

Amber had more words ready in her mind, justifying their need to speak, and her need to come inside to do so, but she didn't need them. Lily stepped back from the door, allowing Amber to walk inside. It was even more impressive in the giant hallway than outside.

"Come through. But I don't have long."

Amber followed Lily through the house to an enormous and beautiful kitchen. She tried to make sense of it as quickly as she could. Apparently Lily had been in here, working on her laptop, since it stood open on the counter-top of a breakfast bar that overlooked the garden and the river. There was an open bottle of white wine next to it. Lily pressed the lid of the computer down, then indicated a chair at a table, on the other side of the room. She also picked up the bottle.

"Can I get you a drink?"

Amber said nothing, but smiled her thanks, while Lily poured a second glass. She stopped when it was less than a third full.

"Please, sit down." Lily handed her the glass, "you heard about us then?" Her voice was flat and dulled.

"Yes. Billy told me. Before he…" Amber let the end of the sentence drift away. Now she was here she feared if she used the word *dead* her voice would give away that it wasn't true. But it seemed Lily had fewer qualms about describing it.

"Before he killed himself?"

Amber took a moment. She nodded again.

"So what do you want to talk about?"

"I just thought we should talk. To make sense of everything. To understand."

Lily didn't reply, and Amber took a sip of the glass. There really wasn't very much wine in it, and she sensed that when it was gone then so was her time here.

"I went to Billy's memorial service, a couple of days ago. I just – I thought you should know."

Lily did answer this time. "I knew about it. I guess a part of me thought I should go. But after what he did – to that man, to my family. Well I couldn't."

"Do you really believe he did it?" Amber couldn't stop herself from asking.

"Don't you?" Lily looked at her sharply, surprise in her voice. Amber reminded herself this wasn't why she was here. But still she went on.

"It just seems totally unlike him."

"The FBI don't have any doubts. They say Billy perfectly fitted their profile."

Amber didn't answer, but used the pause to check the room, searching for ideas.

"You have an incredible house," Amber said, partly to cover for her glancing around, but also because it was true. Yet Lily simply gave an automatic response, an uncaring thanks. Amber took a sip of her wine, feeling Lily's eyes on her again. Watching her, much more suspicious than she had anticipated. This might not work. This might be impossible.

"You said he hurt your family," she said. "It would help me, if I could understand."

Lily took a long time to answer, a hurtful look on her face. "It's none of your business, but the bombings that Billy was doing drove down the share price on my family's company. So much so that a hostile takeover bid was launched. We could lose everything."

"I'm sorry." Amber said.

"Yes. Well. I'm not even sure if he didn't target me only because of who I am. Another attempt to attack my family's company. I don't know if he ever felt anything for me personally."

"I understand you've got back together with your old boyfriend? James – you were with him when we met before."

"That's none of your business."

There was silence.

"Was there anything else? As I said, I don't have much time."

Amber hadn't even finished her wine, and she felt herself begin to panic. She glanced again at the laptop. She only needed two minutes. She thought fast. Had she misjudged with her timings? *Where the hell was he?*

"He didn't say anything to you? About what he was doing?"

This question seemed to surprise Lily, and she turned away, thinking before answering. A hope flared for a moment in Amber. It wasn't a real chance, not with Lily still in the room, but she only had to keep her talking. Surely it would only be a few more minutes.

"No."

"Why do you think he might have done it?"

Lily seemed to be losing her patience fast now. "Look I don't think he meant to kill, if that's what you mean. If that's what you came for." She said. "I think he had some confused, wrong-headed idea about what Fonchem is, and he set out to destroy it, by any means. But he was wrong. Fonchem is a good company. Well run. And maybe Billy didn't care as much as he liked to pretend. Maybe he didn't care if other people got hurt."

Amber nodded awkwardly. Somehow she'd expected to see Lily in some stage of grieving. That didn't seem to be the case.

The doorbell rang, a deep trilling of an old fashioned device, built to last. Lily looked confused, frustrated. Amber looked at her, expectantly, putting pressure on her to answer it.

"I uh," Lily frowned again. "I don't know who that is?"

"Do you want me to go?" Amber offered, gambling that Lily wouldn't want whoever was at the door to see her leaving at the same time.

"No. I'll… Just hold on. I'll be right back." She got up, and left the room.

Amber got to work at once. She moved immediately to the laptop and pulled up the screen. It took a few seconds to wake from its sleep mode – seconds that seemed to take forever. But while they happened Amber already had the USB drive in her fingers, and was ready to slot it in. The computer sounded a soft tone, and was ready to use. She pressed the drive in.

There were more seconds. *Agonizingly* slow. While Amber heard the front door opening. And then a box popped up, just as Billy had described. It was just like installing any other software, you had to launch it, and let the files copy across, shown by a bar that filled the screen. She wasted a few seconds wondering why it wasn't even getting past zero percent, before realizing she had to click OK on the touch pad before it would start.

"*Fuck*", Amber muttered, knowing she'd made the task even harder. But now the bar was filling, and her mind allowed the sounds from the hallway to filter into her consciousness. Lily's voice, confused.

"I didn't order a pizza."

"What do you mean?" A man's voice, annoyed. "It's all paid for."

"Whatever, I don't care. Please just go away."

Shit, this was going to happen much quicker than she'd planned.

When she'd ordered the pizza, asking it to be delivered at precisely six o'clock, she had thought it might take a couple of minutes for Lily to sort out the mistake, perhaps working out which of her neighbors had made the mistake. Now Amber realized this was wildly optimistic.

"It's vegetarian. The lady on the phone was very specific."

"*I don't care.* I don't want it." There was the sound of the front door being firmly closed. Amber looked at the screen. Ten percent done. Not even close. She delayed another second, wondering whether to yank the USB out now, and just abort, and by then it was too late. Lily was already re-entering the room. Amber – up and out of the chair from where Lily had left her – had no choice but to improvise. She grabbed the wine bottle.

"I was just topping myself up. I'm sorry – I hope you don't mind? This has all been so stressful for me." Amber took the bottle back to the table, and before Lily could reply, she refilled her glass. Her hand shook slightly as she did so, but not as part of the subterfuge.

"Of course," Lily said, her voice was cold and hard. Amber stopped herself from asking about the pizza delivery, that would be too conspicuous. She tried as well, to keep her eyes off the laptop computer on the counter top. The screen was still open, the USB device still sticking out of the side, the files still transferring. If Lily glanced at it this would all be over. And in a way that Amber didn't want to see.

"I have to go out though. You can't be here long."

Amber nodded, and put down the bottle. She took a swig from the glass, letting her eyes glance at the screen as she did so. The wine helped. She was at a complete loss what to say next, but to her surprise Lily kept the conversation going.

"I'm sorry. I guess he tricked you too."

Amber felt herself wanting to weep, and since she couldn't think of anything better to say, she let it happen. But it wasn't the sobs that had hit her when she really thought Billy was dead, it was just nervous, awkward shudders that rocked her shoulders. She realized she could see the screen reflected back at her, in the window at the back of the kitchen. The bar looked about three quarters done. Billy had said that once it was installed she wouldn't have to do anything, the software was designed to be secretive and covert, it would begin hiding itself the moment it was installed, including removing any evidence that it had been installed. All she had to do was remove the USB stick, and get out of there.

"Yeah. I guess he did." Amber took another large gulp from her glass. "Look I'm really sorry. I don't know why I'm here. I just thought… Well I knew that you and he were together, for a while."

The bar showed the files were ninety percent transferred. Ninety-five.

Amber stood up, suddenly fearful that as the bar hit one hundred percent, the computer would sound its soft tone again, announcing the installation had been a success. Amber drained the rest of the wine, ready to set the glass down loudly at the same moment. And then she saw what she had to do. The only way to get the device back.

She waited a few more seconds, and then as she went to replace the glass she let her hand flail out and connect with the wine bottle, sweeping it over and onto the floor. There was a loud crash that drowned out any noise the computer might have made.

"Oh -I'm so sorry. I'm so clumsy…"

"Fu…" Lily brought herself under control, but still looked pissed. "It's OK." She turned to grab a cloth, but Amber came with her, and as she passed the laptop she saw the screen had returned to how it had first looked, the software either running or not, she had no way of telling. She let her hand trail along the counter top as she pretended to reach for a cloth, and she slipped the USB out and into the pocket of her jeans.

"I said it's OK." Lily's voice was aggressive now. She'd wadded up some kitchen roll, and was bending over, mopping up the mess.

"I'm sorry. I should go." And with that she made her way to the front door, and with Lily not far behind her, opened it and stepped outside.

She half walked and half ran, until, once she was a few streets away, she pulled out the phone Billy had given her and called him, using the encrypted app.

"You got the software in?"

"I think so. I don't know. "

"No, you did. I'm listening in right now. She's on the phone to James. I've got her whole system. You did great."

* * *

The next stage of the plan was more simple. Billy was able to listen in to Lily's laptop even when it was off – the microphone could record and send the audio just as long at the computer had an internet connection and power. Lily might notice that her battery was running down quicker than usual, but that would likely only prompt her to keep it plugged in. Otherwise, the software was invisible. As a result he was able to call Amber when he knew that James was at her house, though the first two times this happened Amber was at work, and wasn't able to act on it. On the third time, however, she was.

The hardest part was to break into James' apartment. In theory, this was the only difficult part, but Billy had coached her on how to use the lock pick set that he'd owned and practiced on years before. It wasn't difficult, after a bit of practice, to open the transparent practice lock, but it was a different challenge to do the real thing, in a corridor where other students might appear at any moment.

Amber climbed the stairs, wishing she could have Billy on the phone confirming once again that James was still at Lily's house. But he'd only said he would contact her if James left. She got to the door described by Billy and looked left and right. There were four other entrances in sight, but no one visible, so she pulled the pick from her pocket and inserted it into the lock. It was no good, she couldn't stop her hand from shaking, and she had to pull the tool out again to reset. She stood in front of the heavy, wooden door, with the golden circle of metal holding the lock barrel. This was easy, she could do this. But as soon as she lifted her hands again she saw the shake, so instead she went for a walk, up and down the corridor, taking deep breaths to calm her nerves.

Two girls passed her. Giggling and laughing as they went. Neither of them even glanced at her as they passed. Amber waited a few moments and followed them to the stairwell. Watched them down to the ground floor, and out the front door. A lone male came back in, and she flattened herself against the wall – blinking in surprise at how she'd called him a lone *male*. Was she some kind of undercover cop now? He came up one flight of stairs, but then went off into the corridor below her. Amber breathed deeply. She returned to James' front door.

This time she knelt down in front of the door to get a better angle with the tools. The way Billy had shown her, he made it look incredibly easy to use the lock picking tools, but while she had managed to break his transparent padlock in seconds, it was much harder with the real lock she'd practiced on. And she simply hadn't been able to try out her new skills on a standard door lock – there was no door she could practice on without being seen.

But she inserted the tension wrench into the bottom of the lock, and with the same hand applied just a little force. The idea was to take the pressure off the pins that held the lock closed. Then she inserted the pick above the wrench, and began pressing, and twisting and gently lifting, trying to get all of the upper pins to line up, and thus open the lock. She felt the lock's tension reduce – at this point the lock should turn, but when she tried, it was still stuck, and she had to start over. All her focus was on the lock, she simply hoped that no one was going to come and see her here.

The tension reduced again, and this time she was more careful. Slower, but more careful, which was the way Billy had told her to do it. This time she used the tension wrench to turn the cylinder, and – as easy as if it had been the key itself – the lock turned.

Not quite believing what she'd done, Amber pulled the tools out and bundled them quickly into her bag. Then she took a deep breath, and pushed the door open.

Inside James' apartment it was quiet, and dark. He had the drapes closed. She felt an urge to call Billy, and confirm again that he was definitely not there, and that no one else was either, but she resisted it, and instead looked around for where he kept his phone charger. Billy had given her two different options, and there was one in particular he hoped she could use.

She checked the kitchen counter. It was where she charged her cellphone at home, but there was nothing there. Nothing in the living room either, so she stepped into the bedroom. Here, by the side of the bed, she saw the telltale white cable. It was perfect. The body of the charger was hidden away under the bedside table, so he wouldn't even see if it was a slightly different type. And when she pulled it out to check, she didn't even need to worry about that. It looked identical to Billy's charger. She switched them over. And couldn't quite believe she was done. There was an urge, a strong urge to check around the apartment further, to try and find some incriminating evidence.

She went back to the kitchen, pulling open drawers to see what there was. She wondered if maybe there would be a pressure cooker – she could photograph it, maybe even take it away. But no. What was she thinking? What the hell was she doing? She had the charger in place. That was enough.

She slipped out of the front door again, and let the lock close behind her. For a second she was hit by panic when she thought she'd left her bag inside – with the lock picks in it, but then she realized it was hanging on her shoulder. It was just the stress, the nervy excitement of what she'd just done, playing with her head.

She called Billy again when she got home, but he didn't know if it had worked. He needed James to go back, he needed someone to be making noise in the apartment to see if it was being picked up properly. But the next morning Billy called her back. He sounded happy. James hadn't stayed at Lily's, he'd returned to his own apartment around midnight. And he'd plugged in his phone to charge, meaning Billy had been able to access it through the dummy charger and install new software onto it. Now James' cellphone would record every conversation he had, whether using the phone or not, and track his every movement.

Amber still wasn't quite sure how all this was going to help, but Billy was delighted.

CHAPTER FIFTY-SEVEN

A week went by, and Amber went back to her normal life. Or tried to. She had to pretend that nothing had changed. That Billy was dead, and that she was in mourning. Albeit in mourning for a friend who had turned out to be a criminal and a murderer. But even playing that part was difficult. The new friends and colleagues she had met in Boston hadn't ever known Billy, and while they were interested at first in her connection to the young man on the TV news who had bombed the chemical company, the story had no staying power, and so their interest hadn't either. By the time the next weekend rolled around, no one she knew had asked again, no one even seemed to remember.

For Amber of course the situation couldn't be more different. She burned to know what Billy was hearing, and whether he'd picked up anything that demonstrated his innocence, and she phoned him several times to ask for updates. But each time he sounded vague and would only tell that the audio was coming through just fine.

The issue, Amber decided after a while, was that Billy was nervous about saying too much using the pre-paid phones. Although he had installed software that he said was completely safe, he'd also said he couldn't know for sure if the Government had a way of breaking through the encryption – if they had it was a secret, but also the type of thing the Government would *keep* secret. She understood, yet couldn't let it go. She simply wasn't able to get on with her life and compartmentalize what was happening with Billy, to just leave him out there and not even know if he was getting any closer to being able to clear his name. But when she suggested visiting him again – by now she wanted to hear for herself what that Lily bitch and her murderous friends were saying – Billy was heavily against it. He clearly still believed her movements were being watched.

But for as long as they'd known each other, she was the one who understood better what being normal meant. She persuaded him, saying it would be normal – it would look more normal – for a young woman in her position to go home more often in the circumstances she was in. She'd need the support of her family. And from her home it would be easy to go for a drive and end up by the yacht. And so, three weeks after she had discovered Billy alive, she once again boarded the ferry for Lornea Island.

She went through a similar security process before coming to the yacht – changing her clothes and shoes, not taking her normal cellphone at all this time, but leaving it on at her parents' house – in fact she lent it to Gracie, so that it wouldn't stay in one place – which might look suspicious – but instead move about the house. Eventually she got to the head of the muddy lane that led down to Bishop's Landing. She stopped the car here for a long time, but the road behind and in front of her was completely empty, so she made the turn and carefully skirted around the puddles, until she came to the flood embankment at the end.

The weather was improving now, and it put Amber in an upbeat mood, which matched the thought of seeing Billy again, a mood which had grown and expanded during the long wait and journey to get here. But the moment she did see him, her mood began to decline. He looked pretty bad. He *smelled* pretty bad too, as did the inside of the yacht. It had only the most basic of plumbing facilities, a marine toilet which drew water from the surrounding creek and discharged it there too. There was a shower, but it ran from freshwater tanks that had long since been emptied. In a normal situation Billy would have needed to move the boat to a marina or fuel station and top them up, but that wasn't possible.

The outside of the little yacht looked unchanged, though there was now a kayak partially concealed behind the work shed where Amber left the car. But inside the yacht things did look different. The place was a mess. Billy seemed to have dismantled most of the other computers she had seen before, and only the new one, which she had bought him, remained on the saloon table. It was running some program and the lights on the front were flashing on and off all the time. The boat's little sink was filled with dirty dishes.

"Well?" Amber asked as she looked around. They'd only spoken so far for Billy to ask if she had brought any food. She had, two bags of groceries – she'd pretended to be buying them for her mom and sister, although she couldn't bring herself to believe anyone was really watching that closely.

"Well what?"

"Well have you heard anything?"

"Like what?" Billy didn't sound interested. He poked around the groceries.

"Like? Anything that's going to help?"

"Yeah. Maybe." He shrugged in response. "I know it's not me, but I kinda need some vegetables. I think I'm getting scurvy."

"What's that?" Amber asked, looking at the screen on the new computer.

"It's this disease that sailors got on long voyages. Before they invented tinned food. They weren't getting enough vitamin C…"

"Not scurvy. I know what that is. What's *that*. What are you doing?"

He followed where she was looking. "I'm just keeping a record of which audio recordings are coming in and who's present."

"Well? Has anyone been there? Have they said anything about the bombings?"

"No. I don't think they're going to now. If they ever did. They'd be pretty stupid to tell Lily. They'd be pretty stupid to talk about it at all."

"What?" Amber felt her frustration burn. "I thought that's what you were hoping for?"

Billy shrugged, and found a bag of carrots. He pulled one out and inspected it. "Well. I hoped they might. But it was just an idea."

"Maybe I could go around again?" Amber suggested. "To Lily's house. I could say something that forces them to talk about it." She thought fast. "I could tell her that you told me James did it. She'd confront him with it, and you'd record it!"

"Yeah." Billy sounded downbeat. Amber didn't understand.

"Well?"

"Well... You could. But he's just going to deny it isn't he? Remember they didn't *plan* for me to die. They thought I'd be caught, and that I'd tell the cops they did it. They were always expecting to have to deny it. To use the false evidence they made that makes it look like they weren't even there. They're not going to suddenly confess."

"But then... What's all this for then? What's the point? I don't understand."

Billy put down the carrot and pulled out a bag of cookies instead. "I like these," he said. "They're not very good for you, but they do taste nice."

"Billy! What the fuck." She rounded on him, and swiped the cookie from his hand. "You made me bug Lily's computer, you had me break into that guy's apartment. I'm aiding a goddamn fugitive. I could go to jail for that too. Are you telling me the whole thing was for nothing? Why?"

Billy looked at her and at the cookie on the floor. He took a deep breath. Then he sat back down behind the computer.

"Perhaps you'd better see this," he said, as his fingers flew over the keys. She came around behind him to see the screen, and realized he was opening a video file. When it was ready to play the starting image was of Amber, sitting nearly exactly where she was now, inside the yacht's little cabin. But it wasn't taken now, she was wearing different clothes – the ones, in fact, that she'd worn the last time she was there. Billy pressed play, and the image of Amber on the screen started talking. Amber listened, intrigued at first, and then increasingly confused.

"I don't remember saying that." She said, after a minute. "I don't remember *ever* saying that."

"You didn't," Billy replied. But before he could explain further there was the unmistakable sensation of a person stepping onto the yacht, tipping it heavily with their weight. At almost the same time the tarpaulin covering the cockpit was ripped clear. Then a gun was pointed into the cabin.

"Freeze! FBI. DO NOT MOVE!"

CHAPTER FIFTY-EIGHT

The first alarm came from the boy's father. His financial history showed he paid for groceries at the SuperU store on the outskirts of Newlea almost every week, using a bank card. Since the supposed death of his son he either stopped buying food there – or apparently anywhere else either – or he'd started paying cash. The question was, why?

Although by now agent's Black and West were only allowed to allocate fifty percent of their week to the case, they were able to establish roughly how much he was spending, from records of cash withdrawn at two ATMs on the island, in Silverlea and in Newlea. And they were able to compare this with two previous periods – when Billy Wheatley had been living with him, and attending high school, and when Billy had been living on the mainland attending college. Of the three periods, his expenditure was highest now. And yet they had no visibility on how the money was being spent, since it was mostly going out as cash.

Accessing financial records was one thing, the agents needed a separate court order to put a tracker on his truck, and they needed authorization from West's boss in order to apply. He took some convincing, but ultimately seemed as intrigued as they were. The judge waved it through without a second look. No body, therefore, no question the boy *might* have faked his death. The two agents returned to the island to fit the device.

It wasn't the easiest to fit. Sam Wheatley lived in a small house right on the clifftop overlooking the wide stretch of Silverlea Bay. He left the vehicle close by the house, clearly visible from the kitchen and living room windows, where he seemed to spend most of his time when at home. There was no easy place to hide out and wait, so the only option was to come in the night, at three am, and hope the guy wasn't an insomniac. It wouldn't have been a problem if they could have used the micro tracker, that could be installed in moments, but it only had a battery life of about three days. So West wanted to use the much larger version which would last indefinitely, but had to be wired into the truck's battery. And *that* meant jimmying the hood open. Working by flashlight it would take at least five minutes. Five minutes when they could be spotted.

However, she was fortunate to have a partner in Black who loved this side of the job. His father ran a garage, and he and his brothers had grown up around cars. She kept watch while he worked, getting it open in less than twenty seconds, and fitting the wires, then feeding them down so the device itself could be fixed on the truck's underside. A skilled mechanic could now do a full service and wouldn't notice anything was wrong, only an electrical auto engineer might wonder what the additional wires were running from the battery. Better hope he didn't break down.

They tracked Wheatley for a week, charting where he went and how long he stayed, building up a picture. He slept at home most nights, but had a girlfriend in Newlea, a woman they identified to be one Milla Reynolds, a nurse working at Newlea General Hospital. They ran the full electronic works onto her, but if she was sheltering Billy Wheatley at her address, she was keeping quiet about it.

Sam Wheatley *was* buying food though, too much of it, and using cash to buy it. They pulled the CCTV from the store to get an idea what he was buying, and those raised more doubts. There was a lot of pasta, dried stuff. Plus bottles of water. Even more odd, he was buying fuel. They watched him fill up four twenty-liter plastic jerry cans, again paying cash. But then they sat there in the back of his truck for three days, while he drove around. Always the same places – home, Milla's place in Newlea, and the boatyard in Holport where his boat was out of the water being antifouled.

Then he went somewhere else.

By then though, frustratingly, West and Black were off the island, catching up with paperwork in the FBI base in Chelsea, having only been given permission to spend three days over there. They watched Sam Wheatley's movements on the screen of West's computer.

"What's at this Moors' Point then?" Black asked, leaning in for a better look. The tracker recorded its routes overlaid on a Google map, but that had little information on where exactly Wheatley had gone, it was just a blank expanse of green.

"I'll get a map from the map room," West said, pushing back in her chair.

Ten minutes later the two of them pored over an old-fashioned fold-out map. It had far more detail, showing footpaths leading up and down the low cliffs from the small parking area. A sandy bay to the south, and, behind a corner of the island, more marshy area to the north. There were no buildings though, no obvious reason why he'd visit.

"Maybe he was going for a hike?" Black observed. "Guy has just lost his kid after all."

"Yeah. Only we're working on the theory he hasn't lost his kid." West replied. She tapped a finger on the map, near to where it showed the parking area. "What's this mean?"

Black checked the legend. "Viewpoint."

"No, this symbol."

"Oh." Black looked again. "Sea caves."

* * *

The second alarm came a couple weeks later. That was the way the system worked. It was designed to get triggered either by a single highly unusual event, or a combination of smaller, less significant anomalies that together could mean something. The way law enforcement was going, soon the whole damn thing would be automated, at least that's what Black said, sounding like he was himself an old-timer, instead of a young guy just starting out.

The trigger was Amber Atherton, the young woman West and Black had interviewed, and identified as perhaps Wheatley's only friend – certainly his closest friend. She'd traveled back to the island to attend his memorial service, and now she was heading back again, three weeks after that. The odd thing – she hadn't been back once in the six months previous.

She had no car, and even if she had, there wasn't enough to get a court order to put a tracker on it, so they had to do it the old fashioned way, flying back to the island and sitting outside her old house, where her mother and younger sister still lived. Since they had her ferry booking in advance they were able to get there in time to watch her arrive. And after that they didn't have to wait that long.

An hour later she'd walked three doors down, and spent ten minutes inside the house of one of her neighbors. From there she'd taken the car off the drive, and headed north. The two agents followed at a distance, the traffic on the island was light enough there was little danger of losing her.

"You think she's going to this Moors' Point," Black asked, looking again at the map. They were certainly headed in the same direction. West didn't reply. They both knew this road now, having been to Moors Point twice. But there'd been nothing there. Just an empty parking area, and a couple of picnic tables. But they came to the turn off for Moors' Point and kept going.

Finally the car ahead had slowed, and then turned off the road, onto a single lane track. West didn't stop but continued past, only glancing casually as the little car trundling sideways away from them towards the area of marshland.

"What's down there?" she asked, as they swept past.

"Not a lot," Black replied. "A place called Bishop's Landing."

They stopped a few hundred meters further on, and waited for a while, studying the map. The lane led only to one place, and there appeared to be no other turnings. So they returned to the turn off, and this time, West pointed the car down the lane, and drove down slowly. Neither of them talked.

The lane ended with the road rising up to an embankment, designed to protect the low lying land from flooding. Atop it sat a wooden building, some kind of workshop, or boat house. The girl had parked her car behind it, but the two agents exited their vehicle on the lane below, drawing their weapons as they crept forward up the slope. West sniffed, as she led the way, picking up the salty smell of the water, and something else.

"Gasoline."

There was a noise too, not subtle, the clatter of a generator, that was coming from the wooden building. Half way up the slope now, West saw there was something else here – a yacht moored up against a rickety jetty that cut out into the creek. It was covered by a tarp, but a power cord ran from the wooden building, down the other side of the slope and out along the jetty.

They checked the building first, pushing open the unlocked door, and quickly ensuring it was unoccupied. They found the generator, working away, plus the same red plastic jerry cans they'd witnessed Sam Wheatley purchase in the previous weeks. West pointed back outside and at the boat.

"The yacht." She mouthed.

The only way to approach it was along the jetty, and they did so with their weapons readied. They heard the voices from halfway along: two people, one female voice, one male. They seemed to be arguing.

"On my signal," West mouthed, and Black nodded. She prepared to board at the very stern, using the rear wire stays to help her aboard. He was ready at the side, where it was easier but he had a less direct route to aim his weapon into the cabin.

"Two, Three, NOW!" Together they stepped onto the boat, feeling it rock underneath them.

"Freeze. FBI. DO NOT MOVE!" West yelled, her weapon secure in both hands.

CHAPTER FIFTY-NINE

There was a scream – the girl, Atherton, as Black stepped beside her.

"She said don't move." He took over, and this time the two occupants of the yacht did what they were told.

"Hands up where I can see them." Black went on. "Do it now, and slowly. Or I *will* fire." He glanced at West, asking permission to step in front of her into the yacht's cabin. She nodded, checking around them in case there were any other threats they hadn't seen, Wheatley's father, perhaps. But around them was quiet. She followed him down into the yacht's cabin. It was dominated by a large computer sat on the saloon table.

"Very slowly bring your hands behind your back," Black was speaking to the male, and West had no doubts it was Billy Wheatley. Even though she hadn't seen him for years, she'd been looking at plenty of photos. He did exactly as he was told, and her partner cuffed him, but he wasn't looking at Black, his eyes were fixed resolutely onto her. It was almost unsettling. She heard her voice read him his rights.

"Billy Wheatley I'm arresting you under suspicion of the murder of Keith Waterhouse. You have the right to remain silent and refuse to answer questions. Anything you do say may be used against you in a court of law. You have the right to consult an attorney before speaking, and to have an attorney present during questioning now or in the future.

If you cannot afford an attorney, one will be appointed for you before any questioning if you wish. Do you understand?"

While she spoke Black had put cuffs on the Atherton girl as well.

"Hello Jess," Billy replied at last. "I was wondering when you'd come."

* * *

Black stared at West in surprise, but she didn't acknowledge him, instead she offered a smile to Billy, failing in her attempt to stop it looking snarky.

"I thought *you* were dead."

He shrugged. "It's pretty hard to stay dead these days."

She turned to her partner. "Call it in. Get some back-up here. We can take them to the police station at Newlea."

"Before you do, there's something I'd like to show you." Billy interrupted. Everyone in the yacht turned first to him, then when he waited, unmoving, to West.

"What?"

"I have a confession. On video."

West frowned. She couldn't help but remember the person in front of her as a young boy, terrified and charming – in truth he didn't look too different even now. But she knew that, charming as he may be, he was now a serious criminal, who had killed an innocent man. "You want to confess? You can say it now, we can videotape it later on." Both would be admissible.

"No. It's not mine. I didn't do it."

West hesitated, long enough that Black spoke up. "In that case you can tell us at the station. We've got a ton of evidence says you did." He tried to get Billy to move, but Wheatley resisted, and in the small cabin was able to do so against the much stronger man.

"Please Jess, I need to show you here. It's vital."

She hesitated again, fearing a trick. But she looked at the pair of them. The girl looked terrified, and both were handcuffed.

"Check them for weapons. Both of them." She ordered, and she watched and waited while Black did so, keeping her gun ready in case either of them tried anything. They didn't, and neither were armed.

"OK. What do you want to show me?"

Slowly, keeping his eyes on West, but her face rather than the gun, Billy sat down behind the computer. He was able to type, even with the cuffs on, and a few seconds later he pointed to the screen. A video file was ready to play. It showed a still of a young man – she didn't recognize who – sitting in what looked like an interview room in a police station. There was another man opposite him, you could tell he was older, even though only the back of this head was visible. A tape deck sat on the table.

"What is this?" Black asked, then added. "What the hell?"

"Can I?" Billy asked, his hand hovering over the play button.

"Yeah."

He pressed play, and the recording began. The camera must have been fixed somewhere high up on the wall. It didn't move as the older man asked the name of the younger man. He gave it as James Richards.

"You know why you're here?" the older man asked.

"Yes. I want to confess to the murder of Keith Waterhouse, and to all the bombings of the Fonchem Chemical company." The younger man, James Richards, spoke clearly and calmly. Then he scratched his head.

"How did it happen?" There was something familiar to West about the older man's voice, but she couldn't focus on it right now.

"I set up my friend, Billy Wheatley. I made it look like he did it. I set up the whole thing to make him look guilty. But now I want to confess. Billy didn't do anything. I killed that man. I set the bomb."

Up to that point the video tape had looked completely real, but at that moment something odd happened. It seemed to freeze – but only *part* of it. The part of the screen showing the older man, asking the questions, continued to run as normal. And then he turned slightly, so his face was visible for the first time. And then suddenly he spoke again. And the whole thing went totally weird.

"Houston, we have a problem."

"What the *fuck*?" Black said. "Is that *Tom Hanks*?"

CHAPTER SIXTY

"Yeah. I didn't have time to finish that part."

There was silence in the little cabin, so Billy tried explaining again.

"I borrowed the clip from that movie. Apollo 13. I've always liked that movie."

It was clear that no one was following him, though Amber seemed to be the closest to understanding.

"You got him saying that?" She cut in now, apparently forgetting she was under arrest, and moving to Billy's side. "You got him confessing? But where is he? It looks like he's in a police cell."

"More like an interview room," West interrupted now. "What is this Billy? What are you showing us?" Everyone turned to Billy, and he waited a few seconds before trying to explain again.

"It's a confession by James Richards. He and a man called Oscar Magnuson planted the bomb that killed the security guard. They made it look like I did it, to frame me."

"But how did you get this confession?" West went on. "And where is it? And what the hell's that at the end?"

"I didn't get it. I *made* it."

"I don't understand." West said.

"Nor do I," Black added, in case anyone was in doubt.

"That's why I need to explain. Here. Before you take me away, so I can show you?"

The two agents looked at each other, both assessing the risk. Any interview done with a suspect was far better carried out in a controlled environment, but at the same time, it wasn't uncommon for suspects to clam right up once they got to an interview room. Furthermore, this one had just shown them a tape of another guy confessing to the crime they'd just arrested him for. This didn't fit easily into the scenarios they'd been trained on. West nodded.

"OK." Black said. "But the cuffs stay *on*. And you make *one move out of turn* – either of you – and this stops. Whatever the hell it is. We take you away and do this by the book. You got it?"

"Yes." Billy replied. Amber said nothing, her round eyes indicating to West that she was just as confused by this as she was.

Billy began by telling them the whole story. How he'd met James Richards and Oscar Magnuson along with Lily Bellafonte – whose family founded and still held a controlling share in the Fonchem chemical company. And how Richards had approached him regarding the site's planned extension, and Billy's opposition to it.
"You probably saw I was running a campaign against Fonchem," Billy said. "A poster campaign, mostly, about the sea-dragons."

"Yeah. We saw. Go on." Black told him.

He told them about the photographs of the dead sea-dragons that he'd been sent, and the plan to fly the drone over the site to search for the telltale heat signatures of chemical leaks. How they had come to the island, Billy renting a car and booking the ferry under an assumed name. He explained how the drone had not worked properly in the snow, and how he'd discovered James and Oscar had cut a hole in the fence, and how he'd felt pressured to go inside and attempt to find the leak on foot. And then how the next thing he knew there was an explosion, and James and Oscar had disappeared.

The two agents listened, mostly in silence, with occasional questions when Billy skipped past details. He got to the part where he was installed in the boat, knowing the world believed him to be dead.

"Dad was bringing me food, and fuel for the generator, until you bugged his truck."

"You knew about that..? How the...?"

"I have a sweeping device. I told Dad to use it every day. So after that he had to take the fuel to the caves at Moors point, and I kayaked down to get it. It was nice to get the exercise actually." Billy turned to Amber.

"It's my kayak, not the one I borrowed before."

The agents exchanged confused glances, which grew deeper when Amber replied.

"What about the…" Amber glanced at the agents, as if unable to work out if there was anything she shouldn't be saying, but she gave up. "You had cameras set up in the road, why didn't you see these guys coming?"

"I had to take the cams. I needed the processing power for the video."

West took the opportunity to bring the conversation back to the video. "What *is* the video? Where is it filmed? And how did you get it?"

Everyone turned back to Billy again.

"I didn't get it. I *made* it."

* * *

"What do you mean, you made it?"

"I made it. Look." Billy turned back to the computer, pulling up a box where he was able to type. He thought for a moment, then turned to Agent Black.

"What's your name?" he asked.

"You *what*?"

"What's your name? And what's your… what's your favorite food?"

"*Huh?*"

"Just tell him Don," West said, impatient to see what Billy was doing. Black replied this time, somewhat chastened.

"Agent Don Black. I like – Jesus I don't know. I like *ice-cream*."

At once Billy's fingers moved rapidly on the keyboard, and a second later the box was gone, replaced by a front-facing image of the same younger man, the one Billy had called James Richards. Billy hesitated before hitting play though.

"Go on," West told him.

The voice came from the computer's speakers, the young man's lips in perfect time to it. It looked *completely* real.

"My name is agent Don Black. I like ice-cream. Strawberry flavor is my favorite."

"I made that bit up," Billy added into the silence that followed.

"What the *hell* is that?" Black was the first to respond. "How'd you do that?"

"I used a type of neural network called an autoencoder. It reduces an image into a lower-dimensional latent space, and then reconstructs that image from the latent representation. But the latent representation contains key features about things like facial features and body posture taken from other sources. That's then superimposed on the underlying facial and body features of the original video, represented in the latent space."

No one spoke for a long while after Billy finished his explanation. Then Black found his voice.

"You wanna run that by me one more time? In English maybe?"

Billy took a breath. "Most people call it deep faking. I've built a computer model of what James Richards looks like, or *would look like* if he were sitting in that room. And now I can feed in any words I like, and make it look like he's actually saying them."

Another silence, while the other made sense of this. Black was the first to respond.

"And Tom Hanks? What's he doing there?"

"Well I haven't quite finished. We had to bug his house – James' house, not Tom's – and hack his social media and stuff, to get images and audio to feed into the model. But I had to practice first, so I used Tom Hanks. There's tons of footage of him online, in films and interviews and stuff."

Black stared, still not understanding. West was the next to speak.

"I've heard of deep fakes." Her voice was slow and thoughtful. "But what you're saying is this James Richards, he *didn't* confess after all, you've just made a fake video of him confessing. To convince us you were innocent?"

"Yes. Only I didn't do it to convince *you*. I wouldn't have explained it all if I had."

"So why *did* you do it?"

"It's the only way I can get out of this. But I'm also going to need your help." Billy stared at West, and for a long time she was silent. Only Agent Black still wasn't getting it.

"So this kid, James, he didn't confess?" Black said. "He didn't do it?"

Patiently Billy turned to him. "He did do it, but he set up fake evidence to make it look like I did it. And he'll never confess to it. So you have a choice. You can either put me in jail for something I didn't do. Or you can catch him."

CHAPTER SIXTY-ONE

"I'll have the veal," Oscar said, speaking sharply to the waitress but not bothering to look at her. He held out the menu for her to remove, and looked around at his friends. Jennifer was sitting next to Lily, who was next to James. Eric was there, but he was fine – the grit in the oyster that produced the pearl. With a dash of irritation he noticed the serving girl was still there.

"What is it?"

"I'm sorry sir, I said the kitchen has run out of veal."

"Run out of veal? What is this..?" He couldn't think of a suitably caustic analogy, so instead he snatched the menu back and looked over the options again.

"Then gimme the fillet steak. I assume you've got some of that?"

"Yes sir. How would you like it?"

"How about properly cooked?" Oscar offered her a sneer, then handed her the menu a second time and leaned forward, cutting her off from the exchange. He poured himself some more wine, muttering under his breath. Jennifer watched him coolly the entire time, and he knew she liked it, delighted in it. And he liked that.

"Should be fresh snow by the weekend." It was James speaking, one of his arms draped casually around the shoulder of Lily. "Anyone up for the slopes?"

"I'm in," Jennifer said, and she glanced at Oscar. Lily's family were members of the Hamilton Club, a private ski resort up in Vermont, owning a large lodge there. The five of them had been many times, and Jennifer was a big fan.

"Sure." Oscar smiled. But as he did so his eye was taken by a couple entering the restaurant, and speaking to the maître d. There was something about their manner that looked wrong. They wore suits, but not the kind you put on to eat here. And they were too assertive, they didn't have the relaxed way of diners. When the three of them – the couple and the maître d – looked repeatedly over to their table, Oscar knew. He allowed himself a deep breath, but still pretended not to notice as they walked closer.

"Excuse me sir," the maître d tried to say, but the woman cut him off, flashing a silver badge in a black leather wallet.

"Oscar Magnuson? James Richards? My name is Special Agent Jessica West of the FBI and this is my partner Agent Black. Do you mind if we have a quick word?"

James stiffened in his place, but Oscar remained quite calm.

"What about?"

The female agent – West – turned to speak directly to Oscar, she let her eyes flash to the other diners at the table. "It might be better if we speak in private sir."

"Why? I don't have anything to hide. What's this about?"

The agent hesitated a second longer. "As you wish. I see you're dining with Lily Bellafonte tonight. You're aware no doubt of the young man who was accused of bombing her family's business premises? One Billy Wheatley?"

"The environmental nutjob? Who killed himself? Jumped off the ferry?"

"Perhaps. Only it turns out he didn't kill himself after all. He's been apprehended."

A ripple ran around the table, shared by Oscar. So that's what this was about. Internally, Oscar smiled, excited about what was to come. On the outside his face appeared to show completely authentic shock. He lifted a hand to cover his jaw.

"Oh my." He glanced at Lily, and noticed James did the same, offering her a sad smile. This was going to be hard on her. Then Oscar turned back to the agent.

"It's good of you to let us know." He tried a dismissive smile, then turned away.

"We're not here to let you know. We'd like to ask you some questions."

Oscar turned back, feeling the beginnings of anger. "What about? It's nothing to do with us."

"I'm afraid Mr Wheatley has accused you and Mr Richards of being involved in the bombings." West didn't take much care to say it quietly, and the entire table fell silent, while the diners on other nearby tables were also now clearly watching. That pissed Oscar off. What fucking right did this bitch have? What the fuck was she playing at? But he suppressed the anger. Suddenly he burst out into laughter.

"He's accused *us*? Oh wow, that's a good one!" Oscar turned to James again, reassuring him with the glance and encouraging him to play along. They were always expecting this, there was nothing to worry about.

"Well that's preposterous. Completely ridiculous." Oscar stopped laughing now. But West didn't reply.

"You can't possibly be taking this seriously? The testimony of that murdering little jerk? Who faked his own death?"

"Just a few questions sir."

"What here?" Oscar looked around at the restaurant.

"We have an interview room at the bureau offices. Two interview rooms." West looked up at James, then fell silent. Oscar broke the quiet.

"And this can't possibly wait? This *nonsense*, until we've had our dinner?"

"It won't take long to clear up, Mr Magnuson."

Oscar glanced at James, giving him a tiny nod that no one else caught, then he shook his head as if in disbelief. Then he removed his napkin and pushed his chair out.

As he got up from the table, Oscar caught the eye of Jennifer. She gave him the tiniest nod of her own, reassuring him this was nothing to worry about.

"What did you say your name was?" he asked the female agent, and when she repeated her name he added.

"I think you're going to regret the way you've approached this, Agent West."

* * *

Outside the restaurant he and James were put into the back of separate unmarked cars, his driven by another woman who didn't introduce herself. The other agent, Black, got into the passenger seat. Then they drove. No one spoke to him on the way, but he asked where they were going.

"FBI regional headquarters." Agent Black replied without turning around. When they arrived Oscar was led inside via a back entrance, and along several corridors until they came to an interview room. Here Oscar realized that Agent Black had gone, and only the woman was there.

"We'll be with you just as soon as we can. Would you like a cup of coffee?"

"I'd like my dinner."

The woman left the room.

Just as soon as they can turned out to be a long time. The woman returned to check up on him after thirty minutes, and when he protested that he hadn't been dragged out of his dinner to sit and wait for nothing, she promised she would ask Agent Black to speak to him directly. He came another ten minutes later.

"What the hell is this? What am I doing here?"

"We told you Mr Magnuson. Mr Wheatley has made certain accusations against you and your friend James Richards. We have to follow them up."

"Then why *aren't you*? Why are you just holding me here?"

"We're not holding you here, you're waiting. We're speaking first to Mr Richards, when we're done there we'll get to you."

"So I can leave?"

Agent Black got up from where he was sitting and opened the door. "You're free to go anytime." He sighed deeply, as Oscar began to rise from his chair. "But we would appreciate it if you could hold on just a little longer. Believe me, we want to get this cleared up just as much as you do."

Oscar hovered for a moment, half-on half-off the chair, then sank back down.

"Just be as quick as you can."

"We'll try sir."

Left alone again, Oscar told himself to calm the fuck down. It was obvious what they were doing, and it wasn't going to work. He was surprised it had come to this, they obviously hadn't completely disregarded what Billy had told them, which was a surprise. But at the same time, it was understandable, they had to follow it up. Otherwise it would be a problem in trial. Billy's defense lawyer would be able to claim he had a defense that was never investigated. So this was nothing. Just the FBI acting like jerks because they could. Stay calm. Answer the damn questions, and then think about suing their asses off for the way they were doing this.

Another hour later, they *finally* came to speak to him.

It was Agent West and Black who came in, the former carrying a pile of papers in a plastic folder, with a tablet computer on top. Black had acquired a toothpick, which poked out from between his lips.

"I apologize for the wait Mr Magnuson, I believe my colleague Agent Black explained our need to interview yourself and Mr Richards separately."

"Sure."

"Have you been offered a drink? Coffee? Iced tea?"

Oscar considered. It wouldn't hurt to be alert. "Coffee."

Agent Black went to get it, while West sat down opposite, placing the papers and computer on the table between them. She said nothing, until Black came back with the coffee, plus sachets of milk and sugar.

"You understand you're not under arrest, but we are recording this interview. You have the right to an attorney present, if you want one, and you do not have to answer any questions if you don't want to. Do you understand?"

"Yeah I understand."

"How well do you know Billy Wheatley?"

Bang straight in. Oscar gave himself a moment before answering. This was the most difficult question he and James had discussed, back when they were putting this plan together. On the one hand very few people had seen them together – but some clearly had. He shifted a little in his chair.

"We met a few times. He became friends with Lily."

"Lily Bellafonte?"

"Yes."

"When was this?"

"A few months back. Maybe six months?"

"What did you think of him?"

Oscar looked at Agent West, then slid his eyes sideways to Black. Both of the agents were looking at him, but not intently. They looked almost bored, he realized. Going through the motions. He relaxed a little.

"I didn't think much of him. I mean, I didn't think about him much."

"OK". West paused for a moment.

"What do you think he was *doing*?"

"Honestly? I thought he liked Lily, that he was trying to break her and James apart."

"He claims that's what happened. That he and Lily Bellafonte were dating?"

"I don't know about *dating*. She and James have a kind of on-off relationship. It's not unusual for them to take a break. Wheatley just got lucky for a few weeks, and thought it was more than that."

West didn't speak for a while. Instead she tapped her fingers thoughtfully on the table top.

"Mr Wheatley claims that was your motive. For setting him up as the bomber on Lornea Island. That James was jealous of him and Miss Bellafonte." She met his eyes and gazed at him, more interested now.

"That's completely ridiculous. That's crazy. He's crazy. I've never been to Lornea Island. I was here when it happened and I can prove it. I have witnesses. I was with James and my girlfriend Jennifer..." he touched a hand to his forehead, reminding himself to stay calm, not to overdo it. "Agent West – you must be able to... I don't know, check my cellphone records. I was here. We were all here."

"Mr Magnuson, I'd like to play you a clip from our interview with James Richards, if I may?"

Oscar frowned, not understanding. He felt a line of tension form in his back. *James better not have fucked this up.*

"Sure." He shrugged. "No problem."

"Thank you." West picked up the tablet, and fiddled with it a while, holding the screen where he couldn't see it. Then she folded its case into a stand, and set it on the table. The screen now showed an interview room very similar to this, with James sitting, obviously facing the camera. West leaned around and hit the arrow in the center, to make the video begin playing. At once there was the sound of the microphone picking up a hum of background noise. Then a voice began – West's – off camera.

"Mr Richards, Mr Wheatley has accused you of framing him for the bombing of the Fonchem chemical site on Lornea Island, and the murder of the security guard, Keith Waterhouse. What do you say to that?"

On the screen James answered at once. "It's rubbish."

"Do you know why he would say that?"

James shrugged, elaborately. With such unmistakable arrogance, that Oscar found himself smiling too. Or perhaps it was closer to a sneer. The video played on.

"Mr Richards. I want to show you something. Could you look at this?"

On the screen, James appeared to lean forward and look at a photograph, or a document that was being held up for him to see. There was a weird moment, when his face changed. It went from relaxed arrogance to one of shock.

"Where did you get that?" James asked, on the screen.

"Never mind about that, Mr Richards." It was West's voice again. "I'm going to ask you one more time. Did you set out to frame Billy Wheatley for the bombing of the Fonchem chemical plant on Lornea Island, and for the murder of Keith Waterhouse?"

On the screen James didn't answer. His face – filmed in high resolution – had gone white. He glanced at the camera, then back at whatever it was he was being shown.

"Shit."

"Mr Richards?"

"Shit. Look I don't know where you got this, but it wasn't me. None of it. The whole thing was Oscar's idea. I was just going along with it, but I didn't know what he was doing. I didn't know he was going to blow up that security guard. I didn't even know about it until I saw the news the next day."

Back in Oscar's interview room, Oscar watched as the blood turned to ice throughout his whole body.

"You're saying Oscar Magnuson was responsible for the bombing? Can you tell me how it happened?"

"Yeah. Sure. I'll tell you. Oscar made the bomb. He made *all* of them. He used a pressure cooker, and he tricked Billy into picking it up. That's how he got his fingerprints on it. *Shit.*" On the screen James covered his eyes for a moment with his hand. When he lowered it again he glanced at the camera again, but then seemed scared by the sight of it. He looked away. "Look, I need to have my lawyer here. My parents have an attorney. I need to use the phone."

West leaned forward and paused the video, leaving James' white panicked face frozen on the screen. And deep inside Oscar's head, all thoughts of staying calm had gone, as if blasted away by the explosion of a bomb.

"What the fuck did you show him?"

West didn't reply, which only added to Oscar's fury. His complete loss of composure.

"What the fuck was that? What did you show him to make him say that? What the hell is this?"

West sat back. Waited a few moments.

"I showed him two photographs we recovered from his Apple iCloud account. The first was of *you* working on what looks very much like a home-made pressure cooker explosive device. The second was of you on the ferry to Lornea Island, with a newspaper in the foreground showing the same date as the bombing took place. It seems he took them both without your knowledge. Perhaps he wanted a little insurance against you, in case things went wrong. He just wasn't very good at hiding it."

The fuck... the fucking idiot. Oscar felt the floor dropping away from him. It really felt like he was free-falling down to a place he didn't know. He opened his mouth to reply, but his mouth was completely dry.

"Look, we know he's lying. We know it was the pair of you, and maybe that he even led it – after all, he was the one with the grudge – Wheatley was dating his girl. But unless you start talking, and *right now*, before his attorney gets here, then we're going to go with whatever version he feeds us. This is an aggravated murder case. That's life without parole. You got one chance to cut a deal. You start talking. Give us your side of what happened. Right now. Or this is over."

Oscar looked at the floor, gray carpet. Cut into squares. Cheap and thin. He hadn't noticed it when he walked in, hadn't seen it the whole time he'd been waiting, so confident he was on top of this. That he and James had outsmarted Billy, the cops, the FBI, and it had been easy. Easy as manipulating the markets, and making more money than he'd ever known. Suddenly the enormity of what James had done was crashing in on him, stopping him thinking.

"It didn't go down the way James said it did." Oscar's voice was croaky.

"Excuse me? Could you speak up a little? For the sake of the camera?"

"It didn't happen like James said it did."

"But you did carry out the bombing? And frame Mr Wheatley for the crime?"

Oscar took one more look at the carpet, at the walls, at the heavy wooden door, firmly shut, and then at the two agents staring back at him, looking much more interested now.

"Yes."

CHAPTER SIXTY-TWO

The two hotel rooms were joined by an interior door, and though neither Amber nor Billy, nor his father Sam Wheatley, who had been picked up a couple of days previously, had been arrested, the door was locked. The rooms were comfortable enough, but by that stage the three of them had been confined there for seventy two hours, with food and water brought to them three times a day by a young agent with very red hair. Every time she arrived Amber or Sam pounced on her, demanding information on what was happening, but she either didn't know or wasn't saying.

"It hasn't worked. It was never going to work." Amber said. She wasn't sure if she meant it, really she just wanted to break the silence that had descended over them, long after there had been anything helpful to say.

"Have faith. They wouldn't have kept us this long if they had nothing," Sam replied.

Billy ignored the pair of them. For the last twenty four hours he'd done nothing but lie on his side on the bed, staring at the wall.

Suddenly there was a knock at the door, then the scratch of a key being fitted into the lock. It swung open. The same agent as before, the red-haired woman was there again.

"Don't tell me," Amber said. "No news is good news right?"

"Uh huh." The woman said this time. "I'm going to need you to follow me."

Billy looked up.

"They're done?" Amber asked. "What's happened?"

"Agent West asked me to fetch you."

They followed the red-haired woman along a corridor and to an elevator, where they descended to the ground floor, emerging into the lobby of the hotel they'd passed through days before. They kept walking, outside, and across the street, into the FBI building where Billy had assisted with the creation of the final deep fake video. They passed through a security barrier, like one in an airport, and then went to another elevator, down a corridor and finally came to what looked, through the small glass panel in the door, like a conference room. The red-haired woman knocked, and opened the door at the same time, and ushered Billy and Amber inside. Two people were sitting down, in front of a tray of breakfast pastries. One of them was Agent West, the other was a man Amber didn't know. Agent Black was standing by the window.

West got up when they came into the room.

"Hey guys. Are you ready for some answers? I'm sorry it's been so long."

The three of them sat down, and were encouraged to help themselves to the pastries, and West got up to pour them each coffee. Then she introduced the man they didn't know.

"This is Special Agent Bernard Chow, he's an expert in fraud and financial crime. He's been sitting in with us over the last couple of days." Chow smiled a good morning. "I've asked him here as well to help explain what this has all been about." West directed her gaze to Billy, and Chow did the same, but Billy was silent. After a while he nodded.

Amber watched, but couldn't stay quiet herself. "Well? Did it work?"

The three agents hesitated. Then Black spoke.

"Did it work? It worked like a charm, a goddamn charm!" He burst into a smile. "Cocky bastard was enjoying the whole thing. Then we hit him with the fake video, and bam! You should have seen his face."

"Well actually you *can* see his face," West interrupted. "Since we have his entire confession on tape."

"He confessed?" Amber said. "He actually confessed?"

"Oh yeah." Black answered. "We spoke to Magnuson first. When he saw the fake tape he totally cracked, blamed the whole thing on Richards. So then we took the *real tape* of that, played bits to Richards, and he started blabbing too. Pretty soon we had both of them admitting to involvement, only saying it was the other one's idea."

West took over the explanation. "That actually happened pretty early on. Which gave us the option of holding them both. After that it was a matter of unwinding what it was all about. That's what took so long. But yeah. Long story short. We now have the both of them admitting their involvement, and exonerating you. It's quite the result."

"That's fantastic," Sam Wheatley said, his jaw open. He looked at Billy.

"You should see the guy's face," Black said again. "The moment we showed him the fake tape. He looked like the whole ground underneath him just disappeared away."

"So what is the story?" Amber asked. "Why did they do it? It couldn't all be just to frame Billy, over that girl, Lily?"

"No. It might have ended up that way, but that's not how it began." West looked across at Chow. "Perhaps you could explain?"

"Sure." Chow leaned forwards, and his eyes sparkled in the morning sunlight that streamed into the room. He looked to be the only one who wasn't exhausted. "What we have here is a good old family feud."

Chow stood up and walked across to the coffee pot, and poured himself a top up. He began his explanation as he came back to the table.

"Lily Bellafonte's father and uncle, Claude and Jacques Bellafonte are business rivals, each running sizable chemical companies, which they both inherited from their father, the tycoon Arthur Bellafonte. Billy, you probably know this already, but maybe the others don't." Chow smiled at Billy, who said nothing, but listened, his face dull.

"You're also no doubt aware that Jacques Bellafonte's company EEC, has recently completed a hostile takeover of Claude's business, Fonchem?" His eyebrows rose in a question, and when he saw the confusion on Amber's face he explained.

"A hostile takeover is where company A buys company B, even though the directors of company B do not wish it to be bought. In this case EEC – controlled by Jacques Bellafonte – made an offer to Fonchem's shareholders to purchase fifty-one percent of Fonchem shares, but with the condition that the Fonchem board of directors be dismissed and replaced by a new board loyal to EEC. Does that make sense?"

"I guess."

"Good. Now you might ask, why would the Fonchem shareholders be willing to accept such a deal, if the board was against it?" He was looking at Amber now, and she shrugged.

"The answer is due to the depressed price of the Fonchem shares. They were trading at well below what they had been fetching in the five previous years. Which leads us to a new question. Why? Why were the Fonchem shares depressed?" This time he waited for an answer. Amber looked to Billy to provide it, but he was silent. She turned back.

"The bombings?"

"Exactly!" Chow grinned.

"Over the last year there's been a series of bomb attacks on Fonchem sites. Every time there was a new attack, the share price dipped. For each individual attack, the effect was not significant, but cumulatively... It added up. And every time the share price dipped, Jacques Bellafonte bought a few tens of thousands more shares in Fonchem. Not enough to attract attention, but enough to help him to persuade and push through the takeover."

Chow turned to Billy and smiled again. But still he was silent.

"I still don't understand," Amber said, after a while. "What's any of this got to do with James and Oscar? If they did the bombings, why did they want to help Jacques Bellafonte?"

"Ah, well this is the clever bit. They got something else out of it too. Have you ever heard of shorting stock?"

"No."

"OK," Chow took a moment to consider.

"Don't worry. I didn't get this either," Black interrupted, looking at Amber. "In fact I still don't."

"It's really simple," Chow ignored him. "A short is when you borrow a stock from a broker, and sell it immediately at its current price. Then you hope the stock's value falls, so you can buy it back at a lower price. You then return the shares you borrowed to your broker, and you keep the difference in price. Do you follow?"

Amber looked at Sam, and knew he wasn't clear either.

"You don't. Let me give you an example," Chow went on. "Imagine I want to short stock from ABC company, which has a current price of $10. I borrow one share, and sell it immediately at $10. I have $10 now, but I owe my broker the one share I borrowed. Then let's say the share price of ABC falls to $6. Now I can buy back my share and return it to my broker, and I can keep the $4 difference. I just made $4." He smiled again, but his eyes really began to shine when he continued. "Now scale that up so that I borrow one million shares, and it gets more interesting. I don't make $4, I make four *million* dollars."

"Is that legal?" Sam asked.

"Absolutely. It's what hedge funds do all the time. But it's *risky*."

"Why?"

"Because the price of the stock might *not* fall. It might rise, and here's the kicker. *There's no limit to how high it might rise.* If you borrow a million shares at $10, and the price rises to $100, well you're in big trouble. If it rises to a $1000 a share..." he whistled. "And there's no upper limit. It could get to a million dollars a share. At least in theory. Infinite losses."

"But if you knew for sure that the price would go down..." Amber began to get where this was going.

"*Exactly*. If you had prior knowledge of something that would cause the share price to drop... say you knew that a bomb was going to go off on one of the company's sites. Well that removes a great deal of the risk."

"And that's what they were doing?" Amber asked looking at West for confirmation. "They were planting the bombs and – what's it called? Shorting the stock?"

"Exactly." Chow beamed.

"How much were they making?" Sam asked.

"Not that much, which in a way was the genius of the operation. Shorting is perfectly legal, but not," he smiled at Sam Wheatley, "as a result of insider knowledge. So if it's done *too* aggressively, or too frequently it'll usually attract attention. Magnuson and Richards were keeping the level low. They were shorting, but not huge amounts, they were going under the radar." Chow sat back, assuming his audience had understood. But Amber protested further.

"But why? I still don't understand why they were working for this Jacques Bellafonte guy?"

"That's what we wanted to know," West took over. "We finally got there last night.

"James Richards and Lily Bellafonte started seeing each other when they were both still in high school. On the face of it, they're both rich kids, but actually they're in different leagues. Her family's money dwarfs his. And though her family generally approve of him, what they don't know is how he's played around behind her back. Sleeping with other girls, pretty much anyone he could it seems. Somehow Jacques Bellafonte got wind of this a year ago, and began blackmailing him. Either he helped out in the scheme to wrest control of Fonchem, or Richards' relationship with Lily Bellafonte would be blown out of the water."

"What he didn't figure on is just how willing Richards was to take part – hence the shorting," Black cut in. "It became a way for him to make enough money to keep up with his much-richer girlfriend. Albeit while destroying her wealth along the way."

Amber happened to glance at Billy as Black was speaking, and saw him flinch at the word 'girlfriend'. She turned back.

"What about Oscar? Why did *he* do it?"

"He's James' oldest friend." West said. "The pair of them grew up together, running minor scams. Stealing wallets, boosting cars. They didn't need to, but it seems they got a kick out of doing it anyway. But after a while small time crime doesn't quite cut it. He saw this as his chance to break into something much bigger. Bigger risk, bigger rewards. And a bigger thrill too."

The room was quiet for a moment, and West went on.

"He also appears to be very much the brains of the pairing. At least, he's doing the better job of trying to cut a deal to get out of this. I'd say we're very lucky to have stopped him now, before he moves on to bigger and deadlier operations."

"Have you got enough to stop them all?" Sam Wheatley asked, and Black couldn't suppress a laugh. "Oh yeah. We got more than enough."

"So is that it," Amber asked, looking around. "Are we done?"

West shook her head. "No. There's one further part which we have to keep front and center."

"What?"

"All the other bombings were carried out on unmanned sites, and they seemed timed to minimize the risk of anyone being harmed. This one was different. A man died."

"Oh. The security guard?"

"Correct. Keith Waterhouse. He had a wife, two children."

"And you need to know whether it was James or Oscar who actually set the bomb? So you know who killed him?"

"Exactly and we suspect it was actually neither. At first they each blamed the other, but then a new name came up. *Henderson*. Does that mean anything to you Billy?"

Billy looked up, as if he was surprised to still be there. Or that anyone else remembered he was there. Amber watched him, worried again for how down and tired her friend looked.

"No." He dropped his head back down to the table. West kept her eyes on him a moment before going on.

"Karl Henderson works directly for Jacques Bellafonte, but doesn't have a role within the company. Instead he seems to fill the role of general fixer. A problem solver. We know he was there on the night of the bombing, Magnuson gave him the bomb before Billy even traveled back to Lornea. His role was to plant the bomb and then help Magnuson and Richards get away. But it seems he may have deliberately targeted Keith Waterhouse."

"Why?"

There was a folder resting on the table, and West opened it now. Inside were color copies of photographs. Carefully she pushed one across the table to Billy, then a second to Amber and Sam. They showed a section of beach, and when Amber looked more carefully she saw a few dead seahorses lying on the sand. Billy's photograph showed a different section of beach, but still had the dead animals.

"Do you recognize these photographs Billy?"

Billy's expression answered before he did. He nodded, but then went back to looking disinterested and tired. West carried on anyway, speaking more to the others.

"They were sent to Billy anonymously in response to his campaign against Fonchem. We found the same images on a camera belonging to Keith Waterhouse, taken a few days after the site suffered a very minor leak – well within the limits allowed by the Environmental Protection Agency. Waterhouse also sent the images to the manager of the site, wanting to be sure it never happened again. It seems news of his concerns may have reached Jacques Bellafonte or Karl Henderson, and he wasn't the sort of employee they wanted when EEC took over the site. The bombing was an opportunity to take him out of the picture. They took it.

"Do you think you'll catch him?" Sam Wheatley asked.

"Catch him? We already have. Karl Henderson and Jacques Bellafonte are both already in custody." West smiled. "We arrested them this morning. It's over. This whole thing is over. And Billy, you're free to go."

Billy stiffened again at the sound of his name, but still his expression was sad. Amber wasn't sure how much of the preceding conversation he'd understood. He'd hardly spoken a word.

"You know Billy," West went on. "From what I've heard about your adventures since we last met, this is kind of an undramatic ending, compared to your normal work. No gun battles, no sunken boats, no major explosions!" She smiled, and tried to coax a smile out of him too. But Billy didn't smile. Instead he stayed quiet, looking down at the table, and an awkwardness spread through the room. Finally though he did speak.

"Yeah maybe." He looked up at last, his eyes level on West's. "Or maybe I'm just growing up."

* * *

The meeting went on for some time, and by the time it broke up Amber saw from the clock on the wall it was already eleven o'clock. She hadn't slept since the previous night, and suddenly she felt exhausted. And after five days without leaving either the FBI building or the hotel opposite, she was finally allowed to go home. Along with Billy.

"Where are you going to go? What are you going to do?" She asked Billy, as the FBI agents gathered up their papers and prepared to leave the room.

It was Sam Wheatley who answered. "He's coming back to the island with me. Just for a week or so, until we sort out what should happen next. How about you?"

"I should get back to work."

Sam looked at her for a while, then nodded.

"Stay in touch Amber. Don't be a stranger."

CHAPTER SIXTY-THREE

One Month Later

    I don't go back to college right away. Even if I wanted to, I wouldn't have the time to do any work. I have to give loads of statements about what happened, both to the police and the FBI, and when they've finished, the TV news and newspapers really want to speak to me as well. For two days they camp on the road outside the house, and we can't really go outside, but then Dad has a smart idea. He gets me to do an interview with the *Island Times*, explaining exactly what happened, and how I was living on the *Caroline* for over a month in the winter. But he tells the journalist we have to do the interview actually on the boat, and he gets them to take lots of pictures. And then, at the end of the article he makes them write about how we're trying to fix her up, but how we can't because so many of the parts are too expensive. And then he gets me to set up a GoFundMe page. And pretty soon after that the donations start coming in. Sometimes it's money, just ten dollars here, or twenty there, but mostly it's actual boat parts. The island is full of boat people, and boat yards and chandlers, and boat people are almost always really kind. And so when the fuss dies down, we spend the next few weeks trying to fit all these pieces together. You might think spending more time on *Caroline* is the last thing I would want to do, but actually it's really nice. It's spring now, and it's beautiful down there on the marshes, and it's just me and Dad, working hard and not even really having time to speak, or even think much, except about which bit goes where, or whatever job it is we're working on. By the time we're finished the boat is freshly painted, with sanded and varnished decks, and polished brass work, and she looks amazing. I mean she looks a bit odd too, like a sort of jigsaw-boat made from a dozen other boats, but she's sturdy and clean and ready to sail, and I think she looks beautiful.

The only interruptions come from Agent West, who visits a few times to keep me up to date with the case, as she calls it. Because James and Oscar both confessed, they don't have to go to trial, but Jacques Bellafonte wouldn't admit to what he did, so he will have to face a trial. And for a while she thought I was going to have to be a witness, which I didn't want to do. But in the end I don't have to. James and Oscar both know more about him than I do, so they can do it. And because they won't be sentenced until they give their evidence, Agent West is confident that they'll do it properly.

But both Dad and I know I can't stay forever. And as Caroline looks better and better, a bit of me gets sadder and sadder, until Dad has another good idea. He decides that instead of me taking the ferry back to the mainland, we'll take *Caroline*. It'll be her maiden voyage. At least maiden for us.

After that it's less bad.

It's a beautiful spring day, when we finally untie *Caroline* from the jetty in Bishops Landing, and motor down the creek towards the sea. Dad gets me to steer the whole way, and as the creek widens into the estuary, we pull up the sails. The new mainsail is a dark red color, it comes from a really old, traditional-style boat, and the foresail comes from an old racing yacht, so they're not exactly matched, but together they work well, and we cut through the water nicely. As we meet the sea there's a swell, but she rides it well. We take turns to helm, and we play music, and drink coffee and sing and play silly games, like I-spy, and guess the animal, which I always win, because Dad only knows the most basic fish, and I hit him with really obscure crustaceans and mollusks. But he doesn't mind, and then he starts to win by making up animals that don't exist, but that his Mom used to make up stories about. It's nice, because he doesn't often talk about his family.

It doesn't feel like eight hours later that we have to start the engine again to motor into the marina in Boston, and I get the sad feeling again, but only for a while because I'm really hungry by then, and it's nice when we do get in, to go for a meal and eat lots. After that Dad asks if I want to sleep on the boat, or go back to my apartment.

I actually got lucky about that too. The university nearly rented it out again, when they thought I was dead, only then the new student dropped out of college, so she didn't move in after all. And then Dad got back in contact with them, and said I'd still need it, because I wasn't dead after all.

I tell him I'd better go back tonight. Or I might not go at all. He just looks at me and nods.

But in the end it's less weird than I thought it would be. Dad comes with me, and I don't know if he had too much beer with dinner or what, but he's full of energy, and suddenly really funny. Guy and Jimbo and the girls are all there, just watching TV, and they're full of questions about what happened. And I answer some of them, but Dad does most of the talking. And Dad can be kinda cool when he wants to be, with the way he tells jokes and goofs about. We ended up talking until two in the morning, and Guy even offered him some of his drugs, but Dad said no. Dad's cool like that too.

The next day I had to go into college to explain why I missed so many classes and tutorials, and find out what was going to happen about it. Dad offered to come with me again, but this time I said I wanted to do it alone. It wasn't just me and Lawrence, it was a proper meeting with the head of the Marine Biology faculty, and two other professors. One of them was Professor Little – do you remember him? The one with the extremely interesting invertebrates, the pistol shrimp? I had to tell my whole story again, and they asked a load of questions, and only when I'd finished did they start asking about my class work. I'd missed about a third of my classes, and I thought they might make me repeat the whole year, which would have been really boring. But they didn't. Lawrence showed them the grades of the work I had done, and they said I could go into the second year, just as long as I complete all the work I've missed. So I'm going to be busy. Oh, and I won't have Lawrence for my tutor next year either. Professor Little said I'll be with him. So that's cool.

I still have to attend my weekly class at the Harvard campus, and it's two weeks later that I bump into *her*. Lily, I mean. I suppose I knew it would happen sooner or later. It's almost exactly like the first time we met too, on the same corner, only this time I'm not running and I don't knock her books to the floor. Instead we both just stop. And Lily speaks first.

"Hi Billy."

I don't know what to say. She's sent me two messages since it all happened. The first said she was glad I was still alive. The second asked to meet up. But I didn't reply to either.

"Hello Lily," I say, and I step to the side, to get around her, and back to my next class, but she puts her hand on my arm.

"Billy, can we talk? Please?"

"I have a class."

"Come on. You'll catch up."

"I am catching up."

A hint of a smile shows on her lips, and then fades away. I try not to watch, because my stomach is churning like I've had eight cups of coffee. She's still so beautiful. It's like I'd almost forgotten how beautiful.

"Let me buy you a coffee."

"I don't think I want a coffee."

"Something stronger then? Come on Billy. We really should talk."

I want to ask what we have to talk about, after she got back together with James just one week after she thought I'd died. But at the same time, I guess it's inevitable that we talk sometime. And I do have someone in my next class I can get the notes from now. Do you remember her? The mature student, Linda Reynolds?

"OK. But I'll just have a water."

"Great. Come on." Lily leads me across the square to where there's a coffee shop.

I sit down in a booth by the window, while Lily goes to get drinks. She gets me a coffee, even though I said I didn't want one. Plus a bottle of water. I stare at both of them.

"I guess you want to know what happened?"

"Not really."

But she tells me anyway.

"I told you about how Dad runs the company, it wasn't bad. He didn't put profits above everything else, above environmental standards.

At least, not completely." She pauses and takes a sip, her blue eyes watching me. I have to look away.

"But the way Jacques ran his business, it was always different. He was only interested in money. He didn't care if people got hurt, or if it did any damage. That's why his company grew bigger than Dad's, over the years. They had massive arguments about it. About what the right way to do it was. About what Arthur would have wanted. But that's why Jacques wanted to take over so much. Jacques could make more money buying another company, but he wanted to prove *his* was the right way, that Dad was wrong."

I really don't care about this. But one thing does interest me. "What's going to happen? With your uncle's company buying your dads, since he did it all illegally?"

Lily takes a while to answer. "I'm not sure. Dad's in meetings with lawyers trying to figure it out. They think it depends if Jacques is found guilty or not. If he is, they'll try and reverse it. But it's hellish complicated. Whatever happens, the lawyers are going to get most of it."

"He will be." I say.

"What?"

"He will be found guilty. That's what Agent West says."

"Oh. I hope so." Lily takes another sip. "Do you hate me?"

I can feel her looking at me, but I can't bring myself to look back. In the end I force myself to.

"No."

"But you're angry? Or upset? That I got back with James? After you…" She doesn't finish the sentence, even though I don't answer.

"You have to see it from my perspective. I thought you'd destroyed my family's company. I thought you'd betrayed me." She reaches across the table, her head is tilted to one side and her hair is hanging down on one side like a curtain. "And James and I… We'd been together so long, it just felt natural. I *believed* him."

"And you didn't believe me?"

"You weren't there, Billy. You weren't there to give your side. Maybe if you'd… If you hadn't disappeared?"

"If I'd let the police arrest me? And get put in jail for a murder I didn't commit? Would you have believed me then?"

I notice a few of the other students in the café are looking around watching us, and I lower my voice.

"I don't know. I honestly don't know."

Then her lips part, and she smiles. The lips that I kissed, not so very long ago.

"Look, I don't wanna... I don't want to lose you as a friend Billy. And maybe, if we take things slow... maybe..." She lets her voice fade out. "Maybe it doesn't have to be over?"

I don't want it to happen, but I feel my heart start beating faster. This is what a part of me wanted, so bad, while another part said it wouldn't ever happen, shouldn't ever happen. But then I think back to my apartment. It's been going so much better with them, since I got back. I think about Linda Reynolds, whose notes I've been using to catch up, and who introduced me to some of the other students on my course. And then I think about Lily, and her amazing house, and that dinner at the yacht club, and her brother and his posh girlfriend. They're different worlds.

I sigh.

"If you want it to, that is."

She gives me more of a smile now. But instead of answering her I get up.

"I have to go. I have a class, then I have to write three months' worth of essays."

"Sure." Lily's smile fades away. She glances at my untouched coffee, unopened bottle of water, but doesn't say anything about them.

"Goodbye Lily," I say, and I turn around and walk away.

I only get to the door, before my cellphone rings. I pull it out and glance at the screen, but then I wait until I'm outside before answering it.

"Hi Sarah," I say. I get that feeling again, my heart beating faster, only it's different this time. It's less fear, less feeling like I'm about to be found out any moment. That this shouldn't be happening, it's more like a feeling of something that *fits*.

"I just wanted to say I'm looking forward to seeing you, tonight," Sarah says, and I glance at Lily, through the window. She's still sitting there, watching me through the glass.

"Yeah," I say. "So am I."

And with that, I walk away.

THANK YOU!

Thank you for reading, and as ever, I really hope you enjoyed this book as much as I enjoyed writing it. I'm a little surprised at how Billy is growing up, and I'm curious to see how he ends up, and what he ends up doing with himself. However, I am going to take a short break before writing any more books in the Rockpools series, and focus instead on a rather different series.

You can find out more about that by signing up to my mailing list if you're not already on it. You'll also get a free copy of my novella Killing Kind, more details over the page.

A huge thanks to my Beta Readers who helped to clean up the manuscript for this book, and remove my messy errors. Any that remain are all mine.

If you're new to my other (non Rockpools) books, there follows a short summary of my previous novels.

Thanks again for reading, and if you liked this, please do consider leaving a review (you can do so from the link below)

https://readerlinks.com/l/1667985

Thanks!

Gregg

ALSO BY GREGG DUNNETT

THE WAVE AT HANGING ROCK

Three boys grow up on the wild coast of Wales. One of them is destined to be a killer, just not the one you think…

eBook and paperbacks:

Amazon / Kindle Unlimited

Audiobooks:

Audible / Apple iBooks / Amazon Audio

* * *

THE DESERT RUN

Fresh out of uni and drowning in debt, an adventurous pair find an unusual way to start their careers…

eBook and paperbacks:

Amazon / Kindle Unlimited

Audiobooks:

Audible / Apple iBooks / Amazon Audio

* * *

THE GIRL ON THE BURNING BOAT

When Alice's businessman father turns up dead, everyone thinks it's an accident. Until her boyfriend discovers evidence that things are not as they seem…

eBook and paperbacks:

Amazon / Kindle Unlimited

Audiobooks:

Audible / Apple iBooks / Amazon Audio

* * *

THE GLASS TOWER

Julia Otley has just achieved her life long dream - to be recognised as a literary star. But some people are just not cut out for stardom....

eBook and paperbacks:

Amazon / Kindle Unlimited

Audiobooks:

Audible / Apple iBooks / Amazon Audio